Our Little Secret

(Epic Gay Love Story)

Laura Jordan

Magic Touch Publishing

Text copyright © Laura Jordan 2023

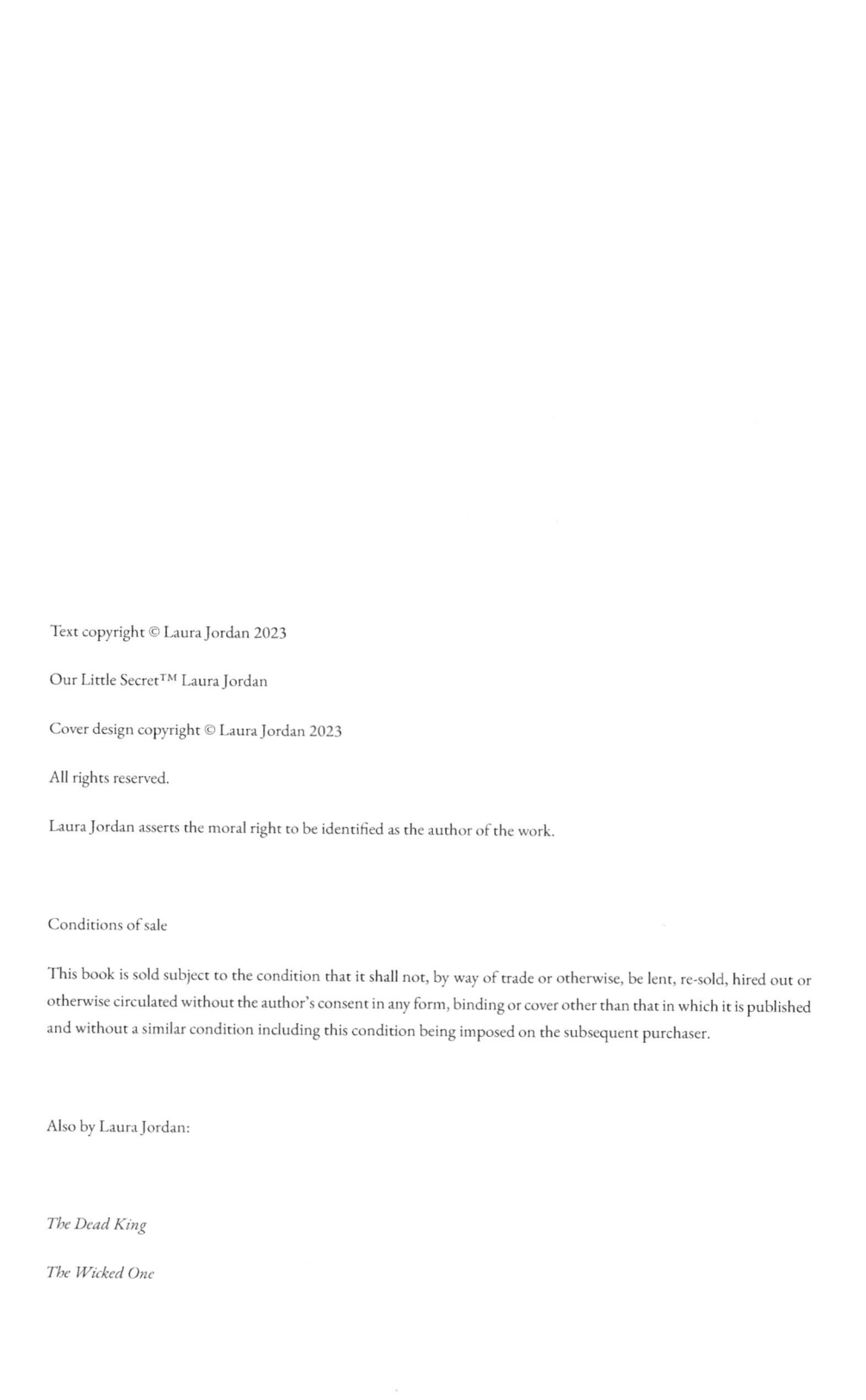

Our Little Secret™ Laura Jordan

Cover design copyright © Laura Jordan 2023

All rights reserved.

Laura Jordan asserts the moral right to be identified as the author of the work.

Conditions of sale

This book is sold subject to the condition that it shall not, by way of trade or otherwise, be lent, re-sold, hired out or otherwise circulated without the author's consent in any form, binding or cover other than that in which it is published and without a similar condition including this condition being imposed on the subsequent purchaser.

Also by Laura Jordan:

The Dead King

The Wicked One

This book contains scenes of a sexual nature. Reader discretion is advised.

Potential trigger warnings for this book:
Sexual harassment
Gay conversion therapy
Depression
Homophobia
Substance abuse
Neglectful parenting

By reading on, you will encounter the topics mentioned above, even if only very briefly. If these are things that you find triggering, please proceed with caution.

This book is for Natalie, who I miss every day.

You gave light to everything and everyone you touched. It was, and still is, a privilege to be your best friend.

I love you, Shmoople.

"Best thing I can do now is post endless thirst traps on Instagram."
— Myself, in the group chat

Chapter One

*I*S EZRA DARLING GAY?

Ezra arches an eyebrow at the headline of the article his sister sent him, amused. He reads on:

NEW PHOTOS HAVE EMERGED OF MILLIONAIRE MILLENNIAL AND NEWLY-BROKEN-HEARTED BACHELOR, EZRA DARLING, COSYING UP TO A MYSTERIOUS MALE HOTTIE. FANS OF THE DARLING DYNASTY WILD CHILD ARE NOT SURPRISED. WE'VE ALWAYS SECRETLY KNOWN THAT HE BATS FOR THE OTHER TEAM. SORRY LADIES!

Ezra scrolls down to said "new picture" and laughs. The pictures are not, in fact, new. They're at least three years old, taken back in his university days. He is at a lūʻau, grass skirt, coconut bra and all, with his arm slung around a classmate in a similar get-up. Ezra is holding his friend's chin in one hand and licking his cheek. The friend's face is screwed up and laughing. Ezra barely remembers most of that night, but that's how he knows it was good.

Grace lets herself into his brownstone, coffee cups in each hand. This morning her curly hair is loose and free. She gives him a grin that promises trouble and it proves infectious because he is immediately smiling too. She's never been one for personal space. Or respecting boundaries. Or using her spare key privileges for emergencies only.

'Did you get to the part where they start analysing your body language yet?' she asks.

'I'm licking his face. I don't think there's much to analyse.'

'True. You're obviously fucking his brains out.'

'Obviously.'

Grace joins him on the sofa, lying back and dramatically draping her legs over his. She gives him his coffee, puts the back of her hand across her forehead and sighs, looking every inch the renaissance painting.

'Whatever will the neighbours think? A *gay* in the family! The Darling Dynasty will be ruined!'

'First off,' he says, quirking an eyebrow at her. 'I'm adopted. So, it wouldn't really be *in* the family.'

Grace sits upright, a look of mock-horror on her face. 'Who *told* you?'

Ezra holds his white hand up to her dark brown skin and says, 'I figured it out on my own, babycakes.'

'Smart boy.'

'And secondly, I'm not gay.'

'I wish you were,' she says. 'Then we could talk about boys.'

'We already talk about boys.'

'True.' She looks at him seriously for a moment. 'Does it bother you? When they write things like that?'

Ezra thinks about it. It isn't the first time a trashy magazine has suggested he's gay and it most likely won't be the last. Grace always tells him that he doesn't exactly help himself, and he supposes that is true. If anything, it entertains him. He always acts camp for the camera and posts selfies to his socials in full glam makeup. He's always spotted at NYC's most infamous gay bar — Judy's — in outrageous outfits, drinking Moët & Chandon with various drag queens. But he's never denied any of it because... well, why defend yourself against something that isn't offensive?

Ezra shrugs. 'Let them have their fun.'

'*Speaking* of fun... did you check your calendar?'

Ezra frowns and opens his calendar app. He groans as he sees a "family meeting" scheduled for 10am.

'I'll give you $50 to tell them I'm sick,' he says.

'Haul your white ass, big bro,' she says, getting off the bed. 'Wear something nice. We're going for brunch afterwards.'

So, he wears something nice — chinos and a navy button down — and he braves 1405 Drury Street where his mom and dad wait for him in their own brownstone dining room. Some people think it's weird that they're all next-door neighbours. Ezra is sandwiched between his sister and parents in 1404, and they all have keys to each other's places. Everyone seems to come and go as they please, so it's as if they all still live together. Kind of. Ezra still isn't sure if he likes the arrangement, but he goes along with it nonetheless because his brownstone is, honest to God, fucking amazing. And besides. They all work together so it makes sense (although, does it really?) for them all to be within shouting distance of each other.

Ezra knows it's serious when he sees both the family publicist and lawyer at the table with his parents. He's twenty-five, but the sight of them all together makes him feel like he's eight years old again. Immediately he assumes he's in trouble and he runs through all the things in his head that could warrant both a publicist *and* a lawyer. He comes up with far too many possibilities.

'Sweetie,' his mom says, a smile overtaking her face. Then a little V forms between her eyebrows. 'Are you alright? You look tired.'

Ezra *is* tired. But that's only because he was up until 3am falling down an unboxing video rabbit hole on YouTube. 'I'm fine,' he promises.

'Are you sick? Do you want tea?' she fusses. She always fusses. 'A snack?'

'I'm good,' he says. 'Just a dumbass.'

She gives him that *my boy* look and chucks under his chin. 'You're *my* dumbass.'

Ezra kisses his mom on the cheek and fist-bumps his dad before taking a seat next to Grace at the Big Table. Ezra always describes his parents as the most intimidating people you'll ever meet. They are loyal, fierce, and never complain at having to work twice as hard at something that a white person would be given on a silver platter. Progressives through and through, firm allies to the LGBTQ+ community, and the first black couple to storm the cover of *Mogul* magazine, Warren and Jacqueline are a force not to be fucked with. They also have boundless, unflinching faith in their children, which Ezra thinks — in his case — is grossly misplaced.

The Darlings never planned to become a famous family. Warren and Jacqueline, once senior partners at a small law firm in Wyoming, supported Grace when she declared she wanted to be a YouTuber. They were even supportive when she dropped out of university to start taking brand deals and collaborating with famous influencers. When she expanded into a family channel, they didn't complain. And when Grace's sex tape was leaked, they stood by their daughter through it all.

The first network that came to them was *Stardust*, requesting a group interview with them all on *Gossip News*. Then came *Global* with a four-part documentary covering the rise, fall, and rise again of the Darlings. By the time *BingeBox* signed them on for their own reality TV show, the Darling Dynasty was already legend.

The best part, in Ezra's opinion, is that it hasn't really changed them. His parents are still the hardest working people he knows. Grace still drinks at the local dive bar with her old school friends. And Ezra —well, Ezra — he's still the same ambitious dreamer he's always been. Only now he has the means to fund those dreams. Whatever they turn out to be.

He risks a glance at their publicist, Ali, who is glaring at him over the top of her coffee thermos. That isn't unusual, but it makes his leg bounce nervously all the same. To her left, their lawyer, Mara, has her ledger out and is writing something down in her perfect handwriting.

'Okay, family,' Jacqueline says, rising to her feet. 'The network have been in touch—'

Grace and Ezra make a show of throwing their heads back and groaning.

'Boo,' Ezra says. 'Hiss.'

'Get off the stage,' Grace adds.

Warren frowns at them, then looks at his wife. 'How did we raise such headstrong children?'

Jacqueline shrugs and says, 'We did our job right.'

Ali narrows her gaze to Ezra. 'You're pronouncing *arrogant* wrong.'

Warren smiles at his kids, proudly. 'They're just wilful.'

'Wilfully stupid.'

'Anyway,' Jacqueline says, bringing them back on topic. 'Like I said, the network got in touch and there has been a... development.'

Grace immediately sits forward in her seat at the same time Ezra gets a sinking feeling in his gut. Their parents exchange an anxious look.

'The Montgomerys would like to work together,' Jacqueline says.

Grace nearly tips her chair over as she springs to her feet, and Ezra catches it in time. 'You're kidding! Tell me you're kidding!'

'I am not,' Jacqueline says. 'But, sweetheart, your father and I aren't sure—'

'They're in the middle of a PR shit-storm,' Ali says, bluntly. She turns her laptop around to face them, showing the open news article on the screen. The headline splashed across the New York Post homepage is simple but damming: LEAKED EMAILS TELL OF MONTGOMERYS' INVOLVEMENT IN GAY CONVERSION.

Grace looks like she's won the lottery, the jackpot, and a consolation prize all at once. 'Oh my God, this is amazing!'

Ezra frowns. 'Is it?'

'Well. No. Obviously, it's awful. But—'

'But our network and their network are pushing for a collaboration to help take some of the attention off the emails,' Jacqueline says. 'However, I'm not sure if this is the best idea. The Montgomery's don't have a history of... playing nicely off camera. Plus David is involved with all that Evangelical stuff with the church...'

'Mom,' Grace says, adopting a voice that she could have only picked up from Jacqueline herself. 'Our biggest rivals have come grovelling to us to help them. This kind of collab would be stratospheric. And it will be on *our* terms because they're screwed!'

'We're just worried that someones going to get hurt,' Warren jumps in. 'People who play with fire—'

'Get ratings,' Grace finishes. 'Get new contracts with networks that aren't dying. Get their own show without having to burden their families anymore.'

'You're not burdening us,' Ezra says at the same time his parents do.

'You guys are done with reality TV,' Grace says. 'This kind of collab can set me up for anything. I don't care how crappy they are. I don't care if I have to play besties with them for a whole season. I'll do it.' Grace looks at Ali with a determined set to her chin. 'What's the storyline?'

Ali shares a look with Mara that makes anxiety settle low in Ezra's gut. Then she says, 'You're marrying Theodore Montgomery.'

Brunch is a terribly grandiose affair, but nobody seems to mind. The rooftop bar is as lavish as it is expensive — and it is *disgustingly* expensive. Ezra finds himself completely redundant as Grace and Iris take charge of the conversation, barely getting a sentence out before the other cuts them off with another. So, he sits, and listens, and busies himself with his bottomless mimosas.

Iris Sanchez-Smith is, for lack of a better word, perfect. She had been Ezra's first love — well, perhaps not *love*, but he'd lost his virginity to her when they were sixteen — and his only love. Everyone had assumed they would get married one day. They'd settle down and buy a house in the suburbs, have 2.5 kids and adopt a dog. Then Iris came out of the closet.

It had been a surprise to everyone, not least herself. They'd parted ways romantically, but she had been a part of his life ever since. That was the thing about Iris. You could never shake her, nor would you want to. They may not have ever really been in love, but Ezra knows that she will always be his biggest loss.

'So, the engagement is officially on,' Iris says. 'God, you're going to get so much hate online. He's legit dreamy. Everyone wants a piece of Teddy Montgomery. Like, literally *everyone*. Even me, and the thought of dick makes me want to vomit.' She turns to Ezra and pats his shoulder. 'No offence.'

Ezra shrugs and drinks his mimosa. He doesn't have anything nice to add to the conversation so he figures he should just keep his mouth shut. His parents had already said everything that needs to be said: The Montgomery's aren't known for their abundance of warmth and joy. The only remotely bearable one is Teddy, and that is being generous.

Okay, look, it's not that Ezra *dislikes* Teddy Montgomery specifically, but he doesn't exactly crave his company either. The thing is, Teddy Montgomery is boring. He's posh, and sulky, and —ugh — British. Which normally would be fine. But Teddy Montgomery is stick-up-his-ass, sandpaper-on-his-dick, piss-in-his-Cheerios *British*. And next year he will be Ezra's brother-in-law.

'It doesn't really matter how dreamy he is,' Grace says. 'It's business, not pleasure. His grandfather's conversion therapy trials were leaked. Instant ruin. The only thing that can save them is collaborating with us on our new season, which both our teams have been pushing for *years*. The engagement is to just distract the public from the whole sordid ordeal.'

'And Warren and Jacq?' she asks.

Grace rolls her eyes and somehow doesn't come off as petulant. 'You know them. They're suspicious of the Montgomerys and worried I'll get hurt. But they respect my decision enough to let it go. Besides, being married to Dreamy McSteamy is no hardship.'

'Yeah, but it's three years of your life, Grace. Three years in a sham marriage, and for what? To appease the network? The viewers?'

'No, it's three years to work on what really matters,' Grace says, with that determination that Ezra both admires and resents in his little sister. 'Three years to expand my own brand, away from BingeBox. With the Montgomerys involved, some of the pressure will finally be taken off me. By the time I'm twenty-seven and our contract with BingeBox ends, it won't matter because I'll already have options. We won't have to renew with them. God knows their platform is dying.'

'I blame the boomers,' Iris says. 'We should never have given them the Wi-Fi password.'

'Then Ezra can swoop in and take over as my manager, mom and dad can retire. Everyone's happy.'

Iris' dark eyes flicker over to Ezra, and she watches him over the top of her extra dry martini (three olives! *Three*!). 'And what about you? Are *you* happy?'

Grace snorts. 'Of course, he's not. He hates Teddy Montgomery.'

Ezra frowns. 'No, I don't.'

'You do.'

Iris nods. 'You do, Ezzy.'

Ezra sighs. He can feel a headache coming on. Grace and Iris seem to have that effect on him when together. The bottomless mimosas aren't helping. 'He's an ass. And he doesn't deserve you. Even if it's just a stunt.'

Grace grins and wraps her arms around Ezra's shoulders. 'My big brother. Always looking out for me.'

Iris quirks a flawlessly sculpted eyebrow at him. 'Are you sure you're not jealous? I mean, Teddy Montgomery is, like, *really* hot.'

'He's not my type,' Ezra says.

'Tall, rich, and handsome isn't your type?'

'*Male* isn't my type.'

'Bitch, I hear that.'

In a desperate — and blatantly transparent — attempt to change the subject, he asks, 'How's work? Are people still in the market for horny art?'

Iris grins. 'Not only is there a market for it, but there is a *demand*. I got a commission yesterday to draw Baz railing Snow.'

He frowns. 'Who?'

'Philistine.'

'Did I see you on Instagram doing a brand deal for Michaels?' Grace asks.

Iris nods and takes a sip of her mimosa. 'They paid me six figures to stand in their oil paints aisle and hold a set of their brushes.'

'Sweet baby Jesus.'

'Speaking of which...'

Ezra tunes out and lets the girls take charge of the conversation again. He orders another mimosa from the cute, blonde waitress and sinks down grumpily into his chair, watching the back and forth between his best friend and his sister, but not really paying attention.

All he can think about is Teddy Montgomery, and his stupid face, and his stupid accent, and his stupid family. Ezra's soon-to-be in-laws.

He continues to stew.

Ezra doesn't particularly enjoy livestreams. He prefers to work scripted. Contrary to popular and ignorant belief, reality TV isn't real. Ever since BingeBox signed them up for *Darling Dynasty* someone has told him where to stand, what to say, and what to feel. It is draining, and he wouldn't do it if it weren't for Grace. It has always been her dream to be famous, not that Ezra can really understand why. The money is amazing, and the special treatment is incredible, and the freebies (good *God* the freebies!) are next-level. But apart from that, it's invasive. It's as if everyone in the world is reading his diary and judging every word.

But it's still better than the anxiety a livestream brings.

Grace is, of course, a natural at these kinds of things. She was born to be in the public eye. She is witty, smart, charismatic — and to top it all off, she is beautiful. Ezra knows he is biased because she's his sister, and to him his mother and Grace (okay, and Iris) are the most beautiful women in the world, but it helps that it's also true. She's just beautiful. Plain and simple.

Grace is done up in full glam and her outfit is Prada through and through. Ezra is wearing smudged black eyeshadow, and Grace has artfully drawn a little heart on his cheekbone in black liner. They look good, there is no denying it. Ezra isn't vain but he can tell when he is having a good skin/hair day, and today is one of those days.

BingeBox has approved the new storyline, and when the cameras start rolling in three weeks' time, the new narrative will be already in motion. Warren and Jacqueline have already — very hesitantly — announced the engagement to the press, and now whenever you Google "Montgomery" the first thing to come up isn't "gay conversion conspiracy" but instead pictures of Grace. It is, Ezra admits, a brilliant plan.

'If there is one thing the press love more than a scandal,' Grace says, 'it's a love story.'

And this is how they came to the conclusion of doing an Insta live. There is a ridiculous amount of pomp and circumstance for one twenty-minute stream. They are at Grace's place, ring lights blinding and boom mics hovering over them ominously. Ali is there, glaring daggers at Ezra because, out of himself and Grace, he is far more likely to say something stupid.

The butterflies in Ezra's stomach turn into a stampede of elephants the moment they go live, but he puts on his thousand-kilowatt smile all the same. Within thirty seconds they already have over 300,000 viewers. Grace does a perfectly polished intro and then dives into the comments section. Ezra isn't really needed, but he's there for his sister to bounce off. They have a dynamic that just *works* on camera and people love to see them together.

The comments flood in.

LittleMissMarilyn: omg girl show us the rock!!!

Shane_Ripley_93: i'm so jealous, had a crush on Teddy Montgomery since forever

xXnoregretsXx: it's obviously a scam guys. his grandad is a homophobe and they want to cover it up

she-doesn't-even-go-here: Ezra you are so fuckin hot pls murder my [cat emoji]

One look at Ali's face, who is watching the comments on a separate monitor, and Ezra knows to ignore that last one. Grace effortlessly takes the lead, picking out the easy questions and giving a somehow vague but, at the same time, wonderfully expansive answer. It usually all ends the same way. *We're so in love! We have been waiting so long to share this news with you! We can't wait to start the next chapter of our lives together!*

Ezra smiles, but inside he is screaming.

Chapter Two

The engagement party is upon Ezra before he can really process it. Three weeks pass quicker than expected because every waking moment of his day is consumed with smash-or-passing wedding dresses, colour themes, cake flavours, and good God the list goes on. Grace, naturally, flourishes under the pressure while everyone flounders. Ezra can't help but become increasingly concerned for their parents who are looking more and more unsettled with each stage of planning.

Ezra looks at himself in the full-length mirror, agonising over which identical blue tie looks better with his suit without coming to a decision. It is, after all, a big deal. It is Grace and Teddy's big night — or at least it is as far as the press is concerned. Two kids from famous families getting married, uniting across the pond, burying all scandals along with the hatchet.

He's met the Montgomerys before. Once at the Teen Choice Awards, another at a charity fundraiser, and another — oddly enough — at a royal wedding. One of the less important side-princesses. Neither of these times has he got on well with Teddy Montgomery. For starters, the man does not drink. Secondly, he doesn't run any of his social media pages himself and therefore doesn't see the fun in taking drunk selfies and posting them with reckless abandon. And thirdly — and this really is the most awful — he doesn't dance. Ezra supposes it's probably hard for him to dance though, what with that giant pole up his anus.

Grace invites herself in, as she always does. She plucks both ties from his hands and instead reaches for a blush pink one in his wardrobe. When he arches an eyebrow at her, she simply says, 'It takes a real man to wear pink.'

The engagement party is being held at The Palace — NYC's most prestigious and pretentious bar — and is closed to the public all night. Just an intimate gathering of family, friends, and a thirty-piece TV crew. Only selected members of the press are allowed in, and Ezra is blinded by the flash of cameras the moment he steps out of his chauffeured car. Grace circles the bar with a genuine confidence that Ezra can only fake on his best days. Instead, he seeks his solace from the open bar, and it's there that he stays for most of the evening.

It irritates him to no end that the Montgomerys show up over an hour after the party has started. David is every part the silver fox in his tux, and Anastasya is beyond glorious in her black cocktail dress. Even their first-born's widowed wife is there, sans kids, and looking magnificent. And then there is Teddy. His sandy blond hair is tousled in that *I-woke-up-like-this-but-I-also-didn't-haha-hashtag-no-filter* kind of way. His suit is impeccable. He turns heads without trying. Has he always been so tall? What a dick.

Anastasya makes sure to smile and greet anyone who so much as looks at her. She's unwaveringly patient while people lose their shit over meeting the Russian ballerina-turned-supermodel. Meanwhile David is shaking hands and clapping shoulders. From certain angles he looks just like the movie star Ezra remembers from his childhood.

The worst part is how good they all look together. All of them. The way Grace just slots flawlessly into their perfect family. The way her and Teddy look like childhood sweethearts all grown up. The Quarterback (do they even have those in England?) and the prom queen. They're both gorgeous. Both effortlessly elegant. His sister loops her arm though his as they make the rounds and accept the well wishes. *Congrats on both being so attractive! An interracial, international couple? How progressive! Gay conversion therapy* who?

When Ezra absolutely cannot bear it any longer, he goes off to make his own fun. A $50 bribe to the DJ grants him access to the evening's entertainment. He swaps out the royalty-free-elevator-smooth-jazz for a 70s, 80s and 90s playlist. By the time an *ABBA* medley comes on, he is three glasses of wine and four tequila shots deep, and very much trying to look as if he is having a great time.

The camera crew never strays far from him as he dances with pretty girls and knocks back his drinks. The dancing becomes sloppy and before he knows what's happening he has a girl either side of him, grinding against him in some kind of horny conga line. He's not complaining though, because they are hot as hell, and their hands are all over him, and the alcohol is making his head buzz in a way that isn't totally unpleasant.

Every time he sees Grace and Teddy coming his way he ducks out into the smoking area, or the restrooms, or even sometimes behind the bar. He can see Grace getting annoyed with him, but the last thing he wants to do is make small talk with Teddy Montgomery, so he figures he'll incur Grace's wrath later instead.

In the middle of a *Grease* mashup one of the grinding girls pulls him into the disabled restroom and is kissing him like he's about to be shipped out to war tomorrow. She fumbles for his belt buckle and tries to sink to her knees, but he catches her by the elbows, pulling her back up. Hurt flashes in her eyes and Ezra simply says, 'You're drunk. And so am I.'

Ezra is surprised when she slaps him and storms off. Nevertheless, he waits for his semi to go down before rejoining the party. He drinks, and dances, and kisses more pretty girls, until a slow song comes on. Avoiding the eye contact of anyone he was dancing with, he skulks back to the bar. The bar is his friend. The bar has more alcohol. Good bar.

By the time Iris joins him, he's every bit as maudlin as he deserves to be. She gives him a look that says something along the lines of *is this wise?* that he pointedly ignores. He orders another tequila shot and an extra for her.

'I have been eavesdropping,' Iris says. 'And involving myself in conversations that I wasn't invited to. I have collected valuable intel.'

Ezra slurs his words. 'Please, oh Wise One. Enlighten me.'

'Teddy Mikhail Montgomery. Born in Britain. Half British on his father's side, half Russian on his mother's side. The homophobe was his *maternal* grandfather, so no surprises there. He's twenty-seven, a Libran, and a whopping six foot three.'

Ezra arches a wry eyebrow. 'I already had all that from Wikipedia, Iggy.'

Iris smiles at his pet name for her, and Ezra is bitterly reminded, once again, how she will always be the best thing he never really had.

'Alright then, how's this? He loves true crime and thrillers. His favourite food is Thai. Pet peeves include: wearing crocs ironically and people referring to their plants as their 'babies'. Supports Tottenham Hotspurs — whatever that is — and is close friends with Instagram model Nick Wesley. Is rumoured to be the next World's Sexiest Man. He cries every time he watches *Titanic*. Also, he has a Golden Retriever called Fred.'

'Iggy, I love you.'

'Of course, you do.'

'And Mr and Mrs Delightful?' he asks. 'Are they just as wonderful as they seem?'

Iris shrugs. 'They were nice to me. She asked me about my art, and he told me about his work with his church back in England. He wasn't what I expected. Less fire and brimstone and more... Mr Rogers? But, like, hot. For a man.'

Ezra grins. 'For a man.'

The barman comes back with their drinks which Ezra downs immediately. His head is buzzing. His extremities feel pleasantly warm and flushed. Wow, he is really drunk, but he's sure no one will notice.

'You're drunk,' Grace says as she joins them.

Ezra frowns. 'Nope.'

'Yep. You need to sober up before mom and dad see you. They'll send you back to the orphanage, you know they will.'

'Where's Harry Styles gone?'

'*Teddy* is talking to his friends,' Grace says. 'You're the only person who hasn't made an effort to talk to him so far tonight.'

'Because I'm the only one who doesn't want to crawl inside his puckered asshole.'

'His parents want to meet you too,' she says. 'They're not like their TV personas, they're really nice.'

'Why? Do they want to convert me to their church?'

'They barely talk about their church.'

'They nearly chewed Iris' ear off about it!'

Iris frowned. 'I asked *them* about it.'

'Have you asked Noel Gallagher about his family's scandal yet?' Ezra asks, his tongue feeling two sizes too big for his mouth. 'Or any of them? I bet they won't be so smiley then.'

Grace's jaw clenches in the way that tells Ezra that she's about to lose her sense of humour. His head is swimming though, so he reckons he's got bigger things to worry about.

'Like it or not, Ezra, next year Teddy is going to be my husband. It's going to stay that way for a while. You're going to have to get over this ridiculous grudge of yours and make nice, otherwise you're going to ruin this for everyone.'

Ezra tries to keep his resolve, but he can see the muscles in Grace's jaw working. This is a big deal for her, and that makes it a big deal for him by default because he loves his sister. More than anyone in the world. He sighs.

'Alright. Alright, I'll go talk to him. But not Mr and Mrs Stepford, they creep me out.'

'Thank you,' Grace breathes out, her jaw relaxing. 'He's really not all that bad. He's a little shy and he's not great at small talk, but he's nice enough.'

'Wow, you're really selling him to me.'

'Go. Smile. Be *nice*.'

Ezra slides off his stool with the grace and elegance of someone who has had seven tequila shots and a bucket of wine. He plucks Iris' shot out of her hand and downs it before plunging into the crowd. Teddy Montgomery isn't hard to find. In a room full of extras, he is, undoubtedly, the leading man. Ezra is livid.

Teddy looks over at him as he approaches, and Ezra watches the flicker of irritation cross his stupidly handsome face. And how dare he? How dare *he* look so annoyed. *Him*. Teddy Montgomery. *Ezra Darling* is the guy who waited in the green room for hours backstage at the Teen Choice Awards with his mom and dad to meet his idol. *Ezra Darling* was the eleven-year-old kid who had travelled all the way to California to meet the older, cooler, taller Golden Child of the Montgomery Empire. *Ezra Darling* was the kid hoping to be best friends with this British kid who had appeared on the front of *Whizz Kid* magazine. A magazine cover that Ezra had saved and practiced introducing himself to for months. And Teddy *Fucking* Montgomery was the stuck-up prick who had walked past him without even saying hello.

'Theodore Montgomery,' Ezra says. He waits for something smarter, more biting, to come to him, but it doesn't, so instead he just stands there. Stupid.

'Ezra,' Teddy says in his plummy, twatty, rod-up-his-rectum accent. 'Please, call me Teddy. It's been a long time.'

It has. Three years since they last saw each other at that stupid royal wedding. Three years, five months and twelve days.

'Has it? I hadn't realised.'

'You're looking...' Teddy looks him up and down. 'Relaxed.'

Ezra smiles. 'And you're looking like the guy trapping my sister into a sham marriage for his own personal gain. But hey, we can't all be perfect.'

Teddy frowns. 'Are you drunk?'

Ezra sways. 'No.'

Something dark flickers across Teddy's face, but it's gone as quickly as it arrives. 'Yes. You are. Might I suggest you switch to coffee or call a taxi home? The last thing you want to do is embarrass your sister on her big night.'

'No, the *last* thing I want to do is let my sister marry you.'

'I rather think that's not your choice.'

'It sure as hell isn't her choice either.'

'Regardless, we're soon going to be a family. So, you'd best get used to it.'

Ezra catches sight of the cameras across the room. They can't get close enough to hear what he is saying but they can definitely see him, so he smiles brightly as he clamps a hand on Teddy's shoulder. It's not as menacing as he wants it to be, because Teddy is so goddamn tall.

'You will never be my family,' Ezra says through a clenched smile.

'Nor would I want to be, if this is how you behave.'

Teddy turns to leave. Before the last working brain cell in Ezra's head can stop him, he's grabbing Teddy's jacket and yanking him back around to face him. There is an audible rip and Ezra doesn't want to think about how expensive the suit is that he just ruined. People are looking at them now. Ezra sways and says, 'Keep your fucking hands off my sister.'

Teddy takes a step closer to him and Ezra has to crane his neck back to look up at him. 'Walk away, Ezra.'

Ezra draws himself up fully to his plucky five feet and nine inches (and a half!). He stares Teddy down, which is hard because Teddy is the tallest human being on the planet, and Ezra feels like a Smurf in his presence. Before he can stop himself, he's jabbing a finger into Teddy's chest which draws more curious glances from the other party-goers. Over his shoulder, he can just about make out his mom's horrified face from where she stands with Anastasya at the bar.

'Why don't you bite my —' is as far as Ezra gets before his stomach churns.

As if Grace can sense what's about to happen — which she probably can, on account that they have practically shared a brain since Grace was old enough to speak — she's making her way over to him, irreplaceable Birkin bag open and ready to catch the inevitable that is sure to make an appearance any moment now. But she is too late, and Ezra empties the entire contents of his stomach on Teddy Montgomery's Gucci loafers.

He is blinded by the cameras flashing.

Ali has skipped anger altogether and has elevated all the way straight to demonic fury. For a woman with giant doe eyes, freckles, and the biggest set of dimples Ezra has ever seen, it comes as a surprise to most that she is, in fact, a five-foot-one, foul-mouthed, caffeine-addicted PR hurricane.

He fucked up. That much he knows. His father is on his third double-shot espresso, fingers drumming anxiously against the table, while his mother slowly runs a rut into the floor with her Louboutin heels. Grace sits beside him, acting like a buffer for Ali's string of expletives. *You goddamn idiot* is kindly translated into *You could have handled it better*. *In front of the entire fucking press* becomes *We can fix this*. And *Do you have any idea what you've done* is interpreted as *It's not ideal but it's workable*.

Ezra doesn't deserve his sister's kindness. He was insufferable last night. Reckless. Selfish. Impulsive. The dumpster-truck-parked-on-his-head hangover is barely penance. But she defends him and sticks by him because that's what Grace has always done. Even though it really should be the other way around. He's the big brother, it should be him protecting her. That's what he had fooled himself into thinking he was doing at the party, but now, when he's painfully sober, he can see what it really was. He was being a dick because he doesn't like Teddy. And now everyone else is paying for it.

Ali slams down a thick stack of printed online articles in front of him. A quick glance at some of the headlines confirms what he already knows. The press — and apparently the entire goddamn world — knows what happened and has already come to their own conclusions.

LOVESICK OR JUST SICK? EZRA DARLING SPILLS HIS GUTS ALL OVER TEDDY MONTGOMERY!

UPCHUCK AND AWAY! EZRA DARLING CAN'T HOLD HIS DRINK *OR* HIS TONGUE!

NICE TO MEET SPEW! EZRA DARLING GIVES SOON-TO-BE BROTHER-IN-LAW A LUKEWARM WELCOME!

Ezra shuffles through the headlines. Most of them aren't even half as funny as they think they are. Nevertheless, the shame and embarrassment is almost unbearable. He wishes Grace would stop being so nice about it. The anger from Ali, he can take. The shock horror from his dad, he can manage. Even the disappointment from his mom, he can stomach. But Grace coming to his defence makes him feel lousy. Yet he lets her anyway, because, to be perfectly honest, he really does need somebody on his side. He vomited all over Great Britain's Golden Boy.

'Here's what we're going to do,' Ali says between stress-chugging her coffee. 'The press are trying to spin a narrative that you and Teddy got into an argument before the... incident.'

'We did,' Ezra says.

'I don't care if he was telling you about his plans to assassinate the fucking president, Ezra! What was said between you two doesn't leave this room! Got it?'

'Loud and loud.'

'From this moment on, you and Teddy are best friends, you understand me? I want you acting like the sun shines out of his goddamn asshole, because as far as you're concerned, it *does*. The Montgomerys are moving into their separate brownstones this week. I have you scheduled for three public appearances each week for the next month. You're going to go out, meet up, play nice for the cameras, and hold your liquor, alright?'

Ezra can't help the sinking feeling in his stomach. Three public appearances a week. For the next month. That is twelve days of his life that he has to give up for Teddy Montgomery. And he has to grit his teeth and bear it. One look at Grace, however, whose face is imploring him to take the deal, and he knows what he has to do.

'Alright,' he says. 'Yeah, alright, I'll do it.

Chapter Three

Ali has sent Ezra a detailed PowerPoint presentation on all things Teddy Montgomery, along with a weekly schedule of their appearances, plus a list of stipulations he must adhere to unless he wants her to — her words, not his — shove her foot so far up his asshole that he can lick her toes clean.

The email that the PowerPoint is attached to is brief and blunt.

*

```
Subject: Don't fuck this up
---
Ali < ali-james@Darlingdynasty.com>
To: Ezra
---
Read this and study it. I want you to know Teddy
Montgomery better than you know your own dick. And I know
you know that thing pretty goddamn well.
Ali
```

*

Ezra debates sending her a reply, but comes to the conclusion that whatever he says, even if it's just a *Yes, ma'am*, will probably just piss her off even more. Instead, he opens up the PowerPoint. It is comprehensive, to say the least. Agonisingly dull to say the most. The slide titles, however, are amusing, ranging from *The Fucking Basics* to *Rich White Family Drama*. He scrolls through most of it, pausing when he gets to a slide called *"Fun Facts"* and *"Talking Points"* — *Grace's suggestion, not mine. I genuinely do not give a shit.*

An unhealthy interest consumes him as he wonders what about Teddy Montgomery could possibly be considered as *fun*. He's not surprised when it rambles on about his music degree (pfft, barely a degree), his charity work (what a suck-up), and his recent crowning as 'Britain's Best Booty' (probably all padding).

Ezra snorts. The whole PowerPoint reads as a what's-what of human bilge. No one person can be that perfect. Which means it's an act. Which means that Teddy is every bit the trust fund baby that Ezra has always suspected. He gets to a bit about a video of Teddy singing to a sick child in a hospice in 2019 and rolls his eyes so hard he nearly sprains something. And then, because he's apparently a masochist, he's Googling the video. He marks it down to morbid curiosity.

The first thing that Ezra is struck by is Teddy's outfit. He's not in his usual immaculate dress shirt and slacks, and shoes that cost more than his house. He's in jeans and a bottle green jumper that makes his eyes pop. His shoes are still expensive (fucking Burberry! Of course, they are) but they're semi-casual. His expression is softer and more open than Ezra has ever seen. He's wearing glasses (since when?) that keep slipping to the end of his nose. The little girl he's singing to keeps pushing them back up which makes him laugh while he sings.

Ezra realises he's singing a Disney song. *Kiss The Girl* from *The Little Mermaid*. He also realises the little girl's head scarf has Ariel and Flounder all over it. She is only around six years old, and is completely besotted with Teddy, and rightly so. Because Teddy is good. Not like the way society has let James Corden think he's a good singer, but actually, devastatingly, infuriatingly, mind-numbingly *good*.

Just when Ezra thinks that Teddy couldn't turn any more into a Disney Prince if he tries, the fucker picks up a guitar and sings a rendition of *Part Of Your World*. The little girl's eyes actually tear up and Ezra feels something thick get stuck in his throat. He remembers, quite suddenly, why he doesn't watch these kinds of videos anymore. Cancer kids being sung to by their idols does not an emotionally stable Ezra make.

Ezra re-reads the PowerPoint again, just to check that he didn't miss anything about Teddy being a serial killer, or a terrorist, or — he doesn't know — maybe someone with a fetish for kicking stray puppies. But nope. It looks like Teddy Montgomery is perfect.

Actually, devastatingly, infuriatingly, mind-numbingly *perfect*.

The morning of Ezra's first official meeting with Teddy and he's not allowed to choose what to wear. They aren't going anywhere particularly exceptional. It's just a little bistro

— it doesn't even have a strict clothing policy. Shirt and shoes. That was pretty much the bar. So why he has tried on ten different shirts with ten different pairs of pants, he has absolutely no idea. Eventually Ali and his mom settle on beige chinos and a white shirt. With a belt. No, without. No, with. And loafers. With socks? No, definitely without. His feet will just have to sweat. The aesthetic will be worth it.

He is driven to the bistro by his chauffeur. Grace and Iris tag along for the ride for moral support. Ezra has the same anxiety he used to feel as a kid when his mom was driving him to the dentist. He absolutely can not fuck this up. He's fucked up enough already. Grace deserves a brother that doesn't fuck up all the time. His parents need a reason not to totally regret adopting him. Ali needs at least *one* PR stunt to go right before she yeets herself out of a window.

This time, Teddy is early. Ezra is already annoyed. Their part of the bistro has been sectioned off and the camera crew is set up and ready to go. Wealthy tourists in the restaurant gawp as not one but *two* celebrities sit down in a booth nearby. They keep in their seats though and try not to be too obvious as they take pictures, lest they be cast out to the concrete wilderness by security.

Teddy forces a tight smile as Ezra approaches. 'Darling.'

Ezra smiles. 'Honey-pie.'

Although Teddy ignores his *hilarious* joke, they shake hands and sit down and the cameras roll. It is horrifically awkward and stiff, and he wonders how on earth the editors are going to make this look anything other than like what it is: two kids that hate each other being forced to go on a playdate.

Ezra orders eggs, bacon, sausage, hash browns, and a mug of black coffee. Teddy orders the eggs Benedict and a pot of tea (milk and two sugars) and Ezra nearly gives himself a stroke trying not to groan. They eat in silence and the awkwardness stretches on for so long that Ezra considers jamming his butter knife into his eye just so that he has something to think about.

Teddy clears his throat. 'So, Ezra. I hear you're doing some charity work for a local rehabilitation centre.'

That certainly gives him something to think about. Ezra was trying to keep that quiet. He looks up, expecting Teddy to be wearing his stage-smile. He's not. His face looks honest and open, so Ezra says, 'Um. Yeah.'

Teddy nods, though not seemingly at anything in particular. 'My sister-in-law runs a charity for recovering alcoholics. Perhaps the two of you could talk fundraisers?'

Ezra blinks. 'Perhaps.'

'I know she has one coming up later this year. It was going to be in London, but since the, uh, move, it will now be here in the city. In the Wright Centre. We would love to have you there. Maybe you could do a talk?'

Ezra wonders if he actually *did* give himself a stroke, because Teddy Montgomery sure as *hell* isn't making small talk with him right now. Is he?

'Um. Alright. Sure.'

'Good,' Teddy says, nodding. He is absent-mindedly pushing his leftover English muffin around his plate with his fork. 'It will definitely improve the turnout. We would appreciate it.'

'You're welcome?' Ezra doesn't mean it as a question, but it comes out as one anyway. And then because Ali is behind a camera giving him the universal sign for *carry on*, he forces out: 'Is it linked with your family's church?'

Teddy's mouth pinches, his hands tightening around his mug. 'It's my parents' church, not mine. And no, it's independent.'

'You're not part of the church?'

Teddy gives him a tight smile. 'The church and I fell out a long time ago.'

Well *that's* not on his Wikipedia page. Ezra doesn't know what to say to that and the conversation lapses back into silence. He is about to open his mouth — not entirely sure what to say — until he hears someone curse.

'Shitting Christ, *cut*,' the showrunner shouts.

Ezra looks over to where he's glaring. A group of girls are causing a scene. One of them has a *Fuck me, Ezra* sign. Another has *Mrs Montgomery* printed on a homemade t-shirt. Not that it matters, because the girl is pulling her top up to show them her breasts. Ezra laughs and looks at Teddy who has gone very, *very* red. It's almost endearing. *Almost*.

'What?' Ezra says. 'You never seen a pair of boobs before?'

Teddy looks at him, his face reddening even more. 'I... *what*?'

'Dude. It's a joke. Calm down. Obviously, I don't think you're a massive virgin.'

Ezra turns back to the scene as the girls are hauled out of the bistro. The showrunner is screaming at the security — a string of profanities that would have even made Ali blush. Well, okay maybe not. But still. Ron is five-feet-fuck-all of pure fury at all times. He has a stupid goatee — that is dyed two shades darker than his actual hair colour, by the way — in a pitiful attempt to cover up the fact that he has absolutely no chin.

'Remind me not to upset him,' Teddy murmurs.

Ezra nods. 'Yeah, Ron is crazy.' He looks at Teddy. 'Anyway, what was that back there?'

Teddy shrugs. 'Just fans I guess.'

'No, dork. I mean the charity stuff. Inviting me to your family's fundraiser. Why did you do that?'

Teddy looks at him like he is stupid. 'No one was saying anything. It was getting awkward. Besides, you probably would have ended up coming anyway. We're best friends now, haven't you heard?

A groan. 'Don't remind me.'

'Also, I would appreciate it if you didn't bring up the church again. Or my parents for that matter.'

Ezra frowns. 'Why? They seem okay.'

Teddy's face is tense. Ezra thinks he might be able to hear his teeth grinding. 'And I suppose you would know after spending all of — what? One evening? — watching them chat up their peers?'

Ezra blinks. 'Have you guys got beef?'

Teddy scoffs into his tea. 'We have the whole butchers.'

Before Ezra can probe him further, Ron comes back and the cameras start rolling again. Much to Ezra's dismay, he and Teddy slip back into an uncomfortable silence punctuated every so often with stilted small talk and the occasional life-saving interruption of a waitress. Just as Teddy might have been getting interesting. He makes a mental note to snoop on the Montgomerys when he gets home.

It is going to be, Ezra is sure, a very long month.

He's not wrong. It *is* a very long month. Every lunch, every dinner, every coffee date and every *hey, it's five o'clock somewhere* boozy brunch, chips away just that little bit more at Ezra's soul. He is empty. Devoid of all joy. A shell of the man he once was. He is also a drama queen though, so he doesn't take himself too seriously.

Ezra has learnt the practised routine of Teddy's small talk. First, he opens with the weather, then he asks about Ezra's family, then he offers some information on what he's been up to since their last meeting. And it's always some kind of knight-in-Gucci-armour bullshit. *Oh yes, I was at a charity event for underprivileged children. Oh, I was raising money at a benefit concert to save the whales. Oh, well, I was swimming the English Channel again to raise awareness for underprivileged whales.*

And at the end of every playdate, Ezra goes home and stalks Teddy's social media pages, not that it gleams much new information. When he exhausts that, he looks at his older brother's Memorialised Facebook page. Leo just looks like an older version of Teddy but with a bit more scruff. He's tagged in several pictures with Daria, his widow. Her Instagram page is mostly of her and the twins — who apparently turned six last week — and her charity work.

Ezra only speaks when spoken too, and doesn't proffer any titbits about himself. Sometimes when the awkward silences stretch on for so long that Ezra is about ready to rip his face off, Ron yells cut and jumps in with some scripted content for them to read from. It's never particularly good, but Ezra loves having something to fall back on, and the lines come so naturally that it almost feels like a real conversation.

Teddy doesn't take to the scripts straight away. It's obvious the man has never acted a day in his life. But Ezra's ease, his breezy tone, his hearty laughs, seem to settle something inside of Teddy. He loosens, even if just a little bit, and there are moments where Ezra can see the man singing Disney songs to the little girl at a hospital.

The media are in love with them, of course. The Wyoming Wild Child and Great Britain's Golden Boy are *total* besties. Every day Grace sends him links to articles from *That's The Tea* or *Idol* or *Celeb News Daily*, each one of them depicting staged, candid, and staged-candid photos of them together. Headlines are unimaginative but positive.

UNITING NATIONS ONE COCKTAIL AT A TIME!

BLOSSOMING BROMANCE AT BRUNCH!

TEDDY MONTGOMERY: GAY OR JUST EUROPEAN? EZRA IS HOPING BOTH!

That last one makes Ezra bristle just a bit. He's used to the media spinning narratives about him and his sexuality, but he suspects Teddy's sensibilities are more fragile than his own (also, when did Ezra suddenly start to care about Teddy's feelings?). But Teddy doesn't seem to take any notice — and if he does, he doesn't mention it — and Grace reminds him that British tabloids are far worse.

Grace also points out that some people have started "shipping" them. Ezra thought that term had died along with Tumblr, but apparently not. When he mentions it to Teddy, he goes that familiar shade of beetroot that Ezra has come to expect whenever Teddy's integrity, intentions, or sex drive are called into question. Ezra is beginning to wonder if Teddy Montgomery actually *is* a massive virgin.

It's on their last scheduled play date that Ezra finds himself oddly morose. He's settled into this routine surprisingly nicely. It's not that he looks forward to — or particularly enjoys — hanging out with Teddy, but it's the structure that this British prude has brought into his life. On Ezra's contract with BingeBox his job title is stated as "TV personality and influencer" which is all well and good, but, in the grand scheme of things, it means nothing. He is someone who thrives on routine, and his life has absolutely none. So, this charade, this forced-fun-friendship with his mortal enemy, has given him more than he had expected. He is terrified at the thought of waking up tomorrow and the day being completely and utterly his own.

Today they are going to Ezra's favourite rooftop bar — the offensively expensive one — for tapas and cocktails. Well, *Ezra* is going to have cocktails. Teddy Montgomery, of course, does not drink, because he's too busy being the most infuriatingly perfect human being on the planet — nay, in the universe! — to allow himself to have even the littlest bit of fun.

They are briefed on their talking points before the cameras start rolling. It is suggested that Teddy asks Ezra to be the best man and that Ezra should enthusiastically accept. He even hams it up for the camera, tears welling in his eyes as he stands and pulls Teddy into a tight hug. People around them *aww* and put their hands to their hearts. Teddy is unbelievably tense in Ezra's arms, but Ezra makes up for it by squeezing him even tighter. He feels Teddy's hands tentatively pat his sides, more like he's airport security checking him for sharp objects than his fake BFF.

'Loosen up,' Ezra whispers in Teddy's ear, keeping his smile bright and joyous for the cameras. 'You're like hugging a lamp post.'

'I didn't ask you to hug me,' comes Teddy's tight reply.

'Are you sure? Then what is that I can feel digging into my hip?'

Teddy immediately lets go of Ezra and steps back. He fusses with his jacket as he sits down, a deep red flush climbing up his neck to his ears. Ezra bites down on a laugh. He knows he shouldn't enjoy ruffling his feathers so much but it's just so *easy*.

He can almost see what Grace would see in him if their entire relationship wasn't just a storyline. There's a certain sweetness to Teddy's bashfulness. He is soft-spoken and gentlemanly. Everything Ezra had once assumed was standoffishness (is that a real word?)

is actually just a deep-rooted shyness. It still doesn't make up for the fact that he is a complete Eton-bred, sober-holic, probably-votes-Conservative, pretty boy. But it's a start.

'Did the twins have a good birthday?' Ezra asks, sipping his bloody Mary that honestly just *slaps*.

Teddy gives him an incredulous look. 'I. Um. Yes, they did. Thank you.'

Ezra enjoys surprising Teddy. 'What did you all get up to?' He knows full well that they flew down to Disneyworld for the weekend from Daria's Insta page, but he asks anyway just to see Teddy's head explode.

'Daria and I took them to Magic Kingdom,' Teddy says, and then his expression goes unbelievably soft at the memory. It makes Ezra smile despite himself. 'Mason was more interested in all the ducks and squirrels running around than the actual rides. I think Margot fell in love with Gaston.'

Ezra nods. 'He *is* pretty hot.'

Teddy gives him a look then — something Ezra can't quite place. He looks like he's about to ask something, when there's a crash from across the rooftop. Ezra turns to see a crazed fan wearing a *Darling Dynasty* t-shirt literally claw her way past security, knocking over a cart of apéritifs in the process, screaming and waving a homemade sign saying *MARRY ME EZRA DARLING*. All in glittery caps. Fancy. She is followed by a small army of similar girls with matching tops and *fuck-me-Ezra-Darling* expressions. And normally, it's not a problem, until one of them tries to bottle a security guard.

Before he can really process it, the Darling's private security team is already ushering him and Teddy away to the staff elevator that will take them down to the basement level where their chauffeured cars will be waiting for them. The last thing Ezra sees before he's shoved into the lift is a girl swinging a punch at Ron. He laughs and looks at Teddy, expecting to see the same glee reflected there, but, of course, Teddy's face is steadily turning scarlet.

'You don't deal with fans well, do you?' Ezra asks.

Teddy looks at him, as if suddenly only realising he's there. He does this, Ezra has noticed. He disappears inside himself. He can't tell if it's a defence mechanism or if Teddy Montgomery hates him so much that he can't bear to acknowledge his existence. The feeling is *very* mutual.

'They're not my fans,' he says, flatly. 'They're yours.'

'The one with the boobs was *definitely* yours.'

'Yes. Well.' Apparently, there isn't an end to that sentence.

'Either way, you start sweating like a hooker in church whenever a fan comes even *close* to you,' Ezra says. 'You didn't realise what you were signing up for when you became famous?'

Teddy frowns and finally turns to look at him properly. A jaw in his muscle twitches, possibly promising that he is about to finally get interesting. 'I never wanted to be famous.'

Ezra snorts. 'Sure.'

'Yes, I'm quite sure. My dad has been an actor since before I was born. My mother went into modelling after her ballet career ended. I was thrown into the spotlight straight away. My earliest memories are of the paparazzi showing up to my birthday parties. Tabloids following me home after school. Having a PR team at age seven. I never even stood a chance at a normal life.'

'Makes sense then why you go singing to children on cancer wards and make sure someone is filming you. Oh, wait.'

'You think I do that to be filmed?'

'Why else?'

Teddy is looking at Ezra like he is a moron. It makes the back of his neck prickle. 'Because those kids have absolutely nothing else going for them. And it costs me nothing to go in there and brighten their day. If a nurse, or a parent, or *anyone* films me and puts it online that's not down to me.'

'And I bet you hate it,' Ezra says. He knows he's going too far. He knows he's pushing it and that Teddy doesn't really deserve this, but his mouth is working faster than all three of his brain cells combined, so he adds, 'God it must be so hard being so *fucking* perfect all the time.'

Teddy shoves him. Hard. Ezra's back is against the wall, Teddy's hands either side of his head. He barely has time to think *fuck me, he's tall* before the lift wobbles and groans, coming to a shuddering stop. He watches, with curiosity, as all the colour drains from Teddy's face. His hands drop to his sides, and he steps back, jaw tight.

Ezra cocks an eyebrow. 'Dude? Chill. It's not like you kissed me.'

'The elevator,' Teddy chokes out. His voice is tight. Panicked. 'It's stopped.'

Ezra nods slowly. 'Yeah. Sometimes that happens. Just hit the alarm thingy and someone will come get us moving again.'

'Right. Yes. Right.'

Ezra watches, utterly bemused, as Teddy rushes over to the panel with the buttons and sharply jabs the alarm button not once, not twice, but three times. One hand runs through his strawberry blond hair, the other undoes his top two shirt buttons. Ezra notices his chest heaving.

'Um... are you, like, okay...?' Ezra asks.

Teddy looks at him. He looks like he's going to pass out. 'I don't do well in small spaces.'

Ezra doesn't expect himself to feel sympathy for Teddy Montgomery, but he does all the same. 'Oh. Sorry, man. That's not cool. But listen, it's fine. Someone will come and get us and then we're outta here, okay? Just, like, don't pass out. I don't know any first aid.'

Teddy nods, but still looks very much like he might faint. Ezra can see his neck going blotchy. Not in the way it does when he blushes — then it's just a steady gradient of pink going all the way up to his perfect hairline. Hives. Teddy's hands go to them and begin to scratch. They're trembling.

'Don't,' Ezra says, stepping forward. 'I mean. Try not to scratch. It'll make them worse.'

Teddy looks beside himself at the thought of having nothing to do with his hands, so instead he wraps his arms around himself in a kind-of self-soothing hug. He leans back against the lift wall and screws his eyes shut, his breaths coming fast and shallow. Ezra just watches him feeling stupid and completely useless. And guilty. Why does he feel guilty? This isn't technically his fault, but he still feels guilty anyway.

'Talk to me,' Ezra says. 'Get your mind off it.'

Teddy doesn't open his eyes. 'What about?'

'Anything. Tell me — tell me how you got into music.'

Teddy nearly smiles. Nearly. 'It was the one choice that both my parents hated, so, naturally, it was the most appealing.'

Ezra is surprised to find himself smiling. 'Wow. Teddy Montgomery, the rebel.'

'It may surprise you to know that I'm not the goody-two-shoes you think I am.'

'You sing to sick children in cancer wards, man. You build hospitals. You're probably going to figure out the solution to global warming in your sleep. I hate to break it to you, my guy, but you are literally the *epitome* of Prince Charming.'

Teddy cracks an eye open. 'Charming? You know, I prefer Flynn Rider. Much more rakish.'

Ezra laughs. He actually laughs. Teddy Montgomery just cracked a joke, and it was... funny? Weird. A silence passes and Ezra sighs. 'I'm sorry. I didn't mean it. What I said about you. I know you don't do it for the camera. I just said it because. Well. Whenever

I do stuff like that it's *always* for the camera. I don't know. I'm projecting. I guess I'm looking for reasons to dislike you.'

Teddy looks at him, more confused than ever. 'Why do you want to dislike me?'

Ezra considers telling him. Then he considers keeping it a secret. Then he opens his big mouth and it all just kind of comes falling out. 'Do you remember the Teen Choice Awards in 2006?'

Teddy blinks. 'I... sorry, is this still the same conversation?'

'Well, you were there, and I was there. I don't think either of us were up for an award or anything. Anyway, I heard you were going to be there, and I begged my mom and dad to get me backstage tickets because, like, you were my idol, and I really wanted to meet you.

'So, they got me the tickets and we flew across the country so I could meet you, and I had my copy of *Whizz Kid* with you on the cover so you could sign it. I was so excited, and I practised what I was going to say, and I sat in that stuffy green room for hours waiting for you.

'Then you finally showed up and I came over to say hi and you just, like, completely blanked me and walked off. And then I cried in front of everyone like a dork, and we went home. And that's why I want to hate you, but every time I see a video of you singing Disney songs to dying children, it gets really hard, you know? So yeah. There you go.'

Teddy's mouth opens, then closes again. Ezra immediately feels stupid (guess it's *his* turn to blush now) and his arms cross defensively over his chest.

Teddy says, 'I'm sorry, Ezra.'

Ezra blinks. 'You. Are?'

'Yes. I'm really, truly sorry. I don't even remember being at the awards. But if it was 2006 like you said then... well, some really awful things were happening to me that year, so I probably wasn't in the best frame of mind. But that still isn't an excuse. I'm sorry.'

'I... um... alright.'

'I hope you can forgive me.'

Ezra feels like the biggest jackass in the world. He's held a grudge for fourteen years and nearly ruined his sister's career because he's too stubborn — too self-centred — to even consider the possibility that someone else might also be having a bad day. This is probably why everyone in his life, apart from his family, dumps him.

'I'm sorry too,' Ezra says. 'That you were having a bad time. And for everything I've done since.'

Teddy smiles. It's his genuine smile — the ones he reserves for sick kids and moments when he thinks no one is noticing him. 'It's okay.'

The elevator groans and shudders again. Teddy's smile drops, his eyes growing round with panic. His legs give out and before Ezra knows what he's doing, he's striding forward to catch him. He holds onto Teddy's elbows and guides him gently to the sticky floor, crouching opposite him. Teddy's hands are shaking again so Ezra takes them in his and squeezes gently.

'Hey,' he says. 'Teddy. It's alright. These things make noises like that all the time. You're alright. Look at me.'

Teddy looks at him and Ezra is struck by how blue his eyes are. He realises they're both wrong. He's not Prince Charming *or* Flynn Rider. He's Prince Eric through and through.

'I can't breathe,' Teddy rasps.

'Yes, you can. You're having a panic attack. Your body is being a jerk and telling you that you can't breathe but you can, alright? You *can*.'

'I... I can't...'

Ezra puts one of Teddy's hands flat against his chest. Teddy's eyes widen and Ezra puts his other hand to Teddy's sternum. He sucks in a big, exaggerated breath and lets it out slowly. 'Like this, see? Feel your lungs expanding. Let all that sweet oxygen in. Like you've been doing so flawlessly for twenty-seven years.'

Ezra starts to wonder if this is going to work at all, but slowly, surely, Teddy's short, sharp gulps begin to even out. His breath judders and catches as he forces himself to take long, measured breaths. After a moment he isn't gasping anymore. Ezra smiles and Teddy tries to smile back.

'Good,' Ezra says. 'That's really good.'

'Guess we're even now.'

'Is that right?'

'You felt like a dork in front of me, now I feel like a berk in front of you.'

Ezra laughs. Wow, Teddy Montgomery might actually be, like, legit funny. Who knew? 'There were no tears. Doesn't count, buddy.'

The elevator groans again and then, blessedly, they are moving. Ezra and Teddy look at each other, hands on each other's chests, and they both start laughing. Ezra stands and pulls Teddy up with him. For a moment, an awkward silence threatens to fall, but then Teddy is reaching into Ezra's jacket pocket and pulling out his phone. He holds it up to Ezra's face to unlock it, then starts tapping.

'What are you...' Ezra begins but Teddy puts the phone back into his pocket.

'You've got my number now,' Teddy says. 'I know this was our last scheduled appearance, but we're kind of in it for the long haul now, aren't we? We might as well make an effort.'

'I... suppose so.'

'Plus, you're in charge of organising my stag do. Best man and all.'

Ezra cracks a grin. 'Sunshine, you're not ready.'

Teddy smiles — his secret smile — again. 'Oh, I believe you.'

Chapter Four

Teddy Montgomery is funnier than Ezra had ever expected. Never before has anyone actually been able to make him laugh out loud via text, but somehow Teddy manages. Sometimes it's a gif. Sometimes it's a one-liner. Sometimes an emoji. However he looks at it, there is no denying that Teddy Montgomery is funny.

It'd taken Ezra over a week before finally texting him. Teddy had saved his name in Ezra's contacts under *Flynn Rider*. It had *also* taken a while for Ezra to find it, but when he did it made him laugh. Harder than he likes to admit.

He didn't text at first because he didn't know what to say. Does Ezra even *want* to text him? What can he say? They're not even friends, are they? *Are* they? Probably not. Are they though?

Their arrangement is over but the promise of what's to come still lingers. They're going to be family. They're going to have to see each other a thousand times and make nice every single *one* of those times until this is all over. There's a certain level of charade they have to keep up now. As far as the public are concerned, Ezra Darling and Teddy Montgomery are best buds. And it has to stay that way.

On a Friday evening, as Ezra is lounging alone in his brownstone, having been abandoned by Grace and Iris — girl's night, no boys allowed — he switches over to the movie channel and snorts as he sees *Tangled* is playing. Finally, he decides to pull out his phone and shoot Teddy a text. **you're on channel 52. also, this is ezra.**

For a while there's no response and Ezra starts to feel like an idiot. Then he sees: **Very funny. You're on channel 66.**

Ezra switches over to channel sixty-six where a rerun of *Phineas And Ferb* is playing. He snorts. **hilarious. which one am i? phineas or ferb?**

A moment later comes: **You're the platypus.**

Ezra barks a laugh. **fucking charming**

And that's how it goes on for a while. They text. They send unflattering pictures of people in various movies to each other with some kind of *hilarious* caption, such as, **didn't realise you were in this movie** or **so brave of you to appear on camera without any makeup on**. One evening when *Labyrinth* is playing, Ezra snaps a picture of one of the goblins and sends it to Teddy with the caption: **can't believe you didn't need any prosthetics for this**. He promptly gets a reply in the form of a selfie which is simply Teddy flipping off the camera, and he laughs so hard his drink comes out of his nose.

In fact, Teddy's texts are the only thing Ezra finds himself looking forward to during the day. Filming only started six weeks ago and he's already sick of it. Grace, of course, is thriving. She doesn't flinch when a camera is shoved into her face. She continues on like they're not even there. Their parents are supportive, erring on the side of caution while simultaneously respecting Grace's decisions. The whole storyline is a living, breathing ick.

The narrative for this season is all focused on the wedding. A crew trails after Grace as she and Teddy meticulously plan every aspect of their big day. Ezra isn't needed for most of it, so he's yet to come face-to-face with Teddy since the elevator incident. Once the camera crews leave for the day, Grace always finds him in his brownstone, alone and watching TV, to tell him how filming went.

He pretends he's only half-paying attention whenever the subject of Teddy comes up. Part of him is secretly curious as to what he is like on camera with her. Scripted. Playing along with Grace's charade as he picks out cake flavours and party favours. He wonders if he ever lets that secret smile of his slip out. If that blush creeps up his neck whenever he's embarrassed. If he still looks utterly terrified whenever a manic fan runs at him with her breasts out.

'Teddy is so sweet,' Grace says as she rummages through his fridge for Chinese takeout leftovers. 'Ali suggested that he kiss me today while we were filming, and he kissed me on the cheek. The *cheek*, Ezra! I felt like I was in *Bridgerton*.'

Ezra frowns at her as she claims the last of his chow mein. He was saving that for when he undoubtedly wakes up at midnight with a hankering for greasy noodles. Does she not have any of her own food? You know, in her own brownstone? 'Maybe he's camera shy.'

'Oh, he's definitely camera shy. It's actually kind of cute. God, he's such a gentleman, I wish American boys were like him.'

'And you're sure you don't have a thing for him?' Ezra asks.

'Oh, positive. He's adorable and stuff. And he has that accent that is just, like, *oh my God*. Plus, he's gorgeous. But, like, nah. Not my type.'

'What *is* your type?'

Grace stuffs a forkful of chicken and noodles into her mouth, thinking about her answer. 'He's got to be mysterious. An enigma. Like he just stepped out of a film noir with a chip on his shoulder and a deep dark secret that he will never tell me.'

'Good to know you're being realistic. Are the public buying it? You and him?'

She passes her phone to him, open on Photos, so that he can swipe through the various screenshots of news headlines she's taken. It would seem, as Ezra flicks through them, that the public certainly *do* buy it. Not only that, they're crazy about it. He scrolls through staged pictures of them at lunch together, at wedding fairs, embracing at their engagement party — pre-Vomitgate.

He stops at a photo of Teddy kissing her on the cheek. It's chaste like Grace had said. Sweet, almost. Something in Ezra's gut twists uneasily and he chalks it up to being protective of his little sister. Because that's what it is. That's all it is. Teddy Montgomery is kissing his little sister on the cheek, and it isn't sitting right with him, and that is okay because this is a perfectly normal reaction to have.

'Do you think he likes you?' Ezra asks, handing the phone back.

Grace snorts. 'I hope so, we're getting married.'

'No, I — I mean *like-likes* you.'

She gives him a look. 'Are we in fourth grade? No, Ezra, I don't think he *like-likes* me. He's never really in the moment when we're together. He's always far away. I don't think he's very happy.'

Something in Ezra's chest pinches. 'Why do you think that?'

'I made the mistake of asking how his parents are,' she explains, spearing a piece of chicken with her fork. 'He went all blotchy and weird. He had to ask the cameras to stop rolling and take a moment off set.'

Okay, well *that* is interesting. Ezra thinks back to how Teddy had behaved when he'd tried to make small talk about his father's involvement with the church and how he'd just shut down. He says, 'He did that with me too.'

Grace shrugs. 'Some people are more private about their home lives.'

'Yeah, if their home lives are shit.'

Grace waves her fork in the air dismissively, threatening to fling noodles onto his couch. 'I think that stuff about the Montgomerys being assholes off camera is just a rumour. They've been really nice to me.'

Ezra makes a noncommittal noise that neither agrees or disagrees with his sister. He turns on the TV and finds an old rerun of *America's Next Top Model* for them to watch. Grace polishes off the chow mein and then goes in search of something sweet even though she's complaining that her stomach is so full it hurts. When she settles on the sofa beside him with a packet of chocolate chip cookies, he puts his arm around her and they settle in to watch Tyra Banks make a bunch of girls half her age cry.

And he does not think about Teddy Montgomery. Not at all. Not even once.

Nope.

Text Thread: Flynn Rider

ezra:
heard you and grace have taken things to the next level. kissing on the cheek. hope you used protection.

Flynn Rider:
I was thinking of you the whole time, I swear.

ezra:
for real though, how's filming been? i know the spotlight isn't really your thing.

Flynn Rider:
I'll get by. How are you?

ezra:
lonesome. grace and iris are having girls' night. i'm a latchkey kid

Flynn Rider:
Whatever will you do without adult supervision?

ezra:
probably watch porn

Flynn Rider:
I regret asking.

ezra:
don't act like you wouldn't

Flynn Rider:
Pornography is actually banned
in Great Britain. The Queen personally
beheads anyone caught with their hands
down their pants.

ezra:
eat shit

Flynn Rider:
I love it when you talk dirty.

And so that's how they go on. They text. At first, it's a few times a week, then every other day, and then every day without fail. Teddy wakes up earlier than Ezra and usually has his equivalent of a *good morning* text waiting for him. Mostly it's selfies of him and his dog Fred (who names their dog Fred? Jesus fucking Christ-on-a-bike) in bed, hair mussed and eyes bleary. Ezra usually replies with a selfie of his own with a filter on. Sometimes he has bunny ears. Sometimes it gives him a beard. One time it showed him what he'd look like as a girl, prompting Teddy to reply: **Fit!**

It occurs to him that he could always literally just walk down the street and see Teddy face-to face. They have a hundred things coming up in the near future that will put them in the same room as each other anyway. Why is he avoiding it? Why does the thought of seeing Teddy in the flesh settle lead in his stomach, but the thought of texting him all day until his thumbs fall off make his cheeks hurt from smiling? He isn't sure what the answer to that is, but he sure as hell isn't going to open that door anytime soon.

Instead, they text, and send selfies, and Ezra is okay with their weird little friendship. If that's what it is. He's content, even. Which is something Ezra never is. Especially when filming. Sunday is his only respite — no camera crews on Sundays — and usually the only day of the week he sees Iris. She is strictly no-cameras, seeing as how most of her life is already documented on Instagram, so when they're filming he sees far less of his best friend than he would like to.

It's one evening, when Grace and Iris have come to commandeer his brownstone and raid his freezer for ice cream, that the subject of Teddy Montgomery comes up. Again. Ezra pretends to be watching the TV, to whatever episode of *Schitt's Creek* is playing, but his hand is tense on the remote.

'I thought he was never going to kiss me,' Grace says around a mouthful of cookie dough. 'Honestly, I was beginning to think he was a wait-'til-marriage guy or something. But *wow*. Wow, wow, wow.'

Iris' eyes widen. 'He kissed you? Like, *properly* kissed you?'

'Mouth and everything. Ron wouldn't shut up about it and in the end he just went for it.'

'Wow. How was it?'

'Kind of amazing.'

Ezra can't help it. He turns to look at the two girls sitting on the sofa opposite. They're in their sweats and university apparel pullovers. The day's makeup is gone, and their hair is pulled up into messy buns. They're cuddling, sharing a spoon, taking it in turns to dip into the ice cream tub. Ezra wonders if men would be less toxic if they allowed themselves to enjoy friendships the same way that women did.

Iris is grinning. 'Do you have a crush, Grace Darling?'

Grace snorts and Ezra feels himself relax a little. 'Jesus, no. I just wasn't expecting him to be such a good kisser.'

'Tongue?'

'Of course not. He's a gentleman.'

'Are you going to fuck him?'

Ezra nearly chokes on his wine. The girls give him an odd look as he has a mild coughing fit. He excuses himself to the bathroom and dabs at the red splodge saturating into his blue shirt. Ugh. It's Prada. When he looks at himself in the mirror, he is mortified to find himself flushed pink. As in *Teddy Montgomery* pink. He splashes some cold water on his face and grips the rim of the sink.

He tells himself he is fine. This is perfectly normal. It is a completely normal and valid reaction to your lesbian ex-girlfriend asking your sister if she is planning on having sex with your kind-of friend. Although is it? He and Grace had gone into far more detail about their sexual exploits before now. Never before has it made him cringe. And he and Iris had done just about everything they could imagine when they were together, so there was nothing to be shy about there.

It's *Teddy*. The issue is Teddy Montgomery. It always is.

When Grace knocks on the door to check if he is alright, he makes an excuse about not feeling well. He waits until he hears the front door click as they let themselves out before he emerges. He considers changing his shirt, but just changes into his pyjamas and refills his glass of wine. *Schitt's Creek* is still playing. By the time it gets to the episode where Patrick is singing to David, Ezra has already finished one bottle of wine and is making his way through a second.

He thinks of Teddy Montgomery. He stews. He tries not to think of Teddy Montgomery. He stews some more. He tries to focus on Patrick and David's wedding but all he can do is think of Iris' question on a loop in his head. *Are you going to fuck him*?

He's almost through his second bottle of wine when his finger is hitting the call button next to Flynn Rider's name. It doesn't occur to Ezra that it's late, or that he's drunk, or that Teddy is probably asleep. It also doesn't occur to him that this is a very bad idea and that he has absolutely no idea what he's going to say. So, when Teddy answers on the third ring, Ezra is just as surprised as anyone to hear himself say: 'Are you going to fuck my sister?'

'Ezra?' Teddy sounds like he's just woken up. 'What's going on? It's nearly three in the morning.'

'Answer the question,' Ezra slurs. 'Are you going to fuck my sister, Teddy?'

'Ezra, are you drunk?'

Ezra shakes his head, not that Teddy can see. 'Listen, I really don't want you to fuck my sister, alright? It's just. It's not cool, man. Alright?'

'I genuinely have no idea what's going on right now.'

'You could have any girl you want, Teddy. You're gorgeous — you're fucking gorgeous. Any girl, honestly. Or guy. Whatever. I don't judge. You can have me if you want. Just not Grace. I'll be really sad if you do.'

A big, British sigh. 'Are you alright? What on earth has brought all this on?'

Teddy's voice sounds genuinely concerned and Ezra's chest flushes with warmth. He chooses not to think about why. 'Grace says you kissed her. She says it was good.'

There was an awkward pause. 'Well. Yes. I suppose it was fine.'

'That makes me feel weird. I don't like it.'

Jesus shitting Christ, Ezra. Shut up. Shut all the way up. Stop talking. Hang up. Flush your phone down the toilet, change your name and move to Peru. Your name is Edmundo now. You sell pan flutes to feed your wife and six kids.

'Oh,' comes Teddy's reply. 'I'm sorry about that. Ezra, how much have you had to drink?'

Ezra shrugs to his empty living room. 'Some. A lot. Maybe. Listen, Teddy, we're friends, right?'

Another pause. 'I suppose so.'

'And friends don't upset their friends, right?'

'Correct.'

'Then please, *please* don't have sex with my sister. I'll be really upset if you do. I might cry. You can't make me cry again.' When Teddy doesn't reply, Ezra asks, 'Are you still there?'

The briefest hesitation. 'I'm still here, Ezra.'

'Promise me, m'kay?'

'Alright. I promise you.'

Ezra smiles to no one in particular. 'Okay. Thanks, man.'

'Think nothing of it.'

A long pause stretches out across the line. Ezra frowns and pulls back to look at his phone to see if the call is still connected. 'Hello?'

Teddy laughs, gently. 'Hello, Ezra.'

Ezra frowns. 'Are you laughing at me?'

'Only a little.'

'You're mean.'

'I do apologise.'

Ezra sighs. 'I'm drunk.'

Another laugh. 'Yes, I know you are. Why don't you go to bed? We'll talk in the morning.'

'Alright. Are you mad at me?'

Teddy sounds amused: 'Not in the slightest.'

'Sure?'

'Positive.'

Ezra smiles again. 'G'night, Teddy.'

'Goodnight, Ezra.'

When Ezra hangs up, the enormity of what he's done doesn't hit him. When he's stumbling to the bathroom it doesn't hit him. When his head is in the toilet bowl and he's emptying the contents of his stomach it *still* doesn't hit him. And when he's lying in his super-king-sized bed, feeling nauseous as the ceiling spins like a turntable he's still blissfully ignorant of just how much he's fucked up.

Ezra's head feels like a stray cat curled up and died in there. He smells worse. He calls out for Grace and Iris but when they don't respond he remembers they went home early. He turns to look at his bedside table, hoping that Drunk Ezra left him a glass of water and a couple of aspirin, but Drunk Ezra didn't, because Drunk Ezra is a dick.

He searches for his phone amongst the covers and finds it somewhere near his feet. He has three missed calls. Two from Grace and one from Iris. There's a text from his mom checking in on him, and his dad has forwarded a dog meme that's at least three months old. He can also see the subject line of an email from Ali that begins: LEARN YOUR FUCKING LINES, DIPSHIT.

He opens his contacts to call Grace back and freezes. His last outgoing call. Flynn Rider. 2:58am. Three minutes long.

Oh fuck. Oh fuck, fuck, fuck, fuck, *fuck*. It all comes back to him in a nauseating blur. He drunk-dialled Teddy Montgomery last night. He called him gorgeous, and offered to rail him, and — oh sweet fucking *fuck*. He is going to be sick. He is going to be the first person in the world to actually die of embarrassment. He is going to rip his own head off and yeet it across the ocean so that he can't say anymore stupid things to anyone. Least of all Teddy Montgomery.

There's a knock at his front door and he staggers through his living room wearing his comforter as a cape. He hopes it's Iris. She always knows what to do in a crisis. Iris is smart.

Iris is calm. She will know what to do. She *will*. And if she doesn't, then that move to Peru is looking more and more likely.

Ezra opens the door to see Teddy Montgomery looking at him. He's wearing jeans, a pullover, and is carrying an *IHOP* takeaway bag. His smile is easy, casual, growing ever-more-so as he looks at Ezra swaying in the doorway in his Super Mario pyjamas. Oh Christ, Ezra is going to be sick.

'I brought pancakes,' Teddy tells him. 'And coffee. And sympathy.'

Ezra has no idea what to do or what to say, so he steps aside to let Teddy in. He closes the door and watches as Teddy Montgomery confidently steps into his open-plan kitchen to busy himself with plating up the food. He moves around Ezra's home like he's been there a dozen times before, and Ezra sinks onto a stool at the breakfast bar in disbelief as a plate of pancakes, covered in maple syrup and bacon, is set in front of him. He looks at Teddy, blinking hard, as a recyclable coffee cup is pushed into his hands.

'Eat,' Teddy says. 'Drink. You'll feel better.'

Ezra gawps at him. 'What are you doing here?'

Teddy smiles. It's his secret smile. 'I told you we'd talk in the morning.'

'But you're here.'

'That's generally how two people communicate, yes. I got your address from Grace; I hope you don't mind?'

Teddy is looking at Ezra with something that he can't quite put his finger on. His head spins and he winces as his headache turns from dead stray cat to total dumpster fire. He's still certain he is going to be sick any moment.

'We have to talk,' Ezra says, cringing so hard that he has to close his eyes.

'Food first. Talk later. Eat.'

Ezra takes baby bites. It takes an obnoxiously long time for him to finish it all, but Teddy doesn't seem to mind. He has a copy of the New York Times and is sitting across from him, reading and enjoying his own coffee. His glasses are on, slipping to the end of his nose every so often. For some reason, Ezra wants to reach across and push them up again. He doesn't though. This whole saga is already weird enough as it is.

Teddy suggests that Ezra takes a shower and freshens up before they talk. The moment the hot water hits his face he feels instantly better. The pancakes are soaking up whatever wine he didn't puke up last night. The coffee has stopped the shakes. By the time he's brushed his teeth and changed into khaki chinos and a sand-coloured shirt he feels a bit more like normal. However, when Teddy smiles up at him from the kitchen counter, offering him a glass of water, all that good work is magically undone again.

'Shit,' Ezra says. 'Shit. I'm so sorry.'

'Ah. You've chosen self-pity.'

'I'm a dick. I'm an asshole. I'm a thunder-cunt of a goddamn shit-show.'

Teddy's lips twitch like he is holding back a smile. 'Do you want to know what I think?'

Ezra pinches the bridge of his nose, closing his eyes. 'No. Yes. No.'

'I thought you were sweet,' he says. When Ezra looks at him, utterly bemused, he continues. 'You were looking out for your sister, Ezra. Yeah, you were drunk, and you could have gone about it a little better, but you were.... well. Kind of adorable.'

Ezra blinks. 'You're not mad?'

'I'm not mad.'

'I'm still pretty embarrassed.'

'Understandable.'

Ezra sits down again at the breakfast bar. He looks into his glass of water hoping to find the right words there. They don't come.

'I'm not going to hurt Grace,' Teddy says, gently. 'I'm not in love with her. She's not in love with me. I like her, and I think she's fun and funny, but it will never be more than a friendship. You needn't worry about my intentions.'

Ezra looks at him. 'You're not into her? At all?'

'She's...' Teddy searches for the right words. 'Not my type. It's strictly business. Not pleasure.'

Ezra feels the ball of anxiety in his chest ease a little. Then he says, because he absolutely has to say it one more time, 'I'm really sorry, man.'

'I believe you.'

'I know you don't like drinking. If... listen, if I've ruined this. Whatever it is. Our weird friendship. Then that really sucks. I get it, but it sucks.'

Teddy looks at him for the longest time. 'Do you know how my brother died?'

It wasn't in the PowerPoint, but it had been on Teddy's Wikipedia page. 'A car crash, right?'

'That's the official story, but it's a half-truth. The other driver was drunk. They found eighteen empty beer bottles in the passenger seat when police arrived on the scene. They said the collision hadn't initially killed Leo. He'd bled out over the course of the next couple of hours, his legs crushed under the dashboard. It was a quiet country lane, so by the time the police found them, both were dead. Leo's last moments were spent in fear and agony because one man couldn't go one night without a drink.'

Ezra hasn't realised his knuckles are turning white around the glass. 'Christ. Christ, Teddy, I'm so sorry.'

Teddy looks at him with a sad expression. 'I don't dislike drinking. I don't begrudge people who like a drink. Sure, I even like a drink on special occasions. But ever since then I can't face getting drunk myself. It's too hard. One time I was at a pub with my friend Nick, and he ordered a Heineken. I saw the bottle, the same bottle found in the other driver's car, and I just fell apart. I thought I would never stop crying.'

'I...' Ezra falters. 'Jesus, I don't even know what to say.'

'Well, whatever you do, don't apologise again. I'm not sorry you called me last night. I'm not sorry you got drunk. You made me laugh. And I'm not sorry that I brought you pity pancakes. I'm just happy that you're the first person not to treat me like glass since it happened.'

Ezra's mouth threatens to smile. 'You're kind of incredible.'

'And you're an exceptionally funny drunk.'

'Agree to never speak of this again?'

'I think it's the only logical option.'

Teddy gives him that smile, his eyes crinkling, his glasses slipping down his nose again, and the ball of anxiety in his chest completely untangles and falls away. Ezra realises, with alarming certainty, that Teddy Montgomery is pretty amazing. And, apart from Grace and Iris, probably his only real friend.

Chapter Five

Text Thread: Flynn Rider

ezra:
are you coming to my thing on saturday?
the party?

Flynn Rider:
Absolutely not.

ezra:
you have to come

Flynn Rider:
I really don't.

ezra:
yes you do
the cameras won't be there

Flynn Rider:
Do I have to dance?

ezra:
dancing is encouraged
also it's themed, you have to dress up

Flynn Rider:
Well, now I'm definitely not going.

ezra:
[crying emoji]

Flynn Rider:
Oh, all right.

ezra:

you're a total babe.

Flynn Rider:
I am well aware.

The annual costume party has long since been a tradition before the Darlings could afford to rent out the Artemis Hotel. Back before Grace's YouTube career, and her scandal, and all the near-miss scandals that his parents had fought tooth and nail to keep out of the press, the annual Darling costume party was a small affair. Friends and family. The occasional work colleague that Warren and Jacqueline were trying to schmooze. Various girls that Ezra had crushes on, who he desperately wanted to see dressed up as a promiscuous cat, or a promiscuous mouse, or a promiscuous dinosaur.

Every year their house was filled with party guests dressed as whatever the theme was. One of his favourite costumes was the year everyone had to dress up like cartoon characters and himself, Grace, and Iris went as *The Powerpuff Girls*. He, naturally, was Bubbles. That was the year the rumours about him at school had started that he was gay. It was also the year when he decided he didn't care what people thought.

As the Darling Dynasty had grown, so had the parties. Venues went from their back yard in Wyoming, to renting out the local sports hall, to a ballroom at an upstate venue, to renting entire hotels for the night. The Artemis kept the first Saturday in March open for them every year. What had long ago started as an intimate gathering is now the soiree of the year. Invitations are coveted. The guest list is kept under lock and key. The press are kept at bay by a small but mighty army of security.

It is the one night of the year that Ezra can really let go. It's the one night that Grace doesn't have to be on her best behaviour for the cameras. It's the one night that Iris doesn't adopt the role of babysitting the Darling siblings, and actually enjoys herself. Honestly, Ezra is so excited he could throw up.

They are getting ready, for a change, in Grace's brownstone. It's somehow exactly the same yet completely different to Ezra's. Of course, the floor plan and the design are the same. But while Ezra's home is minimalist and simple, Grace's is nothing short of warm and cosy. Her sofa is decorated with throws and pillows. Her walls are adorned with artwork and framed photos. There are rugs to break up the laminate flooring, and each room has been given a specific colour scheme. Sometimes it makes Ezra's head hurt.

He looks at himself in the mirror. The white trousers with the red stripe down the seams. The bare chest. The lush red cape and the matching crown. In his right hand — that is adorned with gaudy pseudo-gold rings, courtesy of Claire's Accessories — he holds a "stick" microphone that brings it all together. Not to mention the moustache.

Iris appears at his shoulder as he checks his appearance in the mirror. 'I still think you should have gone for the fake boobs and the leather skirt.'

'You just want to stare at my legs all night.'

'Baby, I just can't help myself.'

Grace strides into her bedroom pulling on a pair of shades. Ezra grins. She and Iris have chosen to go as The Pet Shop Boys. They are wearing matching silver suits, sunglasses, and retro trainers. Slung around Grace's neck is a plastic kid's keyboard on a strap. Iris is holding a clunky eighties' mic. Together they look so ridiculous and so hilarious, and Ezra knows he is so impossibly lucky to have these two amazing women in his life.

'Mom and Dad are still caught up with legal stuff with Mara,' Grace says.

'What have I done to deserve this?'

Grace chooses to ignore Ezra's hilarious and witty joke. 'They said to go on without us.'

'What about your plus one?' Iris asks him. 'Is she meeting us there?'

'Can we guess what she looks like?' Grace asks. 'I'm picturing tall, leggy, and blonde.'

'Really? I'm picturing squat, no legs at all, and bald.'

'Has there been a redhead yet?'

'Yeah, the one who could ride a unicycle.'

'Oh yeah, I remember.'

Ezra watches them go back and forth in the mirror's reflection. When they get going like this it's best not to interrupt. Sometimes, to Ezra, it's like they're speaking a different language. Sometimes they talk so fast that he genuinely can't keep up to even *try* to join in. And sometimes it's obvious that they don't need a third party. Ezra doesn't mind. He understands there's a special bond between his girls that he could not, and would not, want to ever encroach on. He just wishes they'd draw breath sometimes.

He realises that they've stopped speculating and have turned to him, expectantly waiting for the big reveal. He's glad he has his reflection to focus on, because he struggles to look them in the eye when he says, 'Actually, I invited Teddy.'

And there it is. The reason he hasn't told them. The absolute shit-eating grins that they share behind his back makes his eyes roll over into a different time zone.

'Teddy?' Grace asks. 'As in Teddy *Montgomery*? As in my *fiancé* Teddy?'

'He's not really your fiancé.'

Iris puts a hand to her face. 'Oh my God. Oh my God, Ezra has a new friend!'

Ezra pretends to busy himself with the strings of his cape. 'He's not my friend. I just felt bad for him. And you didn't invite him, Grace. I thought it would look weird to the public if he wasn't seen entering the place.'

Grace snorts. 'The press isn't interested in me and Teddy tonight. It's *all* about the drunken celebrities we've invited. They'll be too busy scooting under car doors for crotch-shots to care where my betrothed is.'

'I think it's nice,' Iris says. 'He's sweet and his best friend is back in England. He's probably lonely.'

Ezra's phone buzzes and he pulls it from his pocket. It's a message from Teddy. Just a selfie of him and his sister-in-law, Daria. She's helping him apply blue and red eyeshadow to his face. Something has made Teddy laugh and he's smiling his secret smile, his eyes crinkling. Ezra grins, making a mental note to thank Daria for capturing something that the world hardly ever sees.

Iris and Grace appear over his shoulders, one either side, and peer down at his phone. Ezra tries to pocket it, but it's too late, and Grace plucks it out of his hand. She shows it to Iris, whose hands are back to either side of her face. Ezra scowls and reaches for the phone, but Grace just dances back out of reach.

'Oh my God,' she says. 'You text each other. Like, a *lot*. Every day!'

'No way!' Iris says.

Ezra holds his hand out and waits. 'Phone please.'

Grace scrolls quickly though the messages, showing Iris just how many of them have been sent. Ezra has to admit. It's a lot. A blush threatens to surface that he chooses to strategically ignore. So, what if he texts Teddy more than he talks to his own family during the course of the day? Teddy is funny. Their conversations are funny. It doesn't mean anything.

'Oh my God, there are phone calls!' Grace practically squeals.

'Oh, stop!' Iris' face is an absolute picture.

'Voice notes! *Voice notes*!'

Before Ezra can pretend that he doesn't care if Grace plays them out loud, Grace hits play on the most recent one, and he is tempted to set himself on fire. Anything would be better than enduring their gleeful expressions as Teddy Montgomery's soft voice crackles through the speaker.

Hi. Thought I'd just say hi. You seemed a bit out of sorts today and I was worried. You're a big boy, I know, but you are also a glutton for punishment when it comes to suffering in silence. Anyway, I'm here if you want to talk. Or if you don't. I started watching Schitts Creek. *I get why you like it. If you're still down in the dumps tomorrow, we can watch it together. Anyway, enjoy your evening and don't beat yourself up over whatever it is for too long. Bye. Bye, bye, bye.*

Ezra is ready to hurl himself into the sun. Grace and Iris are watching him, mouths agape. This time, he can't hold back the blush. That voice note is from a few nights ago. Ezra is, indeed, beating himself up over a filming session that hadn't gone well. Ali was on his ass about it and he'd stormed off set. When Teddy had tried calling him like usual — 8pm sharp — Ezra hadn't answered, and Teddy had gotten worried. Ezra had kept that voice note because no one, apart from his family, ever notices when he isn't okay. Most people can't even see the cracks in the mask. But Teddy can.

Iris doesn't know what to do with her hands. One is on her chest. The other at her mouth. Grace is just grinning. Ezra is quite certain that he's having an aneurysm.

'That,' Iris says, 'is the cutest thing I've ever heard.'

'Ezra!' Grace says, brandishing his own phone at him. 'He's, like, legit your best friend!'

Ezra takes the opportunity to snatch his phone back. He pockets it and crosses his arms haughtily across his chest. He realises that this is the exact response his sister wants to get out of him. He doesn't care.

He stays in a somewhat sulky mood for the first half of the limo ride to the Artemis Hotel. By the second half though, the champagne has long been flowing, and the conversation has turned to fond memories of previous parties, and Ezra is already a bit tipsy. Iris has her phone hooked up to the Bluetooth and she is blaring *ABBA: GOLD* and they are scream-singing along, making up the words to the parts they don't know or have forgotten.

When they arrive, Ezra gets out first so he can help the other two out. Cameras immediately blind him, and Grace and Iris loop arms with him either side. Security is there to walk them down the obnoxious red carpet that they don't deserve (honestly, who *does* deserve a red carpet aside from Cher and Bianca Del Rio?) and they look like a weird collaboration that definitely should have happened back in the eighties.

The Artemis Hotel is a hive of depravity and Ezra loves it. He loves the way people can just *be* when the cameras aren't rolling. The way he can let go without worrying that he'll screw up a scene, or ruin ratings, or embarrass his sister. He loves seeing Grace be her most authentic self and not the overly-polished version of herself that lives on the internet. He loves seeing Iris absolutely come alive and thrive on the chaos of it all.

The main event is happening in the West Hall. A live band is playing covers of songs from the seventies up through the nineties. It is packed with guests dressed as various musical icons, dancing, drinking, and celebrating the mere fact that they're rich enough and famous enough to be invited to a Darling Dynasty soiree.

And they're treated like royalty. Because of course they are. They're Darlings and Co. People gush over them, offer to buy them drinks, try to pull them into their circles to mingle. Ezra gets caught up in a drinking game at the bar that he doesn't know the rules to, but he doesn't care because, win or lose, he gets to take a shot. Dimly he remembers what happened the last time he got drunk in public, but he doesn't care because this is his night. *His* night. He doesn't have to worry about the fractures in the mask. Hell, he doesn't have to wear the mask at all.

People flirt with him. Both women and men get drunk and whisper dirty things in his ear as he dances with them. His head is pleasantly warm and fuzzy though, so he lets it happen, and plays along when a man grabs his ass. He knows that if the press were allowed in that his face would be all over the front pages of every gossip blog come tomorrow. He can picture it now: his head tipped back, laughing, as a cute guy dirty-dances with him. Jesus, they would lose their sweet little minds.

At some point in the evening, he is reclaimed by Grace and Iris who are also drunk and who desperately want him to start a conga line, so he obliges. He is leading a train of drunken A-listers around the dancefloor when he spots Teddy Montgomery watching him from the doorway. He's dressed as Ziggy Stardust, his hair quaffed, wearing the iconic striped jumpsuit with the oversized golden shoulder pads. The red and blue lightning strike down his face is expertly done and Ezra knows that Daria is to thank for that.

Ezra breaks out into the biggest smile of his life and is rewarded with one back. He hands over the reins of the conga line to Iris and crosses the dancefloor to meet Teddy. The closer Ezra gets the better he looks. It really is an incredible costume. There is an awkward moment when Teddy goes for a handshake and Ezra goes for a one-armed hug, and one of Teddy's arms gets crushed between them. It doesn't matter though because Teddy is here. Ezra doesn't know why that makes him so happy, but he chooses to not think about it too much.

'You made it,' Ezra says, knowing it's a stupid thing to say. Of course, he made it. He's here, isn't he? Dumbass.

Teddy smiles. His lips are painted red, and it has no right to suit him so much. 'I was guilted into it by a deranged American.'

'You look great.'

'Thanks. Who are you supposed to be?'

Ezra gives him a hard but playful shove. This just makes Teddy's smile widen, which, in turn, makes Ezra feel stupidly happy. 'You're a real dick.'

'And *you* look amazing.'

Ezra grins. 'You're forgiven. Come on.'

Ezra pulls Teddy over to the bar. He expects Teddy to ask for an orange juice and nearly falls over when, instead, he asks for a red wine. When he catches Ezra staring at him, incredulously, he shrugs and says something about it being his night off. Ezra orders himself a beer and an extra shot of tequila for Teddy. When he gives Ezra the side-eye, Ezra explains that Teddy has some catching up to do. He is even more surprised when Teddy doesn't argue and downs it.

So, they drink. They talk. They laugh. Grace and Iris untangle themselves from the conga line that has now, somehow, become a limbo contest and join them. Teddy never seems to expect the warmth that people show him, because when both girls wrap him up in a hug he looks as equally shocked as when Ezra did. Grace takes about a million pictures of them all together. Not for Instagram or for Darling Dynasty. But just for her. For them. The memories.

When a Pet Shop Boys song comes on, Grace and Iris nearly lose their minds. Grace is up first. She grabs Iris' hand, who, in turn, grabs Ezra's. Ezra snags Teddy's hand as he's dragged away, pulling him up with them. The absolute horror in Teddy's big blue eyes is unmistakable as he's led onto the dancefloor. The girls break off from them and start dramatically singing the lyrics to *West End Girls* to each other, dancing in a far more suggestive way than Ezra ever remembers the Pet Shop Boys doing. This just leaves himself and Teddy, who looks like he is going to pass out.

Ezra has always considered himself a socialite. Someone who thrives when thrown into the deep end and expected to mingle, and make nice, and lead conga lines at parties. He is completely at ease and in his element when in the middle of the dance floor, or dancing on a table, or up singing karaoke. He absolutely cannot imagine what it must be like to not feel totally relaxed in this kind of situation. He does, however, take pity on Teddy and nods to the side lines.

'Bar?' he suggests.

Teddy nods, his body visibly relaxing. 'Please.'

They grab more drinks — beer for Ezra and wine and a shot for Teddy — and they head out to the smoking area outside so they can talk without having to shout. Teddy grabs his coat on the way out and Ezra wishes he'd been smart enough to bring one. Spring clearly hasn't gotten the memo yet, and it's still unseasonably cold for March. He crosses his arms over his bare chest and tries not to shiver.

'So,' Ezra says, nodding to Teddy's glass of wine. 'You're drinking.'

For a moment, Teddy looks sheepish. 'Can you keep a secret?'

'For a price.'

Teddy smiles, but it's his public one. Polite and pinched. Ezra is wounded. 'I sometimes have a drink when I'm anxious. I find it helps me to... loosen up.'

'Why are you anxious?'

'I don't do well in big groups.'

Ezra thinks back to Teddy's behaviour at his and Grace's engagement party. The way he walked around with a rod straight back and a tight jaw. How he was at their public appearances, all wooden and twitchy. Every time he looks horrified and flustered when any fan shows him the slightest bit of attention. Ezra realises, immediately, that he's got Teddy Montgomery all wrong. He's not a stuck-up prick. He is just... a normal guy who was thrown into the spotlight too young. Just like Ezra. And who doesn't know how to handle the attention. Whereas Ezra likes to get blackout drunk and make a spectacle of himself, Teddy likes to fade into the background and pray that no one notices him.

Ezra is about to reply when a gust of cool wind takes his breath away. He curses and tugs his cape tighter around himself. He has no idea what Teddy is doing, taking off his coat, until he offers it to him. Because of *course* Teddy Montgomery would offer Ezra his coat. Because that's the most *Teddy Montgomery* thing he could possibly do. Ezra accepts it, nevertheless.

'So,' Teddy says, taking a demure sip of his drink. It makes Ezra grin. 'You and Iris?'

Ezra groans. 'Who told you?'

Teddy's lips twitch in amusement. 'The internet. And Grace.'

'Traitors, both of them,' Ezra says it without malice. And really, he doesn't mind talking about it. Not with Teddy at least. Teddy is different. He is almost so far removed from Ezra's orbit of daily life that he feels he can tell him anything and it won't really matter because Teddy is just a passing comet. Bright but brief. 'Yeah, we were a thing.'

'What happened?' Teddy asks. His voice isn't overly gentle, the way people usually ask, and Ezra appreciates it.

'She realised she was a lesbian.'

Teddy nearly chokes on his wine. 'Goodness.'

Ezra arches a sculpted eyebrow. 'Is that an issue?' Because if it is, that is going to be a definite problem.

Teddy blinks. Once. Twice. 'No. God, no. I was just...' He searches for the right word. It's cute. He settles on: 'Surprised.'

'Me too, buddy,' Ezra says.

Teddy laughs then, and Ezra grins along with him. It *is* pretty funny.

'I thought she was the one,' Ezra tells him. His moustache is peeling off, so he removes it and stuffs it in his pocket. 'Or at least I wanted her to be. Have you ever been in love? Like, *real* love?'

Teddy blinks, obviously not expecting the question. 'No. I suppose I haven't.'

'I thought I was in love with Iris, but I absolutely wasn't. I just really wanted to love her because she was. Well. She's Iris. Fuck, I still really want to be in love. And not just the regular kind. I want movie love, you know? I want Patrick Brewer singing to David Rose, playing the guitar, their eyes meet, and they know this is the moment that changed everything, kind of love. Like Lorelai Gilmore singing *I Will Always Love* You to Luke Danes at the bar. The Dolly Parton version. Does that make sense?'

Teddy's secret smile. 'It does.'

'Why are all the hot ones gay?'

Teddy barks a laugh that Ezra feels the joke doesn't merit but smiles along anyway. 'I have no idea.'

Grace and Iris grab them when they rejoin the party. A drinking game has started and they are two team members short. Ezra finds it both hilarious and adorable (and really fucking predictable) that Teddy has never played a game of beer pong in his life and that he needs the rules explained to him. And for someone who has never played before, Teddy Montgomery is *really* good at beer pong. When he wins the game for them, Ezra wraps him in a hug — a proper hug this time, none of that one-armed shit — and ruffles his infuriatingly perfect hair.

This celebration, naturally, requires a drink. And another. And another. Sometime around Teddy's sixth shot and his fifth glass of wine, the band plays *Starman* and Teddy gives Ezra a mischievous grin before pulling him to the dancefloor. And Ezra has to check that he's not hallucinating, because he's damn sure that Teddy — Teddy Montgomery — is definitely not pulling him up to dance. Except that he is. Grace and Iris let out a loud cheer as they join them on the dance floor, and they all jump around like idiots.

Ezra watches Teddy's walls come down. He watches the façade come away, bit by bit. He watches the flush in his cheeks and smile on his stupidly handsome face, and some part of him realises how privileged he is to get to see him this way. So open and vulnerable. Just enjoying himself like every other twenty-seven-year-old deserves to.

The band takes a break, and the music shifts over to a playlist. *Buttons* by the Pussycat Dolls starts playing and Ezra tips his head back and laughs.

'Oh my God,' he tells Teddy. 'This is the song I had my first lap dance to.'

Teddy chokes on his wine. 'Oh. Goodness.'

'Her name was Vanessa. We were in love.'

'I don't think that was really her name.'

'Vanessa would never lie to me. Our relationship was built on trust. And fifty-dollar bills.'

Teddy grins. 'I'm shocked it didn't last.'

'What about you?' Ezra asks. 'What song did you have your first lap dance to?'

'Uh,' Teddy clears his throat, his ears turning pink. 'Well. I've never had one.'

Ezra feels his mouth fall open. 'What? You've *never* had a lap dance? Ever?'

'Not ever.'

'Oh. Dude. It's, like, a rite of passage. You turn twenty-one, you get drunk, you get a lap dance. What were *you* doing on your twenty-first birthday?'

Teddy thinks about it. 'I think I was training to swim the Channel.'

'Right. Well,' Ezra says, grabbing his shoulders and directing him back to one of the tables at the edge of the dancefloor. 'There's a first time for everything.'

Teddy doesn't seem to realise what's happening until his ass meets the chair. By then it's too late because Ezra is playfully pushing his legs apart and straddling his lap. Teddy swallows gravely, his eyes wide. Ezra sings the lyrics while he pretends to ride Teddy. Grace and Iris are screaming like deranged fruit bats and cheering him on. Ezra runs his hands up and down Teddy's chest, giving him his best porn star pout. Teddy opens his mouth to object, but Ezra puts a finger to his lips to shush him.

Then, he feels it. He feels it and it's so fucking obvious that it's there and pressing into the underside of his thigh. Ezra stops dead, his gaze locking with Teddy, who looks absolutely horrified. For a painfully long moment, neither of them move, and with every passing second Ezra becomes more and more aware of the fact it's just not going away.

In one sure movement — more sure than Ezra has ever known Teddy to be — he is gently but firmly removing Ezra from his lap. Ezra allows himself to be manoeuvred out of the way while Teddy stands, grabs his coat and heads for the exit. It's not until the door closes behind him that Ezra's feet remember how to move, but his brain still can't quite catch up, because he's already going after Teddy before he can decide if it's a good idea or not.

He finds Teddy in the smoking area, hands braced against the railing of the steps that lead down into the staff car park. He has his back to Ezra, but he can see him breathing hard. When the door creaks, Teddy spins to face him, eyes wide. Ezra holds his hands up in a kind of surrender and tries an easy-going smile.

'Don't freak out,' Ezra says. 'Seriously, dude. It was nothing. It means nothing. We've been drinking, and the atmosphere is always, like, super charged at these things. It could have happened to anyone. Really, it's not a big deal.'

Teddy is looking at Ezra like he's an idiot, but in all fairness, he probably is. 'Not a big deal?'

Well, it kinda *felt* like a big deal. But he suspects that Teddy won't find that amusing. 'Same thing probably would have happened if it was Grace or Iris. Really, it's fine.'

Teddy blinks. 'Oh, good God. You really are this thick, aren't you?'

Ezra frowns. He doesn't know what to say. Mostly because he doesn't understand. 'Why don't you come back inside? No one even knows what happened.'

'I know,' Teddy says, voice low. '*You* know.' It comes out like an accusation.

'But it doesn't actually *mean* anything.'

Teddy's eyes darken. 'What if it did?'

If Ezra was confused before then he's completely fucking bewildered now. 'I... *what?*'

Teddy takes a step closer. 'What if it did mean something? What then?'

'I. Wait. *What?*'

Teddy huffs a disgruntled laugh. 'Bloody Americans.'

Ezra is about to retaliate, but then Teddy's hands are capturing his face, and he is leaning down to kiss him. Ezra's eyes widen at the same time his body goes completely boneless. His hands fly up to capture Teddy's wrists, but he surprises himself when he doesn't try to pull him away. Instead, his thumbs brush over the backs of Teddy's hands, his eyes fluttering closed. His brain is like a vinyl record stuttering on a turntable, the same thought just repeating over and over again: *Oh fuck. Oh fuck. Oh fuck. Oh fuck.*

Teddy's tongue sweeps his lower lip and Ezra parts his mouth without thinking. Teddy's tongue meets his and he's surprised by the soft moan that escapes his own lips. He's never been kissed like this. He's never been the one who isn't taking control. His brain is trying to come up with reasons as to why this is a *very* bad idea — and there are a shit ton — but then Teddy's hands are at his bare waist, pushing him back against the brick wall, and Ezra's brain wanders off on vacation.

There's the sound of car unlocking, and the flash of headlights, and Teddy jumps back so quickly that Ezra's body shivers at the sudden rush of cold his absence leaves. They both turn and watch as a woman talking on her phone crosses the parking lot, gets into her car and drives off, seemingly none the wiser. Teddy looks back to him; his jaw wound so tight that Ezra is worried something is going to snap.

'Teddy,' he tries, but Teddy is already turning, walking down the steps.

This time Ezra doesn't follow. He simply watches Teddy disappear around the side of the building out of sight. For a long while he stands there, back against the wall, shivering. His fingertips go to his lips, and he feels something twist in his stomach.

Oh fuck, he thinks.

'Oh fuck,' he says.

Chapter Six

Teddy Montgomery has fallen off the face of the planet. It's been over a week since the kiss in the smoking area, and Teddy Montgomery is ghosting him. *Him.* Ezra Darling. America's most eligible. The Wyoming Wild Child. If Ezra isn't so paranoid that this is all his fault — which, let's face it, it probably is — then he might actually be angry with Teddy. But instead, he is far, *far*, too busy being completely, utterly, restless.

Teddy isn't replying to his texts. He's not answering his calls. Ezra manages to get his email address from Ali, muttering some excuse about needing it for scheduling, and eventually Ali gets so annoyed with his pestering that she relinquishes. Ezra doesn't know why he expects a reply, when Teddy hasn't replied to his twenty text messages, but he tries anyway.

*

```
Subject: please can we talk?
---
Ezra < Ezra-Darling@Darlingdynasty.com>
To: Teddy
---
teddy please can we talk? i'm freaking out here. i'm
sorry if i read the situation wrong, but i want to make
things right. please just call me.
ezra
```

*

```
Subject: teddy??
---
Ezra <Ezra-Darling@Darlingdynasty.com>
To: Teddy
---
```

```
come on, this is dumb. let's just talk about it. we
can't avoid it forever. it was just a kiss. i've kissed
a bunch of people when I'm drunk. it's not that deep.
call me.
ezra
*
Subject: hello???
---
Ezra <Ezra-Darling@Darlingdynasty.com>
To: teddy
---
was it bad?
*
```

He regrets that last one the moment he hits send. Never, *ever* (seriously, ever) has Ezra been the needy one. He's always the one being chased. He's always the one that gets approached at the bar, the one that men and women want to take home at the end of the night. He's always the one breaking hearts by saying no. He's never been the one who sits by his phone, with the volume on high just in case he gets a text, checking the screen every five minutes to make sure he hasn't gone deaf and missed a notification.

To make things worse than they already are — which is pretty damn bleak, to be honest — Ezra can't even go over to Teddy's brownstone because Teddy is no longer in the country. The official story is that he's visiting friends back in the UK, but Ezra knows it's because of what he did. Of what *they* did. In the smoking area, outside the West Hall, in the Artemis Hotel.

Oh fuck-fuck-fuckity-fuck.

So, Ezra is left with absolutely nothing to do but sit and fester in his own bad mood. It doesn't go unnoticed. He accidentally ruins a scripted family dinner on set by starting an argument with his dad when the subject of Teddy Montgomery is brought up. Warren merely passes a comment on his surprise at Teddy's sudden absence, and Ezra comes to his defence way quicker and *way* more defensive than necessary. Ali is looking at him like she wants to set him on fire, but Ron just rubs his hands together, cartoon dollar signs rolling in his eye sockets.

Grace tries to bribe it out of him with boozy brunch invitations. His mom and dad tag team on gently trying to coax out answers for his foul mood, like he isn't twenty-five and allowed to sulk all day if he damn well wants to. Which he *does*. Iris gently prods him with daily **everything okay?** texts that he appreciates but doesn't reply to.

Because, no. Everything is categorically not okay. Teddy Montgomery kissed him and then ran off back to Britain and is now ignoring him. And all Ezra can do is wonder how he could have messed everything up so badly and wait for him to come home so he can throttle him.

And, of course, he can't stop thinking about it. The kiss. Teddy's possessive grip on his face. His strong hands on his waist. His lips that were way softer than they had any right to be, and his tongue (oh my *God,* his tongue), and his booze-soaked breath that Ezra hadn't minded because, like, Teddy's lips were *really* soft.

He keeps thinking about Teddy's jawline, and how sharp it is. How it is nothing at all like a girl's, and how he really didn't mind at all. How there was a slight scratch of stubble on Teddy's chin, and how that only excited him more. How Ezra's head had tilted back to accommodate Teddy's mouth, because Teddy Montgomery was a damn supermodel with legs that just went on and on. Oh God, those *legs*. Those broad shoulders. That neat waist. Those long fingers—

Ezra has to take more cold showers than he cares to admit. He is also becoming increasingly aware that he should delete his search history on his laptop, lest Grace comes over to borrow it without asking, like she so frequently does. He changes his password anyway, just to be sure. The last thing he needs is his sister knowing he's been Googling things like: **am i bisexual? how to tell if i'm bisexual? i'm a guy and my guy friend kissed me. is teddy montgomery bi? is teddy montgomery gay?**

Ezra isn't proud of those last two searches. It's really none of his business if Teddy is bisexual or gay. Except that it kind of is. Because he kissed him. In the smoking area. Outside the West Hall. At the Artemis Hotel. But it's not the *internet's* business. But he hopes the internet will know the answer anyway. Because he's a hypocrite now too.

Of course, all the Google search brings up is a string of Teddy Montgomery's suspected past lovers. All of them are women. Socialites, actresses, models. All statuesque and beautiful and very, *very* much not men. Not Ezra Darling. He comes across a photo of Teddy kissing a Victoria's Secret model at Ascot and Ezra thinks, quite smugly, that it looks nothing like their kiss. It's polite. Chaste. Proper. *Their* kiss had been hot, and heavy, and steamy, and Teddy's hands had grabbed Ezra's waist, and his tongue (that *tongue*) had been—

More cold showers. More brooding. More invitations to brunch from Grace, and family meetings with his parents so they can casually float the idea of Ezra going back to seeing his therapist. They're worried he's slipping back into his old spirals. He assures them he's not and he's just having an off week that he can tell they don't believe by the way they glance anxiously at each other.

More texts from Iris both morning *and* night asking if he's alright. More tetchy moments caught on camera that make Ron salivate at the prospect of *actual* drama. More snapping at his family members that don't deserve it. More guilt over unnecessarily worrying his parents. More Googling. More image searches of Teddy Montgomery. It seems to go on and on.

Until of course, it doesn't. During one of their impromptu Project Runway binges, Grace casually drops it into conversation that Teddy is back in New York, and that's all Ezra needs to hear. He makes an excuse about wanting to go pick up some food from the Thai restaurant at the end of their block — despite only having eaten an hour ago — and leaves Grace on his couch, wide-eyed and slack-jawed.

And that is how Ezra ends up standing outside Teddy's brownstone in the rain for twenty minutes deciding whether or not to knock. That is how he ends up pounding his fists on Teddy Montgomery's door at 10:35pm, refusing to give up until he is let in, even though he's not sure if he even wants that or not.

When Teddy eventually wrenches the door open, expression wild and bags under his eyes, Ezra realises that he has no idea what to say, and he curses himself when all that comes out is: 'What the *fuck*, Teddy?'

Teddy drags a hand over his tired face. 'Ezra, this really isn't the best time.'

'Don't care,' Ezra says, pushing past him and into Teddy's living room. He's dripping all over the ivory carpet, but he's also past caring about social niceties. 'We need to talk.'

Teddy watches him for a moment, the door hanging open, before sighing and shutting it. He slides the deadbolt over and stares Ezra down, both hands on his hips. 'Go on then.'

Ezra blinks. 'Teddy. You kissed me. We *kissed*. Then you ghosted me.'

'I didn't ghost—'

'Yes, you fucking did. You kissed me, realised it was a mistake, and disappeared faster than you can say *gay panic*.'

'Ezra—'

'Like, was it *that bad* kissing me? Was I really that terrible?' Ezra is aware he is working himself up, but he doesn't care. It's been a few long weeks of anxiety, and regret, and cold showers, and weird Google searches, and worried looks from his family, and existential crises, and he can't pretend that he doesn't care anymore. Because he actually really does. 'Am I such a horrible mistake that you literally had to *flee the country?*'

Teddy scrubs a hand over his face and leans back against the door. He lets out a long, withering, I'm-so-tired-of-this-bullshit sigh. All Ezra can think is, *Yeah, me fucking too, sweetie.* It's then, however, that he notices the dog collar in Teddy's hand. He realises, too late, that he wasn't instantly mauled by an over-excitable Golden Retriever when he walked in. When he looks around the brownstone, a box of packed-up tennis balls and squeakers and an empty dog bed are all the clues he needs.

Oh. *Oh.* Ezra is such an asshole.

When Teddy takes his hand away from his face, Ezra can see his eyes are red. Something in his chest twists so painfully, so *suddenly*, that he feels like his legs might buckle. He doesn't know what to say, so he keeps his dumb mouth shut for once.

'You aren't a mistake,' Teddy surprises him by saying. 'I don't regret what I did. And I admit, I could have handled it better. But I — I don't know. I panicked. And then all I wanted was to talk to my best friend, face to face. It was stupid, and impulsive, but I took the family jet back to England. I needed to get away. I should have replied to your messages. I'm sorry. I didn't know what to say.'

Ezra frowns, because this is *so* not the most important thing anymore. He's spent the last three weeks shamelessly stalking Teddy's Instagram page, being careful not to like any pictures from three years ago — because if he did then he may be the first person to die *twice* from embarrassment — enough to know that Teddy's dog is his baby. *Was* his baby.

'Teddy,' he says softly. 'Are you okay?'

For a horrible moment, Teddy's lower lip wobbles. Then he draws himself up to his infuriatingly impressive height and clenches his jaw. The old British-stiff-upper-lip. 'Yes. I'm fine. Thank you.'

'It's okay if you're not really fine.'

'Well, I am.'

'When did it happen?'

'Daria called me this morning. He'd taken a funny turn in the night. I came home as quickly as I could, but he was already gone.'

Ezra wants to go to him. He wants to ease the tension out of his jaw with a kiss. He wants to remember what it feels like when Teddy Montgomery pushes him against a wall and claims him with his mouth. Instead, he says, 'I'm so sorry.'

'Thank you.'

'I can go?'

There's a long stretch where they just look at each other. 'Stay,' Teddy says.

Ezra swallows. 'Alright.'

'You aren't a mistake.'

'Oh.' Ezra thinks that there is no good goddamn reason why this should make him so happy, but it does. 'That's good right?'

'You tell me.'

Ezra is still dripping on the carpet. They watch each other in silence. He has absolutely nothing intelligent to say, so he settles for: 'Are you gay?'

Teddy arches an eyebrow. 'However did you guess?'

'I—uh. I don't know if I am. Or if I'm not. Or if I'm something else.'

'Alright then.'

Ezra can literally see Teddy shutting down. Closing off. Putting up those walls that all those weeks of late-night texting, and 3am phone calls, and ugly selfies, and shared memes have broken down. He wonders how many people have hurt Teddy to make him so guarded so young. He can't stand to be another one of them. 'No. No, I didn't mean — Teddy. *Jesus*. I *liked* it, okay?'

Teddy's brows knit together, and he looks at Ezra like he's a particularly challenging crossword puzzle. 'Pardon?'

'Christ, Teddy. Do I have to spell it out for you? I liked it when you kissed me. I really, *really* liked—'

And that's as far as Ezra gets, because Teddy is crossing to him in three long strides, grabbing his shirt collar and is kissing him so fiercely that he gasps. And it's good. It's so *fucking* good that Ezra's brain goes offline for a moment. Teddy's hands on his hips bring him back, and it comes to him, with a sudden, jarring clarity, that he was right all along. Teddy Montgomery really *is* devastatingly, infuriatingly, mind-numbingly *perfect*. And Ezra cannot get enough.

His hands push their way into Teddy's hair and when he tugs gently, he is rewarded with a little noise from him that goes straight to the heat building steadily in his stomach. He realises, dimly, that Teddy is manoeuvring them back to the couch. He doesn't mind this at all. He also doesn't mind the slow, deliberate way that Teddy's mouth slides against his, coaxing his lips apart so he can taste him.

There's something in Teddy's sureness, in his confidence in an area that Ezra is — let's face it — totally clueless in, that makes him melt. He is putty beneath Teddy's hands. His strong, sure hands. Ezra is ready to be moulded into whatever shape Teddy wants. Whatever Teddy needs him to be. And right now, Teddy's hands are tugging his shirt out of his pants and. Oh. His hands are on his skin again. Flexing over his hips. And Ezra is absolutely going to die.

The backs of his legs hit the couch and Ezra drops down into the seat, pulling Teddy on top of him. The kiss is broken for a moment and Ezra looks up at the disgustingly attractive man straddling his hips, and he breaks out into a goofy grin that he absolutely hates himself for. Teddy's own smile is soft and honest. His secret smile. He bites his lower lip (dear *God*) and bows his head to kiss Ezra again. Ezra's hips involuntarily buck up and he feels Teddy smirk against his lips.

'Do you have any idea?' Teddy purrs, pressing his lips to the hollow of Ezra's throat. 'How much I've wanted you like this?'

Ezra tries to think of a smart-ass reply, a biting retort, but then he feels Teddy's teeth on his neck and his last brain cell surrenders. His head drops back, his hands gripping desperately at Teddy's thighs, like he is a sailor adrift, and this Englishman is his life preserver. 'Tell me.'

Teddy nips at his throat again. 'Ever since you told me to,' he puts on a surprisingly good American accent, "Keep your fucking hands off my sister".'

'Is that right?'

'Such a *dirty* mouth on you. Whatever will I do with it?'

Ezra can think of a few things. He squeezes Teddy's thighs and says, 'You got a bedroom in here somewhere?'

Teddy swallows. He bites his lip again (sweet Jesus, that *mouth*), this time with anticipation, and nods. He stands and leads Ezra to his bedroom by the hand, looking over his shoulder at him. Ezra's stomach reckons it's an Olympic acrobat. He will probably never forgive himself for the dumbass grin he gives Teddy when Teddy winks at him.

Teddy's bedroom is — well, Ezra doesn't really care what it looks like, because it's Teddy's bedroom and he is standing in it with him. But there is a bed and that is where Teddy is guiding him. They stand at the foot of it and Teddy takes Ezra's hands in his own, his thumbs brushing over his knuckles. Then one hand reaches out and Teddy runs his thumb lightly over Ezra's lower lip, and Ezra kisses it.

'What would you like to do?' Teddy asks, voice husky. 'We don't have to do anything that you're not comfortable with.'

Ezra takes hold of Teddy's hips and pulls their bodies flush together. He's already hard. They both are. 'Well first, I want to take your clothes off.'

'I wouldn't be averse to that.'

'Then I want to finish what you started at the Artemis Hotel.'

Teddy's breath catches. 'Jolly good. After you.'

Ezra is impressed with his hands when they don't shake as he unbuttons Teddy's shirt and pushes it from his shoulders. He is also impressed when he doesn't roll his eyes, because, of course, Teddy is like some kind of Greek God. His body is lean, his shoulders broad, his waist narrow and tight, and Ezra will probably set himself on fire if he doesn't touch him immediately.

He places feather-light kisses on Teddy's chest as he removes his own shirt. It falls to the ground, and he kicks off his shoes. Teddy's hands wind around Ezra's waist as he pulls them both down to the bed. He marvels at the way their bodies slot together so well, like he was always supposed to have Teddy Montgomery pinning him down against a Hermes bedspread. Like Teddy Montgomery's thighs were always supposed to be sandwiched between his.

Teddy kisses him again and it's white hot, stoking something in him that has long laid dormant. He kisses his way down Ezra's body, stopping at the spot below his navel, and Ezra huffs in impatience. It's been three weeks. Three long, hard, fantasy-filled weeks where Ezra has been imagining this very scenario, and Teddy Montgomery is making him *wait*.

Teddy looks up at him through his strawberry blonde eyelashes, and asks, 'Sure?'

Ezra is going to murder him in cold blood. He grabs Teddy's hand and presses it to the rock-hard shape in his pants, and says: 'Pretty sure, yeah.'

Teddy grins. His movements are slow and languid as he unbuckles Ezra's belt and pulls the zipper down with his teeth — which nearly drives Ezra out of his damn mind. He watches as Teddy hooks both index fingers under the waistband of his boxers and unceremoniously yanks them down. He wants to make some kind of remark about British sensibilities, but then Teddy's mouth is on him, and he promptly forgets every word in the English language. Except fuck. Because *Oh fuck*.

Ezra is not religious, but the phrase *Oh God, please* passes his lips more times than he cares to count. His head tips back against the pillow as a steady string of curses jumble and come out of his mouth in one long mess of a sentence. 'Fuck. Oh fuck. Jesus-shitting-fuck. You're so. That's so. Oh. *Oh. Fuck.*'

When he risks a look down and sees Teddy is still looking up at him though his fluttering eyelashes it's all over, and he shouts Teddy's name as his hips buck. When Teddy climbs up his body to re-join him, he is grinning. Ezra pulls him into a kiss that seems to surprise both of them. It's slow and deliberate, and when Teddy pulls back, he has a strange look on his face.

'We can leave it here if you want?' Teddy asks.

Ezra immediately recognises it for what it is: a get-out-of-jail-free card. It's *Run now, while you still have the chance*! It's Teddy watching, waiting, and expecting Ezra to turn him away. To be done with him. And although he is trying to hide how desperately afraid he is that Ezra is going to do just that, he can tell by the pinch in his mouth and the set of his jaw that he is terrified of being rejected. When Ezra finds out whoever has given Teddy Montgomery all these reasons to have so many guards up, he is going to hit them. *Very* hard.

'Not likely,' Ezra says, rolling them over.

The surprise in Teddy's eyes and the amused huff of laughter as Ezra relieves him of his pants, and then boxer shorts, turns into a soft *oh* as he goes down on a man for the first time in his life. And it's hot. It's *so* hot. Watching Teddy's face flush, watching his hands ball in the sheets, watching his lower lip snag between his teeth is almost enough to get him going again. The sight of Teddy Montgomery — demure, modest, polite, Teddy Mikhail Montgomery — coming undone beneath him, head turned and cursing into one of the pillows, is like Christmas.

Teddy collects Ezra into his arms, and they lay tangled in the rumpled sheets for a long time, not saying anything, just breathing hard. Ezra has never been held after sex before. He's usually the hold*er*, not the hold*ee*. Still, it's nice. It's safe, and warm, and when Teddy presses a gentle kiss to his hair his heart lurches in a way that he decides not to pay attention to.

'Are you alright?' Ezra asks.

Teddy's lips brush against Ezra's forehead as he speaks. 'Perfectly. You?'

'I'm doing pretty good.'

'Then why does it feel like you're about to ruin this?'

Ezra looks up and his heart does that annoying sideways thing again when he looks into Teddy's impossibly blue eyes. He's beginning to get the suspicious feeling that Teddy

Montgomery is going to be the death of him. 'It's just that if I don't come back to my place with Thai food this evening Grace will start asking questions.'

'Sometimes I don't know if we're having the same conversation.'

'Basically, she's expecting me. And curry noodle soup.'

'Ah. I see.'

Teddy's trademark this-isn't upsetting-me-although-it-actually-is face is back and it physically hurts Ezra to know that he's the one who put it there. So, he hurries to say, 'I wish I could stay. And I can for a bit. I just can't sleep over. Too many questions. Plus, the cameras are going to be all over you now that you're back. But hey,' he captures Teddy's chin in his hand, 'I *really* do wish I could stay. Really, *really*.'

Teddy smiles his secret smile, and if Ezra's heart doesn't stop its parkour routine against his ribcage, he and it are going to be having some very serious words later on. Because there's no reason for him to like it so much. Not just Teddy's smile, but for being the reason he's smiling in the first place. He has absolutely no right to want to kiss that smile over and over again until his lips bruise. But he does and it's confusing.

When Ezra kisses Teddy goodbye at the door, he can't help the silly little grin that takes over his face. He knows, with absolute certainty, as he walks back to his brownstone in the pouring rain (how the hell is it *still* raining?), that he is in a *lot* of trouble.

He also realises that he really, truly, does not care.

Chapter Seven

So, here's the thing. Ezra is probably bisexual. Like, most definitely, probably bisexual. If he's going by the way he is sneaking into Teddy's brownstone every evening and sneaking out before dawn, then yeah, he's probably bisexual. Most likely. And that's okay. That is A-O-Fucking-Kay. It really is. Ezra is actually surprised by how okay he is with it all.

He is also surprised by how much his thoughts are dominated by Teddy Montgomery. He's *also* equally surprised by how fidgety he starts getting by 8pm, if Grace and Iris aren't taking their cue to leave so he can get an Uber to Teddy's place and rip his clothes off. But. Like. It's nothing to panic about. It's fine. It's all totally fine.

It's totally fine when Teddy sends him a text saying: **I want you.** And it's super-duper fine when Ezra practically flies over to his brownstone to drop to his knees and make Teddy cry out his name, hands swept up in fistfuls of Ezra's dark hair. Or when Ezra is sitting in a family meeting and he receives an absolute thirst trap photo of Teddy, fresh out of the shower, wet hair clinging to his forehead, and Ezra nearly chokes on his coffee. Or when Teddy answers the door to him completely naked and Ezra pins him down and swallows him on the kitchen counter.

But it's more than that. It's more than the amazing (*a-ma-zing*) blowjobs, and the stolen late-night kisses, and the naughty pictures that Ezra has a whole password protected album for on his phone. It's the good morning texts. It's the surprise drop-ins with takeaway and wine. It's the: **you're on channel 39** jokes, and the coffee runs, and the movie nights with Grace and Iris — who are too wrapped up in their secret girl-world to see the way Ezra openly drools over Teddy, and the random *I saw this and thought of you* deliveries from Amazon. It's all this, and the, quite frankly, mind-blowing, leg-shaking, life-ruining orgasms that are all being added to the *totally fine things to happen* file in his head.

Except that it's not fine at all. Because Teddy Montgomery is his sister's fiancé. He's *Grace's* fiancé. And although he knows there would be no love lost between them if their fake relationship broke up, it would ruin the narrative for the new season. It would jeopardise her whole future if she got cancelled by one of the biggest streaming services in the world. And despite knowing all this, Ezra still winds up in Teddy's bed every night. So yeah. It's not fine. But it's totally fine.

Text thread: Flynn Rider [eggplant emoji]

ezra:
currently in world's most boring family meeting. needing a distraction. send nudes.

Flynn Rider [eggplant emoji]:
[ATTACHED IMAGE]

ezra:
oh fuck.
ezra:
[sweating emoji]

Flynn Rider [eggplant emoji]:
[smirking emoji]

ezra:
have i ever told you that you have an absolutely amazing cock? honestly, world class.

Flynn Rider [eggplant emoji]:
Not for at least twenty minutes.

ezra:

you could have an onlyfans.

Flynn Rider [eggplant emoji]:
What makes you think I don't?

All the smirking at his phone screen doesn't go unnoticed. Grace teases him every time his phone dings. *Is that from your boyfriend?* So, he puts his phone on silent, but then he just gets teased for looking at his phone every few minutes. Iris joins in whenever she's around, and that is whenever she's not working on her art or when the cameras aren't around, so that's usually evenings and Sundays.

They have a strict rule that during the day it stays professional. They have to be on camera — not usually with each other, but separately with Grace, or the rest of the Darlings — and if Ezra even so much as looks at Teddy the wrong (or right) way, then Teddy's neck immediately flushes pink and then Ezra needs laser focus not to get hard in front of the entire room. And on the rare times when they *do* have to film together, the air is so thick and heavy that Ezra has no idea how the whole production crew doesn't know they're fucking.

Although, they're not *really* fucking. That is a rickey old bridge Ezra assumes they will cross when they come to it. Or not cross. He doesn't really mind. He is more than happy to keep doing what they are doing. Whatever that is. Bros who blow? Mates who fellate? It's a working title.

There are, of course, several occasions where the four of them — Ezra, Teddy, Grace and Iris — go out for boozy brunch, or rooftop cocktails, or for outrageously expensive meals at The Palace, where they drink, and swap stories, and double over with laughter like they've all known each other forever.

It's at one of these dinners that Ezra feels Teddy's hand squeeze his thigh under the table. Ezra nearly chokes on his duck confit in plum sauce and Grace gives him a bewildered look. When Teddy excuses himself to go to the restroom (he calls it *the loo*, which is kind of adorable), Ezra counts to sixty before making an excuse about stepping outside for some air. Not that the girls are paying attention to him. The red wine is flowing and they've long since been sucked into secret-girl-chatter.

When Ezra knocks on the disabled bathroom door he is yanked inside and pushed up against the wall. Teddy's mouth is on him before he can say anything, but he's not complaining. He takes him by the waist and pulls their bodies together. They both groan as their hips meet and Ezra can feel that Teddy is already rock hard. *Oh God.*

Teddy is making quick work of unbuckling Ezra's belt, and when his hand pushes inside, beneath the waistband of his boxers, his head lolls back. His hips buck in rhythm to Teddy's strokes and when he's about to shout a warning of what's to come, Teddy drops to his knees and catches him in his mouth. This motherfucker is going to be the death of him, he just knows it.

Teddy presses a kiss to his tip, somehow still managing to come off as the perfect gentleman, and stands to claim Ezra's mouth in another searing kiss. And when Ezra's mouth is returning the favour on him, and Teddy is biting his lip to keep from screaming his name, it's so hot that Ezra is going to lose his damn mind.

So yeah. Long story short, Ezra is probably, definitely, maybe, most-likely bisexual. And Teddy is very gay. And they are both *very* much enjoying running headfirst into this total dumpster-fire of a situation without thinking about the consequences. Because, honestly, fuck the consequences. Teddy is just too good — *too damn good* — to give up.

This much is confirmed one evening when Ezra FaceTimes him. He's in a foul mood, stuck in his brownstone with food poisoning, and very much not allowed to throw both of Teddy's legs over his shoulders and swallow what he's given to swallow. Instead, he's in his own, painfully empty bed, sick bucket handy and Pepto Bismol on call.

Teddy answers almost immediately and Ezra's day is already *one thousand percent* better for seeing his freckled cheekbones. He can't contain his smile that blossoms across his sickly features.

'How is the patient?' Teddy asks.

'All the better for seeing you, sweetheart.'

Ezra absolutely revels at the way Teddy flushes at that pet-name. It had started off as a joke. One time when Teddy was going down on him, Ezra looked down, winked and said something along the lines of *So good for me, sweetheart*. And then Teddy had proceeded to give him the most obnoxiously good blowjob of his life. Ever since then, Ezra knows that whenever he calls Teddy *sweetheart* that he will positively melt.

'Well,' Teddy says, clearing his throat. 'I aim to please.'

'You succeed. So, what's it like not having my charming company and sparkling wit to keep you busy?'

'Well, naturally I've fallen into a pit of despair.'

'Naturally.'

Teddy grins. 'And I can hear myself think for once.'

'Fuck you,' Ezra says, but it's undercut with a smile. 'I'm sick, you have to be nice to me.'

'Oh, I will be *very* nice to you when you're all better again.'

Now it's Ezra's turn to gulp. 'I'll pray for a speedy recovery.' He hears noises in the background — voices — and arches an eyebrow. 'Am I interrupting?'

'I'm babysitting the twins for Daria,' Teddy says, holding up a hand to show him his sparkly pink manicure. 'First we played spa. Then tattoo shop. And now I've convinced them to pick out a movie before I'm forced into accepting any more body modifications.'

'Show me that sweet tat,' Ezra says, grinning. 'I hope it's on your ass.'

Teddy switches hands holding the phone to show him the Sharpie pen doodle on his bicep of a robot fighting a giant octopus. His nails on that hand are neon yellow. 'Initially I asked for an anchor. Something manly. Instead, Margot insisted on this.'

'What could be more manly than a robot fighting a kraken? Hey, bright side, Mason's nail painting is really coming along.'

'Yes, except he charges triple the ordinary price and doesn't give his dear Uncle Teddy mates rates.'

'That's capitalism for you.'

There are two whizzes of activity behind Teddy, and he cranes his neck to look at what they're up to. They practically fling themselves down onto the couch beside him, one either side, and suddenly the screen is filled with an extra two faces, both miniature versions of their mom. Ezra realises that this is the first time he's spoken to any of Teddy's family outside of work. And he's certainly never been introduced to the twins before.

Margot peers at the screen. 'Who is that?'

Teddy lovingly strokes the little girl's hair, and the unabashed affection that crosses his face when he looks at his niece makes something in Ezra's chest ache. 'This is my friend, Ezra. He wanted to come over tonight and join us but he's sick.'

Mason blinks up at his Uncle Teddy. 'Has he got the flu?'

'Why don't you ask him yourself?'

Mason turns the full force of his six-year-old stare upon Ezra and repeats. 'Do you have the flu?'

Ezra grins. He's never really liked kids — okay, no, it's not that he doesn't *like* them. He's just always struggled with them. To be honest, he doesn't know how to talk to them. He doesn't want to be patronising, but he also doesn't want to talk about the economic climate, and he's not sure where the middle ground is. These kids, however, both have Teddy's bright blue eyes, so he's already got a soft spot for them. 'Fortunately, not. Just a tummy bug.'

'I hope you feel better soon,' Mason says, and clearly means it.

Margot tugs on the front of Teddy's shirt. 'Uncle Teddy, can we watch the movie now?'

'Of course we can, princess. What did you pick?'

Margot holds up a DVD case (a DVD case! Who watches DVDs anymore?), and Teddy nearly dies choking on a laugh. So does Ezra when she sees what she's picked. *Tangled*. Teddy gives Ezra a look and he just bites his lip and shrugs. 'It's a good movie.'

Teddy nods. He tells the kids to get into their pyjamas and he'll get the movie set up. Mason waves goodbye to Ezra and Margot blows him a kiss, which makes both of them grin. 'I think Margot might have a thing for you.'

'You'll have to fight her for me.'

'Not bloody likely. She's scrappier than she looks.'

Ezra takes a moment to enjoy how Teddy looks right now, in sweatpants and a soft grey t-shirt. One hand is behind his head, the other is holding up his phone. His hair is dishevelled in a way you expect someone's hair to be when they've spent all day running around after two six-year-olds. He's just so unfairly handsome that Ezra isn't sure whether he wants to kiss him or punch him. Instead, he says, 'You're great with them. I wish I knew how to talk to kids.'

'It's a lot like talking to grown-ups, except the subject of *Peppa Pig* comes up a lot more often.'

'What in the ever-loving-fuck is a *Peppa Pig*?'

Teddy snorts. 'Philistine.'

'*Sweetheart*.'

The blush goes all the way up to Teddy's temples. 'Christ. Hurry up and get well soon, will you?'

'I'm trying my best.'

When Ezra hangs up, he's no longer in a foul mood. In fact, he is smiling. Ten minutes later, when he receives a picture from Teddy of him and the twins in matching *Harry Potter* pyjamas, his smile is about as wide as Texas. He snaps a photo back of him posing with his Pepto Bismol bottle and smiles as Teddy just sends back: xoxo.

Something in the back of his head warns him that he might be in trouble here. Ezra, however, very smartly, decides to ignore it until it becomes a problem. Because it's fine.

It's all totally fine.

Chapter Eight

Text thread: Flynn Rider [eggplant emoji]:

ezra:
what do you want for your birthday?

Flynn Rider [eggplant emoji]:
You.

Flynn Rider [eggplant emoji]:
With a bow on top.

ezra:
obviously. what else?

Flynn Rider [eggplant emoji]:
Don't suppose you fancy a trip to London?

ezra:
are you asking me on a date?

Flynn Rider [eggplant emoji]:
I'm asking you to attend the Queen & Adam Lambert concert with me.

ezra:
are you planning to accost me in some sort of seedy hotel after?

Flynn Rider [eggplant emoji]:
I wouldn't call Claridge's seedy.

Flynn Rider [eggplant emoji]:
But yes, I am.

>ezra:
>already booking my flight.

Flynn Rider [eggplant emoji]:
Perfect. Make sure it's a big bow.

>ezra:
>anything for you, sweetheart.

Ezra had not considered how hard it would be to be on an eight-hour flight with Teddy and not be able to touch him. His insides are on fire. His hands keep moving instinctively to rest on Teddy's knee, or his thigh, or higher, and he has to sit on them so that he won't make any sudden moves.

He can feel the same static energy radiating off Teddy, and when he risks a glance over at him, Ezra sees him pointedly looking out of the window, arms crossed tightly over his chest. One of his legs bounces, frustrated, and Ezra can't resist widening his knees so that his thigh presses up against Teddy's. This, in turn, causes Teddy to let out a low hiss that makes everything a thousand times worse.

The girls are blissfully unaware of the fact Ezra and Teddy are in literal hell. They've been vlogging, and drinking champagne, and scream-singing Queen songs for the majority of the journey. Until about halfway over the Atlantic Ocean, when an alcohol-fuelled nap claims them. Grace is pulled into Iris' chest, Iris's chin on Grace's head.

Teddy is already pushing him out of the seat and into the restroom. It's cramped and tight, and they can't make a noise — which somehow makes it so much better. When Teddy comes, Ezra has to silence him with a kiss, and as Teddy shudders and moans into his mouth, that's enough to send Ezra flying too. His legs give out and as Teddy catches him, his elbow hits the flush button, and they have to jam their fists into their mouths so that they won't laugh.

Teddy's best friend, Nick, meets them at the airport. He's every inch the runway model that Ezra is expecting, and its suddenly laughable that Ezra had never even considered the possibility before that he could be bisexual. He'd just assumed that all guys kinda fancied other guys a little bit. Because guys were hot. In the same way girls were. And if he saw an objectively hot guy, it was normal for him to have the same reaction as if he saw an objectively hot girl. He now knows, of course, that he is a dumbass. Because, like, *duh*.

Nick is instantly likeable. Apart from being nauseatingly gorgeous, he has this gentle smile and easy way about him that makes Teddy completely loosen in a way that Ezra has never seen before. When he sees Teddy's face break out into a wide grin as he embraces his oldest friend, he already knows everything he needs to know about Nick Wesley. He's a good guy.

The concert is being held at Wembley Stadium. They, of course, have the private box, kitted out with enough private security to make it look like royalty will be attending. They have time to have drinks beforehand, and Teddy is at war with himself over whether to order a soft drink or not. Eventually he settles on a *lager shandy please* and Ezra absolutely cannot understand why you would ruin a perfectly good beer by watering it down with soda. Still, it seems to get him comfortably tipsy by the time Queen comes onstage.

Ezra is not ready for the sight that is Teddy Montgomery, singing and dancing along to Queen's greatest hits. It should be illegal. *He* should be illegal. The way his Adam's apple bobs as he sings along. The strip of his waist that is exposed as his shirt rides up while he throws his arms up in the air to clap along with *We Will Rock You*. The way the strobe lighting bounces off his striking face, making his cheekbones look even sharper. The way he knows every single word, to every single song without hesitation.

There's a moment when Teddy looks over at him, and his eyes are so bright, his smile so real and happy, that Ezra can't even remember his own damn name. *Oh*. This is how Teddy always deserves to look. Just a normal, happy, slightly-inebriated twenty-seven — well, twenty-eight — year-old, enjoying his birthday with his friends, not worrying about who is next in line to try and crush him. Ezra wants this night to last forever for him. He wants Teddy to be happy like this forever.

By the time they stumble into Ezra's hotel room that night, he's absolutely intoxicated by the sight of Teddy laughing, and singing, and playing air guitar, and if he doesn't kiss every part of him immediately, he is going to explode. They are interrupted briefly by room service who deliver the birthday cake Ezra has organised. It's crude and shaped like a giant penis, but that doesn't really matter when Ezra is painstakingly licking it off Teddy's body.

Teddy is patient while Ezra teases him, even though his body is trembling, and his hips roll upwards whenever Ezra ghosts a kiss across his thighs or higher. Ezra is in no hurry, though. He wants to catalogue every part of Teddy's outstanding body — and if it comes with buttercream frosting then even better. It's not until Teddy is gasping — breathless — and says, 'Ezra. Please. I can't. *Please.*'

Ezra positions himself between Teddy's ridiculously long legs, grins and says, 'Happy birthday, sweetheart,' before taking him into his mouth. Teddy comes with his hands shoved into Ezra's messy hair, his lip caught between his teeth, and Ezra cannot take his eyes off this impossible man.

When Teddy is taking him apart with long languid strokes of his hand, he still cannot take his eyes off him, even though he can never last when Teddy is looking down at him like that, because there is nothing Ezra would rather look at right now than Teddy Montgomery when he's completely laid bare like this.

Teddy means to go back to his own room, but when he tries to leave Ezra catches his hand and says, 'Stay.'

So, Teddy stays, and they make out on the rumpled sheets in one of London's most expensive hotels. When he falls asleep, Teddy has Ezra pulled back flush against his strong chest. Teddy's legs are tucked in behind Ezra's knees. One arm is draped over Ezra's waist, and the tip of Teddy's nose is nuzzled into the back of Ezra's neck.

And, honestly? It's kind of everything.

The following morning, they have breakfast in bed and watch dog videos on YouTube. When Ezra glances at Teddy's face and sees a wistful flicker of pain in his eyes, he reaches for his hand and asks, 'You okay?'

Teddy wraps an arm around his shoulders and replies, 'Getting there.'

'Wanna talk about it?'

Teddy presses a kiss to Ezra's temple. 'You're a darling.'

'Is that, like, a cute nickname or just my surname?'

'Both,' Teddy kisses him again. 'And I'm okay. Besides, he's with George now.'

Ezra blinks. He pulls away and looks at Teddy incredulously. 'Hold on. Fred and George?'

'Yes?'

'You had another dog called George?'

'Have you fallen deaf, love?'

Ezra almost doesn't register Teddy's first use of a pet name for him. Almost. Because, 'Fred and George? As in Weasley? As in *Harry Potter*?'

'Do you honestly think I would just call my dog Fred?'

'Well... kinda. Yeah.'

Teddy frowns. 'Good God, why?'

Ezra shrugs, a little sheepish now. 'Well. Because. I... thought you were a bit boring.'

Teddy drops his croissant on the bedspread. 'You... thought I was *boring*?'

'Obviously, I was wrong.'

There's a long moment where all Teddy can do is stare at him. Just as Ezra is about to tell him to close his mouth or he'll give him something to fill it, Teddy is sweeping the tea tray off the bed. The pastries fall to the carpet with crumbs and a clatter, and suddenly Teddy is pinning Ezra to the bed, a mischievous look on his dumb gorgeous face.

'You,' he says, drawing the words out, 'thought I was *boring*, did you?'

Ezra's chest rapidly rises and falls. This is a side of Teddy he has yet to see, and he doesn't hate it. 'Are you going to prove me wrong?'

'Damn bloody right I am.'

And then Teddy goes on to give Ezra the most devastatingly good — and definitely *not* boring — orgasm of his whole life.

Back in NYC, it's straight back to filming. Grace has her bachelorette party — supposedly organised by Iris, her maid of honour — but actually meticulously planned by Ali and Ron, over many flasks of coffee and sleepless nights. Ron was angling for a wild, dramageddon, girls-gone-wild night out. Ali was arguing that it was not in the Darling Dynasty's best interests to paint their golden girl as a — her words, not his — vodka-soaked, shit-faced, clusterfuck. They settled on flying to Miami, renting a yacht and throwing an intimate boat party of three hundred people.

'Please come,' Grace begs, holding his TV remote hostage, like that will persuade him to change his mind.

Ezra looks up at her from his sofa, eyebrow arched. 'Grace, it's a *bachelorette* party. I'm not a bachelorette.'

'You're as good as!' she says. 'It's Vegas themed! You love dressing up!'

'Why do you even want me there? You've got Iris and two-hundred-and-ninety-nine others.'

'But I want *you*. You're great at parties. You have chaotic energy.'

'I'm not a girl.'

'You basically are.'

Ezra sighs and scrubs at his face. He knows the real reason why he doesn't want to go to the party, but he doesn't know if he wants to face it yet. Because the thing is. The *thing* is. Going to the party is just acknowledging that they're getting closer and closer to the inevitable. The wedding. Grace marrying Teddy. Teddy Montgomery no longer being his. Being his *sister's* husband. The thought makes him ill.

Not to even mention the fact that Grace doesn't deserve any of this. Grace — his biggest cheerleader, and best friend, and partner in crime since forever — doesn't deserve to be married to a man that is sneaking off at night to her brother's bedroom. Even if the wedding is fake, even *if* the marriage is a sham. It's not fair on her, and he knows that, and still he can't stop himself from seeing Teddy even if he tried. Which he isn't.

'Grace...' he draws her name out. 'Please don't make me go.'

'There will be girls,' she says. '*Hot* girls.' Ezra snorts a laugh which draws a bemused look from Grace.

He immediately covers it with: 'I'm not looking for anyone right now.'

'Do it for me,' she says, relying on her secret weapon: the Puss-In-Boots eyes. 'Please, Ezzy.'

'You *do* realise you only call me that when you want something.'

'Only because it works.'

Ezra heaves a dramatic but legit sigh. 'Fine. Yeah, I'll come.'

Grace almost topples the sofa over with the force of her hug. 'Thank you thank you thank you thank you thank—'

'Can't. Breathe.'

Grace pulls back but not before kissing his cheek. 'Wear something sexy.'

'Always.'

And that's how Ezra ends up on a yacht in Miami in a skimpy pair of leather hotpants, thigh high boots, and a bus driver hat. His makeup is full glam, and he has glitter on his chest and in his hair. He drinks whatever is given to him, and he acts up for the camera, and he is so camp that he can already see tomorrow's headlines on the gossip blogs asking *when will Ezra Darling come out of the closet?*

At least it makes sense now. The way he's never been offended or snapped back whenever anyone starts a rumour or speculates that he might be gay. He'd always assumed it was just down to the fact that he didn't care. Because it didn't matter. And, like, it doesn't. But now he knows it is partly because it's true. They could say what they wanted, and it doesn't matter because he knows his truth now.

Grace is positively radiant in a glittering, black, floor-length gown. She is every part her namesake, and she drinks mocktails all night so that she won't make an idiot of herself on camera. That's what Ezra is there for. He knows it, and he doesn't mind.

Iris is also there, even though being on camera outside of Instagram ads is really *not* her thing at all. Despite having the face of a Neutrogena model, she has absolutely no interest in being a reality TV star, and Ezra respects the hell out of that. Her dress is red silk and has a slit up the side that makes people stop and stare. She, however, *is* on the booze tonight, so she and Ezra are the designated chaos demons of the evening.

They play the casino games even though they have no idea what the rules are and lose copious amounts of money in the process. They play all the drinking games, and dance to all of the cheesy 80s hits. A stripper pole has been put up on the top deck, and seeing as Ezra is dressed for it, he gives a show that makes Ron grin and Ali wince. He makes at least three separate toasts to his sister, each one more heartfelt and slurred than the last.

But underneath all the drinking, and dancing, and fifty layers of glitter, there is Teddy Montgomery, stuck in his head without any intent on budging. And Ezra doesn't even mind. He *likes* it when he's thinking of him. He likes being able to look through the pictures he's saved of Teddy on his phone. He has to save photos from Instagram, because Teddy has a habit of going all pink and embarrassed when Ezra tries to snap a photo. He's managed to get a few candid shots, though.

He's in a quiet corner, scrolling through a protected folder named *Flynn Rider,* when he comes across a series of photos he'd taken at the Queen concert. Teddy sipping from his glass of shandy. Teddy's eyes closed, hands in the air as he sings along to *I Want To Break Free.* Teddy with his hands over his heart, eyes glistening as Brian May sings *Love*

Of My Life in tribute to Freddie Mercury. Ezra's chest clinches and his hand goes to his own heart.

He immediately sets that photo as his wallpaper before shooting Teddy a text that says: I miss you. When he almost immediately gets one back that says: I miss you too, love, he really doesn't know what to do with his stomach that is doing goddamn backflips. He is thankful when Iris finds him and drags him back into the party.

So, he dances. And he drinks. And he thinks about Teddy. And he slut-drops with Iris. And he thinks about Teddy. And he makes another speech about how much he loves his sister. And he lets Iris give him a lap dance. And he nearly falls overboard at some point. And he thinks about Teddy.

And when he is lying in his hotel room that night, head swimming, stomach churning, he is still thinking about Teddy Montgomery.

Chapter Nine

```
Subject: flynn rider's shag do
---
Ezra <Ezra-Darling@Darlingdynasty.com>
To: Teddy
---
teddy,
please find attached a link for your costume for the stag do.
https://www.sexycowboycosplay.com/assless-chaps
kisses
ezra
```

*

```
Re: flynn rider's shag do
---
Teddy <Teddy.Montgomery@theMontgomerys.com>
To: Ezra
---
Ezra,
```
I suppose you think you're very clever. You also assume that I don't already have a set of assless chaps. However, it *does* beg the question that if I am to be wearing that, then what will *you* be wearing? May I suggest the following?

https://www.bdsmclothing.com/slave-boy

You would look so delicious.

Kind regards,
Teddy

*

Re: flynn rider's shag do

Ezra <Ezra-Darling@Darlingdynasty.com>
To: Teddy

---

teddy,

so cute of you to assume that YOU are the dominant one in this relationship. when we both know that you completely melt when i pin you down and call you *sweetheart*. i think this is definitely more your speed...

https://www.naughtygirlcostumes.com/sexy-school-girl

xoxo

ezra

*

Re: flynn rider's shag do

Teddy <Teddy.Montgomery@theMontgomerys.com>
To: Ezra

Ezra,

I am highly offended. Not by your blatant disregard for my obvious dominant position in this partnership (please find image of yourself bound with your own belt to my headboard for your reference), but by your assumption that I fall anywhere *near* into the category of 'naughty schoolgirl'. I'll have you know that I was a straight A student and adored by all of my teachers. If any of them wanted to haul me over their laps and spank me, then this is the first I am hearing of it. If either of us fits the definition of 'naughty' it is most definitely you, love. You are, and I mean this with all due respect, a strumpet.

For your perusal:
https://www.daddykinkcostumes.com/male-prostitute
For your reference:
[IMAGE 321_4.jpg]
Warmest regards,
Teddy

*

Re: flynn rider's shag do

Ezra <Ezra-Darling@Darlingdynasty.com>
To: Teddy

---

teddy,

is this your way of telling me that you want me to bend you over and spank you? because that can 100% be arranged. as far as your accusation that i am a "strumpet", these allegations are unfounded and pure speculation. i prefer to think of myself as a very high-end gentleman of the night. and let's not forget that if i AM a *strumpet* then you are the dirty perv accosting me. think about THAT, sweetheart.

p.s. saw this and thought of you:
https://www.coupleskink.com/under-bed-bondage-straps
smooches,
ezra

*

Re: flynn rider's shag do

Teddy <Teddy.Montgomery@theMontgomerys.com>
To: Ezra

Ezra,

I would like to point out that I never got this many migraines before I invited you and your smart mouth into my life. I will, however, allow you to remain a permanent fixture because of all the, quite frankly, incredible and filthy things you have shown you're capable of doing with it.

I'll see you tonight.

P.S. Just bought those straps and am looking forward to using them.

Sincerely,

Teddy

*

Re: Flynn Rider's Shag Do

Ezra <Ezra-Darling@Darlingdynasty.com>

To: Teddy

---

whatever you want, sweetheart.

Teddy Montgomery is not allowed to look as good as he does right now. Because he looks *so* damn good, and Ezra wants to rip his clothes off and fuck his beautiful brains out. He refrains, though, because this is a nice hotel, and a worthy fundraiser, and that kind of thing is frowned upon at such events. Prudes.

He, unfortunately, is not wearing the assless chaps. Instead, Teddy is wearing a three-piece suit with a champagne gold waistcoat and a pocket watch (a *pocket watch*!) tucked into his jacket, the gold chain looping through one of his buttonholes. His hair is neatly combed, his chin is free of stubble, and he looks so hot that Ezra wants to slip his fingers into his posh mouth.

The fundraiser is the one that Teddy mentioned all those months ago at their first forced playdate. The one Daria is hosting to raise money for first responders at accidents.

She makes a touching speech about Leo, and about how his life would have been saved had people been able to get to the scene sooner. Ezra watches as Teddy's body stiffens at the mention of his brother, his jaw clenching in that way he does when he's trying to show the world how tough he is.

They raise an obscene amount of money, but the tickets are $5,000 each, so that helps. Celebrities, socialites, and influencers dig deep into their diamond-encrusted pockets to help the less fortunate, and Ezra writes an offensively large cheque that makes Grace's eyes bug out of her head. He keeps his donation anonymous, like he does with all of them, because only a jerk would make a big deal out of it. Not all of the guests seem to have those same qualms, however.

He finds his gaze constantly being dragged back to David and Anastasya. They sweep through the room, a glorious force to be reckoned with. They smile, they shake hands, they make generous donations. In all the time he and Teddy have spent together, Ezra hasn't brought up the subject of his parents or their work with the church again. The need to make Teddy comfortable and happy outweighs his curiosity every time.

He tries to find something wrong with them, but can't. They are nothing at all like people say. Ezra thinks he might see them slip when a waitress spills a champagne flute down the front of Anastasya's Versace dress, but she merely dabs at it with a napkin and reassures the waitress that she's not angry. She even goes out of her way to find the server's manager to stress that it was an accident.

Iris slides in next to him at the bar without him noticing, and when she speaks he jumps and nearly falls off his stool.

'They're too perfect,' she says. 'They're hiding something.'

Ezra looks at her. 'You've changed your tune.'

'At first I thought they were just nice,' she says, stealing the cherry from the rim of his cocktail. 'Like, because they live in Britain and everyone over there is super polite and stuff. But it's too much. That was a Versace dress, Ezzy. It hasn't even hit the runway yet. It's probably one of a kind.'

'So you think it's an act?' he asks, watching as David ruffles the hair of possibly one of the Kardashians' kids.

'I do,' she says, retrieving her phone from her purse. 'I also did some fishing online and look what I found.'

She hands him her ear buds and her phone that has a YouTube video queued up. He doesn't flinch at the thought of putting Iris' airbuds in like he might with someone else.

There wasn't much either of them could do to gross the other out at this point. He clicks play and watches.

It's grainy and looks like it was filmed on a toaster oven, but Teddy and David's figures are unmistakable. They're being filmed in secret through, what looks like, a hotel room. The person recording must be across the street, just a few floors lower down. Ezra feels guilty for watching it, but Iris must be showing him for a reason.

They're arguing, that much is obvious. Or, at least, Teddy is being argued *at*. His shoulders are slumped, and he's hunched in on himself. He looks like a child getting berated by an irate teacher. Then David grabs Teddy by the lapels of his suit jacket and shakes him. Like, *really* shakes him. Teddy's eyes go round and terrified for a moment before he shoves his dad away from him. Then the video ends.

Ezra watches it a few more times to make sure he's not seeing things, because there is no way — like, *no way* — that David is putting his hands on Teddy. But he is. Teddy, who is gentle and sweet. Teddy, who's humour and quick wit never fails to surprise or impress him. Teddy, who makes an effort to shake everyone's hand, smile, and make polite conversation, despite the fact — and Ezra can see this from space — that he is deeply uncomfortable in large crowds. And his own father is laying hands on him.

Ezra takes out the ear buds and hands them back to Iris along with her phone. He tries to keep his face neutral, but he feels like finding David and shaking *him* down. See how he likes it.

'Well, that's enlightening,' he says, instead.

'It's damning is what it is,' she says, putting her phone back in her purse. 'If one of my moms ever *shook* me, I'd call the kids helpline. I don't care how old I am.'

Ezra gives his oldest friend a long, knowing look. 'So, what's your working theory, Iggs?'

'Don't know yet. But if I had to guess right now—'

'Which you don't.'

'Like, if you had a gun to my head, and I were on a rickety bridge, and you said *one side of this bridge leads to your family, the other side leads to one million dollars—*'

Ezra frowns. 'I think you're mixing up a few ultimatums there.'

'Then I would *have* to guess that they're secretly crab people.'

Ezra blinks, then smiles. 'I love you.'

She grins back. 'I know. Listen, I'm gonna do some more snooping. You keep standing there looking pretty.'

He winks. 'Someone's gotta do it.'

He watches Iris slink back into the crowd and quickly loses her. He is happy to drink his cocktail in peace and people watch. His gaze settles on Daria who is chatting to his mom. Her eyes are tired but her body language is happy and animated. Ezra is surprised by how much he actually likes Daria. She is warm and funny, and she has an obvious soft spot for Teddy. Even though Teddy tries not to talk about Leo too much — the subject makes him curl in on himself — he has picked up enough snippets here and there to put together a pretty good idea of the oldest Montgomery sibling in his head.

The cameras are always rolling, of course. Ezra likes to watch how people react to being on camera. Some clam up. Others show off. Ezra, however, just turns on the big smile and the charm whenever one is pointed at him. He mingles with the other guests, and he makes a speech at Daria's request, and he slow-dances with her because Ali says it will be good for his image. It's a perfectly respectable night. It really is. And it's all just a prelude to the shagathon-spectacular that is to come.

The cameras aren't invited. Even Grace and Iris aren't invited. Tonight is just for Ezra and Teddy. No one even knows they are going out, and Ezra intends to keep it that way. He wants to be selfish with him tonight. Teddy's official bachelor party is later in the month, but seeing as that is some kind of a high tea — probably with top hats and monocles — all caught on Darling Dynasty camera, Ezra wants to give him the full frontal, balls-to-the-wall, bottomless cocktails and orgasms-until-you-die experience. They are going to Judy's.

Ezra finds it ridiculous that Teddy has never been to a gay bar before. Even before Ezra knew that he was bisexual, he was at Judy's every other weekend. Although, in hindsight, there may have been a reason for that. If he's being honest with himself — and he is — there was no denying the flurry of excitement he would feel when a guy caught his eye from across the room.

He probably enjoyed flirting with men at the bar too much for someone who was totally straight. He *definitely* enjoyed dancing with men who would grab at him and feel him up through his clothes too much for someone who was, like, totally and completely straight. He is, in a way, kind of amazed that the rest of the world figured it out before he did. Because he's an idiot.

It's masquerade night at Judy's. After changing into jeans and button downs, they don their disguises. Ezra's mask is glittery and black, in the shape of a butterfly. Teddy's is bright pink with feathers and sequins. And to Teddy's credit, he still makes it look so goddamn sexy.

The bar is overpacked and understaffed when they arrive. Ezra can sense Teddy's body tense up as they enter — the fear of being caught and outed to the world — and Ezra takes his hand, giving it a little squeeze that earns him a smile. They get drinks at the bar and Ezra delights at the sight of Teddy ordering a *Suck, Bang, and Blow* in his sweet English accent, and even more when he coughs after his first sip. Ezra makes it his mission to get Teddy to order as many filthy drinks off the cocktail menu as possible, just so he can hear him say: *Can I get one Creamy Pussy please?* and *One Cock-Sucking Cowboy* and *Bend Me Over, Shirley, when you're ready*. It shouldn't turn his crank, but it really does.

A drag queen called Miss Sheneeda Dickens lip syncs to a medley of Diva anthems, dominating the stage in nine-inch platforms and an eye-wateringly tight tuck. Ezra knows he should be paying attention, but he can't take his eyes off Teddy. He's singing along, respectfully bopping his head in time to the music. Just tipsy enough to enjoy himself, but not drunk enough to let go completely. And it's fine, Ezra is happy to let him move at his own speed.

Teddy catches Ezra watching him, and he grins (Lord have mercy) and leans in to shout in his ear, 'The show is up there, love.'

Ezra nuzzles his nose into the spot behind Teddy's ear. 'You *are* the show, baby.'

Teddy all but liquefies against him and Ezra nips at his earlobe before pulling back and kissing him. He tastes of overly sweet cocktails and Ezra wants to drink him down in front of everyone. Instead, he puts an arm snuggly around Teddy's waist and they watch Miss Sheneeda Dickens fall back into a death drop that makes the crowd lose their minds.

They continue to make their way through the filthy cocktail list, and Teddy's smile goes softer and goofier with each one. When he misses his mouth and dribbles some of his *Tight Snatch* down his front, Ezra licks it off his chin, and for a moment Teddy forgets they're in public, seizing him by his ass and pulling them flush against each other.

'Grabby,' Ezra says.

Teddy proves his point by squeezing again. 'I can't help it if you look particularly ravishing tonight.'

'Does that mean you plan to *ravish* me?'

'Damn right.'

The music changes from up-tempo to sultry as *Cry To Me by* Solomon Burke comes on, and suddenly everyone thinks they're in *Dirty Dancing*. Teddy has a wicked smile on his lips, and he grabs Ezra's hands, pulling him into the middle of the sticky, dry-humping, crowd. Ezra barely has time to cock an eyebrow before Teddy is holding his waist and pulling him close. Ezra swallows hard as he watches Teddy travel down the (not particularly long) length of his body, in a ridiculously graceful slut drop.

He slowly makes his way back, his hands grazing Ezra's thighs, over his hips and grabbing at his waist again, and Ezra thinks he might blackout as Teddy begins dirty dancing with him. And. Oh. *Oh.* He's good at this. Really good. And it's *really* doing it for him. He suddenly remembers Patrick Swayze shirtless and taking Baby's clothes off, and he remembers watching that scene for the first time as a teenager and wishing he was between them. He thinks that he is so fucking dumb for not realising sooner.

Drunk Teddy has rhythm. His hips are loose and confident as they press into Ezra's, and as his lips find Ezra's neck, sucking gently. He can barely hear the screaming of the dancers around them (when had they acquired groupies?) over the rushing in his ears as Teddy Montgomery gives him a hickey. In public. And, oh God, he is so ridiculously hard.

They don't last much longer at Judy's, since they are both sporting the world's most painfully obvious erections. Ezra has booked a seedy hotel room in a part of the city where neither of them would ever be expected to stay, so they go unnoticed as they barely make it to their room in the wake of ripping each other's clothes off.

Teddy's mouth is hot and sweet, and Ezra wants to taste every part of it. Their journey from the doorway to the bed is mapped by various discarded pieces of clothing, like a horny trail of breadcrumbs. Ezra palms Teddy through his jeans, because, apparently, he is a blue-balled teenager, but it makes Teddy moan anyway. Which just one *thousand* percent does it for him.

Ezra is in the mood to worship this man, so when he lays Teddy down on the bed and kisses his way up his thighs, he has every intention of taking him in his mouth and making him scream, but Teddy's hand catches his chin, effectively stopping him. When Ezra looks up at him, he has a strange look on his obscene face.

'You okay?' Ezra asks.

Teddy nods but doesn't say anything. Ezra can literally hear the cogs turning in his overcrowded head, and he waits patiently. That's the thing about Teddy; his mind is always half a mile ahead of his heart. His big, stupid heart. Ezra knows he struggles to say how he really feels, and he knows that when his jaw clenches he wishes he could say it all anyway. He knows that Teddy is also always waiting to be rejected, and that no amount of reassurance on Ezra's part will make those anxieties go away. So instead, he is patient. He is calm and steady for the both of them.

'Kiss me,' Teddy says, breathlessly, tugging at Ezra to join him.

Ezra happily climbs the length of Teddy's body, not knowing where this is going but already buckled in for the ride. He realises, with unnerving clarity, that he would follow Teddy Montgomery anywhere. He bows his head to kiss him, and Teddy's body is so damn responsive beneath his that he almost can't believe there was ever a time that they weren't doing this.

And yet there is something different this time. Teddy's body moves with both a hesitancy and a sureness that Ezra can't place, and he lets Teddy lead him, and touch him, and move him how he wants to. Teddy's legs (those *fucking* legs, Jesus Christ) wind around Ezra's waist and they both groan as their hips meet. Ezra kisses him again, before pulling back a fraction to look at him. And it's unmistakable what Teddy wants him to do. It may as well be written in the sky. He swallows. *Oh.*

'Teddy...' he says, slowly.

'If you want to,' Teddy begins. 'We can. I mean. I know we haven't. Obviously. But, um. Well.'

'Do... do *you* want to?'

'Very, *very* much so.'

Ezra's breath catches. 'Oh. Wow.'

'Do *you* want to?'

There it is again. That fear. The expectation that he's going to be shut down, thrown away, and never thought about again. Ezra can't bear it, and he kisses him until Teddy's jaw softens again. 'Of course, I do, sweetheart.'

'Have you ever...?'

'Not like this.'

'I... wouldn't say it's *too* different to anything you've done before.'

Ezra's lips twitch. 'You're like *nothing* I've ever done before.'

That makes Teddy smile. It's his secret smile, and Ezra is ready to start a religion for this man. He nods to his overnight bag on the floor and Ezra hangs himself inelegantly off the side of the bed to reach it. Teddy fishes around inside and pulls out a condom and a bottle of lube, making Ezra's eyebrow quirk.

'Were you planning on corrupting me tonight, Theodore?' he asks.

Teddy squeezes a liberal amount of lube into Ezra's hand and guides it down between his legs, effectively shutting him the hell up. And when Ezra tentatively teases him open with his fingers, and Teddy's head falls back against the pillows, Ezra is fairly certain that he's forgotten every word in the English language. Not that it matters anyway, because there are absolutely no words that can describe how Teddy looks right now. His face is flushed, his eyes closed, brows knitted together. His mouth is happy, his bottom lip tortured between his teeth.

Ezra works him open and he's a little bit in awe of how ready Teddy's body is for him. How it responds to every touch, every change in tempo. When Teddy's eyelids flutter open, his blue eyes lock onto Ezra's, and he trembles beneath his steady hands.

'*Ezra...*' It sounds like a promise. A prayer.

There is a knot of anticipation in Ezra's stomach as he withdraws and gently nudges Teddy's legs wider. He can't take his eyes off his sweet face, and he lines himself up to where his fingers were moments ago. When he hesitates, it's not because he doesn't want to do it, but because he wants to do it so much that it scares him a little. But it's a good kind of scared. It's climbing the peak of a roller-coaster scared. It's standing at the precipice of a cliff, about to dive scared. It's watching everything you never knew you wanted, lying beneath you naked and wanting and breathless.

'Ready?' he asks, voice horse.

Teddy nods, and when Ezra pushes inside him, his mouth — that posh mouth, that could be so damn filthy when he wants it to be — falls open, his eyelids fluttering closed again. Part of Ezra's mind registers that he's shaking. That they both are. And when he bows his head to bury it in the crook of Teddy's neck, his hands gripping his narrow hips, he feels Teddy's strong hands clinging to his shoulders. Hears a soft: '*Oh...please...*'

And it's so good. It has no right to be this good. And when he pulls back to look at Teddy to make sure he feels the same, he almost comes undone at the sight of Teddy Montgomery completely unravelling beneath him. He can't believe that it could ever be this good for him. For *both* of them. And he pours every ounce of what he's feeling — whatever he actually *is* feeling, because he has no idea — into this. He wants Teddy to know that he doesn't have to worry. That he'll always want him like this.

And when Teddy comes, his body is arching off the bed, his fingernails digging into Ezra's shoulder blades, and Ezra follows him, hurtling head-first into an orgasm that makes his entire body quake. He clings to Teddy, gasping, chest heaving, his heartbeat thundering in his eardrums. He doesn't know how long they stay that way, but Ezra is absolutely certain that his bones have turned to Jell-O. He will never be able to move again. He is destined to languish here, in Teddy's arms, for all of eternity, and he really doesn't mind at all.

When Teddy speaks, his voice is soft, his lips brushing Ezra's earlobe. 'That was...'

'Yeah,' Ezra agrees. 'It was.'

They kiss. It's sleepy and lazy, and the dopamine haze is rapidly descending. When they fall asleep, Teddy's back is drawn in against Ezra's chest. The fingers of their left hands are laced together and resting against Teddy's chest, and the last thing that Ezra can feel before sleep claims him, is the steady beat of Teddy Montgomery's heart beneath his palm.

Chapter Ten

Ezra suspects that waking up next to Teddy will never lose its charm. Even when he's snoring, even when his usually so demure face is smooshed up against the pillow, even when a small patch of drool is collecting on the linen. There is something so intimate about seeing him this way, when he isn't the Teddy Montgomery that the whole world gets to see and scrutinize. When he's so vulnerable, so unguarded. In a way it almost feels more intimate than last night, and last night was just about as *intimate* as it could get.

He reaches out and gently touches his fingertips to his cheekbones — those cheekbones that could cut glass — and traces the smattering of freckles across his skin that you can only make out if you're lucky enough to be as close to him as Ezra is. Teddy's skin is like the night sky, and Ezra wants to spend the rest of his life mapping the constellations across his beautiful body.

'Are you staring at me?' Teddy asks, not opening his eyes.

'Only when I'm not blinking.'

'Rather creepy don't you think?'

'Can't help it. You're gorgeous.'

Teddy cracks open one eye. 'You're incorrigible.'

Ezra grins and shimmies closer to him under the sheets. 'You *love* it.'

Teddy reaches for him, instinctively, pulling their bodies together. His hands gently knead Ezra's sides. 'The jury is still out on that one.'

'Objection your honour, badgering the witness.'

'In England they don't actually say that. It's something more along the lines of *M'lord, if it do please the right honourable gentleman* blah blah blah.'

Ezra nods. 'Plus, they wear those funny wigs.'

Teddy kisses him and Ezra's stomach and his heart switch places for a few moments. When he pulls away, he has a thoughtful look on his face. 'Last night went well, don't you think?'

Ezra smirks. 'I would say it went better than *well.*'

Teddy playfully pinches him. 'I mean the fundraiser. Everyone seemed to get along alright. Mum and Dad didn't offend anyone as far as I'm aware. Ron and Ali didn't kill each other. Plus, Daria said we raised a lot of money.'

And there it is. Ezra's opening to ask about it. To get Teddy talking about his parents. He must be quiet for longer than he realises because Teddy gives his side another gentle squeeze. His smile is kind.

'You look like you're thinking some big thoughts over there,' he says.

Ezra smiles. 'Nah. Just lots of little ones.'

'Well, my therapist says I'm a very good listener.'

Ezra tries to smile but it's dead on arrival. 'Teddy, are your parents, like — are they ever... not good to you?'

Teddy's body stiffens but his face stays perfectly schooled. 'In what way?'

'I guess, like,' Ezra shuffles up so that he's sitting properly. 'Are they, I don't know, unkind to you?'

Teddy's eyes go distant for a moment. 'Yes. I suppose they are.'

Ezra's heart lurches painfully. 'Like how?'

Teddy sighs and sits up too, propping himself on the pillows beside Ezra. 'Exactly how you'd expect; how their off-camera reputation precedes them. They are cruel, and bigoted, and emotionally unavailable. They resent me almost as much as they do each other. It is... difficult to be around.'

Teddy looks so small then, so utterly miserable, that Ezra literally *has* to pull him in for a hug. He presses kisses against his rumpled hair and says, 'I'm sorry. I had to ask. They just seem so... robotic? I guess?'

'I think they're using the show as a chance to reinvent themselves,' Teddy sighs, his arms winding around Ezra's middle, squeezing gently. 'Finding work is getting harder and harder for them. Mum is past what is considered her peak when it comes to modelling. Dad hasn't had an acting gig that isn't a supporting role in a romcom for years — and he used to be a leading man! Once he was even rumoured to be the next Bond. I think they want to be seen as easy to work with.'

'So, it's just an act?' Ezra asks, already knowing the answer.

Another Big British Sigh. 'Yes. They'll slip up soon though. I can see the cracks starting.'

'Jesus. I don't really know what to say.'

Teddy presses a kiss to the hollow of Ezra's throat. 'Tell me something nice.'

That Ezra can do. He smiles down at Teddy. 'Daria said we raised an eye-wateringly offensive amount at the fundraiser. I really like her. She's kind of everything.'

'She is lovely,' Teddy agrees. 'Leo adored her. They were childhood sweethearts.'

'That's *sickeningly* adorable.'

'Mum and Dad could never stand her, which obviously meant that me and Leo liked her immediately. I knew he was going to marry her before he did. Actually, I think he was the last to know that he was madly in love with her. He loved her so much that it was hard to look at sometimes. Like, it was so intimate that no one else should even be allowed to see it.' Something painful flickers across Teddy's features and his jaw suddenly sets like concrete. Ezra wants to kiss him until he melts, so he does.

Somewhere between the kisses and the gentle touches, and the murmured *sweetheart*s that absolutely wreck Teddy, Ezra says: 'Tell me about him. You loved him, and I want to know him. Through you.'

Teddy licks his lips. 'I... don't know. It still hurts.'

'Then you don't have to,' Ezra assures him. 'But when you're ready to talk, I'm ready to listen.'

Teddy watches him for the longest time, his big blue eyes unfathomable and devastating. Then he says: 'He loved *Harry Potter*. Even more than me. When we were younger and I was just a kid, he used to take me to stand outside *W.H. Smith* overnight to make sure we both got a copy. When he got sorted into Hufflepuff he was beside himself with pride, because, according to him, Hufflepuffs are *particularly good finders*.'

Ezra can't help it, he is grinning. 'And here I was thinking *you* were the Hufflepuff of the family?'

'Because I'm the Family Gay?'

'No, because you're the Family Hottie. You're like Cedric Diggory, but if he was even taller, and hotter, and wore Prada.'

That makes Teddy smile properly. And Ezra doesn't know what magical password he must have said, but Teddy lets the last wall built around him and his fragile heart down, because they spend the next hour in bed, cozied up, while Teddy tells him all about his older brother. He tells him about when Leo took him out for the first time on his eighteenth birthday and how he got him *completely wankered* on tequila shots. About how he was terrified to come out to him, for Leo to just nod and say *well yes, obviously* and how he'd held him while he cried his eyes out. About how he and Leo would sneak out of press tours to find the nearest dive bar with the intention of just having *a few bevs* and then waking up the next day on the Isle Of Wight (where?) with killer hangovers and a million texts from their publicists.

Ezra watches as Teddy's expression swings from joyfully nostalgic, to completely pained, to bittersweet and wistful. His face animates when he tells him about the time he and Leo took an impromptu trip to Disneyland with Daria and the twins, then falls slack when he retells the story of how Leo nearly estranged himself from the family when his parents called Daria a *gold-digger and an unbefitting match for the Montgomery name* and how Teddy had to beg him not to leave him alone with his parents.

And Ezra listens to it all. He laughs when Teddy laughs, and he smooths out the frown on Teddy's forehead whenever a dark memory surfaces. But for the most part it's happy, and Teddy's sweet face whenever he laughs about another outrageous thing the Montgomery siblings had gotten up to, makes Ezra's heart throw up.

It's not the kind of hotel that has room service, so they Uber Eats breakfast to their door and Ezra tips the receptionist *far* too much so that she'll stop glaring at him for making her walk down from reception. It's nothing extravagant, but it's greasy and delicious. They watch YouTube videos of influencer house tours, and they kiss, and it's horribly domestic, but it's also really nice.

And Ezra doesn't know why, but Teddy has been so honest with him that he feels he has to give something back, and his mind weighs the pros and cons of telling him the one thing that he never tells anyone. Not only because he's signed an NDA on it, not only because it is, technically, not his story to tell, but also because it turns his insides cold to think about it. But when he opens his mouth, the words kind of, just, tumble out, and he can't stop them.

'It goes without saying that this can never be repeated to anyone,' Ezra says, pointedly not looking at Teddy as he chases the last of his scrambled eggs around his plate. 'Because mom and dad, and Ali, and Grace, and probably even Iris would kill me. But there was a time, a few years ago, when we nearly lost Grace.'

Teddy looks at him. 'Oh. Love. I wasn't aware.'

'That was kind of the point of the NDAs. We made sure that no one knew. When her YouTube career kicked off, and she was starting to make big money, she fell in with the influencer crowd. And some of them were fine, but most of them were assholes. Like the platform isn't toxic enough anyway without these jerks trying to undermine you at every opportunity. It didn't help that she's not white. She was immediately the target. One day it all just got too much and she—' His throat is suddenly clogged with glue. 'She tried to kill herself.'

Teddy's hand finds his. His voice is soft when he says, 'Ezra... I'm so sorry.'

'It's alright,' Ezra tries to shrug it off, but his body feels heavy. 'She's still here. We didn't realise at the time that she was depressed. We also didn't know she was on heroin. When it all got too much for her she tried to overdose. I found her in her apartment, unconscious in her own sick, the needle still sticking out of her arm. I'd never been so terrified.

'Luckily, we got her to the hospital in time. We managed to play it off to the press as an allergic reaction to a new medication she was taking. We sent her to a rehab clinic in the Maldives so we could call it a well-deserved holiday after a traumatic event. And everyone bought it, because we told them to.

'She got better. And she's fine now, obviously. But for a moment there, I really thought we'd lost her. I knew that if she died, I would never have forgiven myself for not noticing she was struggling. She was so miserable, Teddy. Meanwhile, I was getting drunk at parties, and playing camp to the camera because it got views, and making a spectacle of myself at public events, because that's what I knew people expected of me. And I enjoyed it. I liked being the Wyoming Wild Child.

'But I never stopped — I never fucking *stopped* — to even ask if she was okay. Because I was too wrapped up in myself. And, actually, I still don't think I will ever forgive myself, you know? I should have been there for her.'

Ezra doesn't realise his hands are balled into fists until Teddy gently prises them open. 'Life for you wasn't exactly easy back then, either. You're not completely at fault for not realising what was happening.'

Ezra frowns. 'What? My life was literally the definition of easy.'

'You were a closeted bisexual kid barely out of his teens who had suddenly been thrust into the limelight and expected to learn scripts overnight. There wasn't a single day where I can't remember not seeing your name trending on Twitter, or seeing a picture of you in a British tabloid, and I don't think you've realised how traumatising that actually is. Trust me, I've lived it too.'

Ezra looks at him. Really looks at him. How is it possible that this plummy, beans-on-plain-toast-eating lunatic of an Englishman knows him better than he knows himself? He swallows, because his voice has gotten tight all the sudden, and croaks out, 'Well. When you put it like *that*...'

'You're an exceptional brother,' Teddy says, kissing the space between Ezra's knitted brows. 'You're an exceptional *person*. You make the world better by just existing. Thank you for telling me.'

Ezra smiles, weakly. He suddenly feels exhausted. 'Thanks for listening.'

'The rehabilitation charity must sit close to home, I bet?'

'Basically, in my back pocket.'

Teddy takes the tray of mostly empty breakfast plates and puts them on the floor before rolling Ezra on his back and kissing him senseless. He kisses him until all the tension eases out of his body, and then a bit more just for good measure. Ezra isn't sure at what point in the conversation that he became the one that needs comforting, but he isn't going to say no. Not when Teddy Montgomery is kissing the length of his body. Not when Teddy Montgomery is straddling his lap. Not when Teddy Montgomery's head is tipped back, lips parted as he rides Ezra languid and slow.

Probably not ever.

Ezra doesn't know why he is nervous about dinner with Teddy Montgomery's parents off-camera. He isn't Teddy's boyfriend, and even if he *is*, Ezra has never been nervous about meeting parents before. Parents, in general, love him. He's polite, and charming, and always offers to help with the dishes, which literally makes most parents come on the spot. But tonight, as he changes into his third chinos-button-down-and-sports-jacket combo, Ezra realises that he's terrified.

The cameras won't be there, so Iris is joining them. She's practically family at this point. As far as the public is concerned, the Darlings and the Montgomerys go *way* back, and this marrying of families is totally not to cover up Viktor Volkov's gay conversion scandal. Nope. Not at all. In the slightest. No, this is an informal meeting between soon-to-be in-laws, and Ezra has no reason to be gripping the sides of his sink and staring down his reflection, but he is anyway.

When Grace comes to pick him up, she redresses him in the chinos from outfit one, the shirt from outfit three, and the jacket from outfit two. She approves of the shoes, however, and they're soon in the limo, on their way to David and Anastasya's townhouse.

Which, as it turns out, is less of a townhouse, and more of a four-story mansion in a gated community in the heart of Rich White People NYC.

'White people,' Grace mutters as they approach the door. 'Can you have a word with your race please and tell them to get some taste?'

Ezra nods. 'I'll try my best.'

A butler answers the door. Because of *course* a butler answers the door. When you ascend to the level of wealth that is David and Anastasya Montgomery, you absolutely cannot be expected to answer your own door anymore. Opening doors is for peasants and the help.

They are led through a sea of mediocre Georgian decorating before winding up in the dining room, where the Montgomerys are waiting and dressed like they're going to the damn opera. Teddy meets his eyes, and there it is. That smile. And Ezra wants to go to him, but Grace beats him to it and gives him a respectable kiss on the cheek and a *hello gorgeous*, and something inside Ezra just burns.

But he swallows it down and gives Teddy a handshake and quietly says, through gritted teeth while no one is paying attention to them, 'I want to *eat* you.'

Teddy smiles brightly — his publicity smile now, for the sake of anyone who glances their way — and claps a hand on Ezra's shoulder. 'After dessert, darling.'

David and Anastasya make a grand show of greeting their guests, clasping hands and complimenting outfits. Daria wraps each of them in a hug, lingering a bit longer on Iris than necessary. Ezra just keeps liking her more and more, especially as Iris blushes. Like, *actually* blushes.

He tries not to feel stung about the fact his sister is sitting next to Teddy, and not him, and instead tries to focus on the positive that he is jammed between Daria and Iris, who settle into easy conversation like they've known each other their entire lives. Iris tries not to make big, love-sick eyes at Daria, but Ezra can see she is practically drooling into her soup bowl.

Grace rattles off about wedding plans, and Warren and Jacqueline smile and make polite conversation with the Montgomerys. Ezra tries to see the cracks in the façade, but Anastasya continues to smile graciously, and David is gregarious as ever. Ezra does, however, notice how they barely seem to acknowledge Iris. The vibe between them isn't exactly *tense*, but it's not Magic Kingdom either.

When Grace starts talking about the merits of roses over peonies for the bridesmaids, Ezra zones out and refocuses his attention on Teddy. He runs a foot slowly up the inside of Teddy's leg and has to bite the inside of his cheek to keep from smirking as a blush overtakes his pretty face.

He receives a text from Teddy: **You're a bastard** and replies: **aw, sweetheart.** And even that is enough to make Teddy's face go all silly, and when David gives him a strange look and tells him it's rude to have his phone out at the dinner table, he apologises and mumbles something about Google Alerts.

After the main course is served, Anastasya smiles at the hired staff and asks them for a moment of privacy. She has nothing but warm smiles and thanks for each waiter and waitress as they leave the room. The moment the door closes behind them, Ezra actually sees the mask fall away. The temperature in the room cools as Anastasya sits back in her chair and studies them each in turn, her gaze turning sour as she gets to Iris.

'Let's not pretend,' she says, her Russian dialect thick, 'that we are friends when we don't have to.'

The room suddenly becomes very small. Ezra and Grace briefly exchange stunned looks before both turning to their parents. Jacqueline looks completely bemused whilst Warren seems to be frozen with a forkful of filet mignon halfway to his mouth. Daria visibly sinks down into her seat. One glance at Teddy's stricken face warns Ezra to brace for impact.

'We all know why we're here,' she continues. 'My father's history has gotten our family into trouble, and we need you to get us out of it. However, it has come to our attention that your family's values do not exactly line up with our own.'

David addresses them next, hands folded on the table in front of them like he's a principal and they've all been called into his office for a dressing down.

'As you know,' he says in an English accent that has been weather-worn by his years in America. 'My family and I are heavily involved with our church, and we always want to uphold our church's beliefs.'

'David,' Jacqueline says, placatingly. 'Anastasya, you must know that we have absolutely no intention—'

'I wasn't done,' David cuts across her.

Ezra watches his dad bristle in his chair, but his mom's hand on his shoulder somewhat soothes him. At the very least, convinces him not to leap from his chair and strangle the other man.

David continues. 'My family and I have dealt with a great deal of tragedy and unfounded scandal. Throughout all that, our church has stood by us. We will not abandon them now just because our work associates have chosen to bring someone... *untoward* into their fold.'

His gaze settles coolly on Iris, as does everyone else's. Ezra watches his best friend who, for the most part, seems unfazed. There aren't many people that Iris can't charm, but the Montgomerys, it would seem, are going to be the first. Ezra can see the shitstorm before it breaks.

'We cannot be seen associating with a degenerate,' Anastasya says. 'Our church and our conscience won't allow it.'

The evening comes to a grinding, shuddering, shrieking-breaks-on-a-freight-train stop. Teddy drops his fork, a radish spinning over the tablecloth. His mouth opens and closes several times before simply just snapping shut in grim submission.

Ezra can taste bile in the back of his throat. He isn't an idiot; he knows that homophobia is still alive and well. But there is a huge difference between reading about it and seeing it happen on the news, and watching it happen over the main course of your dinner. To your best friend. From your *in-laws*.

Iris clears her throat. 'Well,' and her voice is way more polite than these motherfuckers deserve, 'we actually prefer the term "lesbian". That or just "gay" will do. But yes, I am, essentially, a *degenerate*, as you have pointed out, Mrs Montgomery. However, as I do not appear on camera, I don't see how that's going to be a problem.'

'You cannot see a bad smell,' Anastasya says. 'And yet it still lingers.'

'Mum—' Teddy tries, but she ignores him.

'Besides, you're seen in public with them. The Darlings are guilty by association.'

'Anastasya,' Warren tries to interject. 'We don't view Iris' sexuality as something that needs to be felt guilty about.'

'The Darling Dynasty is a show that supports family values, is it not?' Anastasya has no intention of looking at anyone but Iris. 'Do her... *proclivities*... not threaten that? Because it threatens us.'

Iris arches an eyebrow. 'If you're asking, *does me eating pussy put the Darling Dynasty in trouble*, then no. It doesn't. Not only because the kind of audience who enjoys watching Darling Dynasty aren't homophobic assholes, but also because I give exceptionally good head. So don't worry, there have never been any complaints on either front. But if you're worried about what your church will think if you're seen with me then don't — I sure as hell don't plan to ever be around you.'

Anastasya tilts her head. 'It does make me wonder. What on earth could happen to a girl so young to incline her to such deviancy? Did someone hurt you?'

'Did someone hurt *you*?' Iris replies. 'Did someone drop you on your fucking head as a baby?'

David's hand tenses around his sherry glass. 'Do not speak to my wife like that, young lady. You are a guest in this house.'

'Could have fooled me.'

Jacqueline gets that look on her face that means business, and all Ezra can think is *please mom, make it stop*. 'This is not a conversation that needs to happen. Not now or ever. Iris is part of our family and we expect you to treat her as such.'

'Exactly,' David says. 'She is family. Any association with the Darlings is an association with us. We are aware that this arrangement is temporary and for artificial reasons—'

'To save your asses,' Iris points out.

'—but that doesn't mean that we cannot continue keeping up appearances. As I understand it, your... *inclinations* aren't public knowledge. We would like to keep it that way. We can have NDAs drawn up and sent over to your lawyer.'

Iris smiles, but it is tight and clipped. She takes the napkin off her lap and places it calmly on the table before standing and smoothing her perfectly uncrumpled dress down. 'No need, Mr Montgomery. I don't think we run in the same circles, so I doubt I'll be seeing you again anyway.' She looks at Daria. 'It was great to see you again. You're gorgeous, and if we weren't at a *Chick-fil-A* AGM right now, I'd probably give you my number. But I'm off. I've got a fuck-tonne of pussy to eat, and a family to disappoint, and, I don't know, possibly an orphanage to torch. Degenerate *out*.'

Iris leaves. The room doesn't take a breath. Grace is the first to run after her, followed by Ezra and, a few moments later, Teddy and Daria. They find her standing on the pavement outside, the heels of her palms pushed angrily against her eyes. When she takes them away, Ezra is certain she isn't going to cry. Iris *never* cries. Iris is solid as stone. Iris is—

Iris is crying. Sobbing, actually. And Grace immediately pulls her into her arms. Ezra joins, and they both hold her, their joint best friend. Ezra's legs feel weak. He's never had to be the strong one when it comes to Iris. Iris is always the one keeping the rest of the world together for everyone else.

Teddy looks beside himself. When he tries to speak, all he can manage is a soft, small apology. And he means it. Ezra can see that he means it, and that he is tearing himself up inside. That he is perilously close to flying off the deep end because his perfect jaw is literally wired shut. Daria's hand on his shoulder seems to keep him grounded.

Ezra can't even imagine how it must feel to be Teddy, so deep in the closet he hasn't just found Narnia but everything that lay beyond it too, and to hear his parents — his own parents — say such vile things. Things that they would say about him too if they knew. If they ever took their heads out of their asses long enough to even remember that Teddy exists. And shit. Ezra wants to hold him too. And kiss him. And call him sweetheart, not because it will make his knees go weak, but because it will let him know that at least someone still cares about him.

Iris holds a hand out to Teddy and when he accepts it she pulls him into the fray, bringing Daria along too, and suddenly they're all holding her. They let her take as long as she needs, because this is probably the only time in her life that Iris will ever cry, and it shouldn't be rushed.

Ezra turns as he hears the front door open. He sees his parents behind them. Iris starts to apologise, but Jacqueline and Warren shut her up by pulling her into their own group hug.

'Come on,' Warren says, decisively. 'No one talks to our kids like that. Let's get pizza. The food tastes like ass here anyway.'

And that is how they end up in a grotty pizzeria back on the streets of NYC, that only has one star on TripAdvisor, but is always busy because New Yorkers know what *good* pizza is, even when it's prepared in a cesspool, and will readily overlook any silly complaints like *unclean surroundings* or *unfriendly staff*.

It is also how they end up with the new *WhatsApp* group: **Fancy Meeting You Queer.**

Chapter Eleven

Text thread: Fancy Meeting You Queer

saving grace:
does everyone know what they're wearing to this thing?

ezra:
clothes?

saving grace:
not helpful

iggy:
wear the blue dress

iggy:
you know the one. that makes your tits look amazing

ezra:
please stop talking about my sisters breasts??

Flynn Rider [eggplant emoji]:
I will also be wearing a blue dress

that make my tits look amazing
if that helps?

>ezra:
>don't encourage them

daria:
Don't wear the blue dress, Teddy.
It's far too slutty.

>ezra:
>on second thought can you 100%
>wear the blue dress?

saving grace:
get your own fiancé

>ezra:
>but yours is so pretty

Flynn Rider [eggplant emoji]:
It's true. I *am* pretty.

iggy:
i'm going to wear nothing but a pride flag
and the disapproval of our founding
fathers.

>ezra:
>i swear alexander hamilton was gay?

Flynn Rider [eggplant emoji]:
He was buggering John Laurens every
chance he got.

saving grace:
yeah, but only on days with a Y in them

ezra:
amazing how that didn't make it
into the musical

iggy:
wear the blue dress

iggy:
that goes for you too teddy

Flynn Rider [eggplant emoji]:
I am more than just eye candy.

ezra:
true

ezra:
you're also a piece of meat

Flynn Rider [eggplant emoji]:
Thank you.

For the first time in a long time, Ezra has a real group of friends. One that actually extends beyond just Grace and Iris. And although none of them know about him and Teddy, their group is still a safe place for them to escape to. It isn't that Ezra doesn't have other friends — because he totally does — just not friends that he ever sees. Or can count on. Or can turn to in a moment of crisis. Okay, so maybe not *friends*, but definitely people that like to be papped with him, and people who like getting invites to the annual costume party, and people who sometimes call him the *Darling Token Caucasian* as a, like, totally funny joke. Because, obviously, a successful black family would never have gotten this famous without a white kid as the front man.

Alright. Okay. So yeah, those people are probably not his friends. Probably not even acquaintances. But if he cuts off every casual contact every time they use him, or make him feel small, or are low-key racist to his adopted family, then he wouldn't have anyone left.

Teddy, as it turns out, isn't wearing a blue dress that make his tits look amazing. Instead, he is wearing a navy-blue suit — to match Grace's boob dress — and a contrasting mustard yellow tie, and Ezra has no idea how he is going to last at this press conference for an hour without sitting on his face. To make life easier, Grace sits next to him. At least that way he can't reach across and put his hand on Teddy's knee. Or thigh. Or—

Ezra crosses his legs. He looks around the conference hall for a welcome distraction, but all he is met with are faces of the press, camera lenses and tape recorders. This is the first of, what will be, many more events. Filming is on their mid-season break, and their free time is being put to good use by the press tour. They are starting in NYC, and then covering twenty other states in ten days. He is already exhausted.

Usually, Ezra hates press tours. They're not scripted, and he doesn't have the luxury of getting drunk and playing up to the camera to cover his obvious lack of charisma, uniqueness, nerve, and talent. He also hates that he's been stress-binging *Drag Race*. But at least there's Teddy. And even though Ezra has to smile and tell everyone how totally *psyched* he is to be the best man, and pretend to the world that he isn't just the best man but *the* man in Teddy Montgomery's life, it's still nice having him there. Like a piece of home is on the road with him.

Ali glares at him from the wings. He is used to Ali glaring at him though, so he doesn't pay her much attention. He suspects that she knows Ezra dragged Teddy away last weekend for a secret stag do, and he suspects she also probably heard about their shocking dinner with the Montgomerys, and he also *highly* suspects that she has figured out a way to blame him for it.

Before they'd gone on stage to take their seats, she'd grabbed him by the scruff of his jacket and warned, 'Behave yourself this time, you little turd.'

Ezra knows she's probably referring to last season's press tour, when Ezra had gotten so nervous that he'd emptied the hotel room mini fridge and had shown up so drunk that he hadn't given a second thought at flipping off a journalist who'd asked Grace if she was *planning on keeping her clothes on in this season.*

So, Ezra tries to ignore Ali. And he tries to ignore Teddy. And he tries to ignore every single journalist and paparazzo who tries to catch his eye to ask him a question. Not that many people are interested in him now that Hollywood's hottest new couple are sitting right next to him. When he risks a glance at them, he sees Grace's hand on Teddy's thigh, Teddy's hand resting on top of hers. Something nasty stirs inside him.

'Jacob Wreath, *VIP*,' a bespectacled man in a rumpled suit informs them. 'Teddy, how are you finding America?'

Ezra watches him. Watches Teddy give his tight smile. The press smile. The please-stop-paying-attention-to-me smile. 'I find it very accommodating. Thank you.'

'Samantha Higham, *Buzz Weekly*. Teddy, what's been your favourite part of joining the Darling Dynasty so far?'

At this, Teddy gives Grace's hand a gentle squeeze. He looks at her so adoringly, and so tenderly, and, for a moment, Ezra thinks he might dropkick his own sister. 'It has to be Grace. She is beyond incredible, and I cannot believe I have the wonderful privilege of being the man she will one day call *husband*.'

There are soft *awws* and shuffling sounds of hands being placed over hearts from the crowd. Ezra is going to beat himself to death with a boom mic.

'Rochelle Weiss, *Grapevine*. Teddy, if you had to marry any other member of the Darling Dynasty who would it be any why?'

Ezra might be imagining it, but he swears Teddy's gaze flickers to him for a millisecond. Then he gives another pinched smile and says, 'Well, considering Iris Sanchez-Smith is practically a member of the Darling family, I'm inclined to choose her. But that would, of course, be ignoring the fact that I haven't already found everything I'm looking for. Which I have.'

More *awws*. More heart-clutching. More barely-contained eye-rolling from Ezra. And then, everything seems to slow down for a moment. Grace is reaching out to cup Teddy's cheek. She smiles at him before drawing him in close. Ezra barely has time to register the surprise on Teddy's face before Grace is kissing him. *Kissing him*. Him. His Teddy. His Teddy Montgomery. Something scorching, and vile, and sharp settles like molten lead in his stomach, and his hands ball into fists on his lap.

Teddy tries to catch his eye as he pulls back, but Ezra isn't looking — *cannot* look at him right then. And every time Teddy glances over after that, Ezra refuses to give in, keeps looking forward. He can feel his own jaw wired shut. He can feel a tightness in his throat, an anger that threatens to choke him live on stage. If the rest of the room picks up on it, they do the right thing and don't angle a single question at him. Instead, they let him stew as he listens to Teddy and Grace answer more banal questions with equally banal lies.

When did you know it was love? Are you planning on starting a family? Will you stay in America or are you moving to the UK? How does it feel to be the most amazing heterosexual couple in the whole world? Teddy, if you had to choose between Ezra or a literal sewer rat, which would you pick and why would it definitely be the sewer rat?

By the time it's over and Ezra can march offstage, he is amazed that he hasn't killed anyone.

Ezra is ignoring his phone. Well. No. He isn't. He's looking at it every time it buzzes and reading all of his incoming texts from Teddy. The group chat, that has since been renamed *Queer, There & Everywhere*, is firing off hilarious quips and come backs at rapid speed, either not noticing or not caring that he and Teddy aren't joining in.

He purposefully leaves **Ezra, please talk to me**, and **Ezra, this is ridiculous**, and **Ezra, I'm sorry**, on read, feeling petty but fractionally better. He wants to drain the mini-bar but Ali has preemptively emptied it, lest they have a repeat of last year's Great Middle Finger Calamity. So, instead, he goes down to the hotel bar and orders a whiskey, neat. He doesn't like it and would much rather have a Long Island Iced Tea, but he is feeling maudlin, and whiskey is a drink for when you feel maudlin. So, he sips his whiskey and tries not to pull a face.

Within half an hour, three separate people try to take him to bed. Two girls and a guy. He politely declines and nurses his whiskey that he doesn't like, and stares at his hands curled around the tumbler glass as he waits for the bile in the back of his throat to go away.

'You don't even like whiskey.'

Ezra doesn't look up. He tries to ignore the way his skin prickles at the sound of Teddy's voice. He manages to fight the natural pull that Teddy has over him, like he's the sun and Ezra is the earth, forever in his orbit. He sets his jaw and says, 'You don't even like girls.'

When Teddy speaks, his aristocratic voice is as close to irritable as Ezra has ever heard. 'That's low, Ezra. Even for you.'

Ezra turns on his barstool to face him. 'Did you or did you not kiss my sister?'

Teddy lifts his chin defiantly. 'It meant nothing.'

'Then why did you do it?'

'I don't suppose,' Teddy says, sliding onto the barstool next to him, 'that it makes a difference that *she* kissed me, and not the other way around?'

'Beauty *and* brains.'

Teddy sighs, like Ezra is a particularly tiresome, especially petulant riddle that he can't be bothered to solve anymore. 'It was for the cameras, Ezra. You know that. This is the whole point of the press tour.'

'The whole point of the press tour was for you to put your tongue down my sister's throat?' Ezra takes a sip of his whiskey without grimacing. 'Well, mission fucking accomplished, sweetheart.'

Teddy flinches, as if Ezra has struck him, and Ezra regrets it instantly. 'Please don't call me that when you're angry.'

'Please don't kiss my sister.'

'You do understand that this is unavoidable?' Teddy asks. 'There are going to be times when Grace and I are going to have to touch, or maybe kiss? What did you think we were going to do on our wedding day? High five? And what about after that? We're going to have to move in together to keep up appearances. This,' Teddy gestures at the space between them, 'has always had a shelf life.'

All the air leaves Ezra's lungs. For some bizarre reason he laughs, even as his eyes sting. He sees that Teddy regrets saying it, but it's already been said and Ezra has already been burned. He swallows, thickly. He *will* not bawl into his liquor in a hotel bar like a cliché.

He says, 'Then what the fuck are we even doing, if this means nothing to you?'

Teddy gives him a hard look. 'I didn't say that.'

Ezra's voice is rising, and he can't help it. The bar is loud, and no one is particularly interested in two guys sniping at each other, but they are beginning to draw curious glances. 'You said you would choose Iris over me. *Iris*. My lesbian ex-girlfriend!'

'Keep your voice down, Ezra.'

'Are you trying to hurt me? Are you *trying* to make me feel like shit?'

'Of course, I'm not.'

'Well, you are.'

Teddy glances around them. Those who don't have the self-respect to try and eavesdrop without outright staring at them, are trying to read their lips over the music. 'Let's go upstairs.'

And it looks like Ezra doesn't have a choice, because Teddy is already standing and striding away, and he has no choice but to follow. That alone pisses him off more. He struggles to keep up with Teddy's long gait, which just makes him even angrier, and by the time they make it to Teddy's hotel room, he is ready to start a war.

But then he sees Teddy's face. *Really* sees it, now they're out of the dim lighting of the bar. And he looks miserable. Still a catwalk model, obviously, but his gaze is distant, clouded over. His hair is messy from fingers raking through it over and over. His chin has a hint of stubble that is just so quintessentially *not* Teddy Montgomery. His jaw is set like stone, apart from the slight wobble of his lower lip, and all of Ezra's anger immediately melts away.

'Oh,' he says. 'Sweetheart.'

'How can you bloody well stand there and say that I don't care about you?' Teddy demands, but his voice is hoarse. 'How *dare* you.'

'Teddy... *baby*...'

'All I know how to do is care for you. You are the most sure and steady thing I have ever known. And it kills me — it *kills* me — that I have to pretend that's not true. You really think I want to go around pretending to be something that I'm not? You think that I wouldn't have it any other way if I could? Because if it was my choice, I'd be kissing *you* up there in front of those cameras, but it's not my choice, and it never *has* been my choice, and it never *will* be my choice. All I want is you, and I can't fucking have you!'

Ezra closes the space between them and takes Teddy's wrists in his hands. He can feel his pulse racing. He can see his chest rising and heaving in short, shallow breaths. Teddy's eyes have gone from unfocused to razor sharp, agitated, and Ezra can see the panic attack coming from space.

'Sweetheart,' he says calmly. 'I'm sorry. I was jealous, and I've upset you, and I'm so sorry. Breathe.'

'I *am* breathing,' Teddy all but wheezes.

'Breath properly.' Ezra brings Teddy's hands to his chest, and takes deep, calm breaths. 'Like this, baby. Breathe.'

Teddy sucks in a deep, shuddering breath. Then another. Then another. And when he's finally breathing like he's not trying to inhale the hotel room, he hangs his head. 'Fuck. *Fuck.*'

'I'm sorry. You have enough people in your life upsetting you without me adding to it. I was stupid and jealous. And I didn't mean any of it. Well. Except when I said beauty *and* brains. I meant that part.'

That, at least, earns him a smile, albeit a sheepish one. 'And I really am sorry for kissing your sister.'

'It was a shock, but I should have realised it was coming sooner or later. I'd have preferred later. Like never. But...' Ezra finishes his sentence with a shrug.

'I didn't enjoy it, if it's any consolation.'

'It is.'

'I really do wish I could kiss you in public,' Teddy says, swallowing. 'But — I just — it's just—'

'No one is forcing you to out yourself,' Ezra says, pulling him into a reassuring embrace. 'Please forgive me.'

Teddy kisses his temple and says, 'Forgiven. And I didn't mean what I said either.'

'I know, dummy.'

A beat. 'You really were jealous?'

Ezra pulls back to give him a completely withering stare. 'Yes. Obviously. Have you *seen* you?'

A smile twitches at the corner of Teddy's mouth. 'Tell me.'

A bolt of something white hot strikes at the base of Ezra's spine. His breath catches. 'You want me to tell you how jealous I was when I saw her hand on your thigh? Or when I saw you look at her the way you're only supposed to look at me? Or when you kissed her like a very, *very* bad boy?'

Teddy Montgomery melts. 'Yes.'

'Fuck, you smell like her perfume.'

'I want to smell like *you*.'

Ezra's voice is rough now. 'Tell me who you belong to.'

Swallow. 'You.'

'Good boy,' he kisses Teddy and smiles as he draws a moan from his delicate lips. He adds *praise kink* to the ever-expanding list of things that he knows about Teddy Montgomery that the rest of the world does not. 'Now tell me again on your knees.'

Turns out that absolutely nothing gets Teddy off faster than being told what to do. Ezra learns this as he is pinning Teddy's wrists to the mattress and fucking him hard and fast, all the while repeating *mine* against his mouth. It is also no surprise that nothing else makes Ezra see stars like Teddy nodding and agreeing. *Yours. Only ever yours.*

The rest of the press tour is much the same. Different state, different questions, same bullshit answers. Grace is always either holding Teddy's hand, or has her hand on his knee or thigh (his goddamn *thigh*), or sneaking kisses against the corner of his mouth when the cameras are watching. And every night, Ezra stalks to Teddy's hotel room and jealousy-fucks him until their legs are shaking and they're hoarse from screaming.

And it's killing him. It's actually killing him. And every new state, every new stop, and every conference, he can feel his insides twisting up more and more until he is so knotted and gnarled up that not even Teddy can smooth out all the kinks.

Teddy is suffering too, because of course he is. Teddy is used to pretending to be something he's not, but not on this scale. Not with the entire world watching him as he play-acts the everyday hetero next door. As the week goes on, his face grows gaunter, his skin more ashen. Blue rings appear under his eyes that his makeup artist has a harder time concealing with each day.

They're stuck in this cycle of press, photoshoots, lies, sad-angry-passionate sex. Lather, rinse, repeat. One evening, after Ezra has effectively fucked Teddy's brains out and left him totally jellified and snoring in bed, he untangles himself from the other man's long limbs and heads down to the bar. It's late and mostly empty, and he orders himself a long-awaited Long Island Iced Tea, not caring if it doesn't make him look as brooding as he feels.

He senses someone slump on the stool beside him. Iris. He can tell just by the energy she carries around with her. She just has this way about her. Iris doesn't merely exist, she excels. It's effortless. Everything about her is: from the olive skin down to the jet black hair and dimpled smile. She is everything, and Ezra wishes they could just love each other, because then it would all be so much simpler. Ezra turns to look at her and she is so familiar and so much like home, that he feels the already pretty big lump in his throat double in size.

'Oh, Ezzy,' she says, quietly. 'What the hell are you doing?'

In that moment, he realises she knows. Because of course she knows. That's what happens when you aren't in front of the cameras. Instead, you're behind them, watching it all unfold. Watching it happen in real time. Since there is no point in lying, Ezra replies, 'I don't know.'

'Well, you need to figure it out pretty soon,' she says. 'Because they're getting married.'

Ezra's head falls into his hands. Everything is awful. Everything is just so awful. 'I know. *I know.*'

Her hand gently settles on his shoulder. 'I'm sorry. I know it's hard.'

'How long have you known?'

'About you or about Teddy?'

'Both.'

'From the start.'

He lifts his head to look at her. He is horrified to find that he really wants to cry. 'What am I going to do?'

'I don't know, babe.'

Ezra puts his head back in the comfort of his hands. There's a moment of silence, and then Iris is dragging her stool closer to him so she can drape her arm around his shoulders. And while he doesn't cry, his eyes aren't strictly dry either. Iris orders herself a martini, and they stay there, drinking, and not talking, but still saying so much, until the bar staff tells them it's closing time.

Chapter Twelve

Ezra doesn't normally get nervous for public appearances. He's done enough of them now to have a fail-safe, cover all bases, screw-up-proof script that he can defer to. It isn't like when he has to do Instagram lives with Grace and he is assaulted with questions and comments that mean well but are all, ultimately, complete curveballs. And it isn't like when he has to do a press tour and people are flinging questions at him like: *who are you bringing as a date to the wedding?*

The *real* beauty of public events like signings, fundraisers, parties, and TV interviews, is that — for the most part — they're in a controlled environment and the only people who are there are either die-hard Darling Dynasty fans, or people that have been invited. Which means that Ezra can rely on his script. The blessed tome. The oracle.

Except tonight, he is bricking it. And he wants to lie to himself and say he doesn't know why, but he does, and it starts with *Teddy* and ends with *will be there*. Which normally is, like, yay. Because Teddy is there. But this means Grace will also be there. And it means Grace will be on his arm. Grace will be holding his hand. Dancing with him. Kissing him. And the public will eat it up because they make such a perfect heterosexual couple.

But he has his speech memorised, and his goof-proof small talk of: *so tell me, where are you located now?* and: *we should meet up and discuss at a later date!* and even: *how is the husband/wife/kid/dog/fantasy football league doing?* to fall back on whenever people want to talk to him. And they do. Everyone always wants to talk to Ezra. No matter where he is, people just seem to gravitate towards him. Sometimes it's harmless, just polite mingling. And other times — like, most times — it's clout chasing, or attempts to get him into bed, or people trying to sell a story to whatever gossip blog will buy it. *Ten Things You Never Knew About Ezra Darling! Number Seven Will Shock You!*

But the nerves are there, jangling around in his stomach like used needles (wow, bad analogy for a rehabilitation fundraiser), and as he steps out of the limo, camera flashes blinding him, it only gets worse. He feels an arm loop through his and he turns to see Iris smiling at him, like a radiant life preserver. He lets out a breath he isn't aware he's holding.

'You're gorgeous,' he says.

'You're late,' she replies.

They are photographed to near blindness as they enter the venue. Which, no surprises, is the Artemis Hotel. Once inside, away from the paparazzi they are instead ambushed by the professional photographers hired by the event organisers to *capture the magic of the evening*. Their words, not his. Wow. Ezra is grumpy tonight.

After Iris had caught Ezra drowning his sorrows in a pitcher of Long Island Iced Tea on the press tour, they had devised a plan. Well, kind of. They aren't going to outright lie to the press and say they're dating again, but they aren't going to go out of their way to stop the rumours either.

So, the occasional flirty Twitter exchange, or Instagram post of them at brunch together, or showing up to events together looking like Posh and Becks — well. It is what it is. And it's working. Sliding naturally back into the narrative that he and his best friend are fucking each other's brains out gives Ezra something else to focus on at events like these other than Teddy and Grace. Even if part of him feels sick to his core at the lie. At the thought that he will ever look at anyone else all the while Teddy Montgomery exists.

They make the rounds, mingling and chatting with people who have paid an obscene amount of money to be here just to donate even more obscene amounts of money for people they would ignore if they passed them on the street. Ezra feels the stampede in his stomach settle to a mere riot as he falls back on his lines.

He laughs easily with people he's never met before and people he's met a dozen times and still can't remember their names. He shakes hands, and compliments outfits, and schmoozes, and schmoozes, and schmoozes. He is the master at this. This is his domain. This is his *shit*. And by the time they regroup to the bar (an open bar, thank *God*), he is feeling loose and ready to sink a few cocktails.

They haven't said hello to Teddy and Grace yet, and to be honest Ezra is glad. He's kind of been avoiding him since the press tour ended. Not because he doesn't want to see Teddy, because he does. He *really* does. But every time he thinks of him, he gets this ache in his chest, and he hasn't figured out if that's a good thing or a bad thing yet. He doesn't actually know what he'll do if he has to look at him, face to face. And that alone is so terrifying. And thrilling. And nauseating. And intoxicating. And... and shit.

It's not gone unnoticed either. Teddy has been texting. Leaving calls. He hasn't gone as far as emailing him yet, like Ezra had (not his proudest moment) but he's getting increasingly suspicious. Even tonight, Ezra can feel Teddy's eyes on him as they move around the room with their fake partners, so it really should come as no surprise when he feels Teddy settle beside him at the bar.

'If I didn't know better,' Teddy says, voice low. 'I'd say you're avoiding me.'

Iris pretends she can't hear them and focuses instead on the cocktail menu. Ezra, however, cannot keep his mouth from hanging open. He makes the mistake of looking at him and, like, ouch. His chest is doing it again. Because it's some kind of cosmic joke how hot he looks right now.

'Teddy,' he warns. It's his *we're in public right now* voice.

'Ezra,' he replies in his *I don't care if we're in public right now* voice.

'Later. Please.'

'Only if you can guarantee there *will* be a later.'

'Teddy!' Iris perks up like she's only just realised he's there. Ezra really loves this woman. 'Let's dance!'

Teddy doesn't have time — or, let's face it, the bad manners — to decline before Iris is pulling him to the dancefloor and settling into his arms as *I Can't Fight This Feeling Anymore* mocks them all over the speakers. Ezra pointedly doesn't watch as Teddy doesn't take his eyes off him. He's almost glad when Grace joins him. That is until she asks, 'Are you avoiding me?'

Ezra looks at her. 'What? No.'

'Liar. Are you mad at me?'

'Why would I be mad at you?'

She shrugs. 'You tell me.'

Ezra doesn't like this. He's spent the last hour untangling the ball of anxiety that has been knotting in his chest since this morning, and already it's snarling itself up again. And the last thing he wants to do is upset Grace, or for Grace to worry that he's upset with her. Because he isn't. He's upset with himself. Is it too late to jump back on the escape-to-Peru plan? *Hello, nice to meet you, my name is Edmundo...*

Ezra puts on his well-rehearsed, thousand-kilowatt smile. 'I'm peachy keen, jellybean. Just nervous about my speech. Sorry, I'm being a dick.' It isn't a *total* lie.

Her expression immediately softens, and Ezra feels a hundred times worse. 'Why? You're going to kill it. You always do.'

'Just don't want to let you down.'

A hand on his arm. A smile. All things he definitely doesn't deserve for railing her fiancé on the regular. 'You never do.'

His insides wrench painfully. 'Thanks.'

REO Speedwagon has finished taunting them and Ezra watches as Iris tries, unsuccessfully, to convince Teddy to stay for another. He's already making a beeline for the bar. Ezra downs the rest of his drink, gives Grace a tight smile, and hops off his stool. She arches a perfectly filled-in brow at him.

'Better go give that speech,' he says. 'Before I chicken out.'

He side-steps Teddy and shoots Iris a *thank you* look, to which she returns a *I tried my best*. He can feel Teddy's gaze on his back the entire way across the dancefloor. The anxiety stampede is back as he takes the stage, gripping the microphone hard in his hand. He goes to speak, and a loud wail of feedback makes his ears ring. The DJ gestures for him to step away from the speakers, and he does. This time when he goes to speak, there is no feedback, but also — to his absolute shock horror — neither are any words.

It goes on forever. Just forever. He stands with his mouth hanging open, looking out at a sea of people who could have probably bought a yacht with the money they paid for the pleasure of being there, and time stretches on, and on, and on. He stays like that until the end of time. He mummifies. People will dig up his ruins in a thousand years time and put him in a museum with a plaque that says: *Unknown male. Died as he lived, waiting for an original thought. Was of little consequence to mankind.*

Before he can realise what is happening, Grace is rescuing him. Because of course, she is. She's Grace. She will forever be rescuing her dumbass brother when he makes an idiot of himself. She surreptitiously pulls his speech notes from his jacket pocket and gives an impromptu rendition of what he has spent weeks meticulously writing, rewriting and rehearsing. When it's over, the audience claps, and Grace walks him offstage.

She tries to ask if he is alright, but Ezra is already walking away. He needs to get out of there. He needs air. He's never suffered from claustrophobia before, but the walls of the West Hall are closing in on him and he is going to scream if he doesn't get out of there right now.

He's in the smoking area before he really registers it. Memories of the last time he was there come to him. Following Teddy out there after giving him a lap dance. Teddy kissing him for the first time. Teddy pushing him back against the brick wall. Teddy's hands on his skin like fire melting through ice. Teddy. Teddy. *Teddy.*

'Are you alright?'

Ezra nearly laughs. There he is. He came to check on him. He doesn't deserve it after avoiding him all night (all week), and there he is anyway, checking he's not garrotting himself with his tie. Honestly not a bad option. He spins to look at Teddy and... ouch.

'How bad was it?' Ezra asks.

Teddy tries to keep his face neutral. God bless him. Doofus. 'Not that bad.'

'And the truth?'

'You... may have gawped a bit like a fish. It was a little unsettling. I think a child started crying.'

'Oh, fuck.'

'A very handsome fish, though.'

Ezra runs his hands through his hair. 'I'm so dumb.'

Teddy's voice is gentle. 'What happened?'

'I genuinely have no idea.'

'Is it to do with the reason you've been avoiding me?'

Ezra looks at him, holding his gaze. Christ, those eyes. They make Ezra want to go to war. 'I'm a dick. I know. I'm sorry.'

Teddy steps forward, taking Ezra's hands in his. And it's so risky. Anyone could walk out and see them. But Ezra can't bring himself to pull away, and he lets Teddy's thumbs rub comforting circles over the backs of his hands. 'Talk to me, Ezra.'

Ezra lets out a shaky breath. 'It's just... it's hard, you know? Seeing you together. And I know we've had this conversation before, and I know it's not going to change, but that doesn't stop it from being hard, and, *ugh*. I don't know. I just... I wish I could dance with you. Wow, that's so dumb.'

Teddy is giving him a strange look. For a moment, Ezra suspects that he's shown his hand. Played his cards. Or whatever you did when you played poker, he has no idea. But then Teddy is reaching into his jacket pocket and pulling out his phone. *I Can't Fight This Feeling Anymore* plays from the small speaker and when Teddy holds out a hand to him, Ezra doesn't hesitate in taking it. They hold each other and turn slowly, and when Ezra tilts his chin up to look at Teddy he is rewarded with a kiss. And another. And another.

When Teddy pulls Ezra's hips flush against his, he can feel how much he wants him. Ezra smiles, biting his lip and says, 'Well now.' He shimmies his hips and Teddy's grip on his waist tightens.

'Do not,' Teddy says, his eyes darkening in a way that makes Ezra's knees liquify, 'tease me. I don't think I have the patience for it. Not after you've been avoiding me all week.'

'Maybe I just like seeing you all wound up?'

Teddy makes a rumbling sound close to a growl. 'I should teach you a lesson.'

Ezra is about to say something bitingly witty — he's not sure what yet — but then Teddy grabs him and roughly shoves him against the wall. He kisses him, hard and furious, his hands fumbling with Ezra's belt, and Ezra is reduced to a puddle. Teddy's hand wraps around him and Ezra would be embarrassed by the strangled moan that escapes him, except that it has been a *long* week.

'You've been dodging my calls,' Teddy says, voice low, face close. 'Ignoring my texts. You, Ezra, have been a very, *very* bad boy.'

Ezra swallows. He's aware his legs might be shaking. 'What are you going to do about it?'

'I am going to take you home and tie you to my bed,' Teddy says, leaning in so that his lips brush Ezra's ear. His hand is still stroking, long, languid movements, and it's not nearly enough. 'And I am going to make you *beg* for me.'

Ezra lets out an honest-to-God whimper. 'Oh. Please. *Sweetheart.*'

Teddy groans and kisses him. He doesn't wait for Ezra's permission, sliding his mouth open with his tongue and claiming him. His hips squirm, silently begging for more, but Teddy's hand stills. When Ezra makes a noise of protest, Teddy nips his lower lip.

'Stay still and take what you're given.'

Ezra is going to die. He can't find the words, so he just nods helplessly, and Teddy's hand starts moving again. And Ezra's legs really *are* trembling now. His head is tipped back to the light-polluted sky. He reaches for Teddy, palming him through his Burberry suit pants, and when he groans, Ezra nearly comes on the spot.

There's a squeal of metal as the door handle turns, and Ezra isn't sure who moves first, but Teddy is flying back, turning away. Ezra rips his jacket off and tries to hold it as nonchalantly as he can over his crotch. He thinks he might be blushing. Teddy is *definitely* blushing — Ezra can see the pink creeping up the back of his neck.

Grace steps out into the smoking area and freezes. She looks at Ezra, and then Teddy — who still cannot turn around — and her worried expression melts into something bemused. 'Um. Hi?'

Ezra is aware that his smile is probably far too bright, and his body language way too easy as he lounges against the wall. 'Hey. Hi. Hello.' His voice is about three octaves too high.

Teddy pretends to be deeply interested in the parking lot, but shoots Grace a sheepish smile over his shoulder. He looks so flushed and horny, and Ezra's erection is probably going to take someone's eye out in a minute.

'I came to see if you're okay?' Grace says. It comes out like a half-question. 'You kind of just... bolted?'

Ezra's smile is about to split his face in two. 'Me? Fine! Yep! I'm fine! Just needed some, uh, air?'

'I see...'

'Teddy came out to... check on me.'

Teddy waves over his shoulder again, his face the absolute picture of a teenage boy who's been caught looking at porn on the family computer. 'Yes. That's me. That's what I was doing.'

Grace looks between them both. 'Are you guys high?'

Teddy barks a laugh. 'On life, perhaps!'

Ezra can see Teddy cringing so hard at himself that his eyes close as he physically recoils from his own words. Ezra swallows hard, struggling to keep his plastered-on grin in place. 'I'm fine. Really. My head went blank back there, but I'm okay. Thank you for saving me.'

Grace looks back to him, brow furrowed. 'Do I need to be worried about anything?'

'Nope. Not at all.'

'Sure?'

'Positive.'

A look of exasperation quickly crosses Grace's face, a look that he probably would have questioned had all the blood in his head not relocated and set up camp in his dick, but then it's replaced with something like resignation.

'Right, well,' she says. 'It's freezing out here. You two enjoy being weird.'

She leaves them, the exit door banging shut behind her. Slowly Teddy turns around, locking eyes with Ezra. A cheesy grin suddenly explodes across his face, and then he is laughing. Doubled over. Wiping tears from his eyes. Ezra realises he is laughing too. Cry-laughing. He tumbles forwards, giddy, and clutches Teddy's forearms.

They are still laughing as they call a cab to take them home early. Still sniggering as they tumble into bed. Still dizzy and high on the thrill of almost being caught as they strip each other. And it somehow makes the sex so much better. Even as Ezra slides into him from behind, fingers leaving bruises on Teddy's hips; pressing hot, open-mouthed kisses between Teddy's shoulder blades. Even as Teddy's toes curl and his hands ball into the sheets. Even as he looks over his shoulder at Ezra as he comes. Even as they collapse shakily against the duvet. Even as Teddy collects him in his arms and kisses Ezra's sweaty brow. Even then.

When they decide it's too early to go to sleep, but too late to put a movie on, Teddy surprises Ezra by pulling an acoustic guitar out of the closet. Ezra knows literally nothing about music, but he can't take his eyes off Teddy as he plucks at the strings, tuning it by ear. He is naked, and lean, and lithe, and the guitar lets him coax all manner of sounds out of it. Ezra sits back against the pillows watching as Teddy decides he is satisfied and begins to play. And. Oh. *Oh*.

Teddy Montgomery sits at the foot of the bed, smiling at him, not even looking down as he effortlessly plays *I See The Light* from *Tangled*. His sandy hair is mussed and the muscles in his arms roll beneath his creamy skin as he plays. His blue eyes sparkle in a way that makes Ezra want to go for round two. And then Teddy is singing, and it reaches all the way into a tender place inside Ezra's chest that he hadn't even known existed.

I See The Light perfectly blends into *Can You Feel The Love Tonight*, then *A Dream Is A Wish Your Heart Makes*, *Once Upon A Dream*, *A Whole New World*, *Beauty And The Beast*, and then *Part Of Your World*. And as much as Ezra could listen to him play the Disney catalogue all night, he really needs to kiss him. Like, yesterday. He has the wherewithal to wait until the song is over before kneeling and capturing Teddy lips in a surprisingly chaste kiss. Like Teddy is so precious, so very dear, that Ezra is scared to tarnish him.

Teddy has no such qualms, and the guitar is quickly forgotten about as he pulls Ezra into his lap. They kiss, and kiss, and kiss, and they make love again, with Teddy sitting astride him, hands planted firmly on Ezra's chest. Ezra watches as Teddy's head tilts back. He can't take his eyes off him. Hearing Teddy's voice break as he cries out Ezra's name sends him over the edge, and they wind up tangled in each other's arms again, breathing hard.

Teddy falls asleep with his head on Ezra's chest. Ezra knows he should go back to his brownstone. He knows they shouldn't make a habit of falling asleep in each other's beds. He knows he should wake Teddy and make his excuses, but every time he looks down at him, at his face that goes so soft and light when he's sleeping, he knows that he's not going anywhere. He bows his head to kiss Teddy's rumpled hair. Teddy murmurs something intelligible in his sleep and turns, burying his face into Ezra's chest, and Ezra is so helplessly in love that he cannot breathe.

Chapter Thirteen

Ezra is trying not to overthink it. He is trying not to let it be the only thing he thinks about. He's trying to approach it all from a very logical, very pragmatic, very *calm* place. He's trying not to completely drown in how much he loves Teddy Montgomery. Which, as it turns out, is a whole lot. He's full of it. He's up to his damn neck in love. He can't have a moment's peace from it, because when he's not with Teddy, he's thinking about Teddy, and it's all-consuming. It's eating him alive. And he's letting it because — well — it's *Teddy*.

Teddy with his seafoam blue eyes, and his strawberry blonde hair — who gets annoyed when Ezra calls it ginger, saying *it's honey blonde*. Teddy with his deceptively toned body, and his infuriating 6-foot-3 Grecian God physique. Teddy with his secret smile, and the crinkles around his eyes, and his hearty laugh whenever Ezra makes him genuinely double over. Teddy who trembles when he comes, and gasps when the hollow of his throat is licked, and who loves to be kissed after Ezra has given him head. Teddy with his giant heart of gold, and his tense jaw when he's trying to be brave, and his goofy side that he only lets Ezra see.

Teddy. Teddy. Teddy. Teddy. *Teddy*.

Just thinking of him makes Ezra's chest ache. Being around him is somehow simultaneously both better *and* worse. Every time Ezra makes love to him, he has to near bite his tongue off so that he won't start reciting poetry. If Ezra thought he knew what love was before, then he was wrong. Because this — Jesus. Only real love can burn him like this.

And the worst part is knowing that it *shouldn't* hurt. He should be elated right now. Him and Teddy should be naked on a beach somewhere right now while Ezra feeds him grapes and gives him blowjobs (not necessarily at the same time). But Teddy is marrying his sister. And even if he isn't, Teddy isn't out yet and Ezra has absolutely no intention of pushing him.

Iris is no help, even when she is. She is full of responsible, voice-of-reason advice. None of which includes *grab Teddy and run away to Hawaii*. She urges him to talk to Grace. Talk to his parents. Tell Teddy how he feels before he explodes. All very reasonable pieces of advice, but, ultimately, unhelpful. Because Ezra can never tell anyone. If he tells anyone he'll mess it all up.

Grace needs this narrative to see them through to the end of their BingeBox contract so she can move on. His parents want to retire from the limelight. A forbidden gay scandal will allow anything *but* that. Teddy needs a place to escape to where he can be himself, and that is with Ezra. If he tells Teddy how he feels, who knows what that will do to him? Teddy needs a safe space, not a guilt trip. And if that means Ezra has to suffer in silence, then so be it.

But wow, is he suffering. He's not even pretending to pay attention at the family meeting. He can somewhat make out Ali giving a presentation on her MacBook and talking about public appearances before filming starts again. His phone is in his lap and he's flicking through candids of Teddy.

He pauses over one of him sitting on the ottoman in front of the window in his living room. He's playing the guitar, sheet music and pieces of paper with scribbled lyrics spread out around him. His brow is knitted as he concentrates on the strings, ignoring the hair that flops into his eyes. It's not quite a frown. It's a look he only gets when he's composing. It's a look that Ezra loves.

'Hey, fuckstick,' Ali snaps.

Ezra looks up, because she could only be talking to him. He's not sure when Ali decided that she didn't care about verbally assaulting Warren and Jacqueline's kids in front of them, but it has been the same for as long as Ezra can remember, so he doesn't question it. Neither does anyone else. 'Um. Hello?'

Ali's glare is all *Jesus give me strength*. 'Something you want to share with the class?'

Ezra pockets his phone. 'Nope. I'm good.'

Ali's manicured hands go flat on the table, and she leans across the polished mahogany until her face is inches from his. 'I swear to God, you little shit, if I have to repeat anything I just said because your head was too far up your fucking ass to listen, then I will throw you out of a fucking window. Are we clear?'

Ezra blinks. 'Crystal.'

'Filming starts again in two weeks. I want you on your best behaviour until then. Once the cameras start rolling, I don't give a shit what you get up to, we can pass it all off as

Wyoming Wild Child drama. Keep your head down, keep quiet, and don't start anything that you don't intend to finish. From now on you're the poster child for Bible study, got it?'

Ezra's phone buzzes and he resists the urge to check it. 'Yep.'

'Fucking A, kiddo.'

Ali's tone goes back to being pleasant as she addresses Jacqueline and Warren, and Ezra sneaks a look at his phone. It's a message from Teddy: **Hope you're alright, love. You seemed out of sorts this morning. Miss you.** Ezra's heart clenches, a rock settling in his throat that he can't quite swallow around. He taps out a quick: **all good, gorgeous. miss you too,** and looks up to see Grace giving him a peculiar look.

When Ali dismisses them all, Ezra bolts for the door. Grace calls after him, but he can't trust his voice to be steady, so he just smiles and waves over his shoulder. He's not sure if he wants to cry, or scream, or laugh. Maybe all three. When he closes his brownstone door behind him, he lets out a long, shaky breath. He's going over to Teddy's later and he needs to be a sane person for that.

Walking to the kitchen, Ezra grabs a shot glass and a bottle of tequila from the cupboard. He doesn't have the salt or the lime, but he also doesn't have a clue at the moment either, so he figures it's fine. He does a shot, grimaces, and chases it up with another. When he takes the third and nearly wretches, he hasn't realised that Grace has invited herself in. When he looks up and catches her eye, something like ice settles in his stomach. Her face is stony and prepared to win whatever argument they're definitely about to have.

'It's eleven in the morning,' she says, nodding at the tequila bottle.

Ezra arches an eyebrow. 'You came here to lecture me on drinking before midday?'

'No, I guess not.'

Ezra puts the top back on the tequila bottle and pushes it to one side, which is probably for the best because his head is already kind of fuzzy. 'Well, you're clearly here to say something, so go ahead.'

Grace looks at him for the longest time before asking, 'Do you think I'm an idiot?'

Ezra blinks. Obviously, he doesn't think that. His sister is the smartest person he's ever met. He's not sure if it's a rhetorical question, or if she is expecting an answer. And, honestly, both options feel like a trap. 'Definitely not.'

'Then do you really think I don't know that you're fucking my fiancé?'

Ezra feels all the blood drain from his face. He's lucky there is a stool next to him, because his legs stop working. He's aware of his mouth opening and closing, no actual words coming out, but he's not sure if they could get past the wet cement in his throat anyway. 'Oh.'

'Yeah,' Grace says, arms folded tightly across her chest. 'Fucking *oh*.'

'Grace, I—'

'Don't tell me you're sorry,' she snaps. 'Because you're clearly not.'

'I actually am.'

'Great. Then you'll stop seeing him?'

Their eyes meet. Ezra has never seen his sister look so hurt, and it's killing him to know that he's the reason why. The cement in his throat dries and hardens, and it hurts to speak. 'I can't.'

Grace barks a humourless laugh. 'I can't believe this. I can't *believe* this. This is so typical of you!'

Okay *that* is unfair. 'Yeah, totally. Remember that *other* time I fucked your closeted gay fiancé?'

'You know what I mean.'

'I really don't.'

Grace looks at him like he's an idiot, which, to be fair, he is. 'You can never just let me have my moment, can you? You have to make *everything* about you!'

'Um? Well, no?'

'You pretend you don't want any part of the Darling Dynasty. You pretend you don't want to be on camera. You act like you're doing us all a big goddamn favour being a part of the show, and then you do shit like this!'

'Shit like *what*?'

'Shit that will make sure that you're the only one that anyone cares about!'

Ezra feels like all the air has been knocked out of him. 'You think this is a publicity stunt?'

'Everything is a publicity stunt with you!' she shouts. 'The way you dress, the way you encourage the rumours about you — obviously not rumours, I guess. The way you have to be so *fucking* extra at every opportunity. Even when I was a heroin addict it was all about you! Wow, look at Ezra Darling, getting involved with a rehabilitation charity out of the goodness of his heart, what a real champ! I can't even wreck my own life without it being about you!'

Ezra watches his sister, choosing his words carefully. 'I never wanted to be the character that the show has made me to be. Ron wanted an ambiguous camp character, so that's what I gave him. You don't think I'd rather just be myself?' Ezra can feel his voice raising, but he can't stop it. 'This is why I want out of this thing when the contract is over. I can't live up to everyone else's idea of who they think I am! And don't you dare throw the worst night of my life in my face like that! I thought you were going to *die*!'

'And yet you still managed to make it all about you! Poor little Ezra! He gets another sob story to milk!'

Ezra's eyes are burning. His throat is lined with razor blades. 'Your overdose was never a subplot to me. And neither is Teddy.'

'Except that he is!' she says, suddenly exasperated. 'He's meant to be *my* big storyline, and you can't even let me have that.'

'He's more than just a plot point, Grace.'

'That's not what I meant, and you know it.' She scrubs a hand over her face, not caring if she smudges her immaculate makeup. 'I can't believe you're taking this away from me. Can't you just let me have something for once? Couldn't you just let me have him?'

'Have him?' Ezra almost laughs. 'You don't even love him!'

'Oh, and you do?'

'Yeah! I do, actually!'

All of the air leaves the room. Grace stares at him, mouth open. Ezra waits patiently for the world to fall in around him, and when it hesitates, he reaches out with a shaky hand and pours himself another shot of tequila. He manages to keep it down, even though his insides are threatening to riot. Nothing happens for a long, agonising moment, then Grace joins him at the counter, taking a long drag from the bottle, shuddering as it goes down.

'Grace—' he tries.

'No,' she says. 'No, I get to speak now, Ezra.' She gives him a look that she could have only learned from Ali. It's too close to disdain for his liking. 'I have given up a lot for you. I'm not even the star of my own show.'

'Grace—'

'No, Ezra. This is what you do. You just take and take, until there's nothing left for the rest of us. And we're just supposed to be okay with it? No. I won't make any more sacrifices for you. I just won't.'

Ezra feels his temper flare. 'Sacrifices? Grace, I have given up my *life* to be your co-star.' She scowls. It makes her look young instead of angry. 'What's that supposed to mean?'

'Just that ever since I joined this family, I also joined a storyline I never wanted.'

'No one asked you to be a part of it,' she snaps. 'No one asked you to join us.'

Ezra flinches like he's been slapped. He watches Grace's eyes go wide, her hand pressing over her mouth. 'Wow.'

'I didn't mean it like that,' she says quickly. 'I only meant the show. I—'

'It's fine,' Ezra cuts across her. 'I think you should go now.'

'Ezra—'

'No, really,' he says, nodding at the door. 'You've said your piece. I've listened. I'm done.'

She tries to reach for his hand, but he pulls away. 'I didn't mean having you as part of the family. You're my brother. I love you.'

His lower lip threatens to wobble, so he sets his jaw like Teddy would, and looks away. Don Julio looks back at him from the counter. He doesn't bother with a shot glass this time, instead just taking a long, unenjoyable gulp straight from the bottle.

'You know who's never made me feel like I don't belong?' he asks, grimacing at the burn.

'Ezra...'

'Teddy. Right from day one, from the moment I was a dick to him at that stupid engagement party, he still made an effort to make me feel like I was wanted there. He wanted me to sober up so that I could stay and enjoy my night. Which is so weird, because he didn't know me. He didn't owe me anything. He was just right there with instant acceptance and understanding, even though I didn't deserve it.

'Then there's my own mother — someone who's supposed to love me unconditionally — and she got rid of me the first chance she got. Do you have any idea what that's like? People who literally *have* to love you, who are biologically programmed to have at least some degree of affection for you, still turning their back on you? Or what it's like being the kid who's jostled from one foster home to another because no one wants the scared little kid with anxiety who still hoards food scraps and hides under the bed at night?

'I never felt a scrap of real love in my entire life until I was adopted by the Darlings. And every day since I was given a home here, I have lived in fear that one day you would turn around and say you don't want me anymore. The night before my eighteenth birthday I had a bag packed just in case I was kicked out in the morning.

'I have never felt good enough, or worthy enough my whole life. Until *him*. Until Teddy Montgomery. I didn't try to make it happen this way, I didn't try to fall in love with him or ruin your show, it just happened. I look at him and I feel, for the first time, like I'm home. I know I'm expendable to most people, but not him. Never him.'

Grace looks at him for a long damn time. He can't read her expression. Then, she crosses the kitchen in four quick strides and wraps him up in a hug. He feels himself sag in her small but mighty embrace, and is unsurprised to find that he's crying. That she is too. For a long moment, they just hold each other. Exist in each other's arms. His head swims with tequila as the anger quickly seeps from his suddenly exhausted body and Grace steadies him as he wobbles on his feet.

'I'm so sorry,' he whispers against the curls of her hair. 'I'm so sorry.'

'I know you are,' she says, rubbing his back. 'Why didn't you just tell me?'

'I didn't want you to be mad at me.'

'Oh, well, that worked out great then,' she says. 'I have never been so furious with you in my entire life, you big dummy.'

He nods. 'I know. I'm sorry. I really am.'

'You know, it's really hard to stay angry when you're literally sobbing.' She pulls back to look at him and says, 'Really, Ezra? Teddy Montgomery?'

Ezra wipes his eyes. 'I know. I'm a jerk.'

Grace sighs. 'Yes and no. Sit, we have to talk.'

They sit on the stools at the breakfast island. Ezra can't bring himself to look at his sister. He focuses on his hands which are wringing each other out nervously in his lap.

'When did you realise?' she asked. 'That you loved him, I mean.'

Ezra lets out a shaky breath. 'Literally a few days ago.'

'Lord have mercy.'

'I know.'

'Are you okay?'

Ezra looks at Grace, who has every reason in the world to hate him right now, in astonishment. Who has put up with his bullshit for long enough, and who deserves to be mad as hell at him right now. His throat tightens at the concern in her eyes. He's struck by how much he doesn't deserve her.

'Not really,' he croaks.

'Does anyone else know?'

'Iris figured it out.'

Grace nods. 'Of course, she did.'

Ezra blinks hard against his burning eyes. He looks down at his hands again. 'I am so, *so* sorry, Grace. I can't believe I've messed everything up again.'

'I can,' she says, bumping his shoulder with hers to let him know she's half-joking. 'But you can't undo it, so we have to figure out how to deal with it.'

He frowns. 'Aren't you mad at me?'

'Oh, I am. And I will be for a very long time.' She looks at him, her expression softening. 'But that's not going to solve anything right now.'

Ezra laughs but it comes out as a half-sob. He covers his face with his hands and takes a long, shuddering breath. 'Right. So, what do we do now?'

'Well, you're going to tell him, obviously.'

He looks up at her, brow furrowed. 'What? No, I'm not. That's a *horrible* idea.'

'You're going to tell him,' Grace repeats. 'And then you're going to tell Mom and Dad. And then we're going to figure this all out with the least amount of casualties possible.'

'But what about you? And the contract? BingeBox will drop us if the season finale doesn't have a wedding.'

Grace looks at Ezra like he's an idiot again. Which, again, he definitely is. 'As if any of that matters now. You *love* him, Ezra.'

'*You* matter.'

'I'll be fine. We'll deal. We always do.'

Ezra bites his lower lip between his teeth. 'What if he doesn't love me back?'

She shrugs. 'Then I'll marry him anyway.'

Ezra laughs. Like, genuinely laughs. So does Grace. It feels good to relieve some of the tension in the room. He knows he's a long way from being forgiven, but that's the best thing about having a sibling: you have a guaranteed best friend for life. And Ezra has a lifetime to make things right. The way Grace looks at him — like he's a total dumbass — lets him know that she knows it too.

She sighs and puts her arm around his shoulders, resting her temple to his. They stay that way for a while, Grace swaying them slightly, and Ezra dares to hope that he hasn't ruined absolutely everything. 'Friends?'

Grace snorts. 'Acquaintances.'

'Fair enough. I love you.'

'I know you do.'

'Grace?'

'Yeah?'

He turns to look at her. Somehow his eyes have gotten wet again. When he speaks his voice is small. Tight. 'I'm so scared.'

Grace pulls him into a hug, tucking his head under her chin. Even livid with him, she can't help but comfort him. She holds him and lets him pretend that he's okay. Not for the first time, Ezra thanks all the gods he doesn't know if he believes in for bringing the Darlings to him. Not for the first time he accepts the fact that Grace is better than he will ever deserve. Not for the first time, he lets her comfort him while his entire world is falling down around him.

Teddy looks shocked, if not pleasantly surprised, when Ezra shows up on his doorstep, eight hours earlier than planned. Teddy is wearing well-worn jeans, a soft jumper and his glasses. His feet are bare, and Ezra can see the neon pink remnants of Mason's last pedicure. His hair is messy, and he hasn't shaved yet. In his hands he holds a steaming mug of tea that has *Happee Birfday Unkle Teddy* hand-painted on it. He smiles at Ezra, the steam fogging up his glasses, and Ezra is so in love that it's going to kill him.

'Hello, love,' Teddy says. 'To what do I owe the pleasure?'

Ezra strides into Teddy's living room before he can chicken out. He takes the tea from Teddy's hands and puts it on the coffee table. 'We need to talk.'

Teddy frowns. 'I can't have my tea while we talk?'

'No. I need you to concentrate. And I don't want you to drop it.'

Teddy closes the door and deadbolts it. 'Okay?'

Ezra drags a hand over his face. 'God. Jesus. Fuck.'

'Love, you're worrying me a bit.'

'Could you at least take your glasses off?' Ezra asks. 'Or. I don't know? Wear something less... less... *ugh*.'

Teddy quirks an eyebrow, and even that makes Ezra's heart squeeze. 'You want me to... change?'

'No. Yes. I don't know.' He swallows. 'You're just so. *Ugh*.'

'Right.'

'You look so good.'

Teddy grins. 'And that's a problem?'

'Yes. No. *Fuck*.'

Teddy steps forward, face gentle. 'Darling, what's upset you?'

'You have!' Ezra explodes. 'You're upsetting me! You and your perfect face, and your secret smile, and your homemade mugs, and your *Harry Potter* pyjamas, and your singing, and—'

'Ezra,' Teddy takes him by the shoulders. 'Breathe. I'm sorry if I've done something to upset you. What is it? Let me try and understand so I can fix it.'

Ezra looks at him despairingly. 'You *can't* fix it.'

'Try me.'

'I, like, love you, okay?' Ezra is shouting now. 'I *love* you! And it terrifies me because I don't even know if you love me back. You're either going to be the man I spend my life with or the man who breaks my heart, and I can't breathe. I can't fucking breathe, Teddy. I can't *breathe*.'

It occurs to him that it's true. He actually *cannot* breathe. His lungs are more than capable of sucking in air, but he can't seem to let it out again. And with each short breath he sucks in, his lungs swell up, and he cannot get anything out *or* in. And in the back of his mind, he knows this is a panic attack. He knows it's all in his head, but that doesn't make it any less real. And the more he tries to gasp for air, the more it eludes him. His head swims, his hands shaking. He looks to Teddy, helplessly.

'Darling,' Teddy says, one hand going to Ezra's cheek, another closing around his wrist to feel the pulse thrumming there. 'Love. It's alright. You can breathe.'

Ezra shakes his head. He reaches out and grasps Teddy's sweater, fingers curling, panicked, into the fabric there. 'I—I can't—breathe.'

'Yes. You can.' Teddy gently uncurls Ezra's fingers from his jumper and presses one hand to his chest, and places his other hand over Ezra's heart. Like Ezra had done to him in the elevator so many months ago. 'Like this. In and out. Nice and slow.'

Ezra focuses on the rise and fall of Teddy's chest. Slow and steady, and measured. He tries to copy it. Tries to let the air flow naturally, not force it. In. Out. No rush. Calm. Calm as Teddy's soft blue eyes. Calm as the muss of his sandy hair. Calm as the soft cupid's bow of his lips. Calm as the wall of solid muscle beneath his palm.

'That's it,' Teddy says softly. 'That's it, love. Good.'

Without warning, all the adrenaline that has been crackling around Ezra's body evaporates and his legs give out. Teddy catches him, like he was expecting this, and helps him over to the couch. Ezra barely has time to protest before he's being pulled into Teddy's arms, all the while he murmurs against his hair *it's alright. I've got you.*

Ezra isn't sure how long they stay that way, but when he's sure he isn't going to pass out any time soon, he pulls back and looks at Teddy, whose face is soft and open, and adoring. Ezra swallows. 'Uh. Sorry? Don't really know what happened there.'

'Never had a panic attack before?' Teddy asks, hand still stroking through his hair.

'First time for everything.' A silence stretches between them like a gaping chasm. The longer it goes on for, the worse the gnawing feeling in Ezra's gut becomes. 'Listen. I know that was, like, a lot. I'm sorry. But it kind of hit me all at once, you know? And I know you didn't say it back, and you don't have to, but I had to tell you. And if things are weird now then that'll be really shit, but I'll understand. But I—'

'Do you ever,' Teddy says, with a grin, 'stop talking?'

Ezra blinked. 'Um?'

Teddy chuckles. 'Don't be dense, love. Of course, I love you. I've loved you ever since you sat down and took my hands in that bloody lift. Ever since you brought my hand to your chest and told me it was going to be alright. I've always been doomed to fall madly in love with you.'

Ezra stares. He sits upright as if to get a better look at him. '*What?*'

'I love you, Ezra.'

'Well. Well, *fuck me*. You could have said that earlier!'

'You hardly gave me a chance—'

Ezra kisses him. *Really* kisses him. He feels Teddy laugh against his lips, but takes that as an opportunity to taste him, and his laugh quickly dissolves into a groan. Ezra straddles Teddy's lap, looping his arms around his neck. Teddy's hands push their way underneath Ezra's shirt, fingers flexing over his hot skin. When Ezra grinds down against Teddy's lap, he's rewarded with what's already waiting there for him.

'Make love to me,' Teddy murmurs against his mouth and Ezra nearly loses it.

They barely make it to the bedroom. They're naked before they hit the sheets. Ezra has Teddy pinned beneath them and is taking his time in kissing him breathless. In kissing the man he loves. The man who, remarkably, loves him back. Ezra nips at his jaw and the noise Teddy makes is enough to make an entire nation bend the knee.

'I love you,' Teddy says between kisses.

'I love you too.'

'Bloody well right you do.' Teddy says playfully and rolls them, pinning Ezra beneath him. He grabs his hips and pulls Ezra almost into his lap, his legs spread wide around Teddy's narrow waist. And it's. Oh. Wow. It's different.

'Oh,' Ezra says, his hips rolling. This is new. This is *very* new. He doesn't hate it.

Teddy is watching him with a carefully curious expression. 'Everything okay over there?'

'I—I want this,' Ezra says, terrified but knowing it's true 'I want to try it this way.'

Teddy's face is soft and loving, and so painfully sweet. 'Darling... it might not be something you want to jump straight into.'

'I know. I know we would need to build up to it. I've been experimenting on my own. But I'd like to try it with you.'

Teddy is so careful when he says, 'I don't need it. I'm happy with what we've been doing. Nothing is missing here for me.'

'Me neither. I just,' Ezra searches for the right word. 'I want to share myself with you the way that you do with me. I want you in every way.'

'Alright, love. We can try.' Teddy kisses him, suddenly chaste. 'But if you don't like it then we stop. Okay?'

Ezra nods and pulls Teddy down for a long lingering kiss before a breathless, 'Fuck, I love you.'

After they make out for what feels like hours, Teddy spends the night teasing him open with his fingers and his tongue, taking the edge off with long languid strokes, his fingers wrapped around Ezra with a certainty that Teddy only shows when they're alone. And it's good. It's really *good*. And Ezra is gasping and trembling, and he's never been harder, and when Teddy finally slides inside him, he sees stars.

Ezra's whole body is shaking, so much that it prompts Teddy to look down at him and ask, 'Are you alright? Am I hurting you?'

His throat is strangely tight, so he shakes his head. It doesn't hurt. It's different, this feeling of being full and claimed, but it doesn't hurt. He pulls Teddy down for a soft kiss that quickly turns hungry. He wraps his legs around his lover's middle, his heels pressing into Teddy's ass in a not-so-subtle attempt to get him moving.

'I am going to make it so good for you,' Teddy promises, his hips beginning to thrust. 'So good. I'm going to watch you fly.'

Ezra whimpers. Teddy fucks him slow and deep, and the shaking subsides as Ezra quickly goes pliable. His hands find Teddy's shoulders, nails biting into flesh. There's a moment when Teddy adjusts their position slightly, and Ezra is going to ask if everything's alright, until Teddy seems to hit a spot inside him that makes him light up all over. All he can do is hold on, and gasp and moan, as Teddy gives him a kind of pleasure that he hadn't known existed.

He comes without Teddy's hand on his erection, and for a long moment he soars. He feels Teddy's body stiffen and shudder, hears his guttural moan. It seems to take minutes for him to come down from the high, but when he does, Teddy is there, enveloping him in a hug.

He knows they shouldn't be lazy. He knows they should shower and clean up. He also cannot bring himself to care. His body is deliciously satiated, his limbs and eyelids heavy. The man he loves who loves him back is holding him, whispering sweet nothings against the shell of his ear, and he just *cannot* care.

As they drift off, Ezra curled like a kitten into Teddy's chest, he whispers, 'I flew.'

Chapter Fourteen

Subject: ezra is coming out

Ezra <Ezra-Darling@Darlingdynasty.com>
To: Teddy
---
instead of coming out to my mom and dad, i'm thinking of sending this to them. thoughts?
https://www.so-your-kid-is-gay.com
love you
ezra

*

Re: ezra is coming out

Teddy <Teddy.Montgomery@theMontgomerys.com>
To: Ezra

Ezra,

Whilst informative, I don't think it focuses enough on the 'B' in LGBTQ+. I have done some extensive research on your behalf and have found this site to be both comprehensive and diverse. Please find the attached link.
https://www.bisexual-or-just-kidding-yourself.com
All my love,
Teddy

*

Re: ezra is coming out

Ezra <Ezra-Darling@Darlingdynasty.com>
To: Teddy

---

truly comprehensive indeed. especially liked the page called 'bi or just attention-seeking'. very eye opening. alternatively, i have also found this to forward to them before the family meeting:
https://www.wikihow.com/how-to-accept-your-gay-child
lots of love,
ezra

*

Re: ezra is coming out

Teddy <Teddy.Montgomery@theMontgomerys.com>
To: Ezra

Ezra,

I appreciate the instructional pictures that came with that. How else would someone know the appropriate face to make when their child comes out to them? I have made a note of step five (try not to gasp) in the event that, one day, either Mason or Margot come out to me, and I have to respond appropriately.

In the unlikely event that those helpful pictures aren't enough, I have found a YouTube video that I think might be of use.
https://www.youtube.com/how-i-got-over-my-son-being-gay
All the love in the world,
Teddy

*

Re: ezra is coming out

Ezra <Ezra-Darling@Darlingdynasty.com>
To: Teddy

---

teddy,

see? this is why i love you. well, that and your massive penis. been walking funny all week. had to consult the following:

https://www.the-joys-of-anal-sex.com/aftercare

love and kisses,

ezra

*

Re: ezra is coming out

Teddy <Teddy.Montgomery@theMontgomerys.com>
To: Ezra

Ezra,

I sincerely apologise for any pain our previous engagement may have caused you. I would like to point out, however, that you begged for me to (and these are exact quotes), 'fuck me fucking blind'. While your current discomfort is both unfortunate and sympathised with, I will remind you that we did not have to go three times in one night. That was a choice made by you, not myself and my 'massive penis.'

Nevertheless, please find a link below that should help alleviate any remaining distress:

https://www.happysex.com/soothing-ring-aftercare-cream

Utterly in love,

Teddy

P.S. My 'massive penis' says "hello" and that it "misses you". As do I.

```
*
Re: ezra is coming out
Ezra <Ezra-Darling@Darlingdynasty.com>
To: Teddy
teddy,
sweetheart, we absolutely DID have to go three times in one night. as per my last email, you have an absolutely incredible dick, and I cannot be held responsible for what comes over me when you come over me.
okay heading into family meeting now. wish me luck.
totally loved up,
ezra
p.s. please tell said monster prick that I am thinking of him always.
```

Ezra wrings his hands out as he tries to find the words. His parents wait patiently for him to speak. They aren't used to one of their kids calling a (usually dreaded) family meeting, so they're too concerned to push him. Grace sits beside him, a gentle hand on his forearm, visibly trying to absorb some of the tension rolling off him in waves.

Him and Teddy have agreed that it's okay to tell his parents. They will understand the delicacy of the situation, and they too aren't exactly big fans of David and Anastasya. They've decided that it's best for Warren and Jacqueline to know, and even though the thought of outing Teddy to *anyone* makes him feel sick, Ezra is confident that his parents will keep their secret. His folks are cool.

'The thing is,' Ezra says, looking at his palms, like the answer to all his problems might appear there. 'I'm. Uh. Well. I'm not exactly... straight.'

Warren and Jacqueline barely exchange a glance. His mother says, 'Alright.'

'I'm actually. Um. Bisexual?' Ezra doesn't know why it comes out like a question, but it does.

The corner of Jacqueline's lips quirk. 'Yes, hon. We're well aware.'

Ezra frowns. 'You are?'

'You were hardly subtle about it,' Warren says, also trying not to smile.

'But. Wait. *No*. I only just figured it out a while ago. How did *you* know?'

Jacqueline laughs. 'Hon, you had a poster of Robert Pattinson on your wall as a teenager.'

Ezra remembers the poster vividly. RPatz staring straight at the camera, all brooding and serious. As a teenager, Ezra had reached out and touched it every morning when he woke up for years, and every night before bed. Haughtily, he replies, '*Twilight* was very popular back then.'

'Not to mention your obvious crush on Tom Daley,' Warren adds.

Ezra's arms cross over his chest of their own volition. 'He's objectively dreamy and a good athlete.'

Grace squeezes his arm. 'You also saw *Magic Mike Live*, like, five times.'

He can hardly lie and say it was for the plot, so instead he says, 'Male stripping is an unappreciated art form.'

'The point is,' his mother says, reaching across the table to take his hand. 'We know. We've always known, baby. And it's okay.'

Ezra looks around at each of them in turn. 'You all really knew before me?'

Grace nods. 'Yeah. You're kind of slow.'

'Alright. Well, good. That was easier than I expected.'

Jacqueline pats his hand before withdrawing and preparing to call the family meeting to an official close. Her phone is already in her hand, her thumbs flying over the screen, organising her next meeting — one with actual business partners and not just her kids. Warren rises to his feet too, collecting his iPad from the table, and Ezra can feel his chance to tell them the full story slipping through his clammy hands.

'Actually,' he says, voice small. 'There's something else.'

Jacqueline looks at him over her phone, her face perfectly neutral. 'Oh?'

Ezra looks to Grace for support, and she squeezes his arm, encouragingly. 'I'm... seeing someone.'

His parents break into smiles that Ezra knows won't last for long when he tells them who it is. A prickling starts under his skin, and he doesn't know where to look, so he stares at his hands on the table.

'That's wonderful, hon!' his mom beams. 'We're so happy for you! When can we meet him?'

'You, uh. You've already met, actually.'

Warren cocks an eyebrow. 'We have?'

'Yes. It's. Um. Well.' He takes a long, shaky breath. 'It's Teddy.' When they don't react, he adds, 'Montgomery,' for good measure.

For a long moment, nothing happens. Ezra is sure his parents are both staring at him, but he can't bring himself to look. Underneath the table, his leg starts bouncing. Then, without looking at her phone, Jacqueline dials a number and brings the phone to her ear.

'Mara?' she says. 'How quickly can you get over here?'

It's been three hours. Three. Whole. Hours. And Ezra is ready to pull his hair out. Mara, to her credit, is utterly unflappable in the face of potential Darling Dynasty ruin. She's been their lawyer ever since Grace's nudes were leaked, and when you matched her stoic problem-solving and Ali's no-nonsense firepower, you got a hell of a PR team. Even Ali, to everyone's surprise, is relatively calm. Though her coffee flask smells suspiciously of Kahlua.

Mara has been painstakingly combing through the BingeBox contract, and of three things they are positively certain. One: The season must end with a legally binding wedding. Two: Grace and Teddy's marriage must last the next two seasons, carrying them over to the end of their contract. And three: Outside relationships are strictly prohibited.

Mara suspects that there is wiggle room in the case of Ezra and Teddy's relationship being leaked to the press, and Ezra isn't sure who shouts *no* first out of him or Ali. Grace's nudes being leaked was not her fault and no one could argue otherwise. Her overdose and stay in rehab was a close call but they'd gotten away with it. A forbidden gay romance between the Golden Girl's brother and her fiancé, though — that has *scandal* written all over it.

And yet, all Ezra can think is: *protect Teddy.* The thought of Teddy waking up one day to find out he's been outed to the world, his eyes wide and frightened, his jaw set in stone, makes Ezra's stomach churn. He's not sure at what point in the meeting he has to grab Grace's hand for support, but she doesn't let it go.

He feels his phone buzz and he sees a message from Teddy: **Haven't heard from you yet. Hope you're alright. Love you. X.** His head swims and he holds his temples in his hands while the grown-ups talk around him. Grace rests a hand on his shoulder. At one point Mara suggests Ezra and Teddy stop seeing each other until the contract is over, and Ezra thinks he's going to be sick.

It feels like a betrayal talking about this without Teddy being there. Mara is drawing up contracts for him to sign detailing the timeline of their relationship. Ezra is having to divulge every detail of their relationship so that it can be picked apart. When did it start? Their first kiss. The first time they slept together. How far have they gone? Is it just a hook-up? Is it something more? His parents sign contracts to say they haven't been privy to this knowledge before today. Everyone signs NDAs, not that anyone will blab anything, but Mara ensures them it's just a formality.

All he can think is: *protect Teddy. Protect Teddy. Protect Teddy.*

Ali suggests using their situation to their advantage by spinning a new narrative that BingeBox would prefer to their current one: a star-crossed romance. Enemies to lovers. Make it seem that Grace and Teddy decided to call it quits due to 'unavoidable circumstances' and then start an on-screen romance between himself and Teddy. And again, he says *no* because there is no way in hell that he is going to force Teddy out of the closet before he's ready.

So, it's been three hours and they are no closer to a solution than they were when it started. Ezra's hands are shaking. He feels traumatised. This morning he was in bed with Teddy, kissing him and making him feel good, and everything had been great. And now their relationship — the first relationship that has ever actually meant something to him — is sprawled out across his parents dining table in the form of contracts and nondisclosure agreements. He just wants Teddy. He wants to hold him, and bury his face in one of his expensive sweaters, and to feel Teddy's chin rest on top of his head.

Just when Ezra feels like he is about to start screaming, his parents tell Ali and Mara that they can go. They will reconvene another time. They want to give Ezra a break. Ezra wants to fling himself into the sun. He can vaguely feel Grace rubbing soothing circles against his back, but he's not even really there anymore. Not really. He's far away, looking in at the scene like an outsider, feeling sorry for the queer kid who just wants to go home and kiss his boyfriend.

'Hon,' his mom says gently, dropping into a seat beside him. 'I'm so sorry. That all went on for longer than I expected. Are you alright?'

Ezra looks at her, expression miserable. 'Please don't. Don't ask me to do it.'

'Baby,' Jacqueline takes her son's face in her hands. 'I'm so sorry.'

'Mom,' his voice breaks. 'Please. I love him.'

Warren sits down beside Grace. 'I know, kiddo. And it kills us to see you hurting. But we can't get out of the contract with BingeBox, and if we break it then it has massive ramifications for your sister—'

'I don't care,' Grace interrupts. 'BingeBox thinks they can dissuade other platforms from working with us? I think they're full of shit. Come on, this is *killing* him.'

It is, Ezra thinks. He stays quiet. His phone buzzes in his pocket but he doesn't reach for it. He needs his hands to keep his head in place. Besides, reading another concerned text message from Teddy will tip him over the edge.

'It's not that easy,' Jacqueline says. 'All your father and I want for you is to be able to live your lives however you want once this is over, but we have to get over it first. You know how BingeBox and the media will twist this. We don't want you to get hurt. It's just three years, hon.'

'Three years of living a lie,' Grace says.

'We should have never agreed to working with the Montgomerys,' Warren says, mostly to himself, like hindsight will do anyone any good.

'That's on me,' Grace says. 'I pushed for it.'

'It's on us,' Warren says. 'We didn't like the sound of it from the start, but we wanted to let you make your own choices. We should have listened to our instincts.'

'I can't make you do anything you're not comfortable with, sweetie,' Jacqueline says, her hands still cupping Ezra's miserable face. 'But I can warn you. This isn't just playing with fire, this is starting an inferno.'

'I'm going to be sick,' Ezra moans miserably, pulling away from his mom. He gets up from the table, leaving his family to decide what's best for him as he hauls his body to the kitchen.

He pours himself a glass of water from the tap, and takes small sips, silently willing the ball of anxiety in his chest to shrivel up and die. His phone buzzes again and he fishes it out of his pocket. Ice floods his veins. The glass slips from his hand smashing at his feet as his whole world crashes down around him.

Grace is out of her seat first. The glass crunches under her shoes as she grabs his shoulders, peering at him. He's sure she's saying something, but all Ezra can hear is white noise. Grace pries the phone from his hand and reads the text aloud from Daria.

Teddy's been in an accident.

Chapter Fifteen

Ezra is no longer in charge of himself. His brain switched to autopilot approximately an hour ago when he first got Daria's text, and now he simply sits back and watches, frozen, as his legs power him through the Sacred Hope parking lot. Grace has to jog to keep up with his strides. Daria sent him the ward and room number. His parents are on their way. They'd waited for the family chauffeur, having taken the long route to try to misdirect the paparazzi, but Ezra had run outside and grabbed the closest Uber driver.

The front of the hospital is swarming with press. When he begins shoving and elbowing his way through them it doesn't take long for them to realise who he is. Cameras flash, questions are hurled his way. Paparazzi crowd around them, and Grace clings to his arm to keep him from punching anyone.

Grace, how do you feel? When did you hear the news? Why weren't you with him? Is it critical? Ezra, are you here to support your sister? Who found out first? Is he going to make it? Will he need surgery? Was it a drunk driver like with Leo?

When security spots them, they pull Ezra and Grace from the melee. They ask all sorts of questions that Ezra doesn't have time for. He pushes past them, storming into the reception and Ali steps into his path. He doesn't even have time to be impressed with how she got there first. He doesn't have time for anything except Teddy.

Ezra is surprised by the venom in his voice when he speaks. 'Move.'

Ali arches a sculpted brow at him. 'Do not make a scene. Not with every reporter in NYC out there.'

'I said *move*.'

'Grace goes up first,' Ali says. 'She's his fiancé. You will wait here until she comes back down. You're here to play the role of concerned best friend and brother-in-law. Not a lovesick puppy.'

'I'm not here to play a role, I'm here for Teddy,' Ezra says, trying to step around her. Ali puts a hand on his chest and stays firmly in his way. 'For God's sake, Ali. Get out of my way,' he says.

'Ali,' Grace tries. 'Please. Ezra can come with me.'

'They're only allowing one visitor at a time.'

'Then let him go first.'

Ali looks at her. 'So, the press can report on how Teddy Montgomery's fiancé relaxed in the waiting room while her *brother* ran to his side instead? Not likely.'

'I don't have time for this, I need to see him.' Ezra's throat feels like sandpaper.

'He's about to go into surgery any minute anyway—'

And, of course, that is the *worst* possible thing she could have said, because now Ezra is pushing past her and running. Prince George ward. Room 3A. That is all that matters. He hears footsteps running after him. A hand snags his elbow and he whirls around, eyes wild, to see Ali glaring up at him. She opens her mouth but Ezra cuts her off.

'I love him,' he says. 'I know that's the last thing you want to hear right now, but I love him. And if it's as bad as Daria says it is, and I don't see him before he goes into surgery, and I never get to tell him one last time then I—I—' He can't finish that sentence. His eyes burn and he swallows past the painful lump in his throat. 'Ali, please. *Please*.'

For a horrible moment, Ali's expression stays perfectly indifferent. Then something cracks and she sighs. 'Fuck. *Fuck*. Fine, alright. Go. Me and Grace will talk to the press. We'll say he's already in surgery and you're going up to support Daria. Go. *Go*.'

He doesn't stop to thank her. He doesn't even look at Grace. He spins on his heel and runs for the elevator. When it doesn't come quick enough, he opts for the stairs, taking them up three at a time to the third floor. He hates how lost he feels as he scans the signs, looking for which way it is to the ward. A green line on the floor promises to guide him and he sprints as he follows it along, not caring at the glances he gets from nurses and other patients.

He reaches room 3A just as Teddy is being wheeled out on a stretcher, Daria at his side, holding his hand. Ezra's legs threaten to give out, but he pushes himself forwards. Daria sees him and reaches out, and he takes her hand, falling into step with the stretcher. He looks down at Teddy's barely conscious form. His face — that face that Ezra has stared at for hours, cataloguing every detail to memory — is twisted in agony. He has a large, angry gash across his forehead, another on his cheek. Over his mouth is an oxygen mask. His chest is bare and Ezra's stomach rolls at the already blackening bruise on his chest where his seatbelt saved his life. His hand finds Teddy's and he squeezes gently.

Teddy cracks open his eyes and the recognition, the relief, the absolute love that Ezra sees in them takes his breath away. Makes him weak. 'Hello, love.'

'Sweetheart,' Ezra whispers, not caring who hears.

'Hurts.'

'I know, baby. I'm sorry.'

'I love you.'

'I love you too.'

Ezra can feel Daria looking at him. Can practically hear the cogs turning in her head. Can hear the penny drop. He doesn't care. A surgeon in green scrubs gently takes their arms pulling them to a stop as Teddy is wheeled off down the hallway. Ezra tries to shake her off, but a firm hand is placed on his shoulder.

'I'm sorry, sir,' she says. 'Visitors can't go past these doors.'

Ezra looks at her, helplessly. He knows there is no point in arguing, but part of him still wants to anyway. Something in her soft gaze is soothing though. It's probably a look she's given to a hundred worried family members and loved ones before, and it's probably perfectly rehearsed, but it's somehow everything Ezra needs right then. So, he says, 'Bring him back to me.'

She nods. 'We'll do our best.'

Ezra watches the surgeon and Teddy disappear behind the double doors and something inside him is ready to crumble. He turns and looks at Daria who is ready to burst into tears. He swallows his own feelings and gathers her into his arms. He lets her cry into his chest all the while his eyes burn. If he has to be strong for a little bit longer, just for her, then he will. He can wait until he is alone. He'll have to.

Daria's head is in his lap, all cried out. It's been two long hours. Teddy's doctor has already explained the situation: a driver on their phone had gone into the side of Teddy's chauffeured car. The chauffer was fine, but Teddy had taken the brunt of it. The other driver had died on impact. Teddy is lucky to be alive. He has seven broken ribs, a fractured skull, and internal bleeding. He's lost a lot of blood. The operation is an attempt to save his vital organs. Now, they just have to wait.

They're in the Prince George waiting room. Despite being a private hospital, a few tone-deaf people have still come up to him asking for a selfie. At some point — he's not sure when — Grace had joined them. Their parents too.

No one speaks. No one tries to comfort him. His fingers stroke gently through Daria's hair. Some part of him is aware that he's pretty much adopted her as another sister at this point. When Iris arrives and fixes Ezra with that knowing look of hers, he nearly bursts into tears. He doesn't though, because that will only get Daria going again and she's only just stopped.

It's nearly hour three when the surgeon comes to find them. She clears her throat, and six pairs of eyes turn to her. Daria sits up, her hands clutching Ezra's. She looks tired and harrowed, and Ezra is ready to hear the news that will destroy him.

The surgeon says, 'He's out of surgery. One person is allowed to be there when he wakes up.'

Ezra doesn't even need to ask, because Daria is already pushing him to his feet. She'd cried when Ezra had told her their story, from beginning to end. She'd held him, and wept, and thanked him for making her brother so happy. And now she was sacrificing seeing him for Ezra's sake. He kisses her cheek and squeezes her hand before following the surgeon to Teddy's room. His chest tightens with each step. His hands are shaking and he can't stop them, so he shoves them into his pockets. He takes a deep breath as the surgeon holds open the door for him.

Ezra isn't prepared to see him. Teddy is washed out and frail. His breaths are shallow and there are tubes — so *many* tubes — coming in and out of him. His cuts are stitched up and readily bruising. His chest is still bare, but bandaged up, and Ezra is comforted by the simple act of watching it rise and fall. Still, his heart squeezes painfully in his chest. A nurse is there with them, but Ezra doesn't care. He drops into the chair beside the hospital bed and takes Teddy's hand in his. He feels so weak. Ezra's throat is suddenly full of stones.

Teddy shifts in his sleep, his eyelids fluttering. He mumbles something that Ezra doesn't catch.

'Teddy?' Ezra croaks. 'Baby?'

'Ezra?'

The nurse comes over, paging for a doctor. Panic spikes in Ezra's chest and he wants to ask what's wrong, but he can't bear to hear the answer. A doctor joins them, and Ezra is gently jostled to one side while they fuss over him. Ezra realises, his heart returning to his chest, that they are only checking his vitals. When the doctor is happy, he gives Teddy a gentle smile and promises to see him later during his rounds. The nurse asks if he's comfortable and Teddy nods weakly, and then they leave. And Ezra and Teddy are alone.

Teddy turns his head and looks at him. He smiles — as much as he can with tubes up his nose — and says, 'An angel.'

And Ezra bursts into tears. He's so tired of being strong. He crosses to Teddy's side and gently cradles his face in his hands. His forehead presses against Teddy's as his chest racks with sobs. He can feel Teddy's hands over his, thumbs brushing feebly against his wrists, but that makes him cry harder for some reason.

'Oh, love,' Teddy says, voice weak. 'Please, don't. Please don't cry, it'll break my heart. I can't bear it. Please tell me how to fix it. How can I make it better, love? Hmm? Let me make it better.'

Ezra can't speak, so instead he kisses him. The blinds are drawn, and he's pretty sure that someone wouldn't come in without knocking first, and even if they did, he can't bring himself to care. Teddy is alive. Teddy is here. Kissing him back. That's all that matters. *Teddy* is all that will ever matter.

'I love you,' Ezra says. 'I love you. I love you. I love you.'

Teddy kisses his tears, his cheeks, his nose, and his lips. 'I know, love. I love you too. It's alright.'

'I thought I was going to lose you.'

'Never.'

Ezra pulls back enough to look at him. To take in his sharp cheekbones, his square jaw, his straight nose and blue eyes. He is so overcome with how much he loves him that he can hardly speak. 'You are my forever.'

Teddy smiles, even though it seems to take every ounce of his strength. 'And you are mine.'

They kiss again and Ezra is careful to be gentle. There is a knock at the door, and for a moment, Ezra thinks he won't be able to pull himself away, but he does. The door opens and Daria is there. Her eyes fill with tears at the sight of Teddy and Ezra knows exactly how she feels.

'Oh, Teddy,' she says, her voice breaking. She runs to him, and holds his face in her small hands, much in a similar way that Ezra had.

Ezra gives them space. He closes the door behind him, and every step down the corridor, every step away from Teddy feels like a betrayal. Grace and Iris rise to their feet when he enters the waiting room. They look at him expectantly, like he is supposed to have all the answers. He opens his mouth, though he's not sure what he's going to say. Not that he even gets that far, because all that comes out is a fresh wave of sobs. His legs finally give out and he sinks to the floor gasping for breath.

Iris is there first. Then Grace. Then his parents. They don't try to move him. They just hold him. Try to absorb some of his pain. Some of his tension. They let him cry. They let him shake. They remind him that he *can* breathe when his body tries to trick him into believing that he can't. Through it all, his mother finds his face, holding his chin with gentle hands.

'We'll fix it, hon,' she promises, and Ezra knows she's not just talking about Teddy's accident, but about everything. 'I'm so sorry. I'll make it right, I swear.'

Teddy is in the hospital for ten days before he's discharged. Ezra only leaves his side when Grace drags him away to eat and shower. Ali is making all the doctors and nurses on the ward sign NDAs. Anastasya and David only visit once and bring their pastor with them. He'd spend the entire time thanking God for sparing Teddy's life, all the while Teddy looked like he wanted to crawl out of his skin. Ezra had, very maturely, not pushed the holy man out of the window.

Grace, at Ali's request, does a short Instagram live with Teddy from his hospital bed to show the world he's okay. Iris visits almost every evening to show him the progress on a new commission she's working on. It's Sirius Black and Remus Lupin as teenagers at Hogwarts, making out on the astronomy tower and he, the giant nerd, loves it. When Daria brings the twins to visit, Teddy is so perilously close to tears that Ezra has to step out of the room for a moment. Teddy hates people to see him like that — hence the stubborn tick with his jaw — and Ezra doesn't want to give him an extra audience member to perform for.

Recovery isn't as linear as the movies make it seem. Although Teddy's body seems to be healing well, his emotions are working against him like a weird paradox. On day three, Teddy is elated to discover he can stand by himself, but dismayed by something as seemingly trivial as falling asleep during Ezra's visit. By day five, he can walk — albeit with a cane — but he almost cries when he forgets Margot's middle name. No amount of reassurance on Ezra or the doctor's part, assuring him that this is normal, and the drugs are making him woozy, seems to placate him.

It's not until day seven that Ezra sees a glimpse of the man he knows, when Teddy shyly asks Ezra to help him shower. Ezra does, of course. The wet room attached to his private suite is large enough to hold a small gathering, and Ezra strips them both down before helping Teddy get comfortable in the shower seat. He washes Teddy, slow and lovingly. He massages his scalp, and he washes his hair, wringing all a matter of happy little sounds from Teddy's lips. By the end of it, they're both hard and aching, but broken ribs and a slippery floor is just asking for trouble. And what would the nurses think when they come to rescue them? The idea makes them giggle like schoolboys.

On day ten, his doctors sign the release papers and Teddy is sent home with seventeen staples, a prescription for painkillers, and a follow up MRI scan in two weeks time. Ezra is especially proud of the welcome home party (is it a party if it's just six of them?) that he has, quite literally, thrown together at the last minute at Teddy's place. He's even more proud that he was able to fly Nick in from London. The look of pure delight on Teddy's face when Daria helps him through the front door is worth it.

Ezra steps forward and kisses him, hard, and the others holler and cheer. Teddy grins against his mouth. Because here, amongst their friends, they don't have to pretend to be something that they're not. Here, they get to be just Ezra and Teddy. Two guys who love each other.

'Welcome home,' Ezra whispers against his lips.

Teddy all but purrs and the sound goes straight to Ezra's groin. And as great as it is to have everyone there, and as much fun as they have, swapping stories, and laughing, and getting tipsy, and as much as Ezra loves to unabashedly stare at Teddy while he is in his element, it's even nicer when they leave — continuing the party at Grace's place — leaving Ezra to take Teddy to the bedroom.

Under the sheets and bathed in the moonlight coming through the window, Ezra worships Teddy's body. He kisses the bruises and the cuts that are going to leave scars. He kisses the hollow of his throat because he knows that drives Teddy wild. He works his hand on Teddy's length in between them with delicious, languid strokes. Teddy comes with his head tilted back, lips parted in ecstasy, Ezra's mouth on the pulse at his throat.

They fall asleep holding each other. Teddy drifts off first, but Ezra can't bring himself to close his eyes. Whenever he thinks about how close he came to losing him, his eyes sting. He gazes down at the silly man using him as a pillow and smiles, running his hand through his thick hair. The same mantra from the day he came out to his parents flashes in his mind, and it's still the truest thing he knows.

Protect Teddy.

Chapter Sixteen

Text Thread: Queer Today Gone Tomorrow

saving grace:
if we wear moustaches can me, iris, and daria come to the stag do?

ezra:
which one of you changed the group name again?

iggy:
i did

iggy:
answer the question

saving grace:
it seems only fair since you went on teddy's REAL stag without us

ezra:
you don't want to come. we're painting plates and sampling rare cheeses

daria:
I like cheese.

Flynn Rider [eggplant emoji]:
That is absolutely NOT we're doing.
It's a steak dinner and wine tasting.

                                                                        ezra:
                       i swear that's what i just said?

iggy:
how did we not get an invite
to EITHER stag?

                                                                        ezra:
                                          you're girls?

saving grace:
YOU came to my hen

                                                                        ezra:
                                        under duress

Flynn Rider [eggplant emoji]:
It finishes at 9pm. We can go out
afterwards?

iggy:
COCKTAILS!!!

saving grace:
COCKTAILS COCKTAILS COCKTAILS

daria:
I can get Anastasya to look after the twins.

ezra:
poor twins

iggy:
[cocktails.gif]

Flynn Rider [eggplant emoji]:
We'll pick you up in the limo when we're done.

iggy:
[dancing.gif]

ezra:
you've dug your own grave there, babe.

iggy:
[middlefinger.gif]

ezra:
[laughing emoji]

Filming starts again just in time for Teddy's staged bachelor party. Not *quite* a high tea, but still nothing like their night at Judy's. The night they had first slept together. The night that Ezra suspected he might be falling in love with Teddy but didn't want to admit it. The night he finally discovered what Teddy looks like when he's being made love to. The thought makes heat pool in Ezra's stomach and he swallows hard. He catches Teddy's gaze across from him in the limo, and he feels the spark between his legs threaten to become an inferno. He quickly looks out of the window and thinks about his dead grandma.

It's a small group. Himself — obviously — Teddy, Nick, Warren, and (ugh) David. Who, by the way, looks like he'd rather be out kicking stray cats and burning down LGBTQ+ charity centres than on his way to his son's bachelor party. Ezra hasn't seen him since that awful hospital visit, and for that he is both grateful and livid.

As if David can hear his thoughts, he turns his head sharply to glare at Ezra, and if *that* isn't a boner-killer then he doesn't know what is. Ezra clears his throat and turns his attention to the casual conversation Nick is having with Warren, talking about British politics, and the current so-called-scandal with their youngest prince and his American bride. Ezra thinks people should just leave them alone.

The restaurant is French, far too stuffy, and definitely not Teddy's pick. Months ago, if you'd asked Ezra what he thought Teddy's ideal dinner was he'd have shrugged and said lobster stuffed with caviar (hilarious). But now he knows that it's something called a *chicken parmo*, which is, essentially, a giant chicken nugget covered in cheese. He would have said Teddy's drink of choice was an antique red wine, brought to existence by Jesus H. Christ himself. Now he knows it's actually a shandy. Which is just ew. But it makes Teddy happy and Ezra will forgive him all his alcohol trespasses for that goofy smile Teddy gets when he's tipsy.

When Ezra looks at the menu, the prices are high for even him. He catches Nick's gaze and something passes silently between them along the lines of *Teddy is going to hate this*. One glance at Teddy's tight jaw confirms it.

'Jesus,' Ezra mumbles. 'What were these cows fed on? Golden flakes and compliments?'

Teddy smirks but doesn't look up from his menu. 'Probably also a healthy dose of pretence for good measure, too.'

David looks at his son with a *goodness, what are you like!* expression, that Ezra now knows is only for the cameras. 'Oh, Theodore.'

Warren clears his throat, ready to steer the conversation into safer waters if need be. And it probably will. Teddy has this look on his face tonight that can only mean trouble and Ezra's not sure yet if that's a good or a bad thing. Since the accident, Teddy seems to have less patience for the things and people that irritate him. Ezra can't blame him.

'So,' Warren says, 'Teddy. Your other friends couldn't make the trip from England? That's a shame.'

Teddy shrugs. 'Dad doesn't like my other friends. He only let Nick come because he works in the same circles as mum and Daria.'

Ezra nearly chokes on his glass of water. David's perfect parent façade almost slips as the table goes very quiet. He reigns it back in at the last minute and gives Teddy another *oh, that's my boy!* look.

Warren blinks. 'Oh. I see. Um. Well, we look forward to meeting them at the wedding.'

Teddy smiles warmly at Warren to let him know that his tension isn't aimed his way, as if everyone didn't already know it's targeted at David. 'That's very kind of you. I'll make sure to bring them in through the back door so that dad doesn't have to look at them.'

'Theodore,' David says, this time with a bit of bite.

Behind the camera, Ezra can see Ron practically salivating. He clears his throat and says, 'Well, I think I'll have the short rib—'

'When you booked this place,' Teddy says, addressing his dad but not taking his eyes off the wine list in his hand. 'Did it occur to you that I don't like steak? Or did you just forget?'

David's left eye honest-to-God twitches. 'Theodore, there's no need for theatrics.'

'Dad, our whole lives are theatrics.'

Ezra looks at Nick, arching an eyebrow. Nick just shrugs. The cameras roll, sweeping in to get a close up of Teddy and David. Ezra wants to stretch his leg out and gently nudge Teddy's but he knows he can't. Instead, he fires off a text: **you okay?** Teddy checks his phone and taps a reply which sends David's eyebrows flying up his forehead to his receding hairline. He gets a reply: **Just fed up with this shit. Love you. X**

'Theodore, it's very rude to use your phone at the dinner table,' David says.

'My apologies, father. Would you like to shove it up your arse so that the pole you have wedged up there doesn't get lonely?'

Ezra genuinely, hand on his heart does a spit-take. He's pretty sure Ron just jizzed his pants. Nick sucks in his cheeks so that he won't laugh, and Warren hides his smile behind his napkin. Teddy pretends to be interested in the white wines — that Ezra knows for a *fact* that he wouldn't drink if it was the last thing on the menu — while David gapes at him, mouth opening and closing like a particularly dumb, homophobic fish.

Teddy politely waves the waitress over and orders in perfect French (of course, he speaks *French*), before opening the floor to the others. Ezra orders a glass of the rioja and the short rib in red wine sauce. David's mouth is still hanging open when the waitress gets to him. Teddy orders for him — sirloin, medium rare, glass of Chilean chardonnay — and he pointedly ignores his father to address the group.

'Here's to getting through this—' Teddy pauses to look at him. 'What is it you call it, Ezra? A dumpster fire?'

Ezra nods, wondering if anyone has ever been more in love than he is with Teddy Montgomery right now. 'Dumpster fire sounds good.'

'This *dumpster fire* of a stag do.'

The waitress returns with the drinks and Nick raises his glass, smirking. 'To the dumpster fire!'

Everyone but David raises their glass. 'To the dumpster fire!'

Ezra takes a sip of his rioja, eyes not straying from Teddy's. He watches Teddy lick the pinot noir from his full lips and his legs liquify. *Oh. Wow.* He texts him: **you're killing me, sweetheart.** Teddy replies immediately with: **Damn right I am.** And then Ezra has to spend the rest of dinner willing his raging erection to go away.

After dinner they legit go for cigars — despite the fact that none of them smoke — on the rooftop bar. A waitress brings them multiple rounds of various expensive wines to try. Ezra is not prepared for how good Teddy looks, nose inhaling the scent of a merlot, cigar hanging from his long fingers. He even politely samples the white wine, when Ezra *knows* he hates it, and he can't keep his eyes off Teddy's throat as he swallows. Teddy knows what he's doing, because he shoots Ezra a look that makes electricity crackle down his spine.

Ezra sends him a text that says: **two can play that game, baby.** He proceeds to make a show of wrapping his lips around his cigar and taking a long drag that he hates, but it's worth it for the flush that crosses Teddy's face. He gets a reply: **Do that again.** So, he does, and Teddy's knees nearly buckle, and honestly, none of this is helping his boner situation.

David, at least, keeps his mouth shut. He stays out of the conversation, the tendons in his neck standing out as he struggles not to explode. He's exactly the kind of spoilt brat that Ezra had always assumed Teddy was. How wrong he'd been. Looking at Teddy now, with his arm around Nick's shoulders, laughing about a memory from when they were at university, his eyes crinkled and slightly bleary from the bare minimum of booze, Ezra can't believe how wrong he was.

When it's over, they drop David off first, then Warren, and then they swing by Iris' brownstone to pick up the girls. They bundle into the back with them, arms full of feather boas. A pink one is draped around Ezra's shoulders, and Teddy is fixed with a purple one.

Iris and Grace, who have both already started early on the cocktails, fight to sit in Teddy's lap, smearing his cheeks with lipstick marks. Teddy laughs and indulges them, and Ezra just lets himself bubble over with happiness.

They go straight to Judy's and are guided into a private booth that Grace, thankfully, had the wherewithal to reserve for them. A waiter brings them cocktails with absolutely filthy names and Ezra enjoys watching Teddy sample each one, his sweet face growing warmer and sillier with each sip.

There's a live band called Four Gays And A Guitar covering 90s pop classics. It only takes the first few bars of *Baby One More Time* before Iris is on the table, arms in the air, hips shimmying. Grace pretends that she doesn't want to be dragged up to dance, but everyone knows that she does, and by the chorus she and Daria are on the table with her, scream-singing the lyrics.

Ezra orders another round of cocktails, six *Anus Burner* shots, and a bottle of Moet and Chandon. He passes the drinks up to the girls who down them, cringing, and Ezra tips his head back laughing. A Spice Girls medley starts and suddenly Nick is on the table with the girls doing his best Posh Spice impression. Ezra can't resist putting his arm around Teddy's shoulders as they watch their friends. He knows it's dangerous, and he knows literally anyone can be — and probably are — watching, but he cannot bring himself to give a shit. Teddy Montgomery is *his*. He wants to enjoy that in public at least once before he has to give it up.

When the band transitions into *The Sign* by Ace Of Base, Ezra's arm is almost ripped out of his socket as Teddy jumps to his feet, pulling him up onto the table. And suddenly they're all dancing, cramped onto the rickety counter, trying not to fall off, singing off-key and spilling their cocktails on each other. At some point, someone — Ezra isn't sure who, but he suspects it's Iris — cracks open the bottle of Moet and sprays it over them all. Ezra licks a stripe of champagne off Teddy's cheek and Teddy blushes, and it's *adorable*.

Ezra's not sure how they end up being invited up on stage with the band, but Teddy has somehow got his hands on an electric guitar and is playing *I Believe In A Thing Called Love* by The Darkness, and it's not strictly 90s but no one seems to care. Grace and Iris dramatically throw themselves at Teddy's feet while Nick and Daria dance like kids at a school disco. Ezra hangs back on the side-lines and just enjoys watching Teddy doing what he's good at.

It always amazes Ezra how reluctant Teddy is to let go, and then how much he soars when he finally does. It's like he's waiting for someone's permission to enjoy himself. It's why he doesn't let himself get drunk like this — along with the memories drinking brings of his brother — because when he's drunk, he lets all his guards down. He's no longer Teddy Montgomery, Great Britain's Golden Boy. Teddy, the child-star-turned-household-name. Teddy, World's Sexiest Man. He is just Teddy. Silly, and drunk, and relaxed, and happy.

Around three in the morning, someone — again, probably Iris — gets the terrible idea to go to Liberty Island. So, they do. It's closed and no ferries are running, and they have to bribe a guy with a literal speed boat to take them out there. He does it for a grand, and they break onto the little landmass with the bottles of booze they bought at a twenty-four-hour convenience store. It's pitch black, and deserted, and spooky, and Ezra pretends to be afraid of the dark so that Teddy will hold his hand.

Grace plays music through her phone and they dance, and drink, and dance, and laugh, and kiss. At some point Teddy takes Ezra's hand and leads him off to a secluded bench so he can kiss him silly. And when kissing quickly becomes not enough, Ezra is pulling down Teddy's boxers and sinking to his knees. Teddy's strong hands, gentle as they reach down to stroke his cheek and run through his hair, and then rough as he comes, hips bucking up to meet Ezra's face. And when he returns the favour, he has Ezra's legs hooked over his shoulders, and Ezra climaxes looking up at the motherfucking stars, and it's just too good to be true.

They all stay on Liberty Island until the sun breaks on the horizon, bringing with it a hangover that Ezra can already tell will have him bedridden for forty-eight hours at the very least. Small boats start to come in, and they bribe the same guy as last night to take them back to the mainland. Another grand. Totally worth it.

Ezra and Teddy sit in the back of the boat. Ezra's head is pounding, and Teddy can barely keep his eyes open. His head lulls on Ezra's shoulder, and when Grace looks back at them, she smiles, pulling out her phone. Ezra offers her a lame thumbs up as she snaps a picture. They all still have their feather boas on, though they have switched them around a few times. Ezra now has the yellow one and Teddy has the pink one.

By the time they make it back to Ezra's brownstone — which is apparently where they're all crashing — it's almost eight in the morning. Daria is the most responsible. She gives everyone a glass of water, something to puke into, and two aspirin each before passing out on the sofa.

Ezra has Teddy curled around him in his bed. They're both naked and Teddy's chest is flush against Ezra's back. Ezra knows that Teddy is asleep by the steady exhales against the back of his neck. It's familiar and reassuring and Ezra drifts off into a dreamless sleep. And when his phone starts buzzing like crazy on the floor somewhere he's too tired and too loved up to care.

Chapter Seventeen

[Excerpt from *That's The Tea*, Monday 11th October 2021, written by Tara Young]

True Love Or Lustful Lies?

Grace Darling and Teddy Montgomery have been the hottest topic in America since, well, Hot Topic. All fifty states have been *swooning* over these international love birds ever since their surprise engagement earlier in the year. Some cynics have pointed out that their announcement of upcoming nuptials was conveniently announced after incriminating rumours came to light concerning the Montgomerys, indicating that Viktor Volkov (Teddy's grandfather) could have very well been involved in illegal gay conversion therapy trials back in the early 00s. To them, here at *That's The Tea*, we say 'boo, you whore.'

Or at least we *did*. That is, until pictures of Teddy Montgomery looking cosy with her fiancés brother (YES! BROTHER!), Ezra Darling, at a gay bar in NYC surfaced in the early hours this morning. As seen in the picture (below) Teddy and Ezra (out partying with friends) are looking *pretty* snuggly in that booth together. Is that an arm around a shoulder we see? Hubba hubba! Is that the look of love on Ezra's face, or is it simply just bromance? If you ask *this* gossip queen, no, it's not. We've all known that Ezra has batted for the other team ever since his first appearance in hotpants and fishnets tights on his 21st (right) and now it looks like he is trying to muscle in on his sister's man.

STILL NOT CONVINCED? OH, HONEY. GET READY TO FALL DOWN THE RABBIT HOLE WITH US. HERE ARE TWENTY PICTURES OF TEDDY MONTGOMERY AND EZRA DARLING GAZING ADORINGLY AT EACH OTHER SINCE DAY ONE. WE *DARE* YOU TO LOOK THROUGH THEM AND TELL US THAT THE WYOMING WILD CHILD AND GREAT BRITAIN'S GOLDEN BOY AREN'T *TOTALLY* HEAD OVER HEELS. WE ONLY HOPE THAT GRACE DOESN'T TAKE THIS TOO HARD. LOSING YOUR FIANCÉ? OUCH. LOSING YOUR FIANCÉ TO YOUR *BROTHER?* DOUBLE OUCH!

Ezra reads the blog post, trying to keep his face neutral, while inwardly his mind is stuck on a loop of *fuck, fuck, fuck, fuck, fuck, fuck, fuck.* He'd known putting his arm around Teddy had been a mistake. He'd known it was dangerous. He'd promised his parents that he would be careful while they figured out the BingeBox contract. And now here he is, looking at a picture of himself with his arm slung around Teddy's shoulders, gazing up at him like he's the Angel Gabriel.

'This proves nothing,' he argues.

Ali glares at him. 'It proves you're a fucking moron.'

'How is this any different to other pictures of me with guy friends?' he asks. 'Every time the media digs up an old picture of me with a random guy they run the same story. What makes this any worse?'

'Because you actually *are* fucking him!'

Jacqueline steps forwards. Her hair is tied back, and her usual stilettos are replaced with sensible kitten heels, and Ezra knows that means his mother is close to losing it. Not that anyone outside of the Darling Dynasty would be able to tell. 'Alright. Let's just all calm down. Ezra has a point.'

'You don't understand,' Ali says, pacing. 'When a story like this runs, people start digging. They do their research. The only reason that the other stories about Ezra have dried up is because there's no evidence to back up the claims.'

'Well, there is no evidence to back up *these* claims either,' he says.

Ali pauses, and her head nearly turns one-hundred-and-eighty degrees — *Exorcist* style — to glare at him. 'You *are* the evidence!'

'Look,' says Grace. 'The story is already out there. There's not much we can do about it now except damage control. The public already knows that Ezra and Teddy have a bromance. We just have to play up on that.'

Warren nods. 'It's not ideal. But it's workable.'

Ezra has tuned out. He's looking at the picture again. Whoever took it really captured a moment. He's beaming up at Teddy, eyes bright and shining. Teddy is looking down at him, face full of so much love that it almost seems pointless denying the obvious. He almost doesn't want to. He wants the world to know that Teddy Montgomery — gorgeous, smart, funny, legs-for-days, Teddy Montgomery — belongs to him. But he knows he can't.

'We get ahead of the narrative,' Ali says. 'Grace you'll need to host an Insta live tonight. Get a dialogue going. Ezra you'll make an appearance. Don't make it too obvious it's staged. Act like you're dropping in. Don't bring up the article until you're asked — which you *will* be. If you start denying it before anyone's even asked, you'll just look even more guilty.'

The world *guilty* tugs at Ezra. 'I'm not guilty for loving him.'

Jacqueline puts her hand on his arm. 'Of course not, hon. This is just... well, I'll be honest with you, sweetie, it's a bit of a shit-show.'

Ezra scrubs his face with his hands. He's too tired and *far* too hungover to be facing the consequences of his actions. His sleep had lasted for all of about thirty minutes before Ali had let herself into his brownstone (when did she get a key?) screaming about *what's the point of having a phone if you're not going to answer it, fuckface?*

She hadn't been at all shy about his or Teddy's nakedness as she ripped the covers off them and threw their clothes onto the bed. Teddy had spluttered, grabbed the sheets and turned beetroot red. Ezra had just cursed and rolled inelegantly onto the floor. She'd sent Teddy and the others home and had practically dressed Ezra before dragging him to the emergency family meeting. And now here he is. Getting his dick chopped off.

Grace is nodding. 'I can do that. I'll organise a graphic saying I'm going live at six this evening. Ezra can drop in and we'll answer some questions in the chat. When they ask about Teddy, we'll say it was drunken brotherly bonding.'

Ezra agrees to whatever is asked of him. Mostly he just thinks about Teddy. About how much he must be panicking right now. If Anastasya and David have read the article. If they're giving him a hard time. If he's had enough water today. If he needs someone to rub his back while he empties the contents of his stomach, swearing to never drink again.

He worries that Teddy will be hard on himself. He tries not to drink because it reminds him of Leo, and when he does, very seldom does he get properly drunk. He's probably beating himself up and Ezra isn't there to stop his anxiety from eating him alive.

Ali's phone buzzes and she fishes it out of her pocket. Ezra watches as her expression slides from livid, to confused, then settles on shocked. She opens her mouth and then closes it again. Her fingers start flying over her phone screen and Ezra swaps a worried glance with Grace, wondering which one of them is going to be hung, drawn, and quartered first.

But then his own phone is buzzing. And then so is Grace's. And then everyone is reaching for their phones, and as Ezra looks at his home screen — his wallpaper is still the picture of Teddy at the Queen concert — his heart threatens to force its way out his mouth. With a tremble he opens the article link Iris has sent him. Sent *all* of them.

BREAKING! VIKTOR VOLKOV INVOLVMENT IN GAY CONVERSION THERAPY CONFIRMED IN NEW LEAKED EMAILS

Ezra doesn't read the article. Because he can't. All he can think about is Teddy and what this must be doing to him. They've never spoken about the real reason why their families are partnering up, but it's always there. But speaking about it feels like some kind of betrayal to what they have. And Ezra knows it will hurt him. The only reason Teddy is so far in the closet is because of his homophobic parents. To know that they not only discriminate against you, but also actively torture people like you into submission? Ezra feels bile rise in his throat.

'You have a fucking guardian angel, kid,' Ali says.

Ezra is ready to scream at her, but when he looks up from his phone he stops. She doesn't look relieved, like she should, that all the attention is off him and the photo. Instead, she looks weary. Troubled. Again, he can't speak.

'Jesus Christ,' Grace breathes, scrolling through the article. 'They have the emails. The actual emails. From Viktor and his clinic. It's — shit, it's damning.'

Jacqueline is already on the phone to Mara. She takes the call in another room, kissing both her kids on the head on her way out. Warren has his laptop out and is engrossed in whatever damage control it is that he's doing for the Montgomerys. Ali paces, taking long, unrelenting swigs from her coffee flask.

'Alright,' she says. 'Pros and cons. Pro: no one cares about the photo anymore. Cons: the gay conversion therapy is no longer just a rumour, but a full-fucking-blown circus.'

'What do we do?' Grace asks.

'We could handle rumours. We could handle hearsay. The Darling Dynasty is clean enough to gloss over gossip. But this. *This*! Jesus H Christ on a fucking bike.'

'Do we pull out of the wedding?'

'Yes. No. Fuck. No, that will be worse. Teddy isn't involved in the emails. It will look like you're abandoning him. We have to find a way to make this work that won't tarnish the Darling Dynasty.'

Ezra can barely make out their conversation over the white noise in his ears, but bits of it get through. Anger flares tight in his throat over how they're worrying more about sullying the pristine Darling name rather than how Teddy is feeling. Because that's all that should matter right now. *Protect Teddy.*

'We're not abandoning him,' Ezra says, voice thick. 'If we leave, he has no one. We're not leaving him.'

Grace's hand settles on his. 'We're not leaving him.'

He looks at her and he can see the real meaning behind her words. *You're not leaving him*. He nods. 'So, what do we do?'

Ali is already sweeping her things off her table and haphazardly into her bag, not taking her time to meticulously put everything in its place like usual. Her hair is beginning to fall out of her ponytail as she hoists the *Balenciaga* purse over her shoulder. She doesn't say anything as the front door slams behind her, nose practically touching her phone screen. Then their phones all buzz at the same time, and Ezra sees the new email reminder from Ali for a "strategy meeting" tomorrow morning.

Teddy looks wretched when he opens the door. His skin is grey, and his eyes are red, and Ezra knows better than to ask him if he's been crying, because Teddy will just do that Teddy thing where his jaw clamps shut. Instead, he pulls Teddy into his arms and they stay that way for minutes. Hours. Days. Who knows and who cares?

'Thank you for coming,' he says.

Ezra pulls back to look at him. 'Are you crazy? Of course I came. Are you alright?'

Teddy runs a shaky hand through his hair. 'I don't know. No, I guess. Christ. When did it all get so...' He trails off, looking utterly defeated.

'Baby,' Ezra says gently. 'I know. I'm so sorry.'

Teddy sighs. 'Tea?'

Ezra nearly laughs. 'Coffee.'

He sits at the breakfast counter while Teddy busies himself boiling the water on the stove. He can practically see the tension rolling off him. His shoulders are tight, and Ezra wants to massage them loose. When Teddy presents him with a coffee — black, one sweetener — and sits down beside him, he is unsurprised to see the stubble on his jaw. To the rest of the world, Teddy at his worst still pretty much looks like Teddy at his best. But Ezra knows that stubble on his jaw, or mussed hair, or jeans instead of slacks means that he's unravelling.

'Do you want to talk about it?' Ezra asks.

Teddy sighs. 'I suppose we have to.'

'No, we don't. But if you want to talk, I want to listen.'

Teddy is staring ahead at nothing in particular. His gaze is glossy. 'Did you read the emails?'

'No. God no. Not without your permission.'

Teddy attempts a smile but it's dead on arrival. 'You should. We'll be going over them at the meeting tomorrow.'

'I won't if it will hurt you.'

Teddy swallows. 'Everything they did hurt me.'

Ezra's chest aches and he puts a gentle hand on Teddy's leg. 'Give me the CliffsNotes version.'

Teddy seems to visibly steel himself before plunging headfirst into it all. How the rumours had originated from a disgruntled ex-employee of the Montgomerys. They'd started the gossip and gone to David and Anastasya threatening to release evidence she had to back up the allegations unless she got triple her severance pay. They had called her bluff and it had been the right choice because she'd been lying. There was no evidence. But then, someone had hacked into their family's private email server — most likely the same person — and leaked correspondence between Viktor Volkov and a clinic he was working with, along with patient files. It was all there, in writing, undeniable proof that before his grandfather died, not only was he a complete homophobe, but also a criminal.

'And what about your parents?' Ezra asks. 'Was there anything incriminating them?'

'No. Only grandad and the clinic. They closed down about fifteen years ago, but their big names are under investigation.'

Ezra squeezes Teddy's knee, wishing he could take away the pain for him. He would take it all if he could. 'I'm sorry, sweetheart. It must have been a shock.'

At this Teddy barks a laugh. 'Oh no. I knew what was going on all along. So did my parents. They made me sign an NDA so that I wouldn't talk about it to anyone.'

'Jesus. You just... found out on your own?'

Something in Teddy's body language shifts. He seems to shrink in on himself, pulling himself out of Ezra's touch. Ezra aches to reach out to him again, to hold him, but he's not tone-deaf. He knows when someone wants to be left alone. Instead, he waits, not caring how long it takes. He's got his whole life to wait for this man to be ready. *Protect Teddy.*

When Teddy speaks, his voice is rough, jagged around the edges. 'Not exactly. Ezra, I—I have to tell you something. I hate it, but I need to say it out loud and I need at least one person to hear it.'

Something frigid settles in Ezra's stomach. His hands tighten around his mug, his knuckles going white, but he keeps his face even for Teddy's sake.

Teddy goes on, looking down into his tea. 'There was this guy. He was one of my dad's business partners, and I used to get this really bad vibe off him. I remember I used to dread social events because I knew he would be there. He would sit by me and put his hand on my leg under the table. He would always stand too close to me or put his hands on my waist. I was terrified of him. We were at the Christmas work do when he slipped his hotel room key into my pocket and told me to find him later. I told my parents when we got home. They said I was a liar. They'd found a love letter I had written but not sent to a boy in my class the week before. They said I was trying to seduce him because of my,' he swallows, '*perversion.*'

Ezra is going to be sick. He is sure of it. He wants to take Teddy far away where no one can hurt him ever again. He wants to fight everyone who's *ever* hurt him. He wants to get his hands on this piece of shit and wring his neck.

'But they were adamant they could fix me,' Teddy says, voice hoarse. 'They said my grandfather had helped many sinners like me before. So, they started treatment. It was a new study and they said I'd be the perfect candidate.'

Ezra blanches. 'No. *God* no.'

Teddy finally looks at him. He's utterly destroyed. 'I was patient zero. They hooked me up to the machines and forced me to watch gay porn while puking my guts up. I was thirteen.'

Thirteen. 2006. Teen Choice Awards. Teddy forced to go about his life like he wasn't being completely traumatised and tormented for just being who he is. Ezra thinking he was a dick for not saying hello. Ezra not realising that Teddy was living a nightmare. Teddy having every bit of his dignity, and his happiness and his childhood stripped from him. And he didn't know. No one *knew*.

Ezra needs to hold him. Like. Right now. Instinctively he reaches for Teddy but freezes. He's not sure why. It just seems like he needs permission to touch him. Teddy watches him and his face softens. He tenderly takes Ezra's face in his elegant hands. Ezra will never get enough of those goddamn hands.

'You're not him,' he says. 'You never will be him. I know you won't hurt me.'

'Never,' Ezra promises.

That night, when their bodies come together, Teddy is straddling Ezra's lap, his back bathed in the streetlight from the window. Teddy comes with his face buried in the crook of Ezra's neck and Ezra holds him as he shudders. He can't bear the thought of someone hurting him, and when Teddy pulls back and sees that Ezra's eyelashes are wet, he just kisses away the tears, all the while repeating, *you will never hurt me.*

And he won't. Not ever. And he'll make sure that no one else does either.

Ezra has promised Ali that he will try his best not to scowl at David and Anastasya the entirety of their meeting, but when he receives a text from Grace within the first five minutes saying: dude, are you trying to glare them to death? he knows he's already failed.

David is dressed for Ascot and Anastasya is wearing a white pantsuit and a Panama hat. A *Panama hat*. Indoors. With sunglasses. They both look every part the rich white homophobes that they absolutely are, and Ezra is ready to leap across the table and — well, he's not sure. But it will be something heroic and done in Teddy's honour. David catches his gaze and glares right back, and it takes every ounce of Ezra's self-control not to mouth *fuck you*.

'The press conference is set for tomorrow afternoon at the Artemis Hotel,' Ali says as she hands out a detailed schedule of events. 'Only select members of the press are allowed in — publications that owe the Darling Dynasty a favour. I guess, what I'm saying is, it'll be pretty hard to say something that will backfire.'

Ezra notices Ali directing that last statement at him, and he frowns. 'It's not me you want to be worrying about. What about The Man From Del Monte over there? Last time she opened her mouth she verbally assaulted Iris.'

Anastasya's lips curl into a sneer. 'You'll have nothing to fear from *me* when it comes to disgracing our family.'

Her gaze cuts to Teddy who tenses in his seat at the table. No one is saying anything, but everyone knows what she means. Teddy is too hurt to even blush. He just sits, stares at the schedule in front of him, and grinds his jaw.

'Regardless,' Ali continues, like a preschool teacher trying to wrangle her bickering students. 'This is pretty damn hard to fuck up. The press have already been given a list of questions they can ask and I've just given you all a list of acceptable answers.'

'This is censorship,' David mumbles.

'You'd know all about that,' Ezra says, and Grace kicks his shin.

Ali slams her palms down on the table beside Ezra and huffs out a sound halfway between agreement and exasperation. 'Something you want to share with the group, pencil-dick? Because I'm pretty fucking busy trying to save the reputations of two of the biggest families in entertainment in, oh, I don't know, *the world*. And if you have something you want to say then hurry up and say it, so we can get on with me saving your careers.'

Ezra looks at Teddy who is silently begging him to stay quiet. So, he does.

Ali straightens and continues. 'The official stance is that The Montgomerys had no idea of Viktor Volkov's involvement in these trials. David and Anastasya will publicly denounce Viktor's actions and make it known that they and their church are strong allies to the LGBTQ+ community.'

Anastasya snorts and Grace arches an eyebrow. 'You doing okay there? Need some water?'

God, Ezra loves his sister.

Anastasya scoffs. 'How considerate you are.'

'Wouldn't want anyone here to feel uncomfortable.'

Ali pinches the bridge of her nose. 'Jacqueline. Warren. I am running on three hours of sleep and a six-pack of Red Bull. Please control your children before I dropkick them.'

'Kids,' Warren says, shooting them a glance that says *you're not wrong, but rein it in*.

Ali turns to the side of the table that seats the Darlings. 'The Darling Dynasty will, of course, support the Montgomerys. You will say you knew nothing of the trials and say that you have every faith in the Montgomerys' word that they had nothing to do with Viktor Volkov's affairs. We want to promote a united front. Two families, the Darlings and the Montgomerys against homophobia. Can we all *please* just do that?'

When no one immediately replies, Ali slams her hands down on the table again, her glasses slipping down her upturned nose, and everyone is quick to nod and mumble that they will, in fact, do whatever she says.

When they're finally let out of the meeting, Teddy is wound so tightly that he practically jumps Ezra the moment they get back to his brownstone. Ezra becomes whatever Teddy needs. He lets Teddy pin him down, and make him beg, and scream, and tremble. And when Teddy finally fucks him, Ezra lets himself sink into the white-out bliss that is being so completely claimed by another person. *His* person. *His* Teddy.

His. Always his.

Chapter Eighteen

[Excerpt from the New York Post, Wednesday 13th October 2021]

Darling Dynasty Stands By Montgomerys Amidst Conversion Trial Claims

In a press conference held earlier this morning at the Artemis Hotel in NYC, members of the Darling Dynasty stood alongside the Montgomerys in a show of solidarity against the allegations of Viktor Volkov's involvement in illegal gay conversion therapy trials.

Emails confirming Volkov's involvement surfaced on Monday 11th October 2021, after a leak to the Montgomerys' private email server, validating what was originally rumoured to be true. In these emails, Volkov talks candidly about the trials and his patients at a clinic he was collaborating with in Russia. Attachments in the emails include patient files, including those of a "patient 0" who is said, in the documents, to be only thirteen years of age.

The Montgomerys stanchly denied any knowledge of these trials. David Montgomery announced, 'We absolutely do not condone these abhorrent trials, and neither does our church. Had I known such a thing was going on I would have brought it to the authorities myself, family or not.' His wife, Anastasya, added, 'We are truly shocked to the core that something so horrific was happening under our noses. I always knew my father was a cold man, but I never knew he was evil.'

Supporting the Montgomerys were the Darlings. Grace Darling and Theodore Montgomery presented a united front but refrained from speaking. However, when asked about the leaked emails, he answered, with conviction, 'I am deeply saddened by all those my grandfather has hurt. Especially "patient 0". No child should ever have to go through this. I will be reaching out personally to each of those affected in these repugnant trials and offering my help however I can.' His fiancé gripped his hand and added, 'The Darling Dynasty and the Montgomerys do not tolerate abuse or discrimination of any kind. Those who were hurt, we see your pain, and we will make this right for you.'

The Darlings also denied any knowledge of Volkov's involvement, with Grace Darling adding, 'I will not abandon my fiancé in his family's time of need. They have been betrayed by Viktor's crimes. They were as in the dark as all of us. But when you love someone, you don't just stop when it suddenly gets hard, or a little bit inconvenient. I stand by Teddy, and I always will. I only beg that the public sees his innocence as we do.'

Keeping mostly quiet throughout it all was the eldest Darling Dynasty child, Ezra Darling, who had nothing to add except, 'Volkov was a c**t. Teddy isn't. Next question.'

Ezra is sent to press training, because of course he is. Which is stupid. Because obviously he *knows* he's not supposed to call people *cunts* in press conferences. He knows that. Literally everyone knows that. But he'd been angry, and hurting for Teddy. Hearing David and Anastasya lie so brazenly, and listening to Grace call Teddy the love of her life, and enduring the heartbreak in Teddy's voice had just been too much.

So, he spends two weeks with a PR coach. He makes sure that Ezra knows *I do not condone Viktor Volkov's actions* is good, and *Viktor Volkov is a raging fuck-nugget* is bad. Very bad. Ali sends him emails every morning with various, mildly threatening subject lines, warning him to keep his mouth shut until everyone stops talking about it. She's even changed his social media passwords and is holding his accounts hostage until he can be trusted.

Grace is busy with filming. Her whole life is everyone else's business, and Ezra has no idea how she can bear to have so many people seeing her like that. So open. At least Ezra has his persona to hide behind. Filming also means that Teddy is, unfortunately, kept busy and away from him most days. He's not sure when their strict evening only policy stopped being a thing, but it was probably somewhere after the *I, like, love you, okay?* mark. Or probably before, if he's being honest. Probably around the time he realised that Teddy Montgomery was the only thing he wanted and ever *would* want.

Which means that Ezra spends his days languishing in his brownstone, alone and bored. Iris keeps him company when she's not working on a new commission, which is rare. With Christmas coming up, several people have been making orders via her Etsy store. One night she turns up with her iPad and Ezra watches her sketch out the skeleton of what will be Luc O'Donnell and Oliver Blackwood's wedding day — whatever that means. Nevertheless, it's fun to watch her create.

On one of his nights alone, Ezra finds himself wondering, not for the first time, if he should be doing something more with his life. He thinks about the rehab centres and charities Daria is involved in, and he *knows* he can be doing more. After Grace's overdose, he'd always wanted to set up his own charity. The Ezra Darling Foundation, or something. Dedicated to helping people get the recovery they need. But, as Ali has pointed out to him many times, *helping* a charity is glamorous. *Running* a charity is hard and gritty and yields no screen time. But Ezra is beginning to think he doesn't care about that.

In the evenings he helps Teddy unwind from a day of fake on-screen smiling, with kisses, and caresses, and orgasms. One evening, when Teddy comes home particularly wound up, Ezra lets Teddy tie him to the bed posts and edge him until he's literally begging to be fucked, and Teddy thrusts all of his frustration out on Ezra's compliant body.

At some point Ezra stops going back to his brownstone in the mornings. He knows it's stupid and Ali will probably start sending him two threatening emails a day instead of just one, but he can't bring himself to leave. Part of him loves the domestic bliss of it all. Watching Teddy wander around the kitchen, all grumpy and groggy until he gets a cup of tea.

He likes the feel of Teddy's stubbly kisses in the morning, and likes watching him while he shaves it all off. He likes the sleepy smell of him, and then the citrus smell that replaces it after his morning shower. He likes kissing him goodbye and wishing him a good day. It all just feels so *right*.

Even more so, Ezra likes to be there when Teddy comes home. He doesn't care if he is in a good mood, or a bad mood, or irritable, or horny (especially not horny) or low — he likes every side of Teddy. Ezra wishes he was the kind of boyfriend who could cook — he really can't — but he has a cell phone and more local takeaways on his favourites list than he cares to admit, and he knows all of Teddy's usuals.

In the evenings they watch *Schitts Creek,* or *Gilmore Girls,* or *Game Of Thrones,* and Ezra snuggles up to the love of his life. Because that's what he is. Teddy is *it*. Sometimes, if he's lucky, Teddy plays the guitar. Sometimes he takes requests, and other times he plays acoustic versions of pop's greatest hits. Sometimes he composes and shyly plays bits and pieces for Ezra. Ezra tells him he should release his originals and not just covers. Teddy's music is transcendent. Life-changing. Quintessentially him.

Once the buzz about the email leak dies down, and the public's attention is caught by a celebrity divorce, and Ezra has proven that he can be trusted with his own decision-making again, he is allowed to begin preparations for his birthday. Well, actually, he's allowed to let Grace *tell* him what they're doing for his birthday. Because if Ezra has it his way they would go for dinner at the Palace and drinks at Judy's and then probably wind up at Iris' brownstone singing karaoke that wakes up all the neighbourhood dogs. Which is *fine* for a regular night out, but apparently not for a birthday.

Instead, they are going to New Orleans.

Text Thread: Queer Me Roar

iggy:
are we getting matching tattoos this weekend?

ezra:
absolutely yes

Flynn Rider [eggplant emoji]:

Absolutely no.

> ezra:
> spoil sport

> Ezra:
> how else will we remember our time
> in new orleans?

Flynn Rider [eggplant emoji]:
Photos, I'd imagine.

iggy:
photos AND tattoos?

saving grace:
i'll get a matching tat with you

daria:
Me too!

> ezra:
> will the chaos demons please stop
> corrupting daria?

Flynn Rider [eggplant emoji]:
Daria! What will the twins think?

daria:
That their mother is a... what did
You call it, Iris?

iggy:
a badass bitch?

daria
Yes, that's it! A badass bitch.

>ezra:
fuck me

ezra:
you've broken her

iggy:
honour and privilege

Flynn Rider [eggplant emoji]:
Ezra, control your women.

ezra:
couldn't even if I wanted to

❦

New Orleans is carnage, and Ezra is made for it. He wakes up to a birthday blowjob that has him clinging to the hotel bed's headboard, Teddy grinning up at him from between his shaking thighs as Ezra calls him a slew of names ranging from *angel* to *demon*, and then back to *angel*.

Breakfast is accompanied by morning mimosas, which Grace and Iris insist are a good idea. Daria and Ezra are easily corrupted by the anarchy, but Teddy sticks to orange juice, and therefore is the only one who isn't already tipsy before midday. Ezra has no idea what the girls have planned for him, but he knows it's better to be a little buzzed for it. Grace and Iris have a habit of making birthdays infamous.

Much to Ezra's absolute delight, and Teddy's abject horror, the first activity is airboat racing in a swamp that brags to have more alligator sightings than any other swamp in the area. When Teddy points out that *lots of alligators* isn't exactly a brag, his worries are drowned out by booing, and he sighs and warns them that he'll have no sympathy for anyone who falls overboard and gets eaten.

It's a surprise to everyone when Daria absolutely crushes them all. The bright smile that blossoms across her face when she wins is infectious, and Ezra can't help but notice the way Iris turns into a puddle every time Daria looks at her. Or the way she seems to ascend to a new plane when Daria wraps her arms around Iris in a huge bear hug, kissing her on the cheek. Ezra has never seen Iris come even *close* so shy, but Daria seems to bring out a coyness in her that makes his heart ache happily for his best friend.

After airboat racing, they go on a private, open-top bus tour of the city that takes them right through a parade. It's a pseudo-Mardi Gras put on for the tourists, and the locals probably hate it, and hate them, but it's just, like, *everything*. Carnival music blares from their bus, and the streets are draped in bright colours, and everyone is invited to the party. Their bus joins up with floats, and dancers in showgirl outfits, and Ezra can officially tick *be in a parade* off his bucket list.

He's not sure how, but he has a margarita in both hands, and a dozen beaded necklaces around his neck, and he is standing on a chair, screaming along to *Strong Enough* by Cher, ignoring the fact he absolutely cannot sing. Like, at all. Teddy doesn't seem to mind though, because the look he's giving Ezra is so warm, and open, and loving. And he seems to take a hundred pictures of Ezra having the time of his life. At some point, Iris and Daria start jokingly fighting to straddle his lap and Teddy is laughing the whole time, getting everything on video.

After the parade they have lunch on a steamboat on the Mississippi River, and the food sobers everyone up a little, which, honestly, is good because it's barely the afternoon yet and Ezra doesn't want to be in bed by seven in the evening like he was last year. He gets far more delight than he should do over the sight of Teddy choking slightly on his jambalaya that is spicier than he's expecting. Even though it's making his eyes water, and his brow prickle with sweat, he soldiers on until his bowl is clean, and all Ezra can think is: *I love him, I love him, I really love him.*

There's a birthday cake, because of course there is, and it's three tiers. The top tier is pink, the middle is purple, and the bottom is blue, and Ezra looks at Grace with misty eyes at the not-so-subtle nod to the bisexual flag. Then everyone is singing happy birthday, and the other diners on the boat join in, and suddenly Ezra's cheeks are covered in lipstick marks. Teddy squeezes his knee under the table and promises him a kiss later when they're alone.

Daria is less enthused by their next stop — a tour of the French Quarter's most haunted locations — asking, 'How haunted are we talking?'

Grace shrugs as the horse and carriage stops at Haunt Number one: The Mortuary. 'Probably not demon possession level, but if you're lucky you might get cursed.'

Daria pales to the point where Ezra has to add: 'She's joking.' Or at least he hopes she is.

They pay their entry fee and wait to be assigned a tour guide. Daria stands close enough to Iris that their shoulders brush, and when their guide jumps out at them, she screams and folds into Iris' side, clutching her arm. Iris somehow goes all smug and shy at the same time and Grace grins at her behind Daria's back.

Their tour starts and Daria clings to Iris' arm. Ezra pretends to be scared so he'll have an excuse to hold Teddy's hand. It's a bit like one of the Universal Studios haunted houses where actors jump out at you in the gloom, and various rooms have horror scenes unfolding. By the end of it they're all laughing, and Daria has gone from clutching onto Iris like a life preserver to loosely holding her hand, fingers entwined. No one mentions it.

They have dinner back at the hotel before getting ready to go out. The plan is simple: a bar crawl. Ezra is given an outfit he is expected to wear, which he can only describe as a kind of *sexy jester*, complete with the court-fool hat, bells and all. Teddy is given a much more respectable circus ringleader outfit, a red jacket with tails and a gold trim, a top hat and a cane that gives Ezra filthy ideas.

'Take that home with us,' Ezra says, giving it a firm stroke.

Teddy's eyes darken. 'You're a brat.'

'You love it.'

The girls are dressed as showgirls, with corsets, feathers and frills. They each have sparkly headpieces and dramatic makeup and Ezra and Teddy oblige them in an impromptu photo shoot before they head out. It's a cold night, but alcohol and high spirits warm their bodies. New Orleans by night is basically just New Orleans by day, except on acid, and Ezra is so stupidly happy.

They kind of just spill from one too-loud, too-obnoxious bar into another. Some people recognise them and ask for pictures, but mostly everyone is too intoxicated and enjoying themselves too much to care if a bunch of drunken reality TV stars are partying alongside them. The cocktails come in pitchers and the beer is served in bongs, and Ezra loves watching Teddy's eyes go wide as Iris downs three feet of Desperados in ten seconds, and then horrified when she tries to pass one to him. He sticks to his lager shandy abominations and Ezra loves him so much his heart is going to burst.

Around midnight they wind up in something that is supposed to be an "Irish pub" and Teddy — as the only one of them who has actually *been* to Ireland — points out: 'This place might actually be a little racist.'

Ezra frowns at him over the top of his Lucky Charms cocktail. 'How so?'

Teddy points at a barmaid dressed as a leprechaun. 'Just a hunch.'

Iris nods at a poorly made replica of Dublin's famous Molly Malone statue, but instead of a cart of cockles and mussels, she's wheeling a crate of Guinness. 'It wasn't the bastardisation of Ireland's most beloved fishmonger?'

'That too.'

Grace sighs and takes a sip of her Irish mule. 'Alive, alive, oh.'

Despite the stereotypical décor, they stay because it's open mic night, and the talent ranges from drunken tourists belting out *I Will Survive* to a myriad of incorrect lyrics, to someone in a baseball cap and sunglasses (indoors? At night? Really?) who looks and sounds suspiciously like Harry Styles.

Ezra turns to Teddy to ask if he wants a sip of his *Ass* — a vile, sour apple concoction with a suspicious green hue — to find that he's gone. He blinks and tiptoes up, trying to look over people's heads. He's infuriatingly short, but Teddy is basically Thor, so he shouldn't be too hard to spot. It's not until he feels Grace grab his arm, fingers digging into his bicep, that he sees what she's pointing at. It's Teddy. On stage. Picking up a guitar.

Teddy takes a moment to tune the strings, and Ezra stares, mouth agape. His heart has relocated to his throat. The crowd talks amongst themselves but quietens the moment Teddy approaches the mic. He doesn't even need to say anything. That's just the way he is. He commands attention. In a starless sky, he is a comet. In an eclipse he is the remerging sun.

Teddy clears his throat and smiles sheepishly. 'Um. Hello.'

Iris and Daria are immediately at Ezra's other side, and he's glad because he genuinely needs them to hold him up right now. Because Teddy is about to sing. In public.

'I would like to dedicate this song,' Teddy tells the crowd, but keeps his eyes on Ezra. 'To the love of my life.'

And then his fingers are moving. The first few chords of Dolly Parton's *I Will Always Love You* make Ezra's throat go hot and thick, and then Teddy is singing, and no one takes a goddamn breath, or blinks, or moves, because Teddy is *singing*. And he's amazing. He's everything. And he doesn't break eye contact with Ezra once.

'Oh my God,' Grace whispers. 'Oh my God, Ezra. How are you not crying? *I'm* crying.'

She is. Ezra doesn't need to look at her, he can hear it in her voice. And he doesn't know how he's not crying, because his throat is made of sandpaper, and his eyelashes are glass shards, and his heart is throwing up inside his too-tight chest.

'Oh God, stop it,' Iris says, and she's misty-eyed too.

Iris is crying. And God, so is Daria. And they each hold onto him, cling to him, and they're so happy for him, and they need to stop sobbing because if they don't Ezra is going to start bawling his eyes out.

Teddy gets to the spoken verse, where Dolly is singing about life treating you well and giving you everything you've always wanted. And then he's singing again, his voice beautiful, and sweet, and impossible, promising to Ezra that he will, in fact, always love him.

And then Ezra is crying. Sobbing. Honest to God weeping these big, stupid, happy tears. His girls hold onto him. Iris' head is on his shoulder, Grace has her arms around him, and Daria clings to his hand. Ezra is so in love that he's sure he is going to die from it. It's incredible, and unbearable, and terrifying. Ezra is going to move mountains for Teddy Montgomery. He's going to give him the moon and the stars. He's going to love this impossible man for the rest of his life and then some.

Teddy hits the final note, and his fingers play the last few chords, and then there is silence, and Ezra swears that, for a moment, there's only the two of them left in the bar. Maybe in the whole world. But then there's applause, and Teddy is smiling, a blush creeping up his slender neck, and Ezra is clapping and cheering too, fresh tears spilling over his cheeks.

It kills him that he can't sweep Teddy up in his arms then and there and kiss him and tell him how much he loves him. So, instead he gives him the most platonic embrace he can manage and whispers into his ear, 'You are my new dream.' It's a line from *Tangled*, and it's cheesy as hell, but Teddy gets that goofy smile and Ezra falls in love with him all over again.

Chapter Nineteen

Text Thread: Queer Comes Santa Claus

> ezra:
> are we doing secret santa?

saving grace:
because that worked out so
well last time

Flynn Rider [eggplant emoji]:
What happened last time?

> ezra:
> don't tell him

iggy:
ezzy got himself in the draw and
felt too awkward to say anything so
he ended up without a present.

> ezra:
> IRIS

Flynn Rider [eggplant emoji]:

That is the most adorable and terribly
sad thing I've ever heard.

saving grace:
oh it was tragic. we all opened our
presents and then we realised he
didn't have anything, and he tried
to be all like "it's fine" but then he
went to the bathroom and cried for
half an hour.

>ezra:
>I WASN'T CRYING ABOUT THAT

>ezra:
>I WAS CRYING BECAUSE IRIS
>MADE US WATCH IT'S A
>WONDERFUL LIFE

>ezra:
>AND I'D HAD A LOT OF EGGNOG

iggy:
yeah, that's MUCH better

Flynn Rider [eggplant emoji]:
That is precious.

>ezra:
>this is bullying

daria:
Ezra, would you feel better if I told you an
embarrassing story about Teddy last

Christmas?

Flynn Rider [eggplant emoji]:
Hang about.

ezra:
absolutely yes

Flynn Rider [eggplant emoji]:
Daria, don't you dare.

daria:
Long story short, he had his annual
Christmas sherry, it went to his head,
and he tried to flirt with the actor we hired
to play Santa for the twins.

ezra:
OH

ezra:
MY

ezra:
GOD

Flynn Rider [eggplant emoji]:
Lies. Slander and lies.

saving grace:
is that what does it for you? should
ezra get fat and grow a beard?

iggy:
did you sit on his lap?

Flynn Rider [eggplant emoji]:
I'm my defence, he was a very young, very attractive Santa.

ezra:
i can't believe my boyfriend
has a santa fetish

Flynn Rider [eggplant emoji]:
Don't kink shame me.

ezra:
don't worry sweetheart, i'll jingle
your bells this christmas

Flynn Rider [eggplant emoji]:
JESUS CHRIST!!

Teddy, Daria, and the twins are spending Christmas with the Darlings. Ezra knows he should have prepared himself for the sight of Teddy and the kids wearing matching light-up Christmas sweaters, but he still goes all soupy the moment they come through the front door of their vacation home.

Ever since they were kids, the Darlings have spent Christmas back in Wyoming. The vacation house is vast, and ancient, a converted boarding house from the 1800s. During the other eleven months a year, they rent it out, and let friends and family stay there for free, but in December it's home.

It is, of course, festooned with (totally extra) decorations. Each room has a real pine tree and a colour theme, and some kind of stylistic motif that Grace insists is both festive *and* tasteful. And everything always feels more jolly in Wyoming because, well, snow. And deer, and elk, and the occasional moose.

Iris and her moms join them every year. Considering Rosa Smith isn't Iris's biological mom, she is where Iris seems to get all of her demonic energy from. Rosa is a bundle of unfettered anarchy, usually bundled into skinny jeans, band T's and biker boots, whereas her biological mom, Elena Sanchez — who Iris calls *madre* — is all business, all the time.

Ezra wants to pull Teddy into his arms and kiss him, and ruffle the snowflakes from his hair, but the twins are there and can't keep a secret on account of the fact they're six years old, so he settles for a hug and a promise of kisses later on. Margot tugs on Ezra's hand and beckons for him to come closer. He crouches down so that she can whisper in his ear to ask: *will Santa know how to find us here?* and for the first time in Ezra's life, he gets all broody.

They order dinner from the local Chinese takeaway, and — despite being in their twenties — the millennials are all seated at the "kids table" with the twins, but no one really minds. Ezra keeps Margot and Mason occupied with silly stories, and voices, and jokes, and he gets as excited for Santa's visit as they do. At one point he looks up to see Teddy looking over at him with so much love that he can hardly bear it.

They watch a Christmas movie with the kids. It's not particularly good, but it's corny and it puts everyone in a happy mood. The twins get more and more restless the closer it gets to their bedtime. Teddy offers to put them to bed, and Ezra can't help but sneak away to stand in the doorway and watch as Teddy tucks them in and makes up a story on the spot called: *How Margot And Mason Helped Santa Save Christmas*. It comes with voices, and re-enactments, and even a little dance.

Once the kids are sleeping, the mulled wine and eggnog comes out. Teddy settles at the grand piano — because *of course* he can play the piano — and he plays Christmas hits, singing along while Daria harmonises.

'Can you do Jingle Bell Rock?' Iris asks from where she languishes on the sofa, legs draped over Grace's lap, all eggnog-y and happy.

'No!' Ezra shouts. 'Teddy, say no.'

'Oooh, yes!' Grace says, face lighting up. 'Teddy, can you?'

Teddy frowns from behind the grand piano. 'What's the deal with Jingle Bell Rock?'

'They'll re-enact the entire scene from *Mean Girls*,' Ezra says. 'They do it every year. It's never as funny or as charming as they think it is.'

'Well, now you have to do it,' Daria says, grinning.

Iris points at Daria, a smile overtaking her imbibed face. 'I like her. She's smart *and* pretty.'

'Don't do it, Teddy,' Ezra warns. 'The therapy isn't worth it.'

Teddy looks at Ezra for a long moment, then at Iris. 'What key?'

The girls launch themselves off the couch and Ezra groans, flopping back onto the cushions. They have a whispered discussion with Teddy and Daria before Grace goes in search of impromptu microphones. She finds a hairbrush for herself and a TV remote for Iris.

Teddy counts them in, and the show starts, and Teddy can hardly keep playing from laughing so hard. He doesn't even need to look at what he's doing as his hands fly effortlessly over the keys. Iris tries to climb onto the piano for a big finish, but Daria loops her arms around the little gremlin's waist and keeps her safely on the floor.

Teddy gives them a standing ovation when they bow, and Ezra boos.

'That was wonderful,' Teddy says, giving them both a peck on the cheek. 'I felt like I was at the Palladium panto.'

Ezra arches an eyebrow. 'The what?'

Teddy pats his knee as he sits beside him. 'My little philistine.'

It starts to get chilly as the wind changes direction, working its way through all the cracks and crevices in the old house's walls, and Warren lights a fire. Then he gets out the old record player and his collection of ancient vinyls, and now that Teddy doesn't have to provide the entertainment, he is free to dance with Ezra. Rosemary Clooney sings *Silver Bells*, and Teddy tries to teach Ezra how to waltz, and Ezra steps on his toes and trips over his own feet, and Teddy kisses him chastely in front of their friends and family, his cheeks and nose pinking up.

The Darlings go to bed first, and then the Sanchez-Smiths, and the "kids" are left to drink, and talk, and exchange secret Santa gifts. Teddy looks (adorably) horrified at the thought of opening a present before Christmas day, and Ezra assures him that he can wait until the morning to open the rest. They'd agreed on a spending limit of five dollars, because that was the way it had been ever since they were kids and five whole dollars had seemed like a lot of money. Plus, it's tradition. A tradition that Ezra is getting to share with Teddy.

'Oh my,' Teddy says as he unwraps a pair of plastic candy-cane striped handcuffs from Ezra. Then once more, with feeling, when Ezra looks at him with wide *come hither* eyes. 'Oh *my*.'

Grace makes a vomiting sound from behind her fake beard — a gift from Teddy — and wrinkles her nose. 'Nope. No. Not listening to my brother and my fiancé make sexy talk to each other. Nuh-uh.'

'What a weird sentence,' Iris mumbles as she pulls on her new T-shirt that says "Raised by lesbians and witches" over her head. 'Straight people are wild. Is this on backwards?'

'Yes, you drunken fool,' Grace says, helping her put it back on the right way. 'Ezra's right, I should have just gotten you a cardboard box.'

'Okay my turn,' Iris says, pulling an envelope out of her jeans pocket. She's doodled Christmas elves and reindeer all over the four-by-five surface, and in the middle, in swirly calligraphy, is *Daria*. 'Pour vous.'

Daria takes the envelope with a shy smile. She opens it and pulls out a two-for-one coupon for IHOP. She blinks in confusion. 'The International House Of Pancakes?'

'Will you go on a date with me?' Iris asks, almost immediately sobering.

Grace's hand goes to her mouth. Daria's cheeks turn rosy. Ezra looks at his best friend with wide eyes. There is *no way* Iris just did something that cheesy and romantic. But... she did.

Daria nods. 'Yes. Of course, I will.'

Iris' smile goes all gooey and melty. 'Cool.'

Daria laughs. 'Cool'

When Daria gives Ezra his present, he can't help but feel like everyone is watching him. Because they are. That's the moment he realises this isn't a secret Santa at all, and that they all know what he's got. He has to swallow around the lump in his throat when he unwraps an ugly Christmas sweater matching the ones Teddy and the twins were wearing earlier.

'Welcome to the family,' Daria says, and she gets all tearful as she wraps him in a hug.

And because Ezra is going to get all tearful too, and that is just *not* allowed on Christmas Eve, he suggests they start getting the presents out. So, they get to work unloading the presents from the cars and set them up artfully around the tree in the family room. The twins each have a small mountain waiting for them and bulging stockings to match. Teddy, thankfully, remembers to take a bite out of the mince pie (ew) and a gulp of the milk that's left out on the fireplace for Santa.

Around eleven, Teddy pulls Ezra up to their bedroom. It's not the bedroom Ezra would *usually* stay in, but it's the first time he's ever brought someone home for Christmas, and he wants a room as far away from his family members as possible, and that means sleeping in the other wing where no one can hear them.

Teddy tastes of mulled wine, and sweetness, and promises of filthy things. He guides Ezra back to the bed with a firmness that makes his knees go weak. With Teddy, Ezra never fully knows what to expect. Sometimes he is coy and coquettish, and he wants to be undone slowly and sweetly, and other times he wants to be pinned down and taken hard and fast. Sometimes he is tender, and sure, and he makes love to Ezra like they're in a romance novel. And then there's times like this, when Teddy wants to take Ezra apart piece by piece, and worship him, and make him tremble.

Teddy's movements are confident and mischievous. His smile promises terrible, awful, *amazing* things. His kisses are soft, and hard, and chaste, and bruising all at the same time. Ezra's entire body aches as Teddy takes his time undressing him. Every time he tries to reach for Teddy, to touch or tug his clothes off, Teddy playfully slaps his hands away.

Teddy stretches Ezra out on the duvet and stands at the end of the bed to undress. Ezra can't take his eyes off him. His movements are languid and slow, and he keeps his eyes locked with Ezra's as he lets his shirt fall to the floor, and then his jeans. He stands there in his reindeer boxers (ugh, this absolute *dork*) and Ezra can see the rigid shape of him.

'I want to see you,' Ezra says, voice soft. 'All of you.'

Teddy smiles and slips off his underwear and Ezra barely has time to admire the view before Teddy is climbing over him, stretching his arms up over his head and pinning them there. Their hips brush and Ezra gasps and bucks up, and Teddy claims his mouth in a searing kiss. He kisses Ezra until he is writhing and whimpering beneath him. Ezra knows the noises he's making aren't particularly dignified, but he is too hard, and too horny to care.

'Please,' he whispers, not really knowing what it is he's begging for. '*Please.*'

Teddy smiles against his lips. He seems to know exactly what Ezra is begging for. He brings a hand (*Jesus*, those hands) to Ezra's mouth and commands, 'spit,' and Ezra has no idea how he doesn't come on the spot. He feels weirdly exposed as he spits into Teddy's palm, but immediately stops caring the moment Teddy's hand wraps around him. Because wow. *Wow.*

Teddy's other hand goes to Ezra's mouth and Ezra parts his lips, sucking two fingers inside. Ezra's eyelids flutter closed as those fingers find their way to the most intimate part of him, and his body arches up off the mattress as Teddy teases him open. And it's amazing. Because it's always amazing with Teddy. Ezra's body is so ready for him. He's gasping, and trembling, and it's still not enough. He begs for Teddy to fuck him, and Teddy holds off for as long as he can, enjoying every moment and every noise he coaxes from Ezra's lips.

'Please,' Ezra whispers. 'Please. *Sweetheart.*'

Teddy gives him a look along the lines of *that's not playing fair*, but it works because Teddy is withdrawing and settling himself between Ezra's legs. Ezra cries out when Teddy enters him, and Teddy swallows his moans with open-mouthed kisses. Ezra wraps his legs around Teddy's waist, his hands clutching desperately at his broad shoulders, knowing he's probably leaving marks but not caring.

Every roll of Teddy's hips takes him higher, until he's dangling on the precipice. His erection is trapped between their bodies getting all the friction it needs. His thighs quiver and his spine crackles with electricity, letting him know that he's close. So damn close.

Ezra risks opening his eyes, and the sight of Teddy lost in pleasure unravels him. He turns his head and cries out into the pillow, eyes screwed shut, hands reaching up and clinging to the headboard. Ezra feels Teddy shudder, hears him barely stifle a moan, and catches him as his arms shake and give out.

For a while they lie there, brains short-circuited. Ezra isn't entirely convinced that he's not levitating. He tries to pull Teddy into a hug, but his arms are spaghetti noodles and he ends up just flailing them in Teddy's general direction. When Teddy's breathing returns to somewhat normal, he pushes himself up onto his elbows and looks down at Ezra, smiling. Ezra gives him a blissed-out grin right back. Teddy glances over to the bedside table and laughs, and Ezra follows his gaze to the alarm clock that blinks 12:01 AM.

Teddy bows his head, kisses Ezra softly, and says, 'Merry Christmas, darling.'

Ezra kisses him back. 'Merry Christmas, sweetheart.'

Chapter Twenty

When the twins burst into their room before seven in the morning, Ezra is forced to yank the duvet over Teddy who is nestled happily between his thighs, and smiles like he isn't in the middle of getting a blowjob.

'Santa's been!' Margot squeals. 'Have you seen Uncle Teddy?'

Ezra can't speak, so he shakes his head. They lose interest immediately and run from the room. Teddy's head pops up from under the covers and he grins up at Ezra. Ezra reaches down and ruffles his hair, and Teddy's smile just widens until he looks like a kid on, well, Christmas morning. 'We probably should have anticipated that.'

Ezra grins. 'I'm amazed they waited this long. When Grace and I were kids, we'd be waking mom and dad up before sunrise.'

'You sound like a horribly incorrigible child.'

'Yes,' Ezra ruffles his hair again. 'But cute too.'

Teddy waggles his eyebrows playfully at Ezra before drawing the duvet over his head and finishing him off, making Ezra's toes curl. When they leave their room and trundle downstairs, blissful and still in their pyjamas, it seems they are the last to get up. Grace and Iris give them both the widest, most shit-eating grins possible.

'Enjoy your wake up call, did you?' Iris asks.

Ezra checks the kids aren't looking before giving her the finger.

'I'm so sorry,' Daria says. 'I tried to distract them with waffles.'

Teddy kisses her head. 'We were practically finished.'

Warren slaves away in the kitchen making his annual breakfast scramble, and the smell of fresh eggs, sausage and bacon almost has Ezra floating to the dining table. The twins are restless while the adults enjoy a leisurely start to the day. There is coffee, and orange juice, and something that Iris is calling *the morning martini* that promises regret and shame, and Ezra, of course, takes one.

The twins practically rip their faces off when Daria tells them they can make a start on the presents. And then everything is carnage for the next couple of hours. Wrapping paper is shredded and strewn across the living room, and Daria scurries around collecting it up and apologising, and everyone tells Daria to sit down and stop apologising, but she doesn't.

The twins barely have a chance to enjoy one present before they're unwrapping the next. The adults have significantly less things to open, so they enjoy watching the kids devour their present piles, and occasionally pass each other a gift to unwrap. The gifts are small and silly, because, like, what do you buy a bunch of rich people who can buy themselves literally anything? So, the gifts are either pranks or more thoughtful things like framed photos, favourite snacks, or — in Teddy's case— a personalised blanket of photos of Teddy with Daria and the twins. Ezra knows he's done a good job by the way Teddy's jaw tightens, and he kisses him while the kids aren't looking.

'I did good?' Ezra asks, quietly.

'A-plus,' Teddy replies, eyes shiny.

Once the present-opening ceremony is over, Margot and Mason promptly fall asleep — a side effect of being awake since 4am — and Daria and Teddy carry them back to bed. There are a few hours where everyone is still too tired and too dazed — and some a little too tipsy — to get on with the rest of the day. So, there is a lull, where they chat and doze, and put Christmas movies on the TV for background noise. And by the time the twins wake up again at midday, everyone is ready to carry on.

Warren sets about making the Christmas dinner, which is a grand affair of roast turkey, roast vegetables, stuffing, cold cuts, potatoes and gravy. Daria and Teddy have brought along something they're calling a *traditional British dessert*, that looks like brown sludge with a leaf stuck on top.

Ezra eyes the brown lump with suspicion. 'What is it?'

'Figgy pudding,' Teddy says, setting it in the middle of the table. 'It tastes better than it looks.'

'It would need to.'

Grace peers at it while Iris pokes it with her dessert spoon. 'I don't know if it's a British thing, or a white person thing...'

'It looks sentient,' Iris says. 'Like it knows what I'm thinking.'

'You haven't even heard the best part,' Daria says, putting a bottle of brown spirit down next to the sludge ball. 'First, we douse it in brandy and then set it on fire.'

Grace blinks at her. 'So, it's a British *and* white thing?'

No one says anything while Daria soaks the miserable lump in alcohol and sets it alight. It blazes for a few moments, the smell of burning brady stinging Ezra's nostrils, before flickering out. It looks no happier for being burnt alive. Nevertheless, he takes a helping when Daria hands it to him and allows Teddy to drown it in custard.

He doesn't expect to love it when he takes his first bite. He also doesn't expect to ask for seconds, but he does and practically licks his bowl clean after. There's no use even trying to deny that it was good, although Teddy's smug face makes him want to try.

Teddy grins at him. 'I've never been prouder.'

'I feel like I've eaten a baby,' Ezra says, patting his full stomach.

In the evening, while the kids are busy playing with their new toys and gadgets, the adults get out the board games. Which is where Ezra discovers that Teddy is *beyond* ruthless when it comes to mildly competitive family games. He absolutely slaughters everyone at Monopoly, ending the game after less than an hour and owning over half the board. He then goes on to absolutely destroy everyone at Clue, Ludo, and a *Disney* edition of Trivial Pursuit. For some reason it makes Ezra kind of horny.

When the kids pass out in their beds, and the "adults" settle in the other living room, Iris loudly announces: 'Okay! Drinking time! Time for drinks!'

Teddy frowns. 'Haven't we been surreptitiously drinking all day?'

Iris tilts her head. 'Surreptitiously?'

'Let's put on some music,' Grace says, already hooking her phone up to the sound system. She looks at Daria. 'Will it wake the kids?'

Daria snorts. 'They'll sleep through a tornado. Crank it up.'

Grace selects a playlist called *Pure Xmas Cheese* and hits play. The girls dance together and spin each other around like teenagers at prom. Ezra is content to snuggle next to Teddy on the sofa and watch them, Teddy's arm draped across his shoulders. He watches them, fully aware that there is no shortage of incredible women in his life.

'What are you thinking?' Teddy asks, his lips brushing the shell of Ezra's ear.

Ezra looks up into those big blue eyes and says, 'Happy things.'

'I'm glad to hear it.'

Ezra glances at the window where he can see the snow beginning to fall, then back to Teddy. 'Want to go for a walk?'

Teddy smiles. 'What about the moose?'

'I'll protect you from the moose, sweetheart.'

Teddy kisses him. 'Alright then.'

They bundle up and brace the cold evening. Ezra can't take his eyes off Teddy as he walks with his head tipped back to the night sky, marvelling at the sheer number of stars. You don't get a clear sky like this in New York or London. Ezra can't help but admire his profile in the starlight, all bathed in silver. When Ezra tiptoes up to kiss him, he's rewarded with one of those secret smiles that still, after all this time, make his stomach somersault.

'What was that for?' Teddy asks, cheeks rosy from the cold.

'I just really like you,' Ezra says, and that makes Teddy laugh.

They walk the trails behind the house and Ezra admires the way snowflakes get stuck in Teddy's long eyelashes. When his pink tongue darts out to swipe one from his lips, Ezra thinks he might melt. He tiptoes up to kiss him again, when Teddy stiffens, looking at something over Ezra's head.

Ezra turns and sees the doe and her fawn watching them, less than twenty yards away, and his hand actually presses to his heart. The deer study them for a long moment, before the doe leads her baby away, back into the brush. 'Wow,' Teddy murmurs quietly. 'Never seen that before.'

'Not since I was a kid,' Ezra says. 'Wow.'

Teddy turns Ezra in his arms and looks down at him with a soft expression. 'I want to see all the beautiful things with you.'

Ezra kisses him then, and keeps kissing him until his hands are cold and his chest is warm. When neither of them can feel their toes anymore, they head back to the house. Only Iris and Daria are still up and looking far too cosy in front of the fire to need any company, so they head up to bed. They pass Grace on the landing who is already in her pyjamas, makeup off, hair up in a lopsided bun.

'I found something for you in the mailbox,' she says. 'Looks like it had been there a few days. Probably from *her*. I left it in your room.'

Ezra blinks. 'Oh. Oh, yeah. Shit, I guess I'd forgotten.'

'Might as well get it over with.'

'Yeah, I guess.'

Grace gives them both a kiss goodnight on the cheek before ducking through her bedroom door. Teddy gives him a bemused look but has the manners (of course he does) not to ask about it until Ezra offers the information willingly. Ezra has no idea how Teddy does that. Just gives him space. Trusts Ezra to talk when he's ready. Because if it were the other way round, and Teddy was getting mysterious letters in the mail and Daria was cryptically passing them on, Ezra would be ripping his eyelids off with curiosity. But that's Teddy Montgomery. He is just so damn *good*.

Ezra spots the envelope on his bedside table and freezes. He can feel Teddy watching him carefully, so he tries to keep his hands steady as he reaches for the letter and tears it open. He gives himself a papercut as he pulls the card from the envelope. Teddy joins him at his elbow as he looks down at the four-by-four sheet of folded red paper with gold glittery letters saying *Happy Holidays!*

Ignoring the blood beading on his index finger, Ezra opens the card and reads the perfunctory message in the familiar scrawl. Most of the writing has been done for her by the greeting card company. All she had to do, essentially, was the hello and goodbye, and it still looks like it was too much effort, her handwriting messy and rushed.

dear Ez,

HAPPY HOLIDAYS!

love mom

Ezra stares down at the card and swallows hard. He doesn't realise his hands are shaking until Teddy's fingers close over them. He lets the card fall from his grip, not watching as it flutters to the ground. He realises, with some horror, that his eyes are burning.

'Darling,' Teddy says softly. 'Are you alright?'

'My mom,' Ezra says, focusing on Teddy's hands holding his. 'It's from my mom.'

Teddy frowns. 'From Jacqueline?'

'No. My, uh, biological mom.'

'Oh,' Teddy says. Then, 'Oh, love.'

'I'm okay,' Ezra insists, even though he isn't. 'She sends one every year. I should have been expecting it. I was just — I was having such a nice time with you. I'd forgotten about it.'

Teddy takes Ezra's chin in one hand and gently but firmly pulls his face up to look at him. 'Do you want to talk about it?'

'I don't know.'

'That's okay.'

And then Ezra kind of, just, explodes. 'I don't know why she bothers. She sends me one every year, and she never even writes a proper message. And the only reason she sends me a Christmas card and not a birthday card is because she doesn't actually know when my birthday is. It's probably just to make herself feel better because she feels bad for giving me up, but I don't exist to make her feel less shit about herself, you know?'

Teddy's thumb brushes soothingly over Ezra's cheek. '*Darling*. I'm sorry.'

'I haven't actually seen her or spoken to her on the phone since I first got famous, and she arranged to meet up to ask for money. Which I gave her because I'm an idiot. But when I realised that was all she cared about I stopped bailing her out and she stopped wanting to meet up. That's when I started to get the cards. And she still calls herself my *mom*. Like, how fucking dare she? She lost that privilege the moment she left me on the neighbour's *doorstep*.'

Teddy collects Ezra into his arms and holds him, his lips pressing gently to his temple. 'She's a fool. But her loss is the gain of so many others, including my own. I can't say that I'm not grateful for the path that led you to me, but I wish it didn't hurt you like this.'

Ezra turns his head into the crook of Teddy's neck. 'You should be a writer.'

'*You* should be a swimsuit model.'

Ezra peeks up at Teddy to find him smiling. 'Are you trying to cheer me up with flattery?'

'Is it working?'

'Only slightly.'

Secret smile. 'How about leftovers and snuggles in bed? And a movie?'

Ezra's head tips back and he makes a ridiculously happy little noise. 'Stop it, you'll make me come.'

Teddy laughs and gently shoves Ezra back onto the bed. Before he can sit up, Teddy leans over him and kisses him, saying, 'When I want you to come, you'll know it.' He kisses him again before disappearing, re-emerging fifteen minutes later with turkey sandwiches, cold cuts, cheese, an array of Christmas chocolates, and a bottle of red wine on a tray.

They change into their pyjamas. Ezra just wears plaid lounge pants and a baggy t-shirt, and Teddy, of course, has *Lord Of the Rings* PJs with matching slippers. Because he is a giant nerd. They curl up under the covers with the tray perched across their laps, and Teddy pours them each a glass of wine. They flick through the streaming apps for a while before Teddy settles on *The Rocky Horror Picture Show*. Ezra gives him an incredulous look as Teddy puts an arm around his shoulders, drawing him tightly into his side.

'What?' Teddy asks. 'Why are you trying to inhale the room?'

'*You* like *The Rocky Horror Show*?' Ezra asks. '*You*? As in *Theodore Montgomery*?'

'Yes, love. Why is this news to you?'

'But...' Ezra blinks. 'But it's so camp.'

A smile quirks the corners of Teddy's mouth. 'Yes. And I am *very* gay.'

'But it's *so* camp. And you're not camp. Like. At all.'

Teddy peers down at him, grinning. 'This has really blown your little brain, hasn't it? I wonder what will happen when I tell you that I go and see the show live every time they tour?'

Ezra's eyes go comically wide. 'You do not.'

'I even dress up.'

'No, you do not!'

Teddy laughs. 'No, I don't. I can't pull off the suspenders. I do join in for the Time Warp though.' He trails a finger up and down Ezra's arm. '*You*, however, would look amazing in a corset and little panties.'

Ezra grins. 'Probably.'

They kiss and Ezra is more than happy to focus on the movie and enjoy his snacks and the warmth of being tucked into Teddy's side. Or at least, he thinks so. Like, he probably is. So, he's not sure if it's the red wine or the scene of Tim Curry tearfully singing *I'm Going Home*, but he starts talking again.

'Who leaves a baby on a doorstep?' Ezra asks, tightly. 'I could have died. Or. I don't know. Been carried away by an eagle.'

Teddy looks down at him. 'I'm not familiar with the area, but are eagles known for carrying off infants?'

'There's a first time for everything.'

Teddy pauses the movie and puts his wine glass down on the bedside table. 'Do you want to talk about it?'

Ezra looks at him. 'Do you?'

'I do if you do.'

Ezra sighs and drags a hand over his face. 'I don't know what to say. I should be grateful. I was adopted by the most amazing family I could have ever asked for. Renee was an alcoholic. She probably still is. As far as I know, she still lives in the same house she gave birth to me in, she still works at the same gas station, she still dates the same abusive scumbags. And I get — well,' Ezra gestures at the room around him, 'all this. And you. So, it shouldn't even matter, because my life is infinitely better than it ever would have been.'

Teddy's hand trails idly through Ezra's hair. 'Just because you have a better life than some doesn't mean you're not allowed to feel sad sometimes. And saying you can't be sad because others have it worse is the same logic as saying you can't be happy because others have it better.'

'I know. I just — ugh. I don't know.'

'Tell me about Warren and Jacqueline,' he says, in a transparent attempt to get Ezra talking about things that make him happy. 'How old were you when they adopted you?'

'Three. I'd been in a few foster homes, but I don't really remember them. They'd just had Grace, but it had been a difficult birth and mom had needed a C-section. They weren't able to conceive again after that. They thought they'd be on a waiting list for years but then they heard about a baby left on a doorstep in Orlando three years prior with just a blanket and a note saying my name was Ezra. Like a little Caucasian angel.'

'Does it bother you?' Teddy asks.

Ezra cracks a smile. 'That I'm a cis white male and inherently privileged thereof? I've come to live with it.'

Teddy laughs. 'I mean that it's obvious you're adopted.'

Ezra shrugs. 'Not really. Some people are jerks about it, but that's aimed at my family more than me. When the Darling Dynasty took off, people were saying that the only way a black family had become so famous in America was because they had a white guy up front. Which is dumb, because Grace is literally the only reason we're famous.'

'People are *very* stupid sometimes.'

'I can't wait until the BingeBox contract is over and she can just move on and shine on her own. I hate getting in her spotlight all the time.'

Teddy kisses his forehead. 'Darling, you were thrust into this life. Everything you've done has been to help her. The way that people see you isn't your fault.'

'Still, I want out. I want her to have her moment. She deserves it.'

They're quiet for a stretch. Then Teddy says, 'Leo and I used to wish our parents weren't famous when we were kids.'

Ezra looks at him. 'Yeah?'

'Mm-hm. The other kids at our private school would say things like "Wow, it must be great having famous parents," and we'd agree with them. But we didn't know what it was like to have famous parents because they were never there. It was always the butler, or the nanny, or the housekeeper. And no matter how much we tried to grow up away from the limelight, it just always found us. The press wanted us to be scandalous wild children who did drugs and went to raves. We just wanted to be left alone. So, I understand. I can't imagine what that would be like with the added stress of a constant camera crew though.'

Ezra nuzzles his face into Teddy's neck and inhales the sweet scent of him. It's fresh, and earthy, his cologne slightly spicy. It's so completely *Teddy*. It's home. 'Maybe we should run away together. I hear Peru is nice.'

Teddy's laugh is light and soft. 'I'll follow you anywhere.'

'Anywhere?'

'*Anywhere.*'

They settle down again and Teddy retrieves his wine glass before hitting play. They watch in snuggly silence as they finish the movie. Then, because Ezra has never seen the show live, they find an official recording of one of last year's tour dates on YouTube, and they watch that too. Teddy sings along and shouts out all the right ad-libs at the right times with the rest of the audience, and Ezra laughs at him. Because it's ludicrous — just ludicrous — that he has Teddy Montgomery in his childhood home, watching *The Rocky Horror Show*, and heckling the TV screen. But here he is. And here they are. And Ezra is so unreasonably happy about it.

New Year's Eve is spent back in NYC. Ezra would have happily stayed in Wyoming with Teddy, languishing in bed, having sex, eating turkey sandwiches, getting fat and lucky, for the rest of his life. But the Darlings have been invited to a party hosted by one of the Kardashians and to turn it down is, according to Ali, social suicide of astronomic proportions.

Ezra and Iris ride together in one of the Darling cars because they're supposed to be each other's dates for the evening. They are wearing coordinating navy blue — Ezra in a suit, no tie, top three buttons open, and Iris in a matching, backless cocktail dress. There is no arguing that they look good together, but the reality that neither of them can go with who they *really* want to be with sits between them, tense and heavy.

So, they drink. Iris pulls two hip flasks out of her purse and hands one to Ezra, and they take long, solemn sips as New York City glitters around them. Ezra grimaces every time the whiskey hits his tongue, but it's better than arriving sober, so he gets over it. Iris, however, knocks it back like she's a struggling writer and recovering alcoholic, charged with minding a haunted hotel for the winter.

By the time they make it into the actual venue — after the red carpet, the press, and posing for photos — they each have a telling glaze to their expressions. Iris pockets the flasks, and they head to the bar, not bothering to make the rounds. Which is a shame really, because it's an incredible party. There is a theme that Ezra can't quite put his finger on, but everything is blue and silver, and frosty.

They each order one of the custom cocktails. Ezra's is called *Frosted Tips* and it's pure sugar, and Iris has something with a sparkler in it called a *Winter Warmer*. The face she pulls when she takes a sip doesn't inspire confidence and Ezra resolves to stick to his liquid diabetes for the evening.

Warren and Jacqueline are already there and mingling, carefully avoiding David and Anastasya who are making the rounds. When Daria arrives on the arm of Nick, Iris' hand tightens around her glass, her knuckles turning so white that Ezra takes her drink from her. *He* knows that *she* knows it's just for show. That there's nothing between Daria and Teddy's best friend. But he also knows that hearing it won't make it any better. He proves himself right by slumping in his barstool when Teddy and Grace arrive.

They look perfect. Because of course they do. They're like a *Dior* commercial brought to life. Grace is wearing a beautiful powder-blue floor-length gown. Her hair is loosely pinned back, and her makeup is minimal but impactful. And then there's Teddy: matching powder-blue shirt and pocket square, paired with a slate-grey suit and tie. His sandy hair is tamed, his jaw smooth, his smile strained.

They lock eyes for a moment and Ezra mouths *sweetheart* and that, at least, gets a real smile. Then Grace is pulling him away to talk to a beauty influencer by the champagne fountain, and Ezra watches him deflate. His heart twists painfully, and he nearly crumples in his seat.

'I don't know how you do it, Ezzy,' Iris says, still watching Daria across the room. 'It's only been a week and I already feel like I'm dying.'

Ezra reaches out and takes her hand. 'I want to tell you it gets easier, but…'

'It doesn't?'

'Not really, no.'

'Well, fuck.'

Ezra glances at Teddy who is shaking hands with the daughter of a political figure, making polite conversation. 'When do you think you'll go public?'

Iris sighs. 'Not until after you do.'

His brow furrows. 'Why so long?'

'We're not going to rub it in yours and Teddy's faces that we can be together and you can't.'

He blanches. 'What? No. Iris, that could be three years.'

'Well, let's hope it isn't.'

'Iris, you *can't*.'

She fixes him with a resolute look that says *don't argue*, then says, 'Don't argue.'

'But—'

She puts a hand over his mouth. 'Shut up. Let's get drunk.'

Ezra licks her hand, and she recoils. 'It's a long way till midnight.'

Iris tips her drink to his. 'Exactly.'

It's kind of become an unwritten rule between them now that they all try to keep their distance. Apart from the fact that Ali will castrate them if they don't behave and mingle with other guests as specified in their Damage Control Strategy — also nicknamed *Fixing Ezra's Fuckup* — under section three, paragraph B: *Ezra, Teddy, and peers will strive to be sociable and approachable at all functions and events, and not live in each other's laps.*

It's a simple enough rule, but harder to follow than any of them had anticipated. And with only a month until the wedding, time with Teddy is precious. Even more so than usual. Ezra knows his mom and dad are doing everything they can with Mara to find a loophole in the BingeBox contract, but their time together is literally being counted down. So yeah, he takes up Iris' offer and drinks. A lot. And why not? He's the Wyoming Wild Child, after all.

The cocktails go down far too easily. It's hard to keep count. Ezra and Iris are a horrible influence on each other. They ignore the fact they are both hurting, and focus on laughing too loudly, dancing too obnoxiously, flirting with each other too brazenly — also part of their strategy. Section seven, paragraph E: *Ezra and Iris will exhibit obvious but tasteful public displays of affection whilst in the public eye.* And while there is no kissing, there is touching, holding, embracing. And dancing. Lots of dancing. And Ali doesn't look *completely* horrified by their behaviour, so, like, *yay*?

The DJ gives them a warning at ten minutes before midnight, and then a five-minute warning. Grace starts to fret and collects them all together, so everyone is standing around awkwardly for a while waiting for the countdown to start. Ezra tries to slip away to the bar, but Grace catches his arm and hauls him back, squeezing him between Iris and Teddy. Which is playing dirty, really, because once Ezra is in the general vicinity of Teddy, it's very hard for him to rectify that. Especially when Teddy is looking down at him like that. Because he is. Ezra risks a peep up at him and immediately blushes.

'You look amazing tonight,' Teddy says quietly. 'I wish I could have told you earlier.'

Ezra smiles. 'Are you trying to butter me up?'

'Always.'

A waiter comes around with a tray of champagne and they each help themselves to a flute. Iris slings an arm around Ezra's shoulders and Grace loops arms with Daria. They all huddle together as the DJ announces the thirty-second mark and Ezra takes a deep breath as the familiar anxiety of starting a new year bubbles up in his chest. The pressure to make it a good one. The pressure to make it count. The thought of Teddy's wedding in just over a month's time.

Ten seconds. Five. Four. Three. Two. One. And then everything just kind of explodes. People are cheering. Confetti cannons throw up over their heads. In the distance there are fireworks. The girls are hugging, throwing their arms around each other. Ezra's parents share a chaste kiss. Nick picks up Daria like she weighs nothing (she probably doesn't, to be honest). *Auld Lang Syne* plays and people pretend they know the lyrics. And Ezra just looks up at Teddy. And Teddy smiles down at him. And all the chaos and celebrations happen around them, almost in slow motion. Almost on mute.

'Happy new year, love,' Teddy says, warmly.

'Happy new year, sweetheart.'

Then Ezra tiptoes up and kisses him, and ruins everything.

Chapter Twenty-One

Ezra doesn't realise what he's done until the moment their lips touch. Then he is free falling, panic rising up and crashing down on him. Even through his closed eyes he can see the flash of camera lights. Over the ripple of shock, he can hear the shutters clicking. When he pulls away, all he can see is Teddy's face, pale and stricken. Behind him, Grace's eyes have gone wide. Teddy touches his fingers to his lips, his hand trembling. Ezra is going to be sick.

And then someone is grabbing his arm. Dragging him back. Cameras flash in his face. The room is a sea of phones, recording the single greatest fuck-up of his life. Amongst it all he can see Teddy, standing motionless as people crowd him, shoving their phones in his face. Ezra can just make out the terror in his eyes before Daria is hauling him away. And then he's gone. And Ezra is being shoved through a fire exit door.

The cold air takes him by surprise. He turns to see Ali, face tight with fury, fingers flying over her phone screen. Ezra opens his mouth to speak, not sure what he is going to say, and Ali holds up a finger to silence him. He closes his mouth again, and a few seconds later their car pulls up. Ali grabs him by the elbow and steers him into the backseat beside her, and they are pulling away before Ezra has the wherewithal to protest.

'Wait,' he says, his voice sounding far away. 'Wait. No. We have to go back. Teddy—'

'Teddy is in a car right now with Daria on his way home,' Ali cuts across him, still not looking up from her phone.

'But, Teddy,' he tries again. He remembers the look of dread in Teddy's eyes. He imagines him in his car, panicked and terrified. He thinks of him doubled over, sucking in large gulps of air as a panic attack overtakes him. Ezra blanches. 'Oh, God. I have to see him. Ali, I—'

'Ezra.' She finally looks up from her phone. Her face is hard, but her eyes are weary. And because Ezra has never heard her ever actually use his name instead of an insult, he pauses. 'The best thing you can do right now is not contact him.'

'But,' Ezra swallows around the hardening lump in his throat, 'he must be so scared. He's not out. Oh, God, I just outed him to the world. His parents — *Christ*. His *parents*. And Grace. Shit, where is Grace?'

'Everyone is on their way home.'

'I can fix this,' Ezra says, scrambling for his phone. 'I can fix this. I can—'

Ali plucks his phone from his hands. 'No contact with the Montgomerys. Or social media.'

'But—'

'Ezra,' she says, firmly. Fairly. Utterly exasperated. 'You have just made my life and my job very, *very* difficult. But it's my job. So please, just let me do it, okay?'

To Ezra's utter horror and chagrin, he feels his eyes sting. 'Can you check he's okay? Please?'

'Of course.'

'Oh, god. I'm sorry. I'm so sorry, Ali. I've screwed it all up.'

And then, Ali does something that seems to surprise them both. She pulls Ezra into her arms and holds him. She doesn't let go when he bursts into tears. She doesn't recoil when he sniffles against her shoulder. One hand strokes gently through his unruly hair while the other clenches her phone, her thumb tapping out messages with impressive speed. He'd honestly had no idea that Ali could ever be so gentle. Or human.

Warren and Jacqueline's brownstone is empty when they arrive. Ali turns on the lights and strides over to the drink decanter. She pours a whiskey for herself, drinks it, pours another two and hands one to Ezra. Ezra doesn't want it, but he knocks it back anyway, desperate for something that will stop the tremors running through his hands.

Grace arrives first. Ezra can't bear to look at her. He tries to apologise, but then her arms are around him and suddenly he's crying again, and apologising, and begging forgiveness. Grace holds him and tells him there's nothing to forgive and he just cries harder. He cries until his throat is raw.

He's not sure when his parents got there, but their arms are around him too. His mother takes his face in her hands and forces him to look up at her. Her face is calm and kind, and somehow that makes it worse. He wishes they would just be angry at him. Anything is better than *this*.

'I've ruined everything,' Ezra says. 'I always ruin everything. You should have left me on that doorstep.'

'Ezra Samuel Darling,' she says firmly. Her expression is resolute. 'You are my son. There is nothing you can do that will ever make us regret having you.'

'I'm broken,' Ezra says. 'I'm an idiot. I destroy everything, it's like I'm cursed.'

Ezra sinks down onto the sofa and Warren's hands settle firmly on his shoulders. 'You are not broken. And there's nothing wrong with you. You made a mistake. You are not *the* mistake.'

They all look up as a small tornado that looks a bit and sounds a lot like Iris barrels through the front door. Her high heels are in her hand and her hair has fallen out of its elegant up-do, now yanked back into a ponytail. She throws her shoes to the ground and drops to a crouch in front of Ezra, her hands on his knees.

'He's alright,' she says before he can ask. 'He's a bit shaken, but he's alright. Daria got him out of the party and into a car. She and Nick are staying at his brownstone and keeping his parents away until he's ready to talk.'

'Does he...' Ezra asked, quietly. 'Does he hate me?'

Iris swallows hard, giving him a small smile. 'Oh, Ezzy. He *loves* you. So much.'

Ezra looks at Jacqueline. He feels like a little boy again, waiting for his mom to make it all better. 'Can I see him?'

'No,' Ali says, sharply. She is still on her phone, fingers a blur. 'Not until I speak with Mara.'

'Can I talk to him?'

Ali's phone buzzes and she answers the call, stepping out of the room. Everything is horribly tense while they wait for her to return. Moments later, she is back. She looks ready to pass out, but keeps her shoulders square, her chin defiantly high. It's always been a joke between Ezra and Grace that Ali runs on caffeine, curse words and the blood of her enemies. Now it seems like less of a joke. And, not for the first time, Ezra is immeasurably grateful to have Aliana James as part of the family.

'We're meeting with the BingeBox executives first thing tomorrow,' she says. 'You'll see Teddy then.'

Ezra doesn't sleep. He doesn't even entertain the idea of sleep. Even when Iris drags him to bed and tucks him in, he knows that he'll be awake all night. When she realises this too, she crawls into bed beside him. They cuddle and watch YouTube videos on his iPad, and Ezra lets his eyes glaze over. He's not really watching or listening. Just thinking. About Teddy. About whether he can't sleep either. If he's lying awake next to Nick or Daria, or maybe alone, jaw wound tight.

When his alarm goes off at six-thirty, Iris stirs against him. She, at least, managed a few hours. They get ready in silence and Ezra lets Iris dress him in a smart pair of slacks and a crisp white shirt. When the family car comes to pick him up, she hugs him tightly.

'I wish I could come,' she says, squeezing him.

He tries to smile for her sake. 'You have gay artwork to draw.'

'True. Damen isn't going to propose to Laurent by himself.'

'Whatever that means.'

She squeezes him again. 'Good luck.'

The drive to the BingeBox HQ is quiet. Ali and Mara are meeting them there, so there's not even the sound of phones buzzing or laptop keys clicking. It's just painfully, awfully, quiet. Grace holds his hand the whole journey. She's been put in charge of his phone until he's allowed it back after the meeting. Depending on whether or not they decide he can be trusted.

The BingeBox offices are clean and clerical. Ali and Mara meet them in the reception and an overly polite assistant takes them up to the top floor for their meeting. Ezra has only met Sasha and Conrad Rivers twice before. Once when they were offered the show, and again when they signed the contract. They remind him of his parents, in a way. A fearsome power couple who see business and greet it like an old friend. The only difference is that Warren and Jacqueline aren't elitist robots.

Everything seems to move too quickly. Ezra is ushered from the elevator to another waiting room, and then to a conference room that is all glass and chrome. He's seated and given a glass of water, and Sasha and Conrad welcome them all. He shakes hands with them, and they give him their best executive smiles while their assistants flap efficiently around them. A few moments later there's a knock at the door and Ezra turns in his seat to see the Montgomerys walking in. David. Anastasya. Daria. And. *Oh. Teddy.*

He looks miserable. And smaller somehow. His eyes are dark and red-rimmed, sunken into unusually sallow skin. He hasn't shaved yet this morning, and he looks gaunt. Fragile. He doesn't look at Ezra as he sits down, and keeps his gaze cast downwards into his lap. Ezra moves to stand, but Grace puts a hand on his shoulder.

David and Anastasya are wearing matching facades of calm, but the stiffness in their shoulders suggests otherwise. Ezra can't care less how they're feeling. All that matters is Teddy.

'Thank you all for joining us,' says Sasha once everyone is seated. 'And thank you Ali for getting everyone together on such short notice. I'm not going to insult anyone's intelligence and pretend that we don't all know why we're here.'

An assistant passes her a newspaper and Sasha places it in the middle of the table. And there it is. The biggest mistake Ezra has ever made, laid bare for the whole world to see. Teddy in his grey suit, Ezra stretching up to kiss him, grinning against his mouth like an idiot. Under any other circumstances it would have been a nice picture. The moment was sweet and chaste. And to have their first public kiss displayed and dissected like this makes Ezra's stomach roll. The headline reads: *New Year, New Sexuality.*

'This,' Sasha says, 'as I'm sure you're aware, is a direct violation of our contract. Please, let me finish. Conrad and I aren't monsters. We aren't here to berate you or cancel the show. However, action must be taken, and we would prefer it to be something that suits *everyone*.'

'We're partners,' Conrad adds. 'If one of us is unhappy, all of us are unhappy. We don't want anyone here to be unhappy. Ezra, if you could, in your own words, tell us what happened? That way we can resolve it.'

Ezra goes to open his mouth but Mara steps in. 'My client is not obligated to inform you of any aspects about his personal life that extends beyond what is stated in his contract.'

Conrad's smile is patient but tight. 'Absolutely right. Except that he kissed one of our leading stars who is engaged to another one of our leading stars, therefore disrupting the narrative we agreed upon. I know that I don't need to remind you that this kind of violation is usually settled with a termination of a contract, which is, of course, something we would like to avoid.'

'Of course,' Mara doesn't bother with the fake smile like Conrad does. 'And I'm sure that *I* don't need to remind *you* that making threats to my client's livelihood nullifies any consequences that you think a breach of contract constitutes.'

Sasha puts a hand on her husband's shoulder. 'I assure you that no one is making any threats. We just want to have all the correct facts before we make a decision on how to move forward.'

'I love him,' Ezra says, his voice rough. Everyone turns to look at him. Even Teddy. Mara looks like she might throttle him. 'That's it. There's your story. I love him, and I kissed him. It's not that deep.'

Everyone is quiet for a bit. Then Conrad clears his throat. 'I see. And are these feelings reciprocated?'

'No,' Ezra says before Teddy can answer. 'He had no idea. I got drunk and kissed him. I shouldn't have and I'm sorry.'

Ezra glances at Ali, who, for once, doesn't look furious with him. Just kind of awed. Everyone else is looking at Teddy though, waiting for him to confirm. Ezra doesn't know how anyone could ever believe that Teddy isn't madly in love with him, the way he's looking at him right now.

'Is this true?' Sasha asks.

Teddy opens his mouth and hesitates. Ezra gives him a look that says *please*. He answers, flatly: 'Yes. I had no idea Ezra felt this way. I was just as surprised as everyone else.'

The room seems to let out a breath it's been holding. Ezra is fairly certain that he's going to die if he hasn't already. His palms are slick with sweat, and his leg is bouncing. He wonders if he's too young to have a heart attack.

Conrad lets out a small sigh. 'Alright. Well, that makes our lives a lot easier. This we can work with. A moment please.'

Conrad, Sasha, and their assistants leave the room. Grace turns to Ezra, mouth agape. He wants to scream but he can't find the energy. He doesn't even feel real at this point. Nothing does.

'Why?' Teddy asks, quietly.

Ezra looks up at him and swallows past the glass in his throat. 'It was my mistake. I'm fixing it.'

'Ezra—'

'The boy is right,' Anastasya cuts across him. 'He chose to disgrace himself. He should be the one to face the consequences.'

'He's not a disgrace, mum,' Teddy says, sharply.

Anastasya turns her sneer upon Ezra. He wonders how it is that she can wear her nice-as-pie façade so well in public. 'He's nothing but a filthy pervert.'

There it is. The first glimpse of his life now that he's out. Now that the world knows. The first of many homophobic slurs that will, undoubtably, come his way. Because the world is so obsessed, for some reason, about what genitals people have under their clothes and what they intend on doing with them. Ezra is too hollow to hurt, but he suspects he will hurt a lot later.

Warren is already on his feet, but so is Mara, and her words are quicker. 'Mrs Montgomery, I'll ask you to refrain from verbally assaulting my client.'

Anastasya shrugs. 'Ask your client to not to sexually harass my son.'

'Jesus Christ, Mum! He wasn't harassing me!' Teddy explodes. 'It was a kiss for God's sake!'

'That you didn't want,' David says. 'An unwanted advance is sexual assault. We could sue.'

'But you won't,' Mara says. 'And besides, that is Teddy's choice, not yours.'

'It wasn't sexual assault,' Teddy says, voice quiet with anger. 'How dare you even *say* that after—'

The door to the conference room opens and Sasha and Conrad, and their small army of assistants, re-join them. Mara and Warren take their seats again. Ezra's hands ball into fists in his lap. He prepares himself for whatever punishment they're going to give. Best case scenario: they fire him from the show. Worst case scenario — *shit*, there were too many to even think of.

'We've spoken to Ron,' Conrad says. 'He thinks we can use what happened to our advantage and include it in the new narrative.'

Grace blinks. 'New narrative?'

Sasha beams at Ezra. 'The brother who is hopelessly in love with his sister's fiancé.'

Teddy swallows. 'Um. Wait. I—'

'That way the season can continue as expected,' Sasha goes on. 'The finale will commence with the wedding day, and now Ezra will have a bigger role to play in the show.'

'This isn't a role,' Jacqueline says, hotly. 'This is his life. You can't ask him to use his feelings as some kind of character arc.'

'Believe me,' Conrad says with a smile that is not nearly as sincere as he clearly thinks it is. 'We are very sympathetic to Ezra's situation. But we also believe that it is in everyone's interests that we use it to our advantage. A few longing looks, a couple of heart-to-hearts, a tearful farewell on Teddy's wedding day. This is the kind of thing an audience eats right up. It might even be cathartic for Ezra to get these emotions out.'

'You want to take advantage of our son,' Warren says, voice tight with fury.

'No. We want to play to his strengths. Everyone loves a love triangle. Everyone loves an underdog.'

'And,' Sasha adds, 'everyone loves when the underdog does the right thing.'

Grace shakes her head. 'No. No way. This is Ezra's *life*. You can't expect him to—'

'I'll do it,' Ezra says. He can feel everyone looking at him. He can feel his heart breaking as he says it. 'I'll play the part. The lovesick best man. Whatever you want. I'll do it.'

Teddy shakes his head. 'Ezra—'

'I'm sorry for what I did. I shouldn't have kissed you. I love you. And it's because I love you that I can't be selfish anymore. I broke this and now I need to fix it.'

'*Ezra*—'

Ezra stands on shaky legs. 'Email me any new scenes.'

And then he leaves.

[Excerpt from the That's The Tea, Saturday 3rd January 2022]

Ezra Darling Opens Up About New Year's Eve Kisscapade

What did we tell you? What did we mother-plucking tell you? In the words of the iconic Bella Swan, Ezra Darling is *unconditionally and irrevocably in love* with Teddy Montgomery! And we are so here for it!

Following the New Year's Eve countdown kiss (see below) that sparked hysteria across the globe, Ezra has appeared on *Wake Up New York* to share his side of the story, and honey. Bring the tissues. This one is worthy of being a Jane Austen novel. Sniffle!

Looking very sombre (but also utterly delicious in those tight chinos) Ezra tells the hosts, 'I had no plans to fall in love with Teddy Montgomery. It just kind of happened. And I knew he would never love me back, and I was okay with that because he makes my sister very happy.' Like, c'mon. If that doesn't completely break your heart, then you're either a dementor or Simon Cowell. (Is Simon Cowell still relevant? Eh.)

When asked about the kiss, Ezra says, 'I should have never kissed him. I was drunk and stupid. I risked so much in that one moment. I should have been honest with Teddy and Grace from the start and then maybe this could have all been avoided. The thought that I could have lost the trust of both my sister and my best friend kills me.'

Although Teddy Montgomery and Grace Darling did not appear on *Wake Up New York* with Ezra, both have made statements on the matter. Teddy gave a quote to the *New York Post* saying, 'I should have been more open and intuitive to Ezra's feelings. He is my closest friend and best man. I should have realised he was hurting. I could never find it in my heart to be upset with him about any of this, and we are all looking forward to moving on.' On a more informal platform, Grace took to Twitter to say, 'I ask everyone to please respect my family at this time, especially my brother Ezra. He made a mistake. He is human. Teddy and I are as much to blame as he is for not seeing what was going on. The kiss was not an act of defiance or malice. It was a misstep — one that, as far as we are concerned, doesn't even require forgiveness. There is no bad blood between any of us.'

Winner of the Most Understanding Sister Award goes to... Grace Darling! (Duh.) Because if my brother was macking on (do people still say 'macking on'?) my non-existent fiancé, I don't think I would be quite so understanding. And Winner of the Most Clueless Best Friend Award goes straight to Teddy, because how — just HOW — did he not realise Ezra was completely in love with him? We could all see it!

Clearing up any final rumours, Ezra finished his interview on *Wake Up New York* by saying, 'Of course, the wedding will still be going on as planned. Grace and Teddy love each other, and I am not going to stand in the way of that. True love is so rare these days. They deserve to be happy, and I will strive to be happy for them.'

Sob. Sniffle. Wail. While we at *That's The Tea* can't say that we're shocked by Ezra's declaration of love, we can say we had no idea it was so one-sided. And now what will become of all of us Tezra (possible OTP name?) supporters? Our ship sank before it even had a chance to sail. God, it's like the Titanic all over again! At least we'll always have Kisscapade to tide us over.

Sigh.

Chapter Twenty-Two

Ezra and Teddy are on a temporary contact ban. That includes both physical and remote, and Ezra cannot even be trusted to keep hold of his devices. Ali has given him a pay-as-you-go burner phone that has hers and his parents' numbers in it, but that's all. And it's killing him. The way Teddy had looked at the meeting with the BingeBox executives, so desperate and hopeless, is seared into Ezra's consciousness. He wants nothing more than to see him. Hold him. To tell him it's going to be okay. But no one will *let* him.

Iris is burdened with the job of babysitting Ezra so that he not only doesn't try to sneak over to Teddy's brownstone when no one is looking, but also so he doesn't try to throw himself off the roof. Because, honestly, tempting. She's also his last lifeline to Teddy. Every day she gives Ezra an update on how he's doing. It's always the same: *he's fragile but fine*. But *fine* isn't good enough. Teddy deserves to be happy. It kills Ezra that Teddy still doesn't realise that he *deserves* to be happy.

Iris, of course, is a paradigm of stoicism. Because Iris only has two modes: Sonic the Hedgehog and T800, and absolutely nothing in-between. And all the while Ezra is falling apart (quite flawlessly, he might add) he needs her strength. He needs her to drag him out of bed in the morning. He needs her to shove him into the shower and put his breakfast in front of him. He needs her to ride out the anxiety attacks with him. He needs her to be there in the middle of the night, when he wakes up gasping, covered in cold sweats. He needs her to keep him together.

Except she's hurting too. It's obvious. She misses Daria. Ezra wants to be a good friend to her but he's so wrapped up in his own misery that he can't find the strength to be strong for anyone else. Not that Iris even wants his strength. Or his pity. When she's in T800 mode, it's all about efficiency. Not emotions. Which is hard, because Ezra is literally *only* emotions — and none of them particularly good.

It isn't until one evening, when Iris gets in from collecting their takeaway, when she finds Ezra on the bathroom floor, quiet sobs wracking his body, that she makes a decision.

Ezra doesn't blame her when she leaves. He wouldn't have stayed with himself for this long. This isn't who he is.

Before Teddy, before he'd fallen in love for the first time and had his heart broken, Ezra had prided himself on being strong. For himself. For the people he cared about. Before Teddy, he can't remember the last time he'd cried. The last time he'd had anyone or anything worth crying for. Without even trying, Teddy had completed him and shattered him, all at once. And now, Ezra is broken. Beyond repair. And alone.

He hears the door click as Iris leaves. Doesn't bother hauling himself off the bathroom floor. Twenty minutes later when he hears the door clunk again, he's managed to get his breathing under control. Managed to get his hands to stop shaking. He wipes his eyes roughly with the sleeves of his Christmas sweater from Daria — which has become the most comforting thing that he owns — and stands on dead legs.

'Iris?' he calls, his throat raw. 'It's okay, I'm not Tobias Funke-ing it anymore. It's safe to come in.'

Ezra doesn't know why he's trying to be funny. It just feels like the right thing to do. She's chosen to come back after all. He's not sure he would have come back to himself if given the chance to walk away. He shuffles down the hallway, following the smell of their dinner and the sound of her shoes on the kitchen floor.

'I promise not to weep uncontrollably into your teriyaki soba,' he goes on. 'Unless you're into that. In which case, I'm sure I could muster up my third mental breakdown of the—'

Ezra freezes. Because it isn't just Iris in his living room. It's Teddy too. He wears his sweatpants and an oversized sweater. His sneakers are mismatched, like he'd left in a hurry. His glasses have slipped down to the tip of his nose, revealing his naked, red-rimmed eyes. He has stubble — practically a beard — and his hair is a tangle of untamed strawberry blonde.

'Nice jumper,' Teddy says, quietly.

A broken, '*Sweetheart.*'

Ezra isn't sure who moves first, but then they are in each other's arms. Ezra buries his face into the crook of Teddy's neck and, to his surprise, does not cry. Neither of them say anything. They just hold each other. Hands clutching. Desperate. Missing each other even in the circle of each other's embrace. Ezra hears his front door click again as Iris lets herself out. He makes a mental note to send her literally *all* the muffin baskets for arranging this. For risking Ali's wrath. Risking whatever punishment BingeBox is capable of inflicting.

Eventually, Teddy pulls away and holds Ezra's face in his hands. 'I missed you.'

Ezra swallows. 'I missed you too.'

'I... I can't believe you did that for me.'

'I love you,' Ezra says simply.

And then Teddy is kissing him. It's slow, and sweet, and just —*oh*. It's just *everything*. Ezra clings to him, hands gripping his waist, and some part of his mind tells him to never let this man go ever again. No matter the cost. Just never let him go.

'I love you too,' Teddy murmurs against his lips. '*So* much.'

'Sweetheart. *Baby*.'

Teddy's kisses become rougher. Harder. Ezra opens himself up to him. He lets himself be whatever Teddy needs him to be. And right now, Teddy needs to hold him. Claim him. Be rough with him. Ezra is driven backwards towards the couch, and they fall back together against the cushions. Teddy catches Ezra's lower lip between his teeth and the sound it elicits from Ezra is halfway between pain and pleasure.

Then Teddy draws back. Ezra's eyelids flutter open and he looks at the absurd man leaning over him. He looks so lost, so hopeless, and Ezra can't stand it. He reaches up and touches his fingertips gently to Teddy's cheek. 'Sweetheart. It's alright.'

Teddy shakes his head, jaw clenching. 'No. It's really not.'

'Want to talk about it?'

For a long moment, Teddy looks like he decidedly does *not* want to talk about it. Then he sighs and sits back, and Ezra sits up. Teddy scrubs at his weary face with one hand, and Ezra notices that it's shaking. He reaches out and holds it steady in his own.

'I hate this,' Teddy says, softly. 'Ezra, I *hate* it.'

Ezra's heart is breaking. 'I know, baby. I'm sorry.'

'I'm never going to be allowed to be who I am, am I?'

'You can always be yourself around me.'

Teddy swallows hard. 'Christ, I wish my parents had the same outlook.'

Ezra's face goes a little slack. 'You told them you're still gay?'

Teddy stands, hands going to his hips. He begins to pace, nervous energy radiating from him in thick waves. Ezra wants to pull him back down to the sofa. 'Yes. I figured I owed it to myself and to you to set the record straight. *Again*.'

'Jesus. How did that go?'

Teddy lets out a bitter bark of laughter. 'About as well as you'd expect.'

'Oh, sweetheart...'

Teddy strides over to the far wall and braces one hand on the mantle over the fireplace. The fake flames illuminate his stricken face in warm shades of amber and gold. 'I knew it wouldn't be fun. But. Christ. It was... so *bloody* awful.'

Ezra's voice is gentle. 'What happened?'

'Well, I told them I'm still very much gay, despite all their therapy. They told me I'm confused. I told them I am, quite in fact, as gay as a picnic basket. They told me they hadn't wasted five years of illegal trials on me for me to continue sinning. I told them that this is who I am, and they need to accept me. They told me that I am no son of theirs. I told them that I cannot change who I am, even if I wanted to, which I don't. Then,' another cold laugh here, 'they said that they wouldn't allow me around the twins anymore until I go back to a clinic. Like I'm some kind of *predator*.'

All of the air leaves Ezra's lungs. 'Oh. Teddy.'

Teddy turns away. His fist connects with the wall and even across the room Ezra can hear his knuckles cracking painfully. Teddy swears and slams his palms hard against the exposed brickwork. His chest is heaving, and his shoulders are hunched. Ezra can't see his face, but he knows his jaw will be wired tight, the way it always is when he's trying to keep it all inside.

Ezra crosses the room in four strides and wraps his arms around Teddy from behind, burying his face into the nook between his shoulder blades. It's then that he feels Teddy's shoulders shaking. Then he hears his breath catch. Ezra realises, his heart breaking into a million pieces, that Teddy is crying. Sobbing. And he absolutely cannot bear it.

'Sweetheart,' he whispers, pulling Teddy around to face him. Teddy doesn't want to be seen though. One hand covers his face, the other resting diplomatically on his hip. Ezra can see his throat working, and he tries again. 'Teddy, sweetheart. Please.'

Then he just crumbles. Teddy surges forwards, clutching at Ezra, hiding his face in his shoulder. Ezra holds him and lets him cry. He has no idea how long they stay that way, but he can feel his shirt becoming damp, and he just holds him closer. He's murmuring words of comfort in his ear, not really paying attention to what he's saying. He's too busy thinking about all the ways he can hurt the people who have caused Teddy this much pain.

When Teddy's knees buckle, Ezra guides him over to the sofa and sits him down gently. He sits beside him, pulling him into his chest. He kisses his forehead, runs a hand though his sandy hair, and tells him that it's alright. Everything is going to be alright. Even if he doesn't believe it himself right at that moment.

By the time Teddy stops shaking, by the time he's cried himself out, they're just existing in each other's arms. Ezra tenderly runs a thumb over Teddy's prominent cheekbone. His eyes are red and raw, his lips endearingly swollen. Ezra kisses him anyway and Teddy melts beneath his touch and whispers, 'I'm sorry.'

Ezra's heart genuinely can't take anymore. Teddy doesn't deserve to carry all this guilt and sadness around with him for simply just being himself. 'Sweetheart, don't. You have nothing to be sorry for.'

'This isn't your baggage to carry.'

'Teddy Mikhail Montgomery. Your past, your present, and your future are my privilege to be a part of. Besides, baggage is always easier to carry with another person.'

Teddy pulls him into a bruising kiss. Ezra doesn't complain. He kisses him back, holding him with a fierce protectiveness that makes his chest ache. He's so disgustingly in love with this devastating man, it's almost a joke.

'Take me to bed,' Teddy says.

Ezra does. He takes him to bed and makes love to him. He covers Teddy's body protectively with his own and touches him in all the ways that he knows will make him gasp and shudder. He takes his time teasing him, kissing his way over Teddy's body, ignoring where he wants to be touched the most. He skates his fingers against the insides of his thighs, relishing the way Teddy's hips rise off the mattress in a silent plea.

It's not until Teddy is writhing and moaning that Ezra takes him into his mouth, sinking all the way down to the hilt, making his eyes water. He takes his time drawing all sorts of wanton noises from the man whose thighs he's nestled between.

Afterwards shower together. Ezra takes his time washing Teddy's body, lovingly sponging and kissing him all over. He gives Teddy a pair of pyjamas to wear, and they're far too short for him, but he rolls up the legs into three quarter lengths and still, somehow, manages to look like a Gucci ad.

They reheat the pad Thai Iris left them with and eat it on the sofa watching *Schitts Creek*. At some point, Teddy bursts into tears again. Giant sobs that take over his whole body and Ezra just holds him. Kisses him. Promises that everything will be okay in the end. And he means it. He will do absolutely everything he can to make sure that everything will be okay for Teddy. Even if it means sacrificing himself. His own happiness. Everything.

They fall asleep on the couch while David and Patrick get married in the background, Ezra stretched out and Teddy sprawled over him. Teddy's head rests on Ezra's chest, cheek all smooshed up against his pyjama top. When Ezra wakes in the night, he doesn't have the heart to move him, and instead he lays there, looking down at the man in his arms.

He strokes an errant curl of hair from Teddy's brow and bows his head to kiss his temple. He will make this right. He'll do anything for Teddy. It's a certainty, and a wish, and a prayer, and a promise.

Protect Teddy.

The next morning Teddy is gone, a note left in his wake, in his calligraphic handwriting:

My Forever Darling,

I didn't want to wake you. One, because you looked adorable, and two because I knew you would be upset. I've gone back to England to sort through a few things. I have lawyers that I want to speak with, and I want to investigate the possibility of pressing charges against my parents for what they put me through as a child. I won't be gone for longer than a week, maximum. Not just because that's when I'm expected back on set, but because I may die if I am to be separated from you for any longer.

There is coffee in the pot and an omelette in the fridge. All you have to do is heat it up. Call me as soon as you read this, because I'll probably already be missing you. And, at the risk of sounding frightfully dramatic, I would advise you destroy this letter once you've read it. If it gets into the wrong hands and my parents find out what I'm planning, they will come after me with their legal team.

I don't know what will happen once this is all over. All I know is that I love you, and I want you. I have never, and I will never, want anything more than I want you. What I do know, is that one way or another, I will be with you. I've cowered in the shadow of my past for long enough. I am not scared to be seen anymore, and I want to be seen as the man who is loved by you.

Please don't be angry with me. I couldn't bear to say goodbye. Also, you're very grumpy in the morning.

I'll be home soon, and hopefully with good news.

I love you more than what is considered sane or safe.

Yours, always,

Teddy

P.S. You look gorgeous. I know I can't see you, but I just know you do.
xxx

Chapter Twenty-Three

Subject: love letters straight from your heart

Ezra <Ezra-Darling@Darlingdynasty.com>
To: Teddy
---
teddy,

i know it's only been a day, but i really fucking miss you. i think i miss you even more than i did when we were apart. i was going to text you, but then i realised that i had too much to say. and i actually really like getting emails from you. you write them like letters. i feel like a damsel in a jane austen novel.

i just want to say that i think what you're doing is really brave. everything that you've *already* done has been really brave. you have such a big strong heart and i love it. and whatever happens, whatever your parents do, i'm with you the whole way.

daria said they had a joint conniption when they found out that you'd gone back to the uk. don't worry, she said you were just hanging out with nick while you're not needed on set. and i think they prefer that than the idea of you cavorting with me.

as you can probably tell i've been allowed my devices back. now that you're on the other side of the world (well, kind of) i can, apparently, be trusted. i don't think i've ever had so many notifications. apparently the whole world was in a really big rush to point and say 'i told you so! i knew he was gay!'

i'm making some kind of statement later on all my social media platforms about my sexuality, because apparently that is necessary. why don't straight people have to come out? announce who *they* like to fuck? hardly seems fair. but yeah, tonight i'll be releasing a statement that i'm bisexual. i think i'm a bit terrified. i don't know why, it's not like anyone will care.

wish you were here for good luck hugs and kisses.

i really miss you.

love you

ezra

xoxo

*

Re: love letters straight from your heart

Teddy <Teddy.Montgomery@theMontgomerys.com>

To: Ezra

Darling Ezra,

Leaving you was the hardest thing I've ever had to do. More so than coming out to my parents. More than fleeing the country to see if I can press charges on my own family. More than I had ever imagined possible. But I know it will be worth it, because I am making a better future for us. I couldn't go to our family's lawyers, so Nick put me in contact with his. I will soon be discussing not only the ins and outs of suing my own parents for abuse and neglect, but also looking into — at the very least — disowning them and perhaps having a restraining order put in place.

I'd be lying if I said I wasn't completely petrified. The moment this goes ahead, there is no way I'll be able to keep it from the public. I'm not going to do anything until we've figured out how to get out of the BingeBox contract. I would never want to hurt you, or Grace, or the show. I just want to have a plan for when I can finally come out to the world. It's a nice thought knowing that no matter what my parents do, I'm going to be prepared. They can't hurt me anymore.

I'm so sorry for everything you're going through. I wish I was going through it with you. This is supposed to be a partnership and I'm letting you take all the hurt alone. I'm sorry you've been forced out before you were ready. Thank you so much for sparing me from that. I cannot begin to tell you how grateful I am for your courage, and your selflessness, and your love. You are the best person I have ever known.

I am with you, always.

Forever yours,

Teddy

X

*

Re: love letters straight from your heart

Ezra <Ezra-Darling@Darlingdynasty.com>

To: Teddy

---

teddy,

i did what i did because i love you, and i would do it again. i will never stop wanting to make things right for you.

i hope nick's lawyer takes good care of you. i also hope he is fat and balding and has a tiny penis.

grace and iris send their love, but not as much love as me.

so yours,

ezra

xoxo

*

Re: love letters straight from your heart

Teddy <Teddy.Montgomery@theMontgomerys.com>

To: Ezra

Darling Ezra,

Nick's Lawyer is forty-five, grey-haired and named Lawrence Lahey. Lawrence Lahey the Lawyer. I'm quite sure you have nothing to worry about in regards to me running off with him. At any rate, Nick assures me he is very nice. He's not mentioned anything about his penis though.

I can't wait to hold you again, and kiss you again, and do all manner of filthy things to you again.

Until then, I am thinking of you. Fondly and always.

Utterly enamoured,

Teddy

X

*

Re: love letters straight from your heart

Ezra <Ezra-Darling@Darlingdynasty.com>

To: Teddy

---

you sassy bitch. go and make history. love you.

xoxo

Chapter Twenty-Four

A week without Teddy Montgomery, Ezra is steadily realising, is a week of pure hell. Which he knows is stupid, because he's gone without Teddy for longer than a week before, and without any communication at all, but at least then he was only a few blocks away. This time there is a whole ocean between them, and even though it's going to make things better (please, God, let things get better) in the long run — the *very* long run — it still stings.

It's not made any better by his filming schedule, which is a jerk at best, and a raging bitch at worst. Ezra has to film the scene where he explains his feelings for Teddy three separate times, because Ron says his tears didn't look real enough. Finally, Ezra snaps and screams at him, and then angry tears come, and all Ron says is: 'Roll camera.'

They text, and they email, and video chat. Ezra loves the video chats in particular because he gets to stare shamelessly at Teddy's stupid face, and also because they usually end up getting naked and orgasming. And while cybersex isn't *nearly* as good as the real thing, there's something incredibly hot about Teddy instructing him how to touch himself from almost 4000 miles away, and Ezra not being allowed to come until Teddy lets him.

His 'coming out' statement on Instagram gets over one hundred thousand likes in the first two minutes of being posted. His livestream with Grace to assure the public that there are no hard feelings between them is flooded with hearts and other supportive emojis. Along with a few hateful messages aimed towards Grace about how she's standing in the way of true love, that Ali had pre-emptively warned them to avoid at all costs. He even goes on a podcast — Inside The Influencer — where two social media moguls ask him all kinds of pre-approved questions that Ezra has pre-approved responses for.

And then, there's the part that Ezra has been dreading. The unkind comments. The verbal abuse in public. The threatening messages in his DMs. On a morning coffee run to his local Starbucks, a middle-aged man across the street calls him a *fucking queer,* and if Iris wasn't with him to drag him away, he suspects he would have made a spectacle of himself. It's not later, until he's in the privacy of his brownstone, and after he has told Iris a dozen times that he's *just fine,* that he lets his eyelashes grow damp. Then he emails Teddy to ask about his day because that's an instant shot of serotonin.

It's on Friday, five gruesome days into Teddy's absence, that an email from Anastasya Montgomery pops into Ezra's inbox. He's tempted to delete it without reading it — because, honestly, he doesn't want to hear anything that woman has to say — but the subject line gets his attention. `Clearing the air.` So, he reads on. And that, unfortunately, is how he finds himself going to David and Anastasya's house for afternoon tea.

It's a totally abysmal affair. The housekeeper (is that what he is? Butler?) lets Ezra in and shows him to the *downstairs* drawing room, which would imply that there is also an *upstairs* drawing room, and if Ezra is being completely honest with himself, he doesn't even really know what a drawing room is. A quick Google on his phone while he waits for Anastasya to join him confirms that it's a room where guests are entertained. Ezra doesn't feel particularly entertained. Just awkward and bored.

When Anastasya appears, she is, of course, in an impeccably tailored pantsuit, navy blue with pinstripes. Her blouse is white, and her cravat (a fucking cravat?) matches her suit. The shoes are Louboutin and devastating. She takes a seat at the top of the table and snaps her fingers at a staff member who hastily comes to attend them.

Ezra assures the staff member that he doesn't want any tea, and Anastasya assures her that he *does*, in fact, want tea. So, to spare the poor girl, who looks like she's about to have a meltdown, Ezra accepts the tiny cup and saucer, then proceeds to not drink it. Anastasya watches him over the rim of her teacup, eyes sharp. She waves away the servant, so that she and Ezra can enjoy their awkwardness in peace. Or maybe so she can murder him without any witnesses present. Both are equally likely.

'I suppose,' Anastasya says, her accent thick and rich, 'that you think you know everything about my son.'

Ezra draws in a deep breath, because he suspects he's going to need it. 'Reckon I've got a pretty decent idea, yeah.'

'He's probably told you about all of his little indiscretions.'

Ezra arches an eyebrow. 'Are you being exceptionally vague for a reason, Mrs Montgomery?'

Anastasya smiles, and she doesn't deserve to have those dimples. Bad people aren't allowed dimples. 'The thing you need to bear in mind about Theodore, especially when he's telling you all his little stories, is that he tends to exaggerate.'

'Why don't you tell me what it is you're talking about, and I'll tell you if he's been exaggerating?'

A pause. 'Does the name Robin Waterslade mean anything to you?'

'Should it?'

'Well, that depends.'

'On?'

She takes another dainty sip of her tea. No big, inelegant slurps like when Ezra's mom drinks her coffee. 'On what version of events he's told you. I expect the story you heard was of poor little Theodore and his father's big bad colleague.'

Ezra's stomach rolls as he realises what she's talking about. 'If you're about to invalidate your own son's experience, Mrs Montgomery, then we're going to have a problem.'

'Theodore was always a dramatic child,' Anastasya says. 'And he was the instigator in the whole sordid affair.'

'Don't,' Ezra warns. 'Just... don't.'

'Theodore likes to think that Robin wanted something inappropriate from him. That Robin was *interested* in him. But we know what really happened. Robin had always been like an uncle to Theodore and Leonid. He would have never hurt those boys. He has a wife, you know, and three beautiful, grown-up children. He remains one of mine and David's closest friends to this day, despite how Theodore almost ruined everything with his *perversions*. You see, Ezra, you think Theodore is innocent. But he was trying to seduce Robin Waterslade to satisfy his own disgusting desires.'

Ezra's hands are gripping the edge of the table, his knuckles turning white. He's glad he's sitting, because if he was standing, he isn't sure his legs would keep him upright. 'I think,' he says, trying to keep his voice as calm as possible, 'that you should stop talking, Mrs Montgomery.'

'He quickly realised that we could see through his lies,' she goes on. 'He wanted Robin to be the villain in some silly story he'd made up in his head.'

'Stop talking, Mrs Montgomery.'

'All Robin ever wanted was the best for him. Both of the boys. He's ready to forgive Theodore, you know. If Theodore just apologises to him.'

'Mrs Montgomery—'

'But Theodore always has to be the sacrificial lamb. Always the centre of the universe. He wasn't getting enough attention, so he made up this whole charade of a perfectly good man propositioning him—'

And then Ezra is shouting, because that's all he can think to do. Because the volume of his voice is the only thing he can control anymore. 'He was a child! He was *terrified*! And when he came to you for help, your solution was to call him a liar and torture him!'

Everything goes very quiet. After a long, painful moment, Anastasya puts down her cup and saucer and gives him a contemptuous look. 'He wasn't terrified of Robin.'

'Yes, he was, and you know it! And you did nothing about it because you care more about your relationship with that scumbag than your own children!'

Ezra isn't sure when he'd gotten to his feet, but there's suddenly so much electricity sparking through him that sitting still seems impossible. He suspects he's always known he would go to war for Teddy Montgomery. The question was only when. And now here is. Alone on the battlefield for the man he loves. He swallows hard, clenching his jaw in a very Teddy-esque way.

Anastasya regards him with barely veiled disgust. 'I wouldn't expect you to understand. You're just as bad as he is. Maybe even worse. You have the *choice* to be normal. To be with a woman. And still you choose to be a sinner.'

Ezra nods. 'Yep. Got me there. But you know what? I'd rather be a sinner than a tone-deaf homophobe like you. I love your son, okay? Which is more than you or David can say. And I'm not going to let either of you or anyone else hurt him anymore.'

She sneers. 'You think I don't know about your lie? Your pathetic attempt to spare him? I know who Theodore is and I know what you've been doing together. I'm not stupid. And I will never let him, or you for that matter, disgrace the Montgomery or the Volkov family name.'

'You've already done a wonderful job of that yourself.'

'You don't want to start a war with me, Ezra,' Anastasya warns. 'Least of all, over Theodore.'

'Oh yes, I do.'

Anastasya studies him, and for a split-second Ezra can see where Teddy gets his thoughtful gaze from. She says, 'Has Theodore ever told you how his father and I met?'

Ezra arches an eyebrow. 'Is it relevant?'

Anastasya pours herself another steaming cup of tea. She blows on it daintily before taking a sip, making Ezra wait for story time to begin. 'My father's first clinic was rather inclusive; it was considered very progressive for its time. Don't give me that look, you know what I mean. They welcomed all sorts of sinners through their doors. Men *and* women, men who thought they were women, women who thought they were men — they took in all sorts.'

Ezra snorts. 'How generous of them.'

'My father was a very religious man and up until he opened his clinic he never much bothered with science.'

'Gay conversion therapy isn't science, it's torture,' Ezra says bluntly.

Anastasya doesn't even acknowledge that. 'It wasn't until he had a reason to be personally invested that he took an interest. After all, I was his only child and heir to the Volkov legacy.'

Ezra feels his brain buffer. He blinks a few times, rapidly. 'You...?'

'I met David Montgomery on his first day at the clinic. He was so timid; you wouldn't believe it even if you saw it. I was already six months into my treatment and showing great promise. My father thought we'd be an excellent match together and paired us up. That was one of their strategies, you see. Matchmaking. We entered that clinic as sinners and left it engaged.'

Ezra can barely hear Anastasya over the white noise in his head. He considers that he might be having a stroke, because there is no way — *no way* — that he is hearing this correctly. 'You and David...' he says, slowly, 'are both gay?'

Her eyes narrow into slits. 'Did you not listen? I said we're not sinners anymore.'

'Jesus Christ,' Ezra says, running a hand through his mop of hair. 'No wonder you're both so miserable all the time.'

'David and I have had a perfectly functional marriage for almost thirty years.'

He looks at her then. Watches her stoic face. 'You're the world's biggest hypocrite. Both of you — it's all just lip service. Wow. No wonder you resent your own kid. You can't even love yourselves, so you take it out on Teddy.'

Anastasya's nostrils flare, and for the briefest of moments she isn't beautiful. 'Teddy is our penance for our past mistakes. We must do right and fix him.'

'He isn't broken.'

Her jaw sets. 'He was born broken.'

And that's about all the bigoted bullshit Ezra can handle for one afternoon. He moves back abruptly, knocking the table with his legs and spilling the contents of his tea onto the Versace tablecloth.

'I think we're done, Mrs Montgomery,' he says. 'Thank you for the tea, it was awful.'

Ezra is almost at the door before he hears: 'Wait.'

He doesn't know why he turns back. He thinks maybe it's because he's hoping to see regret or remorse in Anastasya's eyes. Instead, he is met with the same cold stare as always and something inside his chest deflates.

They look at each other for a long, drawn out few seconds. She reaches into her suit pocket and pulls out a small, rectangle card. She holds it out to him. Against his better judgement, he takes the business card and genuinely recoils. It reads: *Dr Robin Waterslade. Waterslade Medical.* Followed by an email and phone number.

'What the hell,' Ezra says slowly, 'am I supposed to do with this?'

Anastasya sips her tea. 'Unlike Theodore, Robin is willing to let go of the past. He understands that Theodore was young when he made his mistake. He is willing to give him therapy to relieve him of his perversions, but Theodore won't speak to him. Perhaps you can call on his behalf.'

Ezra blinks. He really *must* be having a stroke, or an aneurism, or some other thing that sets your brain on fire, because there is *no way* he is hearing this right. 'You want me to call the man who harassed your son to ask him if he'll give him even *more* trauma?'

'I'm giving you a chance to help Theodore. If you really care for him, like you say you do, you'll want the best for him.'

'And you think this is the best for him, do you?'

She watches him, face serene and eyes cold. 'Yes. I do.'

Ezra crumples the business card in his hand and drops it on the table. 'Thank you for having me, Mrs Montgomery.'

And then Ezra gets the hell out of there, because the last thing he, Grace, or the show needs, is for him to make a scene.

───

Teddy is coming home. Teddy is coming home. Teddy is coming right the *hell* home. His parents and Ali think he's getting in a day later, but he's coming home tonight so that they can see each other without anyone else getting in the way. Because, really, they're both still not supposed to be fraternising with each other. But what Ali and the press don't know won't stop Ezra and Teddy from reuniting like a lover and a soldier just returned from war.

Ezra prepares. He showers and washes his hair with the watermelon-scented shampoo that he knows Teddy likes. He shaves his face and other areas that make his eyes water at the possibility of. Well. Yeah. Because *ouch*. He tousles his mop-hair into some semblance of a hairstyle and brushes his teeth for an inordinate amount of time. The cologne is something Grace bought him for his birthday. The first time he'd worn it Teddy had buried his face into his neck and fucked him against the wall with remarkable vigour.

He doesn't know whether to dress up or just tie a ribbon around his dick, but in the end settles on his usual chinos and button down combo. And then, he waits. Which is the worst bit. He tries to watch some TV but the stampede in his stomach won't let him focus. He makes himself tea — English breakfast tea — because he always has a box of *Twinings* in his kitchen cupboard now thanks to Teddy, and nibbles half-heartedly on a bag of potato chips. He's hungry but he wants to order takeout when Teddy gets in.

When his phone beeps he almost drops it in excitement, but not before seeing the message flash up on his screen: **Landed. See you soon. Love you.** Quickly followed by: **Famished.** And Ezra grins. Daria is picking him up from the private strip so he should be home in about half an hour. God. That thought. Teddy being home. And with good news. And the promise of a future for them. Maybe not a future that starts right now, but soon. He doesn't want to think about how everything else is also coming soon: the season finale, the wedding, losing Teddy to Grace. As long as his parents and Mara keep working through the contracts, and as long as Ezra keeps clinging desperately onto hope, it's almost enough. Or, at least, very *close* to almost enough.

Ezra considers ordering the food to coincide with Teddy's arrival, but he's kind of hoping that Teddy's first port-of-call will be the bedroom. Or the couch. Or the kitchen counter. Hell, he'll even take the hallway. So, instead, he settles in for an episode of *The Good Place* and tucks his feet underneath him on the couch. Twenty minutes pass, and then the doorbell rings.

Ezra all but flings himself off the couch. His heart is in his throat as he nearly rips the front door off its hinges and almost throws himself into the arms of a complete stranger. Ezra blinks, looking at the man on his doorstep. He's tall and broad. Probably older than he looks. His tan looks natural, like he spends most of his life in the sun, and his suit does nothing to betray the fact that he clearly takes care of his figure. He is, undoubtedly, a silver fox. Attractive, but definitely *not* Teddy, so it's all wasted on Ezra.

'Oh,' he tries not to sound utterly disappointed, but it's hard. 'Can I help you?'

'I hope so,' the man says in a posh English accent. 'May I come in?'

Before Ezra can say, *uh, no, not really*, the man is already stepping across the brownstone threshold. Not quite pushing Ezra out of the way, but not really giving him much of an option apart from stepping aside. Ezra watches the man in his hallway, unsure if he's supposed to shut the door or not. When the man disappears into his living room, Ezra decides, *fuck the door*, leaving it closed but on the latch as he follows his unwelcome house guest.

The man is sitting on Ezra's sofa, one leg crossed over the other. He looks perfectly at ease, one arm stretched over the back of the couch. He smiles up at Ezra, his grey eyes glinting in a way that makes Ezra twitchy.

'Sorry,' Ezra says, lingering near the hallway. 'I don't mean to be a dick. But... who are you?'

The man smiles. 'A friend of the Montgomerys. Anastasya has told me all about you. Dr Robin Waterslade, pleased to make your acquaintance.'

Ezra can taste copper. Can smell burning rubber. His world tilts for a moment and he has to grab a side table to keep himself upright. He can feel a flurry of emotion inside him battling for dormancy, trying to be the one that guides him into action. Disgust and rage seem to be neck and neck, and Ezra draws himself up to his full, unimposing height.

'Get out of my home, Dr Waterslade,' he says tightly.

Waterslade gives him a look. 'Come now. I came here to talk.'

'I have nothing to say.' It's a lie. Ezra has *plenty* to say, most of them expletives. But he wants him gone. 'And I haven't given you permission to come inside. Teddy will be here soon.'

'Then I'll wait until he arrives,' says Waterslade. 'I haven't seen the boy in a dog's age, and it's about time we let water pass under the bridge. I forgave him a long time ago.'

Ezra swallows bile. 'You... *you* forgave *him*?'

'He could have ruined my career with his lies. Everything I worked so hard for. I could have lost it all. Not to mention the embarrassment he caused my poor wife and daughters. But he was young, and foolish, and I accept that he made a mistake.'

'The only mistake Teddy made was trusting his parents to keep him safe from you. Please leave my home, Dr Waterslade.'

'The boy has always been perverted,' Waterslade says, having the audacity to look sad. Like he actually gives a shit about Teddy. Ezra wants to hit him. 'Such strange proclivities. All we wanted was to help him.'

'There is nothing perverted about being gay,' Ezra says, voice hard. '*Terrorising queer kids* however—'

'You've painted me as the villain,' Waterslade cuts across him. 'Of course you have. Someone's got to be, right? If you're the hero, and Theodore is the damsel in distress, you need someone to be the big bad wolf. But, I assure you, I'm not sat over here twiddling my moustache and plotting Theodore's demise. And neither are his parents. We love the boy.'

'You don't get to say that,' the words are acid in Ezra's mouth. 'None of you know what love is. You don't get to pretend to care about Teddy because you never have, and you never will. You made his life miserable. It's a miracle he's not completely messed up. But that's just how strong he is — everything you put him through, and everything you did to him, and he still has the biggest heart out of everyone I've ever known.'

Waterslade laughs. The motherfucker actually laughs. Like they're having a great old time. 'You make it sound like I abused the boy.'

'You sexually harassed him,' Ezra bites out. 'You invited him to your hotel room when he was a teenager.'

'Theodore tried to seduce me,' Waterslade says, firmly. 'I don't know what version of events he's told you, but I never wanted to lay a finger on him.'

'You traumatised him.'

'You don't know what you're talking about.'

'You destroyed him. You *ruined* him. It's taken over a decade for him to even *begin* to put his life back together. He was just a *child*.'

'We tried to help him,' Waterslade says. 'We all did. But this... this perversion got into him too deep. There was no saving him. The best we can hope for now is that he at least tries to conceal his true nature.'

'Is that why you're here?' Ezra asks. 'Did Anastasya send you to scare me off? To let him stay in the closet with Grace as his beard?'

'I'm merely here to help you to understand—'

'I understand very well,' Ezra snaps, 'that you're a monster. Probably why you get along so well with Anastasya and David. And now, I want you to get out of my home before I call the police.'

There is a long stretch of silence, where neither of them moves. Then Waterslade clears his throat. 'Alright then. I best be on my way.'

'You best.'

Waterslade stands and smooths down his suit. Ezra tries not to let out a sigh of relief as he passes him in the hallway. He has every intention of letting the man see himself out, but then Waterslade stops, turns. He gives Ezra a dirty look that scrunches his face into a sneer. Suddenly, the charming silver fox façade is gone, and Ezra is given a glimpse of the man that Teddy had been terrified of as a kid. His gaze rakes over Ezra with distain. Like Ezra is nothing. A lesser being.

'You must be very pleased,' Waterslade says. 'The apple of Theodore Montgomery's eye. You must think you've won the jackpot there.'

Ezra opens his mouth to deny it, but stops himself. Waterslade knows Anastasya and David. He knows the situation. So, instead, he says, 'Teddy is a human being, not a trophy.'

'Well, if he was, he'd be a consolation prize. And what does that make you? A runner up? You must feel so very *special*.'

'I feel privileged to be loved by Teddy Montgomery,' Ezra's tone is resolute. 'Something you, or Anastasya, or David will never experience.'

Waterslade watches him, lip curling. Then he asks, almost petulantly: 'What is it about you, hm? What makes you so much better than the rest of us?'

Ezra nods to the door, so very *done* with this conversation. Teddy will be home soon, and he wants this creep gone. 'There's the door, Dr Waterslade.'

Waterslade sneers. 'Don't get me wrong, I can see the attraction. There's a novelty to you. Like a shiny new toy.' Waterslade's gaze drags unkindly over Ezra like he's looking at a pile of dog shit he's stepped in. 'Somehow not put off by the accent. And he certainly doesn't need the money.'

Waterslade takes a step forward and Ezra takes one back without thinking. 'I'm telling you to stay away from me, Dr Waterslade.'

A deep, mocking laugh. 'Or what?'

'Or you might embarrass yourself even more.'

Something in Waterslade's expression shifts. He stalks forwards, this time with purpose, something akin to hatred blazing in his grey eyes. Like he wants to throttle him. Ezra has never been in a fight before, and he doesn't intend on starting now. He retreats until he feels the back of the couch up against him. And then somehow, he is trapped, the only exit behind Waterslade. Door on the latch. So close and yet so far, like it's taunting him.

Ezra crosses his arms over his chest because that feels a little better, like a shield almost. Then he uncrosses them because it occurs to him that he might need his hands ready for — Jesus, for *what*, exactly? Waterslade isn't going to hit him. He's a grown man. A doctor. He's not going to come in here, pretend to be all polite, and then start a goddamn fight with him. Except that he *really* looks like he is. He looks furious. And shit. Ezra really doesn't want to get into a fight. He would, for Teddy, but he doesn't relish the idea. He doesn't even know *how* to hit someone.

Waterslade jabs a blunt finger into Ezra's chest, like a bully in the school yard picking on the short kid. Just because he can. That's when it dawns on Ezra — that's what Waterslade is: a bully. A bully who grew up and put on an expensive suit, who expected Ezra to back down the moment he squared up to him. Only, Ezra *isn't* backing down, and now Waterslade is having to make good on his word.

'Do you think he won't get bored of you?' Waterslade all but spits. 'You think he's going to stay in America and play house with the Darling Dynasty fuck-up?'

Ezra's voice threatens to rise, even though he knows that won't help anything. Everything Iris has told him about her self-defence classes tells him that, right now, he needs to be diffusing the situation. Placating Waterslade. Avoiding confrontation. But Ezra gave up logic a long time ago when he fell in love with Teddy Montgomery, and instead he finds himself saying: 'Take your hands off me, Dr Waterslade.'

'You don't tell me what to do,' Waterslade snaps and gives Ezra's chest a hard shove. It shocks him. 'You're a kid. A fucking *kid*.'

Ezra frowns. 'That can't be true, otherwise you'd have slipped me your room key by now.'

It's the wrong thing to say. It's obviously the wrong thing to say. Ezra has never known the *right* thing to say. The back of Waterslade's hand connects with his cheekbone before he can see it coming. Pain explodes across the side of his face and he nearly laughs. Waterslade slapped him. *Slapped* him. Like he's a virginal maiden in a Catherine Cookson novel and Ezra is some sort of scoundrel. It's *galling*. And kind of funny. But not at all funny. And it has no right — no good goddamn right — to hurt as much as it does. But it does. And it's shocking.

Ezra blinks hard before looking at him. This time he sees the slap coming and his own hand comes up to block it. He wants to catch Waterslade's wrist, like a badass, but that takes a level of coordination and coolness that Ezra just does not have. Still, it knocks his hand away and the look of surprise on Waterslade's face is glorious. For a moment they're both still, staring at each other. Ezra gets the impression that Waterslade thinks they're in the middle of a pissing contest. They're not.

'I said,' Ezra says, softer now. Calmer. 'I would like you to leave, Dr Waterslade.'

There's the sound of a throat clearing. Waterslade turns and Ezra looks past him to see Teddy at the door, suitcase beside him. It's raining out and he's wet. Water drips from his hair and runs down his face. He looks every inch the superhero. A very angry superhero. Ezra steps to the side, putting some distance between himself and Waterslade. He doubts Waterslade will hit him again, but his cheek still smarts, and he doesn't want to risk it.

'Hello, love,' Teddy says, not taking his eyes off Waterslade. 'Pop the kettle on. Our guest is just leaving.'

There's a long, drawn-out moment where Waterslade doesn't move, and Ezra wonders if they will actually have to physically remove him from his house. Then he huffs out a laugh. A scoff, really. He dusts down his immaculate suit and strides for the door. He stops in the doorway, coming face to face with Teddy. They're almost the same height — Teddy just a bit taller. Waterslade seems almost surprised by how big he is. Like he never expected Teddy to grow up one day.

He opens his mouth to say something, but Teddy beats him to it. 'Don't say anything. Don't even think about it, Robin. Just leave.'

Waterslade's lip curls. He steps out the door that Teddy is holding open. The rain pelts down on him as he turns to go.

'Robin?' Teddy says, facing him.

Robin Waterslade pauses. He turns back just in time to see Teddy's fist collide with his face. It's not a particularly skilled punch, nor is it very well executed. But it lands. Does it ever fucking land. There's a kind of crunching sound, and Waterslade's nose explodes, blood quickly drenching his mouth and chin. He howls in pain and Teddy closes the door on him, pulling across the deadbolt. Ezra wonders if Waterslade will start knocking again, screaming and demanding to be let in. Or that he'll threaten to call the police. But there's just an eerie silence that seems to fill his brownstone.

There's a few moments where Teddy doesn't move. Ezra watches his chest heave and waits. He can be patient. He can wait a lifetime for this man to be ready. When Teddy finally checks the spyhole and turns to face him, Ezra watches as his whole body shifts. Anger easily gives way to concern. And love. So much love. Then, Teddy is marching over to him. Instead of kissing Ezra, like Ezra had hoped, he holds his face gingerly in his hands and inspects his cheekbone.

'You're bleeding,' he says. 'Christ. Are you alright? Did he—'

'No,' Ezra says. 'Just slapped the shit outta me. I'm okay. How's your hand?'

Teddy frowns. 'My hand?'

Ezra gently takes Teddy's hand in his and inspects the already swelling knuckles. Teddy blinks in surprise, like this is news to him. 'Oh. Yes, of course.'

'Ice,' Ezra says, leading him to the kitchen.

He sits Teddy at the kitchen counter and rummages around in his freezer for a bag of frozen peas, wrapping them in a clean dish cloth. Teddy hisses as Ezra presses the compress to his hand, but doesn't pull away. His free hand goes to Ezra's cheek again, tenderly inspecting the damage.

'I can't believe he hit you,' he says, quietly.

Ezra laughs. 'I can't believe *you* hit *him*. It was kinda sexy.'

'I don't feel sexy,' he admits. 'I feel kind of ridiculous. And guilty? Why do I feel guilty? He's a bad person. I hit a *bad* person. Jesus, I've never hit anyone before. Never even thought about it. It bloody hurts. How do people do this for a profession? I—'

'Teddy,' Ezra says, softly. He gives his good hand a squeeze. 'You're rambling, baby.'

Teddy nods. 'Yes. I am. I think I might be in shock.'

'Probably. Do you think your hand needs an X-ray?'

Teddy shakes his head. 'No. I broke my hand when I was a kid falling off a horse. It was agonising. This isn't like that. I don't think your face will need stitches.'

'Thank God. It's my money-maker.'

Teddy's jaw winds tight and his throat works hard to swallow. 'I'm so sorry.'

Ezra pulls him into an embrace that he's been dying to give him all week. 'Not your fault.'

'If it wasn't for me—'

'No,' Ezra says firmly. 'Don't. You're not responsible for other people's shitty actions.'

Teddy's lips graze his ear as he replies. 'I hate that he hurt you.'

'I know the feeling.'

Teddy pulls back so he can press a soft kiss to his lips. All Ezra's earlier desires about ripping Teddy's clothes off and taking him to bed take a backseat. All he wants to do is hold him. They order from the new Turkish place down the road and Teddy patches Ezra up while they wait. It's a surface wound, and all it needs is cleaning, but Ezra is happy to let Teddy fuss over him. It's nice to be cared for like this.

They don't rip each other's clothes off after dinner, but they're not in a rush, and that's a nice feeling. They have the whole night together and Ezra plans to savour every moment with the man he loves. They curl up on the couch and flick over to YouTube to watch an Irish gamer they both like play The Sims. Every twenty minutes Teddy reapplies his makeshift ice pack, but his knuckles still look angry and swollen. It's not long before Ezra ends up curled into Teddy's side, face pushed into the crook of his delicious neck.

'Tell me something good,' he says.

Teddy's fingers trace gently up and down Ezra's back. 'Well, my lawyer thinks I have good grounds for suing my parents and getting a restraining order. He also says I can charge them for criminal neglect, but I don't know if I will go that far. The last thing the twins need is the trauma of having their only grandparents locked away. Getting them out of the picture is enough for me.'

'That's good,' Ezra says, not removing his face from the hollow of Teddy's throat. He smells so damn good. 'When can you start?'

'As soon as I want. But, for Grace, I'll wait until this season of filming is over.' He pauses, taking in a deep breath. 'We also spoke about opening an investigation into Waterslade.'

That makes Ezra look up. 'Really?'

Teddy nods. 'There's no smoke without fire. And there is a *lot* of smoke.'

'I'm with you,' he promises. 'Always. All the way.'

Teddy kisses him. 'I should have done this a long time ago.'

'Trauma has no timeline, sweetheart,' Ezra says, reaching up and gently tracing a fingertip across Teddy's jaw. 'No rule book. You have to do what's right for you.'

Teddy watches him for a moment before saying, 'God, I missed you.'

Despite it all, Ezra smiles. 'I missed you too.'

Later they kiss. Later, they make love. Ezra lays down and pulls Teddy over him. His hands are grabby and desperate, wanting Teddy to make up for the time they lost while they were apart. But Teddy wants to take his time, kissing every new expanse of skin uncovered as he peels off Ezra's clothes at an agonisingly slow pace. Ezra is stupid enough to think that once he is undressed that Teddy will get to the good bit, but then Teddy is climbing the length of his body to kiss him again. It's all barely there grazes of lips on skin, and featherlight touches.

Teddy kisses him in places that Ezra didn't realise he likes to be kissed. The insides of his elbows, his wrists, his calves. Each touch sends a lick of fire through his body. Teddy's hands stroke Ezra's sides, his thighs, over his hips, ignoring the part of him that painfully wants attention. Ezra is about ready to rip off his own skin when he hears Teddy finally pop the lid on the lube bottle. He nearly weeps with relief.

Teddy's fingers soon find their way, and Ezra's head drops back against the pillows as he finds that spot inside of him that makes him fly. When he grabs Teddy's hand to still him, it's not because he wants to stop, but because he's going to come. And that's not allowed without Teddy being inside of him.

Ezra pulls him down for a searing kiss that makes Teddy groan against his mouth. And when Teddy finally slides home, Ezra makes an obscene noise of pleasure. His eyelids flutter close, and his back bows, chest arching up to meet Teddy's. Ezra's lower lip snags between his teeth as he tries to bite back a moan. His heels press into Teddy's lower back and his toes curl. Teddy reaches between them to make sure they can come together, and they see stars, and constellations, and whole goddamn galaxies.

Afterwards, Teddy holds Ezra close under a mountain of blankets. His body is pleasantly satiated, his mind blissfully empty. Against his will, his eyelids droop and Teddy laughs softly, pressing a kiss to his temple. It's getting light out, and if they were back in Wyoming, they'd be able to hear the birds singing. Instead, they drift off to the sounds of New York City waking up, and Ezra sleeps restfully knowing that Teddy is home, with him. Where he belongs.

Chapter Twenty-Five

Ezra is okay. Well, no, he isn't. But he will be. He just has to get through this one dinner. This one stupid dinner. And then, at some point, he will be alright again. This is what he tells himself as he showers. Brushes his teeth. Dresses. He picks a loud shirt that he hopes will distract from the cut on his cheekbone. There's no swelling like with Teddy's poor hand, but an angry bruise has the audacity to flare up.

His throat is made of glass and wrapped in wet wool whenever he thinks of the speech he is supposed to be giving. And every time he looks at Teddy — which is all the damn time, because it's *Teddy* — he wants to drag him back to bed, build a blanket fort, and pretend the rest of the world doesn't exist.

And fuck. *Fuck*. What is he going to tell his parents? Grace? Iris? Ali will probably sock his other cheek for arriving on set with a smashed-up face. He wonders how Ron will spin the story. Probably another drunken Wyoming Wild Child tale where Ezra can't hold his liquor. That's all he will ever be in the Darling Dynasty storylines: the fuck-up.

As if Teddy can hear his thoughts, he wraps his arms around Ezra from behind, looking at him in the full-length mirror. He kisses the spot behind Ezra's ear that turns his insides to soup and Ezra feels his body loosen. Because Teddy Montgomery has magic powers, apparently.

'We'll get through it,' Teddy says softly. 'We're the endgame here. You and me.'

Ezra closes his eyes. Teddy is so sweet that it breaks his heart. 'I know.'

'Want me to make an excuse for you?' he asks. 'I can say you're sick.'

'I can't do that to Grace.' He turns to face Teddy and kisses him. 'Or you. You're like a baby bird at these things.'

Teddy's smile is coy. 'I think I can spare you for one evening.'

'I know. But anyway, I'm contractually obliged to be there.'

Teddy's smile wavers. 'I'm so sorry to put you through this. It must be killing you. Any news from Mara on a loophole in the contract?'

'Sweet F.A.,' Ezra sighs. 'She says it's so tight that she could have drawn it up herself.'

Teddy catches Ezra's face tenderly in his hands and kisses him again. 'We'll find a way, love. I promise.'

Ezra laughs, half-heartedly. 'Before or after you marry my sister?' Teddy's face crumples and Ezra regrets it instantly. 'Shit. Babe, I'm sorry. I didn't mean—'

Teddy silences him with a kiss. 'I know. I just don't like hurting you.'

Ezra doesn't know how to tell Teddy that it's not him that's hurting him, but the rest of the world. That it's the show. The situation. BingeBox, Ron, and Ali. Even his parents and Grace, although they don't mean to. But not Teddy. Teddy is as far up shit creek as Ezra is, without a paddle, or map, or a clue how to get back. So, instead, he kisses him. He kisses him, and kisses him, and tries to put everything he wants to say into his kisses. And if the hungry way that Teddy accepts them is anything to go by, Ezra thinks he understands what he is trying to say.

When there's a knock at the door so hard that it threatens the integrity of his deadbolt, it can only be Ali. Teddy gives Ezra a *gentleman, it's been a privilege playing with you tonight* look, and Ezra squares his shoulders. Teddy stays in Ezra's bedroom and Ezra checks his living room for any signs that Teddy has been there before letting her in. Ali flies into the apartment, nearly knocking him on his ass, coffee flask in a death grip.

'Is he in here?' she asks, storming into his lounge. 'What am I saying? Of course he's here. Where else would he be? You know, if you want me to have a heart attack there are quicker ways to go about it than this.'

Ezra watches Ali look behind the couch, like Teddy might actually be hiding there before moving onto the kitchen. 'Ali, can we talk—'

Ali rummages around in the bin, triumphantly pulling out a used Twinings tea bag. She holds it aloft and barks a laugh. 'I knew it. I fucking *knew* it. Can you not keep your chode of a dick inside your skid-marked pants for five *fucking* seconds?'

'Um. Ali—'

'I hope he's not naked wherever he is, because I am dragging him out of—' She pauses as she finally looks at him. There's an uncomfortable moment where Ezra can't read her expression, and then her face darkens. 'What happened?'

Ezra swallows. This tiny woman could bring the Punisher to tears. 'I can explain.'

'I fucking hope so,' she snaps, stalking forwards.

Ezra scrambles back, because it's not above Ali to dump her coffee over his head. She's done it before. He'd smelt of hazelnut oat latte for a week. 'Listen, Teddy—'

'Teddy what?' Her voice is deathly quiet when he asks: 'Did he do this to you? Did Teddy do that?'

Ezra literally recoils from the idea. Because *God no*. He looks at Ali, face incredulous. She's wearing an expression he's never seen on her before. It takes him a while to register that it's a look of concern. For *him*. He blinks several times, because this is rapidly turning into the weirdest morning ever. 'Jesus, Ali. No. God, no.'

'Who?' she demands.

'Ali, I—,' he scrubs a hand over his face, and instantly realises his mistake as his cheek throbs. From a slap. A goddamn *slap*. 'I just need you to trust me.'

'Shitting Christ,' Ali says, stepping forward, hand outstretched to inspect him. She takes his chin in her hand and turns his head to get a better look. 'I hope you gave them hell.'

Ezra laughs but it's humourless. 'No, but Teddy did.'

Ali's hand drops. 'Are you two in trouble?' she asks, voice hard. 'Whoever they are, we can fix this. I can call Mara right the fuck now, if that's what you want. Or the police.'

'We need,' Ezra says, taking a deep breath, 'to think. And not to have this go any further than here until we know what we're doing.'

'And what *are* you doing?'

Ezra's mouth is a hard line. 'I can't say. Please, I just need you to trust us. *Please*.'

Ali looks as though she hates this plan, but she nods and pulls her phone out. Her fingers fly over the touch screen and before Ezra can ask what she's doing, there are footsteps in the hallway and Teddy sheepishly joins them. Ali, seemingly remembering her reason for coming, salvages her anger at the sight of him. Then she surprises them all by saying: 'You're supposed to keep him safe.'

Teddy takes Ezra's hand. 'I know. I'm sorry.'

'Don't be sorry,' she snaps. 'Just do a better job.'

'He is keeping me safe,' Ezra says. 'And I know you don't want him here, and I'm really sorry. But—'

Ali seems to suddenly notice Teddy's swollen hand. Her eyes blaze. 'Theodore Montgomery, I swear to God—'

'He got it from the guy who did this,' Ezra says, quickly, pointing at his cheek. 'Besides, look. It's his right hand and my right cheek. It doesn't match. The other guy was a leftie. Teddy hurt his hand breaking the other guy's nose.'

Ali watches Teddy for a long, drawn-out moment. Then she nods once, and says, 'Good. I hope he cried.'

'There was some definite squealing,' Teddy confirms.

Ali is still glaring at him. 'Still do better.'

'I will,' he promises.

Ali sighs and checks her phone. 'The makeup artist will be here in ten minutes.'

Ezra finally looks at her, frowning. 'I'm not getting ready on set?'

'You said this doesn't go any further than here,' Ali says. 'You need to cover up that bruise before you get to the rehearsal dinner.'

And in that moment, Ezra could hug her. He doesn't, because, like, he's not an idiot. That would be like hugging a grizzly bear on steroids. But he *could*. He lets out a gruff laugh and says, 'I always thought you hated me.'

Ali looks at him like he's deranged. 'I never hated you, dipshit. I think you're a shit-for-brains cockhead with all the appeal of a pile of monkey jizz. But I feel that way about all my brothers.'

Ezra blinks. 'You think of me as family?'

Ali doesn't seem to want to dignify that question with an answer. Instead, she just gives them both a *don't be fucking late and don't show up holding hands* glare before leaving, slamming the front door behind her. It's then that Ezra realises that Ali has been on their side all along.

The makeup artist doesn't ask any questions and does a good job of concealing the cut and the bruising on Ezra's cheek. He tries not to wince when she dabs at his face with the makeup sponge and ruin all her good work. The foundation is heavy and gives his skin a weird, waxy feeling. But when she holds up a hand mirror, he looks fresh-out-of-the-box good. Her idea to give him a bit of eyeliner and mascara to detract people who got too close from noticing the slight swelling has him looking like Adam Lambert, and Teddy salivating like he wants to devour him.

When she's packed up and gone, two separate cars come to pick them up, ten minutes apart, and they are taken to The Palace for the rehearsal dinner. Ezra's leg bounces nervously as he rides in the back of the estate car. He reaches for his phone to text Teddy, and right as he unlocks his phone, it buzzes. **It's going to be okay. Love you.** Ezra doesn't reply. He doesn't need to. Teddy already knows what he's thinking.

Grace greets him with a wary expression. It's before midday but they're all dressed in evening wear to film the rehearsal dinner and pretend it's the week before the wedding, when in reality it's still just under a month away. A *month*. Ezra swallows down his anxiety, letting it sit like a damn rock in his gut, and forces a smile.

'You look beautiful,' he says, kissing her cheek. And she does. Her cocktail dress is cream with gold trim and her hair is loosely pinned up. She is radiant, and Ezra desperately wants so much more for her than this. He swallows hard, again.

'Are you alright?' she asks like she already knows the answer is no.

Ezra smiles in a way that he hopes is reassuring. 'Yes. Happy for you.'

Grace looks like she wants to push it, but she lets it go. He lets her drag him into the first round of mingling with guests and approved press while the camera crew preps. He tries to keep his face neutral as Teddy arrives, but all he really wants to do is collapse into his arms.

Then he notices Teddy's face. Like, really notices it for the first time since he's come back. His eyes are bleary and sunken, his skin taking on an unusual grey tinge. He's forgotten to shave. He meets Ezra's eyes and Ezra nearly chokes. Teddy is hurting. *So* damn much. He hadn't noticed it last night with all the drama. And there's nothing Ezra can do about it. *Baby,* he mouths. Teddy smiles and silently replies: *love*. And it's risky, and anyone could have seen it, but it makes the tightness in Ezra's chest ease just that little bit.

With Teddy present, Ron announces that they are about to start rolling. The press are asked to leave before they begin, and Ezra can barely suppress a sigh of relief as the last camera bulb flashes his way before being jostled towards the exit. They take their seats at the round table, Ezra finding himself between Grace and Iris, as usual.

There are half-scripts to follow in between speeches and jokes. Grace gives a saccharine speech written by Ron better suited to a *Disney* movie, about finding true love, and being so lucky to have found it, and about all the ways she's going to cherish it for the rest of her life. Teddy's speech is vague, at best. He mumbles about how he is looking forward to their next adventure, and about the memories he's excited to make. The kind of speech a valedictorian might give at a high-school graduation to his peers, not to your future wife.

Nick's speech is, of course, hilarious. He tells stories about Teddy as a teenager that make him blush, and make Ezra fall in love with him all over again. Daria says a few words about Leo and how much she knows he would want to be here. Ezra's throat closes up as he sees Teddy's jaw tighten. Grace squeezes his arm and Ezra tenses. That should be *him* comforting Teddy.

Iris looks bewildered when she's prompted to make a speech. She stands up, holds her wine glass aloft and recites Ross Geller's: What Is Love (L.O.V.E.) speech from *F.R.I.E.N.D.S.*, before sitting back down. People applaud, purely out of politeness, but Ezra knows their reaction shots will have to be re-recorded later on. Or Iris' speech, depending on whether or not they can get the rights to it.

Then it's his turn. And he's been dreading it all night for good reason. Because his speech might be the only scrap of truth in the whole night. He pulls the sheet of lined A5 out of his jacket pocket, that has his whole heart splashed across it, and smooths it out against his leg. His hand holding the microphone shakes.

rehearsal dinner speech (don't fuck it up)

~~websters dictionary defines "love" as a strong affection for another, arising from kinship or personal ties.~~

~~in their 1984 album, foreigner said "i want to know what love is." looking at grace and teddy, i know the answer.~~

~~he's supposed to be mine.~~

i wish i had a better way to open this speech than to say i am so ~~fucking~~ happy for my sister. it's cliché, i know. but it's the truth. ever since she was a kid, she wanted the full fairy tale. the happy ending. the knight in shining armour. and she grew up being able to give herself all of that. she worked hard to make sure she could get her fairytale. she worked even harder to make sure she got the happy ending. and she showed up every ~~fucking~~ time to be her own hero when she needed it. and now she has someone to share her queendom with.

it's hard for a brother to admit when someone is good enough for their sister. but i have no doubt that teddy montgomery is the greatest man i have ever ~~loved~~ known. he is kind, compassionate, and infinitely ~~loving~~ caring. someone i am proud to be able to invite into my ~~heart~~ family. when i look at him, i see ~~my future~~ someone who will do anything to protect the people he cares about. i see someone worthy of grace. i trust him with ~~my heart~~ her heart. and i trust grace to take care of him ~~like i want to~~ too. ~~we~~ they might not make sense to everyone, but they don't need to. because true love doesn't need to answer up to anyone's ~~fucking~~ expectations. it just has to be real. i know what teddy feels ~~for me~~ is real.

i know i have a reputation as a ~~dick~~ troublemaker. and i know this engagement hasn't been without it's bumps, and i'm not stupid enough to pretend that it's not been, ~~totally~~ in part, because of me. the truth is, i love teddy. i loved to hate him, then i loved him as a friend, and then something more. that will never go away. but i love grace too. and if this is all i can give to her, then so be it. because her and teddy's happiness means more to me than my own. and i guess that's what true love is. being able to withstand any kind of pain if it makes the people you care about happy. and more than anything, i want ~~teddy~~ them to be happy.

~~so yeet me into the fucking sun.~~

so, raise a glass. to two of the greatest people i have ever known. and how much they deserve this and everything else good in the world.

thank you.

Ezra doesn't look up from the paper until it's over. He immediately knows he's done an awful job because Grace is crying. Jesus, almost everyone is crying. Even Iris — *Iris*, who doesn't even cry at *Old Yeller* — is choked up. Teddy's jaw is made of granite, his eyes glassy. Just as Ezra is about to apologise, Grace stands and throws her arms around him. Then there's clapping. A shit-ton of applause. And when Ezra risks a glance over Grace's shoulder, he can see people on their feet. A full-on standing ovation for the hardest speech of his life. And if that doesn't just make his throat close right up.

'I'll make this right,' Grace whispers in his ear. 'I promise.'

Ezra holds her a little tighter. 'I believe you,' he says, even if he doesn't. The lead in his stomach promises absolutely nothing good. At all. Not where his heart is concerned. But she doesn't need to hear that, and he really doesn't need to say it, so he doesn't.

They are saved by a server approaching them to inform them that the starters are ready. Ezra is so relieved he could kiss the ground she walks on. Because even though the food turns to ash in his mouth, and his stomach wants to heave with every bite, it's a welcome distraction. So, bring on the stuffed mushrooms.

Ezra feels himself switch onto autopilot for the rest of the evening. He eats. He mingles. He chokes out his scripted lines for the cameras. He resists the pull of the open bar because he knows he can't handle his drink and he can't bear the thought of disappointing his family yet again. He doesn't talk to Teddy because if he does, he's going to shatter.

At some point, Iris coerces him into a dance. He tries to give her an encouraging smile as she loops her arms around his neck, watching him with concerned eyes. She's always been too perceptive. They sway and Ezra is unusually stiff and clunky. His feet barely shuffle.

'Holding in there, Ezzy?' she asks softly.

He smiles. 'Always.'

'Liar.'

'It's that obvious?'

Iris sighs. 'I'm worried about you.'

Ezra lifts Iris' arm and twirls her under it before pulling her back to him. 'This isn't forever.'

'Except this is. He *is* your forever. I know your folks are trying to sort this out before the wedding, but what if they don't? This can't be the end of it for you, Ezzy. It's killing you.'

Ezra looks at her and he can't speak. Because she's right. Of course, she's right: she's Iris. She's the only thing that makes sense anymore. He looks over to Teddy and Grace who are chatting animatedly to a recently *un*cancelled YouTuber and his boyfriend. As if Teddy can sense his gaze, he looks over at Ezra. His eyes grow so sad and weary that Ezra has to look away.

'I can't stay here,' he says quietly. 'Cover for me?'

Iris gives his shoulders a little squeeze. 'Always.'

No one notices him slipping out of the party, and if they do no one cares. He gets an Uber back to Teddy's place because he can't stand the thought of being alone in his brownstone. He lets himself in with the spare key Teddy gave him weeks ago. He has his own drawer in Teddy's bedroom too. And a toothbrush in the bathroom. And his dairy-free milk in the fridge. And if that doesn't scream *forever*, then he's not sure what does.

It's gone midnight by the time Teddy returns. His tie is undone, his hair mussed like he can't keep his hands from running through it. One of his little ticks. One of the many reasons why Ezra loves him. One of the *many* reasons why this is going to suck.

'I knew you'd be here,' Teddy says, joining Ezra on the couch. He drags a hand down his tired-looking face, and sighs. 'Right, let's get this over with quickly, shall we?'

Ezra frowns. 'You don't even know what I came here to say.'

Teddy laughs but it's hollow. 'Yes, I do.'

Ezra turns in his position on the sofa and looks at Teddy Montgomery. The man is ridiculous. A damn joke. Ezra wants to commit every sharp line and angle of his face to memory. He wants to create a collage of him in his head. He wants to be an encyclopaedia dedicated to this man.

'Here's the thing,' Ezra says, voice thick. 'We have less than a month until the wedding.'

Teddy looks at him. 'I'm well aware.'

'And we need to start thinking about what if we can't get out of this contract.'

Teddy's eyes go hard. 'I see.'

Ezra takes a deep breath. 'This is killing us, Teddy. It is, and you know it. I know it too. And at some point, we're going to have to decide which hurt we can live with; the one where we carry on like this, or the one where we don't.'

Teddy's jaw tenses, the cords in his neck jumping. 'It sounds like you've already decided for both of us.'

Ezra can't bear to look at him. Not when Teddy's face is all pain. So, he takes his hands instead. 'I haven't decided on anything yet. But I know that whatever we decide to do about this is going to be forever.'

'I'm only supposed to be married to Grace for three years,' Teddy says. 'Nothing is forever.'

'How I feel about you is. That's forever.'

'Then don't do this,' Teddy all but begs. 'Don't ask me to choose.'

Ezra takes Teddy's face gently in his hands. He wants to kiss him so badly. But kissing will lead to everything else, and Ezra really needs his brain online for this. 'Baby, I'm not. I promise. But I have to make a choice for myself. And I want to choose you, I do. But I'm the only one who can fix this.'

'Nothing needs to be fixed,' Teddy says, grasping Ezra's hands and holding them to his chest. '*We* don't need to be fixed. There's nothing wrong with us.'

'I know, babe. I'm not saying that. But I've screwed this up enough by falling for you. Now I've got to do the right thing.'

'Are you really going to pretend that you're the only one who's done the falling? Ezra, I'm in love with you, for Christ's sake!'

Ezra's eyes burn and he closes them. 'I know. I'm in love with you too. But there's so much that I can mess up for you: your reputation, your career, your family, your lawsuit. You have everything to lose. I already lost everything a long time ago.'

Then Teddy's hands are on Ezra's face, tender and strong. 'You haven't lost me.'

Ezra swallows. His throat is suddenly full of cotton wool. 'Of course, I haven't. You were never mine to begin with.'

Teddy brings their foreheads together. 'I have *always* been yours.'

'Please,' Ezra whispers. 'Please let me do this.'

'I can't.'

'Please. I have to let you go.'

'I won't let you.'

Despite the thickness in his throat, Ezra opens his eyes. Because Teddy deserves this at least. And Ezra can give him this. 'Teddy Montgomery, I love you so much.'

Teddy's eyes shimmer. His voice is hoarse. 'Please. Don't.'

'And it's because I love you that I can't be careless with you.'

'Please... *please...*'

'I have been so reckless because I love you *so* much,' Ezra lets himself cry now. Lets himself feel his heart break just that little bit more. 'But we deserve more than this. *You* deserve more than this. We both knew this had a shelf life, we just didn't want to admit it. I can't ask you to sacrifice everything, and you can't ask me to wait for you.'

'I just need more time.' Teddy's eyelashes are wet. 'Please give me more time.'

'I *can't*. Sweetheart, I can't. We can't go on hurting each other like this.'

Teddy holds back a desperate sob. 'I'll break it off tomorrow. I will. Ali can schedule a press conference. I'll take the consequences for both of us.'

'No,' Ezra says, swallowing hard. 'You can't out yourself for me. You have to do it for yourself.'

Teddy's eyes close against the tears. 'Is this it? Is this really it?'

Ezra wants to wrap him up in his arms. He wants to say *no. He* wants to take it all back. Tell him that this will all be better in the end, and if it's not better yet then it's just not the end yet. He wants to take away Teddy's pain. Kiss it away. Hold him until he stops shaking. But he can't.

'I have to go,' Ezra's voice wobbles. 'If I don't leave now, I never will.'

Teddy's lower lip trembles. Ezra wants to steady it with a kiss. 'Stay.'

'Baby.'

'Stay.'

'*Baby.*'

And then Ezra kisses him anyway. He tries to put everything he feels into it. All his love, and pain, and sorrow, and hope, and wanting. Everything. Because Teddy Montgomery deserves everything, and Ezra wishes he could give it to him. Teddy clings to him, and Ezra isn't sure if the salt he can taste is from his own tears or Teddy's. Gently, he uncurls Teddy's fingers from his shirt and peels his hands away. Teddy shakes his head, really crying now.

'No. Ezra, please.'

'Shh, baby. It's alright.'

Ezra stands and presses a gentle kiss to Teddy's forehead. Teddy clutches desperately at Ezra's hand, trying to pull him back down to the sofa. Ezra thought his heart was broken before, but this is something else. A new level of pain that he almost can't comprehend. It's like he can't breathe. It's like he is ripping his own heart out and leaving it beside Teddy. And maybe he is, because Ezra feels like he's dying.

He can't look back at Teddy as he leaves, because he knows that will end him. He lets the door click shut behind him before he allows himself to fall apart. He is barely aware of his feet moving him down the steps to the street. He is unusually grateful for the rain. It lashes down hard, pummelling his neck and shoulders, giving him a new hurt to focus on.

He makes it halfway down the street before stopping to slump against a streetlamp. His breaths come in ragged gasps. Part of him knows that he is perilously close to a panic attack, but another, more sensible part of him, reminds him that he is in public. And although it's dark out and he can't see any paparazzi, he doesn't want pictures of himself looking like a wreck showing up on the gossip sites tomorrow morning. He pushes away from the lamp post and forces himself on.

'*Ezra!*'

Ezra closes his eyes. He doesn't know whether to laugh or cry. He doesn't know if the universe is giving him a second chance or just laughing at him. Because he knows, before he turns, what he's going to see. And fuck. There's Teddy. Looking like a goddamn seven-course meal, and Ezra is starving. Famished.

Teddy all but stumbles down his brownstone steps. And then he is striding along the street, bare feet splashing through the puddles. Ezra is already marching towards him before he knows what he's doing. Or maybe running. It's hard to tell. Because Teddy is running too. And when they collide, Ezra feels his heart — Christ, his whole *world* — crash back into him. His arms are full of Teddy, and how on *earth* had he ever thought he could give this man up?

Then they're kissing. And kissing. And kissing. And the rain seems to come down harder, but they don't notice. Or they don't care. Or maybe both. Because all that matters is Teddy. Teddy Montgomery, who can't let him leave. Teddy Montgomery who refuses to stop loving him. Teddy Montgomery who kisses Ezra like he's his lifeline. And Ezra meets him kiss for kiss. This man is going to be the end of him. And the beginning. And everything that comes after.

He's not sure who leads them back inside Teddy's brownstone, but that seems to be suddenly where they are. Ezra is cold and dripping on the carpet. He trembles as Teddy leads him to the shower. He lets Teddy gently peel his wet clothes off and push him back under the spray. Ezra can't help but gasp as the hot water hits his back, and Teddy swallows it down as he kisses him again. And again. And again.

Teddy's body is hard and insistent against him. Ezra lets himself be crowded back against the shower wall. The coldness of the tiles has him yelping, a complete contrast to Teddy's body that seems to be almost vibrating with anticipation. Their bodies press and drag together, and Ezra's head tilts back. Teddy's mouth finds Ezra's neck and lavishes it with hot, open-mouthed kisses.

Just as Ezra is about to beg for more, one of Teddy's hands — God, one of his *hands* — wraps around them both at the same time. And in that moment Ezra is kindling and Teddy is the spark that ignites him. Together they burn. They burn until the fire is too much. Too hot. Too bright. And Ezra isn't sure who cries out first, because it's drowned out in the heat of the water, and their kisses, and their desperation.

Teddy's knees almost give out, but Ezra keeps him upright. He holds him against his body. Teddy presses his face into Ezra's neck, and they stay like that for a while. At some point they start murmuring nonsense to each other. Apologies. Proclamations of love. Promises to never let go. It's only when the water starts to run tepid that they actually get out.

Ezra doesn't argue when Teddy leads him to bed. Nor when Teddy pulls him under the covers. Nor when Teddy instigates round two, which has them on their sides, Teddy's back to Ezra's chest, Ezra's fingers digging into the underside of Teddy's thigh. He comes with his face pressed into Teddy's sandy hair, and they hold each other while they doze in and out of proper sleep.

'Don't,' Teddy says quietly, through their post-orgasm haze, 'ever do that again.'

Ezra holds him closer. 'I won't. I promise.'

I promise. I promise. I promise.

Chapter Twenty-Six

Ezra knows he's not going to like the reason why his phone is ringing before seven in the morning before he even glances at the screen. He reaches blindly for the nightstand, knocking over a bottle of water before his fingers close around the familiar rectangle. He's tempted to decline the call until he sees Grace's name flash across the screen. Shit. That's even worse than Ali.

'Grace?' Ezra answers the call.

'Ezra,' her voice is distant. Hollow. 'What have you done?'

Ezra immediately sits up. He realises that Teddy is awake, sitting at the end of the bed. His phone is in his trembling hands. His gaze is fixed on the far wall, face slack. Anxiety curls in Ezra's stomach as he reaches across and slips the phone from Teddy's hands. And if Teddy even notices him doing it, he doesn't say anything. Doesn't stop him. Just keeps up his remarkable impression of a statue.

Ezra looks at the open email on the screen and freezes. It's from Ali. There's no text. Not even a subject line. Just pictures of himself and Teddy from last night. Outside in the rain. Kissing. *Kissing*. He feels his stomach roll.

'Ezra?' Grace's voice floats back to him somewhere through the fog. 'Ezra, are you there?'

'I'm here,' he says quietly, suddenly understanding Teddy's fascination with staring off into the distance.

'Ali is sending a car over to you. Iris is coming too.'

'Alright.' Ezra looks at Teddy, whose skin has taken on a greenish-grey tinge. 'I'm worried about Teddy.'

'What's he doing?'

'Nothing. I think he's in shock. I'll see you soon.'

Ezra hangs up and tosses the phone across the bed. Scooting to sit beside Teddy, he tentatively touches his arm. Teddy doesn't react. Doesn't move. His hands won't stop shaking though, so Ezra takes them in his.

'Sweetheart,' Ezra tries. 'Say something. Please.'

Teddy blinks a few times and then looks at Ezra. 'I love you.'

Ezra frowns. Not the response he was expecting but he'll take it. 'I love you too. Are you alright?'

Teddy kisses him. 'I love you, Ezra.'

'Babe, that's great and everything. But you're scaring me a little.'

Teddy stands and Ezra watches him as he picks out his clothes for the day. He takes them with him into the en suite and Ezra hears the shower turn on. Minutes later, Teddy emerges, dressed and with damp hair. He picks up his phone and starts firing off text messages. Ezra just watches.

'Um,' he says, not sure what is going to come out of his mouth next. 'Are you...? Like. I mean. Are you okay? Obviously, you're not okay, but. Uh. You're not about to yeet yourself off a bridge or anything, right?'

The look Teddy gives him then is beyond tender. He bows his head to capture Ezra's mouth in a sweet kiss. 'Of course not. I promise. Get dressed, love.'

Ezra blinks. Well, okay then. He dresses and barely has time to brush his teeth before Iris texts him to say she's outside. They find her leaning against the chauffeur car, coffee in one hand, bagels in the other. She gives them a look halfway between sympathetic and *I told you so*. If she notices the cut on Ezra's cheek (and she probably does, because she's Iris), she, thankfully, doesn't say anything.

On the way to BingeBox HQ, both Ezra and Teddy are silent. Ezra knocks back his coffee like it's a shot and Teddy sips contemplatively on his latte as he looks out the tinted windows. Neither of them are up to eating however, and the bagels go untouched. At some point Ezra's leg starts bouncing of its own volition, and Teddy gently places a hand on his knee to settle him.

Security personnel are ready to greet them as they park in the underground lot and escort them up to Sasha and Conrad's office. Ezra's hands become increasingly sweaty the longer they're in the elevator. By the time they're let out on the top floor he's at serious risk of sweating through his shirt. When he glances at Teddy though, his expression is unreadable. And honestly, like, it's weird. Really weird.

Through the glass walls, Ezra can see that everyone is already there. Grace and his parents. Daria and Teddy's folks. Sasha and Conrad. Ali and Mara. Ezra nervously licks his lips and looks at Teddy, realising they haven't even decided how to play this yet. Which they really should have done. They need a game plan, like, yesterday. But to Ezra's surprise, Teddy just takes his hand.

'Do you trust me?' Teddy asks Ezra quietly, eyes on his parents.

What a dumb question. Of course, he does. Ezra would blindly follow Teddy into battle without asking questions. And, he supposes, that's kind of what this is. But with less horses and javelins, and more homophobes. He nods.

Teddy gives his hand a little squeeze. 'You are my new dream.'

Ezra doesn't have time to grin, or call him an idiot, before Teddy is leading them through the door, Iris in tow. And Ezra actually feels the temperature in the room drop as everyone's gaze settles on them. On their joint hands. On the cut on Ezra's face. The roiling in his stomach is back as Anastasya tries to melt him with the power of her bigoted glare.

Teddy keeps hold of Ezra's hand as they sit down, resting their laced fingers on the table. A statement. And dear God, if Ezra makes it through this meeting without someone flaying him alive, he might just marry this ludicrous man.

Then Teddy Montgomery says: 'I hope this is important. We were in bed.'

Iris covers a laugh with an unconvincing cough. Ezra has to pick his jaw up off the goddamn floor. Anastasya may actually combust. If their whole careers weren't in dire peril, Ezra suspects that would have turned him on. Maybe it still did. A little.

'Let's cut to the chase,' Sasha says, evenly. She is a facade of calm in a Louis Vuitton pantsuit and a well-rehearsed CEO smile. 'For all our sakes.'

Conrad pushes an envelope across the table that has been neatly torn open. Teddy reaches for it and Ezra leans in to look at the letter he pulls free. Attached with paperclips are several photos of himself and Teddy last night. Kissing on Teddy's street. Ezra grips his hand a little tighter.

Teddy reads aloud. The letter is short, the message clear: 'I have a video too.' Teddy blinks, then says, 'If they're trying to blackmail us, they forgot the key part where they actually extort us.'

'Hold your fucking horses, kiddo,' Ali mutters. She looks like she hasn't slept in days. She probably hasn't.

'They also sent this,' Conrad puts a burner phone on the table. It's cheap. Something you could pick up at Walmart or Target with a twenty and still have change leftover. 'There's only one number on there. It's saved as "Call Me".'

'Obvious question incoming,' Iris says. 'Did you?'

'We did,' Sasha nods. 'Surprise surprise, they want money. Fifty thousand dollars or the video goes to every drama channel on the internet.'

'Pay it,' Anastasya barks. Her gaze is still firmly on Ezra and Teddy's joint hands. 'Pay it and be done with it. Your show will make the money back.'

Sasha calmly folds her hands across each other on the table. She looks so nonchalant that Ezra wants to shake her. Shake that mask loose. Know how much shit they're really in. Which is, let's face it, a lot. 'You see, it's not that simple. We could, very well, pay the demanded fee and in return they can give us the video and the photos. But there is no guarantee that they don't have copies and that they won't keep demanding more.'

'So, what is your plan?' David asks. Where Anastasya is chewing on rusty nails and used band aids, he prefers a silent rage. It's unsettling. 'Just let this *reporter* — if that's what they even are — spread these lies about our son—'

'They're not lies,' Teddy says, and the room goes pin-drop silent. Ezra gives his hand a gentle squeeze because it's started to shake again.

'What did you say?' David asks slowly, because even with photo evidence he still needs it spelling out for him.

'I said,' Teddy's voice barely wobbles, 'they're not lies. Christ, dad, look at the photos. Look at this.' He holds up their joint hands for a moment. 'What more do you want?'

'Photos can be doctored,' Anastasya says. 'So can videos.'

'I'm sure they can, mum. But these aren't.'

David's voice raises for the first time in — well — ever. 'Listen to me, boy—'

'No,' Teddy cuts across him, finally looking at his father. 'You are going to listen to *me*. For the first time in your life, you are going to listen to someone else. Dad, I'm gay.'

David turns his glare onto Ezra. 'This is his fault. It's his influence. You were perfectly normal before we moved here.'

'Dad, I've always been gay. You just didn't want to admit it.' Teddy looks at Ezra, and his expression goes soft. 'And there's nothing wrong with me.'

'Everything we did to prevent this!' Anastasya snaps. 'How could you do this to your family?'

Teddy's gaze darkens. 'You mean the illegal gay conversion therapy? Or the emotional abuse? Or not believing me when dad's colleague came onto me when I was thirteen?'

Well, shit. The pause before anyone speaks is so pregnant that Ezra is amazed no one actually goes into labour. And no one is expecting Mara to be the one to break the silence when she says: 'If we are to continue with this line of conversation, I would recommend everyone's lawyers be present.'

Conrad clears his throat in a desperate attempt to regain control of their meeting. 'Personal matters aside, we need to focus on the correct steps to take now. Ezra and Teddy have clearly violated their contacts and betrayed the network's trust by indulging in this unscripted affair. Action must be taken.'

'We have two options,' Sasha continues. 'The first option is we pay the fee — out of Ezra and Teddy's royalties — and spin the narrative that these photos and the video are doctored. Any following demands for money will also come out of their royalties until the authorities can track down who is behind this.'

'And the second option?' Ezra asks, already knowing he's not going to like it.

'You deny the video is fake,' Sasha says. 'And we will terminate your show. You will have to buy yourself out of your contract with us, and all further business between us will cease.'

'So,' Jacqueline says, using the mom-voice that Ezra and Grace learned to avoid inducing growing up. 'Let me make sure I have this perfectly clear. You are asking our children — our *children*, Sasha — to lie about who they are. About the most important thing in their lives. Or to condemn their careers?'

Sasha gives her a look that she must think is placating, but Ezra knows that it will have the complete opposite effect on his mom. 'We understand that you want what's best for your children. But contracts have been signed, and those same contracts have been violated. We must decide—'

'Theodore will deny the validity of the photos,' David says, decisively. 'We can say that Ezra is behind it. Jealous that his deviance couldn't sway Theodore. No one needs to know the truth.'

'But I'll know the truth,' Teddy says. 'For God's sake, dad. Is it really so bad that I'm gay? That I'm in love with another man? Do you really hate who I am that much?'

David looks sharply at his son. 'We will get you help. We can talk to our church. We—'

'It's *my* fucking life!' Teddy suddenly explodes. 'I don't need help! I don't need fixing! There's nothing *wrong* with me!'

'Watch your language!' Anastasya barks.

'Why can't you just love me?' Teddy demands. His jaw is winding up tighter than a piano string. Ezra can see his throat working. Over a decade of anger, and pain, and misery threatening to rip free. 'All I ever wanted was for you to love me! As I am! Ezra does! Leo did! Why can't you?'

'Your brother would be ashamed of you,' David says, eyes hard.

'He wasn't. He knew. And he loved me anyway.'

'Better him dead than to see you now.'

Ezra can almost hear Teddy's heart break. He watches helplessly as all the fight leaves his body. His shoulders sag, his hand going limp in Ezra's. Wordlessly he stands, and Ezra wants to follow him as he leaves, but he knows that if he doesn't say something right now that he'll always regret it. So instead, he squares his shoulders, takes in a deep breath, and throws himself onto the battlefield.

'How dare you,' Ezra's voice is quieter than he'd have liked. But. You know. Baby steps. 'How dare you take away the last part of his brother that he has. How dare you refuse to give him the basic love and affection a child deserves from their parents. How *dare* you make him feel any less of a person because of who he loves. How can you be so heartless?'

David's nostrils flare. 'This is a family matter. It has nothing to do with you.'

'It has everything to do with me. Mr Montgomery, I am in love with your son. And he's in love with me. And, seriously, fuck you if you can't be happy for us.'

David rises to his feet, fists balling at his sides, but then so does Warren. And it takes Ezra by surprise. Because he's used to his dad being the quiet mediator. The voice of reason. So, seeing him standing there, looking like he's about ready to start throwing hands, is unreal.

'Do not,' Warren says, tone lethal, 'even think about threatening my son — or your own, for that matter — ever again.'

David's face goes an alarming shade of purple. Behind their dad's back, Ezra shares a *what the actual hell* look with Grace.

'I will do as I see fit when it comes to my family,' David snaps.

'We are not your family,' Warren says, resolutely. 'And going by the way you treat Teddy, neither is he.'

'And neither am I,' says Daria.

Well, double shit.

Anastasya looks at her daughter-in-law. 'I beg your pardon.'

'Love is supposed to be unconditional,' Daria's voice is soft but determined. 'You only love the idea of who you want Teddy to be. Not who he really is. And Leo would never be disappointed in him for loving Ezra. Same as he wouldn't be disappointed in me for loving Iris.'

Triple shit. Ezra looks from Daria to Iris, who's chest is so puffed up with pride and affection it's a surprise she hasn't burst. Ezra puts a hand out to squeeze her shoulder and she spares him a grin. Holy hell, this woman. The first and only girl he ever loved. Couldn't have picked a better ex-girlfriend if he tried.

Ali clears her throat. She's been unusually quiet this whole exchange, and Ezra has half-forgotten that she's even there. Now though, looking at the grim determination on her face, he can see that she's just been gearing up to something. And God help them all.

'If anyone wants the opinion of a publicist with over twenty years in the game — the same publicist who is paid to give you said expert opinion...' She starts slowly. Ezra can feel her building up to the kind of ball-crushing-comeback that he has come to both love and fear from her. 'Teddy and Ezra just gave the Darling Dynasty the biggest twist of the whole season. Not to mention a cliff-hanger that would not only guarantee a return audience for the next season but an increased audience.' A pause. She looks at Ezra. 'However, if you want my opinion as a trans woman who is openly pansexual and completely fucking *done* with the politics and bigotry in this room?' And then Ali smiles. And it's wonderful. 'Go get your man, Ezra.'

And he does. Ezra leaves BingeBox HQ and does exactly that. And it too, is wonderful.

***

Teddy is so predictable. Just like when Ezra doesn't know where to go and ends up at Teddy's, Teddy is waiting for him on Ezra's couch. And wow. Because this is it. Ezra is looking at his whole damn future right now. Teddy on the sofa, already changed into a pair of sweatpants and a baggy t-shirt. His feet are bare and propped up on the coffee table. On his TV, *Mamma Mia* is playing. Teddy is humming along, steaming cup of tea in his hands. He looks up at Ezra, and his smile can power all of New York City.

'Honey,' he says. 'You're home.'

Ezra flops down beside him, careful not to jostle his tea. 'You're surprisingly...' he searches for the right word, '...chipper?'

Teddy smiles and presses a kiss to his temple. 'I've had time to think.'

'Uh-oh.'

'Behave,' Teddy's tone is stern, but there's a quirk to his mouth. 'Like I said, I've been thinking. And I think I'm ready to come out. I know we'll have to pay out the BingeBox contract and we'd have to check with Grace first, obviously. But if she's okay with it, and if you're okay with it,' Teddy's tone goes tentative, and it's adorable, 'then I would like to tell the world that you're mine.'

All the air leaves Ezra's lungs. 'Oh. Wow.'

'Good wow or bad wow?'

Ezra kisses him. 'Definitely a good wow.'

'I'm not going to fool myself into thinking it will be easy. I know it won't. Mum and Dad will have their opinions. It will immediately cut off career opportunities — not that it's such a bad thing. I never wanted to be part of the reality TV world. But I'm tired of pretending to be someone I'm not. And I'm tired of pretending that I'm not hopelessly in love with you.'

Ezra kisses him again. Because. Like. Duh. How can he *not* kiss him after that? On the screen Sophie and Skye are singing about laying all their love on each other, and Ezra feels it all the way to his bones. His phone buzzes and he really doesn't want to look at it, but after the chaos he's just left in his wake at BingeBox, he knows he probably should. It's from Grace, and simply reads: **eta 5 mins. don't be naked please.**

She's there in four minutes, tops. Enough time for Ezra to change into his pyjamas and put on a fresh pot of coffee. Because Grace coming over probably means an all-nighter. Which normally would be, like, yay. But Teddy is there, and all Ezra wants to do is rip his clothes off and tie him to the bedposts. But, seeing as how he (and his dick) may have ruined his sister's career, he (and his dick) will have to get over it.

He pushes a mug of coffee into her hands the moment she enters so that she can't hit him. Then again, he realises that she could just throw the mug at him. Luckily, instead, she sits at the breakfast counter and grins at them both.

'You two,' she says, 'are something else. You know that?'

Ezra looks from his sister to Teddy. 'Does she look like she's going to murder us? Is she lulling us into a false sense of security?'

Teddy nods. 'Definitely. That's why she didn't bring Iris. No witnesses.'

'Why is she smiling at us like that? It's creepy.'

'Truly harrowing.'

'That was quite the shit storm you left behind,' Grace says. 'Teddy, I think your mom had an aneurysm. Especially when Daria got up and kissed Iris in front of her. Your dad nearly coughed up a lung.'

Teddy barks a surprised laugh, joining them at the kitchen island. 'She did what?'

'She dipped her like in that famous V Day photo, and just, like, kissed her,' Grace says, sipping her coffee. 'Your mom called them deviants and told Daria she wasn't welcome in the family anymore. Daria told them they weren't welcome around the kids until they,' Grace clears her throat and puts on her best (still quite awful) English accent, 'revaluated their bigoted notions and pulled their twin sticks out of their puckered rectums.'

Teddy's mouth hangs open. 'She didn't.'

'Oh, she did.'

He looks at Ezra. 'Let's send her a muffin basket.'

'*Then*,' Grace goes on, and Ezra has to pour himself another coffee, because this is obviously going to be a story. 'Ali said that she would no longer represent people who are incapable of accepting true love when it doesn't conform to their heteronormative predispositions.'

Ezra frowns. 'That's unusually calm of her.'

'Then she called Anastasya an uptight jizz sock and told David to lick a battery. Then she flipped off Sasha and Conrad and called an Uber.'

Ezra blinks. 'We'll send her a muffin basket too. And Mom and Dad?'

'Are so proud of you they could burst.'

Ezra's eyes unexpectedly burn. 'Well. Alright then.'

Teddy sighs and leans against the counter. 'Grace, I am so—'

'Don't you dare apologise,' she says, holding a hand out to stop him. And Ezra can tell from the look of steely determination on her face that she isn't allowing room for argument. 'You did what you had to. I respect that. And it's something I should have done for you months ago, if I was any kind of a true friend or sister.'

'Grace—' Ezra tries.

She shakes her head. 'No. This is on me. I could see how much you were both hurting, and I didn't do anything. That was really shitty of me. But I was so focused on getting this season out. I was scared that losing our contract with BingeBox would blacklist us from working with other networks. I couldn't see further than whatever script they gave me. And I am so, *so* sorry.'

Ezra wraps an arm around his sister's shoulders. She allows herself to sag into him for a moment before straightening her shoulders and lifting her chin.

'So,' Teddy asks, hesitantly. 'How much trouble have we gotten you in with BingeBox?'

'None,' Grace smiles. Ezra doesn't believe that for a moment. 'I told them, in very plain terms so that they couldn't get confused, that we won't be denying the authenticity of the video.'

Teddy and Ezra share a look. Teddy says, 'I don't understand.'

'I'm not going to ask you to pretend anymore. And I'm not going to work with people who ask you to. I've bought us out of the contract. I agreed to do an interview with them for the last episode of the season so that they can make up the numbers. But after that, that's it. We're done.'

Ezra gapes at her. 'But. But your show. Your *career*—'

'Will be fine,' she says firmly. 'I'll find something else. Or I won't and I'll go back to YouTube.'

'Grace, we can't let you do this,' Teddy says.

'You didn't. I did it of my own choice.' Grace gives a truly world-weary sigh and reaches for them both, grabbing both their hands. 'Ezra, you have given up your whole life for me. You never wanted this, but you did it for me anyway. Let me do this for you.' Then she looks at Teddy, her smile fond, like she is looking at another brother. 'And Teddy, consider this an early wedding gift from me. You were willing to give up your happiness to help out someone you didn't even know. Now it's my turn to give up something for you.'

Teddy's jaw clenches and he nods tightly. 'Thank you.'

'Really,' Ezra adds, squeezing her hand. 'Thanks. You're amazing.'

'I know. Now, for what I *really* came here to do. Teddy?'

He spares a quick glance at Ezra, before answering. 'Yes?'

Grace grins. 'I think we should see other people.'

Chapter Twenty-Seven

Teddy is cute when he's nervous. Like, a-box-of-kittens-wearing-bows cute. Ezra watches him fiddle restlessly with his tie as he stands in the wings to the press conference stage, and eventually Ezra has to still his hands with his own. Standing this close to Teddy, looking up at him, Ezra can feel the anxiety vibrating off him. His muscles are so tense beneath his Burberry suit, and Ezra wants to take him home and indulge him in a bubble bath and a massage. And later, he will.

'You don't have to do this,' Ezra gently reminds him.

And then Teddy looks at him with so much tenderness that Ezra's insides wobble. 'Yes, love, I do. For you. For *us*. For our future.'

Ezra brings Teddy's hands to his chest, just like all that time ago in the broken-down elevator. He hopes that Teddy knows it's beating for him. 'You're my whole world, Theodore Mikhail Montgomery.'

Teddy's smile is truly life-ruining. 'And you are the best worst decision I've ever made, Ezra Samuel Darling.'

Ezra tiptoes up and kisses Teddy's nose. 'Ditto, sweetheart.'

Teddy melts a little, going pliant against him, just as a woman comes over to mic him up. Everyone on the Darling Dynasty team has been briefed on their relationship, and have all signed NDAs to not talk about it. So, when Ezra gives Teddy a heated look while the press team preps him, he can live in the comfortable knowledge that he doesn't have to give a fuck who sees. And Christ, it's a good feeling.

Ali joins them, finally looking well rested for the first time in, well, probably ever. She nods at them both as she takes a sip from her thermos that smells distinctly Kahlua-less. Ezra makes a note to suggest to his Mom and Dad that she be given some leave after this. Or a raise. Or both.

'Okay, Prince Harry,' she says. 'They're all ready for you. They're all Darling Dynasty friendly publications. They know there are no questions. It's live streaming on the Darling Dynasty Instagram and Facebook pages. Don't fuck it up.'

Teddy goes conspicuously pale and clammy. He looks at Ezra with his Bambi's-mom-about-to-be-shot face, and Ezra gives his arm a gentle squeeze. 'You're too hot for the closet, baby.'

Teddy relaxes the barest of fractions. The woman who'd attached the lapel mic to his jacket reappears and gives them a patient smile. 'Ready when you are, Mr Montgomery.'

Teddy thanks her and looks back to Ezra, who can't help but grin up at him like an idiot. Because, when it comes to Teddy, he is. 'Wish me luck?'

Ezra pulls him in for a quick kiss. Just the barest brush of lips. A promise of what's to come later. 'I'll be waiting right here.'

And then, Ezra watches his whole heart walk out onto the stage and change their lives forever.

[Excerpt from the Darling Dynasty Newsletter, Saturday 12th February 2022]

Full transcript of Teddy Montgomery's speech at the Sterling Centre Press Room

Thank you for joining me today.

I've never been good with words unless they're song lyrics, so I won't waste your time and I'll get straight to the point. I will no longer be marrying Grace Darling later this month. The reason that I will not be marrying Grace is simple: from the start, our relationship was a charade, a narrative created by BingeBox that would bring myself and the Darling Dynasty together. Our networks had been pushing for our families to collaborate for years, and until recently, when my family came under speculation for something that I am not currently at liberty to talk about, we have always said no. Until we said yes.

The plan was for Grace and myself to be married by the time this season's filming wrapped, and to stay married for three years, until the Darling Dynasty contract with BingeBox was complete. That, however, will no longer be happening in the light of the fact that I am irrevocably and unapologetically gay. And while I won't apologise for being gay, I will apologise for lying to our audience. It was not in mine, or anyone else's, interest to deceive you. We were stuck between a contract and a hard place, and I respectfully ask for your forgiveness if you feel that myself or anyone at Darling Dynasty has betrayed your trust. This was not our intent.

This of course, brings me to the matter of Ezra Darling. Earlier this year, Ezra was forced to make a series of public statements about his sexuality. Statements that would not be necessary had we been honest from the start. The truth of it is, that Ezra and I have been in a sexual relationship with each other since early 2021. I am ashamed of myself for allowing him to take the brunt of the public speculation. He was trying to protect me. I was still closeted, and he didn't want me to be forced into coming out. Because that's the thing about Ezra Darling: he is the most caring, warm, genuine person you'll ever meet. And I suppose it should come as a shock to no one, least of all myself, that I fell in love with him.

Falling for Ezra Darling was a mistake. A mistake I was privileged to make. A mistake that I will continue to make for the rest of my life. I know what love is, because I have him. A lot of people have asked me to give him up. I have been shamed by my own family, coerced by people in better positions of power than myself, threatened and blackmailed. But all of that pales in utter comparison, because the fact of the matter is: I choose him. I will always choose him. Every time. Without fail. Without thinking. He is my choice.

And now, I must humbly ask that you respect my choice. I am aware that I have done nothing to earn it, but I ask for it all the same. I am not naïve enough to think that I can say a few polite words, and that everything I've done will be swept away. I have to earn the trust of my audience again, and that of the Darling Dynasty audience that welcomed me with such open arms. I will strive to do better every day.

I can only apologise for the pain I have caused and promise that it will not happen again. I cannot and will not be forced back into the closet. I understand that not everyone will accept this, and that is their prerogative. I don't ask that anyone change their beliefs or opinions just because I fell in love with someone of the same gender. What I *do* ask for, however, is your kindness. Not just for me, but for anyone else out there who is different. Anyone else you may encounter who is struggling with themselves. There is so much more going on than what we can just see on the surface, and the greatest honour we can do to each other is to be kind in the face of our differences.

Please believe me when I say I will take my own advice today. Once more I apologise, and I thank you for your time.

Thank you.

Ezra's eyelashes are damp as Teddy re-joins him in the wings. Teddy wraps him in a hug that threatens to cause serious internal bleeding, but Ezra doesn't care. He also doesn't care when Teddy grabs his legs and lifts them up, securing them around his waist. Suddenly they look like all those videos of soldiers coming home from missions abroad, their partners clinging to them like spider monkeys. Ezra doesn't mind being a spider monkey.

Then they're laughing. And kissing. And maybe crying. But definitely kissing.

'You did it,' Ezra says between kisses. 'You did it, baby. I'm so proud of you.'

'I love you,' he says. His voice is still shaking. *All* of him is shaking. 'God, I love you.'

Ezra genuinely can't stop kissing him. 'I love you too. Always.'

'Jesus, I feel like I'm on Gay Porn Hub,' Ali says, joining them.

Teddy almost drops Ezra, a blush starting at his neck and creeping all the way up to his ears. He clears his throat and smooths down the front of his suit jacket. His cheeks pink up too as Ezra wraps an arm around his lower back, but he still melts into the touch. Ezra can practically feel years of repressed emotion and self-loathing seeping from his lean body.

'Spend a lot of time on Gay Porn Hub, do you?' Ezra asks.

Ali gives him an arch look. 'I have a thing for leather daddies.'

Poor Teddy chokes like he's swallowed a spoonful of cinnamon powder. Ezra gives his side an affectionate squeeze. He rescues him by saying: 'Thanks for organising this. And for being in our corner this whole time. We really appreciate it.'

Ali physically recoils from the sentiment. 'Ew. Fuck off.'

Eager to join in, Teddy gives her a sincere look. 'We're lucky to have you, Ali. You mean so much to us.'

'Seriously, fuck off. Stop it. I *will* choose violence.'

Ezra leans into Teddy's side and smiles up at him. 'To repay you we wanted to ask if you'll be the godmother when we adopt.'

'If I still had a penis, I'd tell you to suck it,' Ali says. Her phone buzzes and she fishes it out of her pocket. She makes a pleased sound before turning it around to show them the screen. 'Say hello to your coming out party, Harry Potter.'

A lump catches in Ezra's throat as he peers at the screen. It's a series of screenshots from Twitter where an outpouring of support and pride flag emojis flood the feed. Pulling out his phone he opens his own account to see himself and Teddy trending, along with *#HeIsMyChoice*. Ezra looks up at Teddy, who's jaw is so tense that the tendons in his neck pop. He takes Teddy's hand in his. This man. This goddamn man.

'I meant it,' Teddy says. 'I will always choose you.'

And Ezra kisses him. Because how could he not? 'Proud to be your choice.'

And holy hell does he mean it. If Teddy Montgomery chooses him, then Ezra will spend the rest of his life proving that he deserves that privilege. Earning the right to be the one that Teddy tells the world he's in love with. The right to be the one that sees Teddy at his best, and his worst, and everything in between. Ezra knows he has to be the best choice Teddy has ever made. And he swears to God he will be.

They walk home holding hands. Because they can. They get less than halfway down the street from the Sterling Centre before the first photo snaps. Then another. Then another. And for the most part, people aren't intrusive. They watch from a distance. They try to take sneaky photos from across the road. And then there are people who call their names. People that stop them to ask for selfies. People who gawp at them: the Wyoming Wild Child and Great Britain's Golden Boy holding hands.

A car goes by and a girl in the passenger seat rolls down her window and shouts, "He is my choice," giving them both a wave. They laugh. Because it feels so good to not have to hide anymore. To not care who sees, or what people will think. Teddy has the dopiest grin Ezra has ever seen on him the whole time. Ugh. He's so adorable. Ezra is simply going to die.

They walk past the road that leads down to The Palace and Teddy pauses. His expression is tender as he looks at Ezra, chucking him gently under the chin. 'Do you think The Palace will have a table free?'

'For you, baby?' Ezra says, grinning. 'They'll make one.'

Teddy smiles down at him, and Ezra's knees are suddenly made of rubber. 'Good. I want to take you on a date.'

Ezra could die from sweetness overload. In fact, he's pretty sure he already has. He's a goner. Have him cremated. Send flowers. He swallows down an incoherent babble of nonsense that threatens to bubble out and nods. 'Sure. I want dinner before I put out.'

Teddy grins devilishly. His fingers hook into Ezra's belt loops, and he pulls them flush together. 'Ezra, love. We both know you're a sure thing.'

'Not tonight, I'm not. This is our first official date and I'm treating it like one. You want to get into my pants then you're going to have to *work* for it.'

Then Teddy honest-to-God growls. And it might be the sexiest thing Ezra has ever heard. He ghosts his lips across Ezra's and whispers. 'As you wish.'

Teddy steps back and holds his arm out to Ezra. He waggles his perfect eyebrows and Ezra laughs, taking his arm. They make their way leisurely to the restaurant, grinning up at the sky as it starts to snow. The Palace staff practically fall over each other to prepare a table for them in the back where they won't be disturbed. Teddy pulls Ezra's chair out for him, and Ezra nearly swoons. He's never been on a first date quite so formal. But it's, like, really nice. To be taken care of in the way Teddy wants to take care of him is so special, and Ezra's heart is so full.

They pretend like it really is a first date. Teddy asks him where he grew up, and Ezra asks him what he does for a living. Teddy asks if he's a cat person or a dog person. Ezra asks what his hobbies are. Teddy asks about his family. Ezra asks what he wants for the future. They hold hands across the table and talk, and talk, and talk. When the bill comes they both make a show of wanting to pay for it before agreeing to go halves and leaving a generous tip.

Teddy offers to walk Ezra back to his brownstone and Ezra pretends to be coy when accepting. They link arms again and huddle close as the snow comes down harder. When they find themselves at Ezra's doorstep, Teddy gives him a chaste kiss on the cheek, and Ezra's whole body warms despite the cold.

'So,' Teddy says, rubbing Ezra's arms in a futile attempt to keep him warm. 'How did I do?'

Ezra grins. 'Well, you were very charming. Funny. Attentive.'

'So, not boring then?'

Ezra groans. 'You're never going to let that go, are you?'

'Not for a good long while, no.'

Ezra bites his lip and looks up at Teddy. 'Teddy, would you like to come in?'

The door is barely closed behind them before they're kissing. And wow, are they kissing. Ezra can feel himself steadily thawing out as Teddy crowds him into the wall, hands searching out his coat buttons, pushing their way under his sweater. Teddy claims him in a way that he hasn't before. His mouth is needy against Ezra's, his tongue insistent.

All Ezra can think is that there's too many clothes. Too much in between them. Ezra's hands are clumsy as he pushes off Teddy's jacket, fingers going to his shirt buttons. He feels Teddy shudder against him as his palms meet his abs. Teddy's lips move from Ezra's mouth to his jaw, and then down his neck. He briefly stops his assault to pull Ezra's sweater over his head, and then his mouth is back on his neck.

Ezra's eyes flutter closed as Teddy's kisses steadily migrate south, trailing down his collar bones, his pecks, stopping briefly to tease at his nipples. And then lower. And lower, and Ezra's abs tighten in anticipation as Teddy undoes his belt buckle. He makes the mistake of looking down at Teddy as he shucks Ezra's boxers and takes him into his elegant mouth.

He curses, his hands threading into Teddy's hair, tugging in the way that he knows Teddy likes.

Teddy plays with him. Edges him repeatedly, only to draw back and smile fiendishly up at him. His lips are kiss-swollen and wet, and Ezra wishes he had a camera. Teddy is just too hot like this. Needy, and eager, and undeniably toppy. Even on his knees.

When Teddy stands, he immediately reclaims Ezra's mouth. Ezra can taste himself on Teddy's lips and it sends an electric sizzle down his spine. He kicks his boxers to one side so that Teddy can grasp his thighs and lift Ezra's legs around his waist. He pushes Ezra against the wall, gasping as their bare chests and other places meet. Rub together.

'Bedroom,' Ezra breathes.

And like the goddamn Greek God that he is, Teddy carries him like that to the bedroom. Like Ezra doesn't weigh anything. And Ezra marvels at his coordination as he doesn't break the kiss, except to lay him down on the duvet. He looks up at Teddy, breaths coming in hard and fast. Then Teddy starts to undress properly, and Ezra nearly loses his mind.

Crawling over Ezra's body to kiss him, Teddy slots himself snuggly between his thighs. He kisses him slowly. Languidly. Almost lazily. And it's not long before Ezra's body is arching, his back bowing up to meet Teddy's.

'Now,' he pants. 'Please. Now.'

Speech seems beyond Teddy's capabilities, because he just nods. He reaches for the condoms and the lube on the bedside table. Ezra barely needs any prep before their bodies finally meet, Teddy bottoming out with ease. Ezra's head drops back against the pillow and Teddy's lips are on his neck again, biting and sucking as his hips find a rhythm that has them both gasping.

When Teddy pulls back to look at him, Ezra can hardly stand the sight of him. His eyes — those Lake Tahoe blue eyes — are dark and intense. Pools of want, and love. Ezra can't get enough. He reaches up and puts his hands on the flat plains of Teddy's chest. Just skin, and skin, and skin. It's all his and it doesn't matter who knows it. Teddy Montgomery is his.

Ezra wants to say *take me* but it comes out as *love me* and Teddy obliges. And Ezra feels so loved and so desperately happy, and he can't believe his luck. That this silly man loves him. Teddy loves him slow and deep. He loves him with every long thrust and every roll of his hips. He catches Ezra's gasps and moans as they escape his lips, swallowing down his pleas of: 'God. Yes. Please. Please. There. Yes.'

Ezra wraps his legs around Teddy's waist, pulling them closer, and it's still not enough. All of Teddy will never be enough. And even when Ezra is clinging to him, head thrown back, crying out Teddy's name as he comes, it's not enough. Forever with Teddy Montgomery will never be enough. But it's a good start.

Chapter Twenty-Eight

[ARTICLE FROM CELEB BUZZ, SUNDAY 13TH FEBRUARY 2022, WRITTEN BY ALEXIS LUNDY]

<u>TEN #HeIsMyChoice TWEETS ABOUT EZRA DARLING AND TEDDY MONTGOMERY THAT PERFECTLY SUM UP HOW WE ALL FEEL RIGHT NOW</u>

1. "I KNEW IT I KNEW IT I FUCKING *KNEW* IT!!! #HeIsMyChoice"
@QueenQuinn

2. "kind of happy for them, also kind of sad i'll never have a chance with teddy. #ohwell #HeIsMyChoice"
@memewhore

3. "Not me shipping Teddy and Ezra harder than I ship me and my own girlfriend #HeIsMyChoice"
@Tim_Is_Sleeping

4. "it's the 'fuck you' to the homophobes, for me [rainbow emoji] #HeIsMyChoice"
@alice_holmes

5. "I'm not crying, YOU'RE crying [crying emoji] #Tezra #HeIsMyChoice"
@sad_gay_amber

6. "so when is the wedding and are we all invited? #HeIsMyChoice #LoveIsLove"
@this_is_ben

7. "To all the homophobes upset about Teddy Montgomery's press release, can I suggest you get the fuck over it? There are worse things in the world than boys kissing boys. For example, your existence. #HeIsMyChoice"
@MorganMcNamara

8. "my little queer heart can't take it [rainbow emoji] #happytears #lovewins #HeIsMyChoice"
@EmmaTweets

9. "Welcome to the rainbow club, Teddy [rainbow emoji] #HeIsMyChoice #Tezra"
@BigGayAlan

10. "i love the smell of gay pride in the morning #HeIsMyChoice"
@pizzaslut

[Excerpt from That's The Tea, Monday 14th February 2022, written by Tara Young]

He's Here, He's Queer, What Now For His Career?

Who else had Teddy Montgomery coming out of the closet on their 2022 bingo card?

Just WEEKS before Teddy Montgomery and Grace Darling were due to get hitched, Teddy comes out and says he's been sleeping with her brother this whole time. And it's more than just that! It's love! L.O.V.E.!

The kind that Michael Bublé sings about and Taylor Swift wishes she could write better songs about. And here at That's The Tea, we stan.

According to Teddy's press release on Saturday, Teddy has struggled with coming out due to restrictive contracts with BingeBox, and pressure from his family to stay closeted — and yes, this is the same family accused of being involved in illegal gay conversion therapy trials. And, I'm not going to lie, this reporter did get a bit tearful watching his speech live on Darling Dynasty's Insta as Teddy told the world that he chooses Ezra Darling. (Do you think he knew at the time that he was creating one of the most iconic hashtags to trend on Twitter in history? #HeIsMyChoice.)

But, what happens now? Well, there have been rumours that BingeBox have dropped the Darling Dynasty and are scrambling to put together a season finale harder than the makers of Love Is Blind for season three. And what of the Montgomerys and Great Britain's Golden Boy? Gossip over on Reddit says that he is estranged from his homophobic family (thank you, Jesus) and is seeking a solo career — in what exactly, we have no idea. Anyone else think he'd have a remarkable career in singing? We've all seen those hospital visit videos, right? Our hearts! They can't take it!

As for the Darlings themselves, everything has been suspiciously quiet. After Teddy's press release, Grace Darling tweeted a short and sweet "#HeIsMyChoice" but so far, that's it. Here at That's The Tea, we are placing bets on when the official Darling Dynasty statement will come out and what it will say. Anyone else reckon they knew all along? At any rate, everyone in the office here is waving their rainbow flags in solidarity.

We're rooting for you, boys.

[Excerpt from the New York Post, Friday 18th February 2022]

Montgomery Press Conference Confirms Family Scandal

Following a recent press conference at the Sterling Centre, NYC, where Theodore Montgomery came out as gay, the youngest Montgomery child has spearheaded another conference where he publicly disowned his parents. Theodore claims this is due to parental neglect, coercion in his family's gay conversion therapy trials, and for emotional abuse that he suffered as a child. Standing alongside Theodore was his partner, Ezra Darling, and his sister-in-law, Daria Montgomery. Although neither made a statement, Theodore made it clear that both Daria and the entire Darling family stand by him.

In what was a very tense and emotional speech, Theodore spoke about the torment he suffered throughout his childhood. He claims that when his parents discovered his homosexuality, they made him 'patient o' in his grandfather's illegal conversion trials. He says he was exposed to homosexual pornography while attached to a machine that would make him sick, all the while being underage. He then went on to tell the story of how his father's business colleague attempted to groom him, and of his parent's neglect when he turned to them for help.

Theodore broke down several times during the emotionally charged conference, as did several members of the attending press. Theodore went on to say that he has requested a restraining order against both of his parents. It was also made clear that contact between his parents and Daria Montgomery's children is strictly prohibited at Daria's request.

The conference ended with Theodore announcing his new charity that himself and Ezra Darling are founding to protect LGBTQ+ children and young people. PRIDE is a non-profit organisation that will launch early spring and will be spearheaded by Theodore himself. He encouraged the public to "give generously and love openly."

[EXCERPT FROM THE DARLING DYNASTY NEWSLETTER, SATURDAY 19TH FEBRUARY 2022]

To our incredible Darling Dynasty family,

Firstly, we want to thank you all for your amazing support of our show. It sounds ridiculously corny to say, but we would be nothing without our loyal fans. BingeBox may have given us a platform, but you gave us a voice. By wanting to hear what we had to say, you gave us the greatest gift of all, and we are so unbelievably grateful.

Secondly, we want to apologise. We have not been honest with you. We have no excuses. We must own our mistakes, because that's what you deserve. At the start of this season's filming, our own Grace Darling entered into a fake relationship with Teddy Montgomery for the sole purpose of creating a narrative for our show. It was also in the best interest of the Montgomery family who was amidst a torrent of ugly rumours that were, unfortunately, true. More on this can be read about by clicking here.

We want to make it abundantly clear that everyone at Darling Dynasty is entirely supportive of Ezra and Teddy's relationship, and Teddy's decision to publicly come out. We also fully support his decision to disown his parents considering the troubling charges that have been made against them, and also in his decision to press charges against his father's colleague. We fully embrace Teddy Mikhail Montgomery and his sister-in-law, Daria Montgomery, as family.

Lastly, we want to talk about the future. By engaging in a romantic relationship, Ezra and Teddy directly violated our contract with BingeBox. And while Ezra and Teddy do not regret their actions, and while everyone at Darling Dynasty respects their decision, we would be lying to say we are not sad to see an end to our partnership. BingeBox have been good allies and friends to us and those close to us, but at

Darling Dynasty we believe that true love and living authentically are both more important than reality TV. We are unsure where this leaves the Darling Dynasty, but we have no doubt that we have made the right decision.

From the bottom of our Birkins, we want to thank you all so much. For your support all these years and your support now. We couldn't have done it without you.

We hope to see you very soon.

Love,

Darling Dynasty

#HeIsMyChoice

[Statement released on Twitter from BingeBox, Sunday 20th February 2022]

@BingeBox_USA

Dear Bingers,

It is with a heavy heart that we have decided to part ways with our long-time friends at Darling Dynasty. While we have worked together successfully for a number of years, we all feel it is time that we moved on. We have no doubt that the Darlings are onto new adventures, and we look forward to seeing what they create in the future. This season of Darling Dynasty will be the last to air. The season finale will go ahead as planned, but instead will entail an in-depth interview with Grace Darling on the events of the last year regarding herself, her family, and Teddy Montgomery.

For more details, please click the link in our bio.

[Partial transcript from Good Morning New York, Monday 21st February 2022]

[Audience cheering.]

Fletcher Fawkes: Alright, alright. You're going to scare off our next guests before they even come out to play! Ladies and gentlemen, please welcome to the studio: Ezra Darling and Teddy Montgomery!

[Applause. Cheering. MONTGOMERY and DARLING join FAWKES in the studio. They sit on the sofa, holding hands.]

Fletcher Fawkes: Welcome! Welcome! How are you both?

Ezra Darling: Hey! Great, thanks. Good to see you again.

Teddy Montgomery: Thank you for having us.

Fletcher Fawkes: All the better for having you both here. So, tell me: is it love?

Ezra Darling: [Laughing.] Oh, I'd say so.

Teddy Montgomery: If not then we've created a lot of trouble for nothing.

[Audience laughing.]

FLETCHER FAWKES: TEDDY, YOU SAID THAT EZRA IS YOUR CHOICE. SINCE YOU CAME OUT AT YOUR PRESS CONFERENCE, YOUR WORLD SEEMS TO HAVE EXPLODED — BOTH PUBLICLY AND PERSONALLY. DO YOU STILL STAND BY THAT CHOICE?

TEDDY MONTGOMERY: OF COURSE. I WOULD STAND BY EZRA ON THE EDGE OF A CLIFF WITHOUT A SAFETY NET. I WILL GO WHEREVER HE LEADS ME, REGARDLESS OF HOW DIFFICULT THE JOURNEY IS. I LOVE HIM.

FLETCHER FAWKES: AND HAS IT BEEN DIFFICULT, COMING OUT? I KNOW THERE HAS BEEN BACKLASH FROM SOME FAMILY MEMBERS.

TEDDY MONTGOMERY: IT'S BEEN A BIT OF A MIXED BAG. THE SUPPORT FROM THE PUBLIC AND FROM EZRA'S FAMILY HAS BEEN OVERWHELMING, AND THANKS TO THAT IT'S NOT BEEN AS DAUNTING AS I'D ALWAYS FEARED. BUT, LIKE YOU SAY, THERE ARE SOME FAMILY MEMBERS WHO ARE LESS THAN HAPPY FOR ME, AND IT'S CAUSED A RIFT BETWEEN US. IT'S BEEN HARD, BUT NOT IMPOSSIBLE.

FLETCHER FAWKES: AND EZRA, IT MUST BE A RELIEF FOR YOU TO NOT HAVE TO HIDE YOUR FEELINGS ANYMORE?

EZRA DARLING: A RELIEF FOR BOTH OF US, HONESTLY. WE NEVER WANTED TO LIE TO ANYONE, BUT WE WEREN'T BANKING ON FALLING FOR EACH OTHER, EITHER. I'M NOT GOING TO LIE; IT WAS HARD PRETENDING THAT I WASN'T HEAD-OVER-HEELS FOR HIM. EVERY TIME WE WERE ON SCREEN OR IN PUBLIC TOGETHER, IT JUST FELT LIKE EVERYONE COULD TELL. SNEAKING AROUND IS NEVER ACTUALLY AS FUN AS THEY MAKE IT LOOK IN THE MOVIES.

FLETCHER FAWKES: WHICH, OF COURSE, EXPLAINS KISSGATE.

[DARLING LAUGHS AND COVERS HIS FACE WITH HIS HANDS.]

EZRA DARLING: OH, GOD. DON'T REMIND ME.

[AUDIENCE LAUGHING.]

Fletcher Fawkes: [Laughing.] Run me through what happened there.

[Darling points to Montgomery.]

Ezra Darling: He's what happened. Look at him! He's gorgeous!

[Audience laughing.]

Teddy Montgomery: [Laughing.] I think I was just as surprised as you were.

[A picture of Darling and Montgomery kissing on New Year's Eve shows on the screen behind them.]

Fletcher Fawkes: The picture that went viral in less than two minutes.

Ezra Darling: Well, of course it did. Look at him. He's beautiful.

Teddy Montgomery: Yes. You are.

[Montgomery puts a hand on Darling's knee. The audience claps.]

Fletcher Fawkes: You two are killing me. What you have seems so strong. What's your secret?

Teddy Montgomery: No secrets. Not anymore!

[Audience laughs.]

Ezra Darling: We're not going to pretend to be perfect. It's not been easy to get here. Some days it felt like I was drowning under the weight of it all. The pressure, the secrets, the fear — they really take their toll after a while. Plus, I was learning so much about myself, my sexuality. And we're not deluding ourselves into thinking that it will be easy from here on out. But what we've found has been worth fighting for. And we will always fight for each other and the right to love each other.

Teddy Montgomery: That, and we take turns taking Buffy out for walkies.

[Audience laughs. A photo from DARLING'S Instagram shows on the screen behind them. It shows DARLING and MONTGOMERY posing with a Golden Retriever puppy. The audience coos.]

Teddy Montgomery: There she is. Our baby.

Fletcher Fawkes: She's gorgeous.

Teddy Montgomery: She has Ezra's eyes.

Ezra Darling: And my attention span.

[Audience laughs.]

Fletcher Fawkes: You've settled quite quickly into domestic bliss.

Ezra Darling: We've waited so long for this. It didn't make sense to wait any longer.

Teddy Montgomery: I agree. I've waited my whole life for you.

[DARLING takes MONTGOMERY'S hand again. The audience applauds and coos.]

Fletcher Fawkes: It's too cute. It's officially too cute. Alright, before we all get a cavity, we're going to cut to a commercial break. When we're back we'll be talking more to America's favourite couple and hearing all about their new charity, PRIDE. See you in a bit!

Chapter Twenty-Nine

The way Teddy looks when he wakes up should be illegal. He's like a goddamn Disney princess with his parted lips and fluttering eyelashes. His hair is messy, but in that *on purpose* way. Because Teddy Montgomery really does wake up like this. Like all of Ezra's birthdays, Christmases — and possibly Hannukahs — in one. And then he smiles. The ludicrous man smiles at him. All silly, and sleep-drunk, and so pretty that Ezra is fairly certain he's going to combust.

He kisses him. Because he has to. He can't *not* kiss Teddy when he's smiling at him like that. He feels Teddy's body open up to him as he goes soft and pliant beneath Ezra. He feels Teddy surge up to meet him, and they both moan unabashedly as their skin makes contact.

A small, indignant yelp breaks them apart. Ezra laughs and pulls back, looking down at the foot of the bed where Buffy is being jostled about. The disgrace of it all. When they had first brought Buffy home, a week ago, they had tried keeping her in her own bed on the floor at night. But she'd cried so much that they'd agreed to let her sleep on the bed with them. For just one night. And of course, now she sleeps in bed with them every night. Which is fine all the while she's little. But if her paws are anything to go by — and the Internet says they are — then their sweet little princess is quickly going to grow to the size of a polar bear.

'Hello, sweet girl,' Teddy says, propping himself up on his elbows. 'Were we ignoring you?'

Buffy clumsily plods across the duvet, tripping over her too-big paws several times on the way. She democratically plops herself down exactly between Ezra and Teddy and rolls over in a silent demand for belly rubs. Of which, she receives many.

'You're a cock block, little miss,' Ezra says without even a trace of annoyance in his voice.

'Thank God for doggy day care.'

'Maybe we need to get her a little pair of noise cancelling headphones?'

Teddy gives Ezra a wicked look. 'Or get *you* a gag.'

Ezra groans and drops back onto the mattress, arm flopping (deservedly) dramatically over his face. 'You're killing me here.'

Teddy laughs as he scoops the wriggling puppy up into his arms. 'I'll take her out to do her business. You hop in the shower, and I'll join you in a bit once I have her distracted with breakfast.'

Ezra looks at him. 'Promise?'

'Only if you're good.'

Ezra bites his lip, groaning, as he rolls over to push his face into the pillows. He hears Teddy laugh as the bedroom door closes behind him and he allows himself a few moments to be lazy. The last few weeks have been — well — they've been. And then some. And today is their first day in weeks where they don't have a press conference, or a TV appearance, or an interview. It's their first day off since they'd let the world into their relationship, and it's being commandeered by the group chat — which *someone* (Iris) — has renamed to *Everybody Queer Wants You*.

When Ezra hears the front door open and close, and the sound of puppy chow being poured into a bowl, he leaps out of bed. Teddy's shower is far less temperamental than his own and he gets the water to the perfect scorching temperature before stepping under the spray. When Teddy joins him in the bathroom — cheeks and ears pink from the chill outside — Ezra rolls his eyes like he's been waiting for him forever.

'Took you long enough.'

Teddy joins him and says, 'Stop moaning or I'll give you something to moan about.'

'Don't threaten me with a good time.'

And then Teddy proceeds to not only threaten Ezra with said good time, but to drop to his knees and follow through. And by the time Ezra is pulling Teddy to his feet and pushing him against the shower wall so that they can come together, the water is running tepid. Their thighs shake. Teddy's mouth is kiss-swollen, his collarbones covered in love bites.

'You,' Teddy says, once he catches his breath, 'are going to be the death of me, Ezra Darling.'

'And *you*,' Ezra grins up at him, 'love it.'

The rooftop bar at The Palace is freezing, but it's also, as Grace insists, *highly* Instagrammable. So, they sit at a table, under a space heater, wrapped up in their coats and scarves as Grace takes pictures of them all. They patiently let her take a photo of their brunch before they dig in, and there are four separate attempts of them getting the *perfect* Boomerang of them all clinking their glasses together. But they put up with it, because it's Grace, and she's incredible. She threw her career under a red London bus for Ezra and Teddy, and Ezra would do anything for his sister.

'So,' Grace says, once the waiter has taken away their empty plates, brunch quickly descending into day-drinking. 'I have news.'

'Ooh!' Iris grins as she rests her head on Daria's shoulder. They're wearing matching beanies. 'So do we!'

Teddy clears his throat. 'Uh. So do we, actually.'

'Okay,' Grace says. 'Well, me first.' She motions politely for a waiter to come over. He brings with him a bottle of Moët & Chandon and five champagne flutes. She pops the cork herself and pours everyone an overly-generous amount. She lifts her flute, beckoning for the others to copy. 'Following an extremely awkward and slightly homophobic interview with BingeBox for the Darling Dynasty season finale, I am now officially unemployed!'

Ezra gives Teddy a strange look that he reciprocates. Which is good. It means Ezra's not being stupid.

'Um,' Iris says. 'I think I'm lost.'

'Me too,' Daria agrees. 'Being out of a job is a good thing because…?'

'Because it is allowing me to move on,' Grace says. 'To bigger and better things. And *speaking* of,' she pauses for dramatic effect. 'Stream Me got in contact. I know they're pretty new and small right now, but they want to talk to me about starting my own show on their streaming service. I've said I'll meet with their executives next week.'

Suddenly Ezra is standing for some reason. His chair nearly topples back but Teddy catches it. And then he is pulling Grace into a hug over the table, because wow. *Wow*. He hasn't *totally* messed up his sister's career. And are those tears in his eyes? They might be.

He blinks hard before releasing her. The tip of his scarf is in his champagne flute, but he doesn't care as he holds Grace's grinning face in his hands.

'I am so proud of you,' he says, and means it.

'I know you are,' she says. 'And I'm looking for a partner in crime. Someone to help me keep on top of social media and all those kinds of things?'

'As long as I get to stay behind the camera.'

'Promise.'

They hug again before sitting down. Ezra can't stop grinning.

'Well, now our news feels stupid in comparison,' Iris says.

Grace waves a hand at her. 'Absolutely not. Every celebration is a celebration. Go.'

Iris takes Daria's hand in hers and smiles at her in a way that feels so intimate that Ezra has to look away. 'We're going to come out officially as a couple.'

Suddenly Ezra is standing again. Except this time so are Grace and Teddy. And then they're all piling on Daria and Iris. Smothering them in hats, scarves, and coats. Somewhere beneath it all Daria is laughing, and Iris is making hissing cat noises.

'Unhand me, you heathens!' Iris demands, swatting at their arms.

It's Grace's turn to have tears in her eyes as she sits down again. 'Oh, God. Sorry. I'm so happy for you both.'

Teddy's jaw is tight as he says, 'Congratulations.'

Ezra squeezes Teddy's hand, because he knows he's thinking about Leo. How proud he would be of Daria. How much he would love Iris. How happy he'd be that she's moving on.

Daria looks at Teddy. 'Do you think Leo—'

'I think he would be delighted for you,' Teddy interrupts her, voice thick. 'Really, I do. He loved you so much.'

Daria's smile wobbles. 'I'll always love him. You know that.'

'I do.'

Iris puts an arm around Daria's waist. Pulls her in close. Ezra does the same with Teddy. Things tip dangerously close to sombre until Grace raises her champagne flute. 'Right. Teddy. Ezra. What's your news? I swear to God, it better not make anyone cry.'

Teddy gives Ezra a self-conscious look. Then, 'I've decided to focus on my music and write an album. Ezra is going to help me with the PR side of things. All the proceeds will go to PRIDE.'

There was no point in any of them sitting down because all the girls are standing. Again. Ezra laughs as Teddy suddenly has a lap full of girls, and he can't resist pulling out his phone to take a photo. It's probably the only time Teddy will ever be covered in women. When they come away, Teddy has lipstick marks on his cheeks in three different shades and Ezra has to take another photo.

'And he'll be singing tonight at the party,' Ezra says.

'Not originals,' Teddy adds, quickly. 'And not all night. I'm just going to do a few covers between the band's sets.'

Daria reaches across the table and takes Teddy's hand. Gives it a little squeeze. 'Leo would be happy for you too.'

Teddy's throat works. 'Thank you.'

'To us!' Grace announces, champagne flute aloft. 'May we all continue to fucking *slay*.'

Ezra laughs as he joins the others in the toast. 'To us!'

Teddy looks at him. He says quietly, privately, as the girls lapse into conversation, 'And to you. My love.'

Ezra clinks his glass against Teddy's. 'And to you.'

Despite it happening every year, the annual Darling Dynasty costume party always seems to creep up on Ezra. And this year the theme is cult classics. Iris has appointed herself as group costume organiser, and Ezra is seriously beginning to regret ignoring the group chat (*Lets Queer It For The Boy*) as they each chose which *Rocky Horror Show* icon they want to be. And while there is no denying that Ezra looks bomb AF in the corset and suspenders, it's a *bit* chilly.

Teddy appears behind him in the mirror, dressed in a suit with a bowtie and glasses. The perfect Brad Majors. His eyes rake over Ezra with a kind of hunger that lights him up and burns him from the inside out.

'Oh?' Ezra asks, cocking a carefully sculpted eyebrow. 'Is this doing it for you?'

Teddy kisses his neck, just above his pearl necklace. '*You* do it for me.'

'Don't give me a boner in these panties, everyone will see.'

'Good. Let them.'

Ezra turns and loops his fishnet-gloved arms around Teddy's neck. 'Why'd you get to be Brad while I got Frank?'

'You're the one who looks good in stockings,' Teddy grins. 'Speaking of which, I cannot *wait* to peel those off you later.'

Ezra tweaks Teddy's bowtie. 'And I can't wait to gag you with this.'

'Christ,' Teddy drives Ezra back towards the bed, toppling them both down. Ezra is laughing but not pushing him away. As if. 'Just a quickie.'

There's a knock on their door, and then Iris' voice: 'You better not be fucking! I swear to God, Ezra, if you ruin your makeup, I will castrate you!'

Ezra groans. She has a point. His makeup is too good to ruin. And the hair. He is every part the *perfect* Dr Frank N. Furter — albeit a bit updated so as not to look *quite* so seventies. And he only has to make an appearance at the party. Then he can drag Teddy back to bed and do very, *very* filthy things to him.

'Dammit, Ezra!' Iris continues. 'I don't care what dick is in what hole, but if you don't come out here in the next five seconds, I am coming in!'

'We're coming!' he yells, willing his erection to wither and die.

'Wow,' Teddy says, glancing down. 'There really is no hiding it in those little things.'

Ezra gives him a half-hearted shove as they get up. Hanging on the back of the bedroom door is a long back cape with a silver collar. Ezra drapes it around his shoulders and pulls it closed over him, effectively hiding the tent he's pitching.

'Magic,' Ezra says, grinning.

Teddy opens the bedroom door to a small, angry Iris dressed as Magenta in a sexy maid's uniform. Her usual sleek hair is crimped and wild, and her fishnets have great ladders in them. Her hand is raised as if she was about to punch the door down.

'If you two are quite finished sword fighting with your cocks, we need to go. The limo is here.'

Ezra frowns at her. 'I don't think you understand how gay sex works.'

'I don't understand how *any* sex involving a penis works.'

In the living room are the rest of them: Daria looking sweet in a baby pink dress as Janet. Grace is donning sequinned hotpants and a sparkly gold top hat for Columbia. And as Eddie, dressed in jeans, scuffed biker boots and a leather jacket is Nick. Ezra can't help himself as he grins at them all, and then Teddy. Because this is it. These are his people. These absolute weirdos are his *people*, and it's unreal.

And then, because his throat is getting tight, Ezra says, 'Well, I'd fuck us.' And everyone laughs, and he can breathe again.

The limo ride gets messy in a hurry. Iris pops the cork on a champagne bottle that immediately overflows, getting everyone's shoes sticky. No one seems to care. Every time Teddy wraps his lips around the neck of the Dom Pérignon bottle Ezra thinks he might actually melt. Grace is sitting on Nick's lap, tipping his chin back and pouring the champagne past his lips. Iris and Daria are kissing. And everything is kind of perfect.

At the Artemis Hotel, the party has already started. Paparazzi call their names and take pictures as a team of security guards escort them inside. Not before Ezra kisses Teddy in front of the cameras. Just because he can. And his chest goes all warm and fluttery as he looks over his shoulder at the crowd, seeing a sea of rainbow flags. Bisexual flags. Homemade signs that say *#HeIsMyChoice.*

Inside is ridiculous and amazing. Another infamous Darling Dynasty costume ball. Ezra spots at least two Mia Walshs dancing with their Vincent Vegas, a handful of Jack Burtons, and at least one trio of Heathers. The music is loud and obnoxious, and no one cares. People dance. Laugh. Hug each other. Drink.

Their group is noticed before they even make it halfway to the bar. People wanting to say hello. Congratulate them. Buy them drinks. Offer support. It's almost too much, but at the same time it's okay. Because this is how things are. The way they've always been. And Ezra isn't stupid, he knows how lucky he is to be in this situation. So, he drinks it all in. He holds Teddy's hand as they mingle. Make small talk.

Every time Ezra looks at Teddy, out and proud, Ezra's chest nearly bursts with joy. And when he catches Teddy looking at him, eyes so goddamn happy, mouth soft and smiling, Ezra gets the sudden and irrational urge to propose to him on the spot. Because that's what loving someone does: it changes everything you know about yourself. It gives you the courage to run when you didn't even realise you could walk. It's all-consuming, and wild, and selfish, and selfless, and intoxicating.

They finally manage to regroup at the bar and Grace orders everyone an array of cocktails, named after favourite cult classics. Ezra sips his *Cry Baby*, smothering a grin as Teddy suspiciously eyes his *Priscilla Queen Of The Desert*. He has some whipped cream on his chin, and it takes all of Ezra's restraint not to lick it off. Restraint that Nick, clearly, does not have, as he slurps Teddy's face clean, and they double over laughing as Teddy nearly drops his glass in surprise.

Teddy politely declines a round of shots, and Ezra knows he will probably switch to soda after he's finished his cocktail. As much as Teddy is learning to let himself have fun, he still has his reservations, and Ezra loves him for that. In spite of that. Because of that. Teddy catches Ezra gazing at him for the dozenth time and gives him the most indulgent, knee-wobbling, earth-shattering smile. In that moment, he realises that Teddy has it all wrong. It's *him* that's going to be the death of Ezra. And Ezra doesn't mind one bit.

The band announces that they're going to take a short break and invite Teddy to the stage. Ezra gives him a good luck kiss in front of the whole room, because it doesn't matter who sees them. His legs go rubbery on Teddy's behalf as he takes the stage, and he doesn't know why. Well, no. He does. Because this is the first time Teddy has officially played in front of a crowd of people. And at least *one* of them needs to have the jitters about it.

People clap and cheer as he approaches the microphone, guitar resting in his strong arms. Ezra's chest is so full it's going to erupt before he even gets to the first song. Teddy gives the room a shy smile and a wave, and Ezra is molten.

'Hello,' Teddy says. He speaks into the microphone like a natural. Like he was always meant to hold a crowd's attention. 'I hope you don't mind if I sing you a few songs.'

Everyone goes wild. Because of course they do. It's Teddy Montgomery. He plucks at the strings idly for a few moments, tuning. Then he seamlessly launches into his first song. *Kiss The Girl*. It's his own version. His own arrangement. It's soft and slow, and his voice has a huskiness that gives Ezra goosebumps. And he's not the only one, because the room is silent. Watching. Soaking it in.

When he finishes, he goes into a slow version of *Simply The Best*, and Ezra remembers watching that episode of *Schitts Creek* together. Then he sings *Love Of My Life* and Ezra realises that Teddy is singing all of their songs. *I See The Light. I Will Always Love You. Cry To Me*, and so many more. Ezra's throat is suddenly two sizes too small. And his smile is threatening to split his face in two. He is one hundred percent looking at engagement rings online tonight.

When Teddy finishes up his set, he gets a standing ovation. His cheeks and ears burn, and he quietly murmurs thanks into the microphone. And wow. He is so good at this. He's barely off the stage before Ezra is wrapping him up in an embrace, kissing him hard. He can feel the slight tremble in Teddy's body. Nerves. Adrenaline. Pride. Ezra feels it all too. The band starts up again. Something upbeat. Not quite a song, just something instrumental.

'You were amazing, sweetheart,' Ezra says, kissing him again. For, like. Good measure.

'Did I black out?' Teddy asks. 'I feel like I blacked out.'

'Nope. You bossed it. Didn't even look nervous.'

'I felt like I was about to pass out. Still do.'

Ezra literally *has* to kiss him again. 'I am so proud of you.'

'Actually,' Teddy untangles himself from Ezra, 'I have something for you.'

'I hope it starts with "d" and ends in "ick".'

Grace slaps the back of his head. Teddy reaches inside of his jacket and pulls out a rolled-up magazine, only slightly crumpled. Ezra arches an eyebrow at him as he takes it. Then immediately forgets how to speak as he unrolls it, sees the cover. It's an old copy of *Whiz Kidz* from 2006. On the cover is a teenage Teddy, smiling self-consciously at the camera. Ezra looks from the magazine in his hands, up at Teddy.

'Is this…?' he asks.

'Your copy?' Teddy says, smiling. 'Yeah. I asked Grace if she thought you still might have it. She did some snooping and found it under your bed. I thought it was about time I signed it for you.

'Wow. Um. Okay, wow.'

'Open it to my interview. Page—'

'Forty-two. I remember,' Ezra says.

He opens it up to the right page and smiles at the double page spread. *Great Britain's Golden Boy*. Next to a photo of Teddy is his loopy handwriting:

Ezra love,

Sorry I was such a prick the first time around. Say "yes" and let me make it up to you for the rest of our lives.

Love

Teddy

Ezra looks up. And then has to look down. Because Teddy is on one knee. He's on *one knee*. And there's a little velvet box in his hands. The music has gone all soft. The whole room seems to still. Ezra forgets how to breathe. Behind Teddy, Grace has a hand clamped over her mouth. Daria is trying not to cry. Iris grins like an imp on crack. And Teddy. Well. Teddy just smiles up at him. Cheeks pink. So damn earnest. So damn *Teddy*.

'Ezra Darling,' Teddy says. 'I am so recklessly in love with you. Will you—'

'Yes,' Ezra blurts out. His hands are shaking.

Teddy laughs. 'You didn't let me finish.'

'Yes, I'll marry you.'

He grins. 'Are you sure?'

Ezra hears himself laugh. And maybe cry a little. He can't speak so he just nods. Teddy pops the box open and the simple band sparkles at him. He lets Teddy slide it onto his finger. A perfect fit. Then he is pulling Teddy to his feet and their lips meet to the sound of applause. And for a moment, Ezra is flying. Soaring. The band starts up a new song and it takes him a few moments to realise what it is. *Love Is In The Air*. He breaks the kiss to grin up at Teddy.

'Oh, this is corny,' Ezra says. He can't stop smiling. 'Did you request this?'

Teddy grins. 'You love it.'

'I love *you*.'

'Dance with me?'

Ezra kisses him again. 'Forever.'

Teddy sways Ezra in his arms. And everything is good. As the song reaches its first chorus, they are really dancing. Grinning. Laughing. And the others crowd into them. Grace. Iris. Daria. Nick. And it turns into a group hug. And they're all still dancing. Except they're also kind of crying too. Happy tears. And Ezra is surrounded by all the people he loves the most, and who love him back.

And he realises, with brilliant clarity, that they've won.

They've won.

Also by Laura Jordan

The Wicked One

Chapter One

'INCUBUS! I-N-C-U-B-U-S! *INCUBUS*!'

Olivia watched, bemused, as Professor Flannigan flicked through the various images on his crude presentation, each more grisly than the last.

'Male sex demons that prey on sleeping women. Derived from the Latin "a nightmare induced by a demon". These creatures have a sole purpose of impregnating women in the hopes that their offspring will too have supernatural abilities.'

Olivia felt a headache coming on. She let her eyelids drift closed. Darkness felt good. It was only 10am, and she had barely enough patience to tolerate her Paranormal Folklore professor, let alone take notes on things she already knew. This headache had the potential to become a migraine.

'Some believe that the incubus can be identified by a particularly large, cold, penis,' Flannigan bellowed.

Okay, that made Olivia open her eyes. She picked up her pen and wondered if she should write that down. But did she really want the words "large, cold penis" in her notebook? Probably not. She put her pen back down.

Flannigan glared at the students who dared giggle at the mention of such a word, and went back to his slides. 'Though many accounts claim the incubus to be bisexual, others argue that the incubus is strictly heterosexual, and views intercourse with men as either useless or detrimental. That is where the succubus comes in.'

The slide changed from a squat, ugly imp to a tall, stacked Goddess, and Olivia frowned. Did the demon-lady *have* to be ridiculously hot? Why would a demon-lady need to be hot? She's a demon. All powerful. She could be a fat little troll like the other guy, it wouldn't make a difference.

Probably painted by a man.

Olivia nodded. True that. She picked up her pen.

Flannigan pointed to the succubus. 'The female counterpart to the incubus. It is said, in folklore, that to penetrate a succubus is like entering a cavern of ice.'

Olivia put her pen down once more.

'Now, who can tell me when the earliest reference to an incubus was made? Come along, it was in your reading assignment.'

Olivia watched all the introverts wilt into their seats, begging not to be called on. The biggest introvert of them all, Kian Kelly, was sat a few seats down from her. He shrank down more than all of them. Olivia knew what was about to happen. She suspected Kian did too.

'Mr Kelly!' Flannigan snapped. A nasty smile bloomed on his wrinkled face. 'Would you enlighten us please?'

In a small voice, Kian said, 'I don't know, Professor.'

'Pardon? Speak up, Mr Kelly. We are humans, not dogs.'

Kian flushed. 'I said, I don't know, Sir.'

Flannigan tried —and failed— to suppress a grin. 'You don't know? Did you not do the reading?'

'Yes, Sir. I did.'

'Did any of the larger words confuse you, Mr Kelly?'

'No, Sir.'

'Then why don't you know?'

Kian looked down at his hands in his lap. 'I just can't remember.'

Olivia couldn't take much more of this. She put her hand up and without waiting to be chosen she said, 'Mesopotamia, 2400 BC.'

Without taking his beady eyes off his prey, Flannigan replied, 'I wasn't asking you, Miss McQueen.'

'I know, you weren't,' she said. 'Because I actually know the answer. You're asking Kian because you know he *doesn't* know the answer.'

That got his attention.

Bad move. Abort mission.

Flannigan looked at Olivia and licked his thin lips. 'What are you saying, exactly, Miss McQueen?'

Don't do it, Liv.

Olivia sucked in a deep breath. 'Well, Sir, when you asked the question, at least ten people in here put their hand up. That's ten people who think they know the answer. But you didn't pick any of those people, you chose someone who didn't have their hand up. This isn't the first time, either. This is almost every lecture.'

It was around that point that Olivia got the feeling she should stop, because Flannigan had that *I'm going to eat you alive* look on his face, but she had already dug herself in deep enough by that point. Might as well keep going until she hit China.

'That begs the question,' she continued. 'Do you enjoy watching your own students squirm more than you actually enjoy teaching us?'

Dear God, this parachute is just a backpack.

Olivia continued, 'I don't know if it's a sadistic thing, or a power thing. Probably the latter. Probably the same reason why you make us all call you *Sir* or *Professor* — which no other lecturer does by the way. My guess is it's your way of setting yourself up as the Alpha-male. King of the classroom. Head Honcho. So tell me, Darragh — oops, sorry, I mean *Sir* — did I get it right? Hit the nail on the proverbial head, as it were?'

Flannigan stared at her. So did the rest of the lecture hall. His puckered anus of a mouth opened, as if to come back with some kind of biting retort, and then closed again.

The bell on his desk rang.

Olivia rose out of her seat and slung her bag over her shoulder. She smiled at Flannigan. 'Cool. Also, your fly has been open this whole lecture. Thought you'd like to know.'

Olivia left the lecture hall with a bigger headache than when she'd entered, but at least she was smiling. Well, on the inside, anyway. She made her way down the stairs and out of the Parnell building. It was late afternoon and the Irish sunshine was still beating down strong. It was an unusually warm day for early October, but she wasn't complaining. She had been studying at Dublin Community College for three years now, and she still hadn't adjusted to the weather. She missed the long, warm days back in the South East of England — but that was the only thing she missed.

She made it halfway across the quad before she heard someone call her name. She pretended not to hear. Kept walking. But her pursuer was persistent.

'Olivia!'

She heard the thumping of feet and puffing of breath, and Kian Kelly came into her peripheral vision. His face was still red, this time from exertion. He smiled at her. It was a nice smile. He was a nice-looking boy. Everything about Kian Kelly was perfectly *nice*. That's what made him such an easy target for people like Flannigan.

'Hey,' he puffed. 'You didn't hear me calling you?'

Olivia kept up her pace. 'Sorry. Uh... I was thinking.'

'Oh,' Kian said, struggling to keep up with her long legs. 'Right. Well, anyway, I just wanted to say thanks. You know, for back there. Flannigan's a dick.'

'That he is.'

'I don't think anyone's ever stood up to him like that before. Ever. After you left he just stood there, staring at the door. Then he went berserk! He threw his laser pointer on the ground and screamed at us all to leave. Just as I was walking out he picked up that Lilith bust he has on his desk and drop-kicked her into the wall. Well, he tried to. I think he may have broken his foot. Anyway, it was *deadly*.'

Olivia smiled. 'Cool. Hope it hurt.'

'Yeah. Anyway, I figure I owe you a drink or something? You know, as a thanks.'

Uh oh.

Olivia shook her head. 'You don't owe me anything.'

'Sure, I do. That look on Flannigan's face was worth at least a first round. Maybe a second one too.'

'Seriously, Kian. It's fine. Forget about it.'

'Well... maybe not a drink then? Maybe lunch? There's a café just off campus. Domhnall's. They do everything. Full Irish, Spanish omelette, cakes, pastries—'

'Kian, stop,' she said, pausing.

Kian trundled on a few steps more before he realised they had stopped walking. He turned and looked at her, a hopeful smile on his perfectly nice face. Olivia knew that it wasn't going to last, because she was about to be unforgivably rude, because that's just what she did. She didn't enjoy upsetting people — she wasn't a twat — but it was easier to deal with people's disappointment at her rather than their expectations of her.

'I don't want to go for lunch with you,' she said, flatly. 'Or drinks. Or an open mic night, or whatever other thing you're about to suggest. You don't need to thank me, alright? I know what you're trying to do here, you want to start something. A friendship. Whatever. I don't know. But I'm not interested.'

Kian frowned. 'You're not interested in having friends?'

'Not really, no.'

'I was just trying to be nice.'

'Well, I don't want you to be nice to me.'

Ouch. Even she knew that was harsh. But everyone knew what happened to Icarus. Not that Olivia was arrogant enough to think of herself as the centre of the solar system, but she was certainly as destructive as the sun. Maybe more so.

Kian's forehead only creased more. 'I don't understand you. We've been in Paranormal Folklore for three years together, and you've never spoken to me. Not once. Or anyone else, as far as I know. You keep to yourself, you only speak when spoken to, and even then it's like it's too much effort. And then today you swoop in and save the day, and when I try to say thank you, you blow me off? You just go back to being the moody loner who doesn't talk to anyone? Why? I don't understand.'

Olivia started walking again. 'I never asked you to.'

Kian fell into step beside her once more. 'You want to know what I think?'

'No, but I can tell that you're going to tell me anyway.'

'This? The whole too-cool-to-care thing? It's an act. A façade. You push people away so that you don't have to let them in, because that would make you vulnerable. And the last thing that the moody loner — who spends six nights a week at the campus gym lifting dumbbells — wants, is for anyone to think that any part of her is vulnerable.'

He's kind of got you there.

'Kian, I think you're wasting your time in Paranormal Folklore. You're much better suited to psychology.'

'It wouldn't kill you, you know,' he said. He stopped walking and watched her go. 'To let people in. What's the worst that could happen from having a friend?'

You have no idea.

***

Olivia was no expert at makeup — not by any stretch — but she knew enough to get by. She could apply mascara without smudging black all over her nose. She could fill in her brows without looking like a cartoon character. Most importantly she could cover up her scar. An angry slash across her left cheek, curving like a waning crescent moon. A bit of foundation and powder and it was gone. Magic.

You didn't need to be particularly dolled up to get into The Betsy. As long as you had a shirt and proper shoes, that was good enough. The bar was small, and packed well over legal capacity, and the jukebox played eighties pop while the band set up on stage. The vibe was good. It always was.

Olivia made a beeline for the bar, and waved her favourite bartender over. If she had anything even close to a friend, it was Tadhg. He saw her and stopped flirting with a cute guy. He sauntered over in jeans tighter than Olivia's and dropped his elbows to the counter, his head in his perfectly manicured hands.

'The Prodigal Daughter returns,' he said.

Olivia smiled. 'I think the expression is "the Prodigal Son".'

'Nu-uh. Gilmore Girls, season six, episode nine.'

'You're so gay, it hurts.'

'So, what will it be?' he asked. 'Sex On The Beach? Pornstar Martini? Slippery Nipple?'

'Diet Coke with lemon, please.'

Tadhg rolled his eyes. 'You're so boring.'

'No, I'm just sober.'

And if you drink, you're not one hundred per cent in control.

'As a judge,' he said, filling a pint glass with draft cola. 'Why exactly do you even want to be sober anyway?'

'I like to be prepared. For anything.'

'Expect the unexpected?' he asked, popping a lemon slice into her glass and handing it over.

'And then some.'

Tadhg smiled. 'So, I heard you practically bit Flannigan's head off today?'

Olivia took a sip of her drink. 'Where'd you hear that?'

'Aoife told Niall, Niall told Cara, and Cara told me. Is it true you called him a Wankenstein?'

'Not even remotely.'

'Shame. Because he is.' He reached out and turned Olivia's necklace over in her hands. 'Sell this to me.'

'It's priceless.'

'Then give it to me.'

'Family heirloom.'

He sighed and let go. 'Your family has taste. My nanna collects thimbles.'

Olivia looked down at the necklace. It was simple, just a gold disc on a thin chain with a squiggle engraved into it.

Not a squiggle. An insignia.

'The symbol means alliance,' she said. 'My mother gave it to me. She said to remember its meaning when faced with confrontation. Alliance breeds triumph.'

'Looks kind of like a pair of titties to me.' Tadhg's gaze flickered to something over Olivia's shoulder and his eyes widened. 'Oh my God.'

Olivia stiffened. 'What? What is it?'

'Oh my *God*.'

'Tadhg, what's wrong?'

'Behind you.'

'What? What's behind me?'

'He's a ten. *Definitely* a ten. Maybe even an eleven.'

A guy.

It took everything in Olivia's power not to hit him.

'It's just a guy?' she asked.

'Total hottie.'

'So, there's nothing wrong? It's just an ordinary man?'

Tadhg snorted. 'I wouldn't call him ordinary. Oh my God, he's looking at you.'

'No, Tadhg, he's probably looking at *you* wondering why you're gawping at him.'

'He's coming over!'

'Brilliant.'

Tadhg looked at the guy in the seat beside Olivia who was minding his own business and smiled. 'Hey, sweetie. Why don't you show me your best banana impression?'

The guy looked up from his phone, his game of Candy Crush on pause. 'Pardon?'

Tadhg's smile dropped. 'Split.'

Before the guy could argue, Tadhg was shooing him away with his tea towel. The guy gave Olivia a confused look, and she tried to smile apologetically before glaring at her —kind of— friend.

'Did your last two brain cells die?' she snapped.

'I love it when you talk dirty to me.'

'I'm going to kill you.'

He winked at her. 'You can thank me at your wedding.'

The seat beside her was only empty for the briefest of moments before the mystery man sat down. Olivia didn't look at him, kept her angry gaze on Tadhg who was giving the new guy his best smile.

'What'll it be?' he asked. 'We have signature house cocktails. Juicy Lucy? Grow-A-Pear? Sand In The Crack?'

'Just a Diet Coke please,' said the man, his voice like liquid velvet.

Tadhg's smile disappeared. 'God, you're made for each other.'

He slung his tea towel over his shoulder and meandered off. Olivia counted how many seconds it would take before the man said hi. She got to eight.

'I think we're being set up,' he said.

Olivia huffed a laugh. 'Don't feel special, he does this every weekend.'

'I'm Roman,' he said, holding out his hand. 'Roman Wylder.'

And so it begins.

Olivia turned on her stool and met his eyes. She was pleasantly surprised. Tadhg was right, he was attractive. A shock of copper hair and green eyes. Early thirties. Leather jacket. She shook his hand.

'Olivia McQueen.'

'Nice name. Is it real?'

'I guess you'll never know.'

Tadhg returned with Roman's Diet Coke. 'Don't drink it too quickly now.'

Roman paid for his drink and offered to pay for Olivia's too, but she declined. They sipped in silence, while Tadhg looked between them, clearly unimpressed.

'So,' Roman said, putting his glass down. 'What do you do, Olivia McQueen?'

'I'm studying at DCC,' she said. 'Paranormal Folklore. Masters Degree.'

Roman arched an eyebrow. Not sceptical, but interested. 'Paranormal Folklore?'

Olivia nodded. 'The study of paranormal events and entities in folklore throughout history.'

'Sounds interesting.'

'It's alright.'

'Do you believe, then?'

Olivia frowned. 'Believe in what?'

'In paranormal events and entities?'

She smiled. 'You don't have to believe in a subject to study it.'

Roman nodded. 'True. Though it might make it more interesting.'

'True.'

'At any rate it makes my psychology degree sound boring.'

Olivia shrugged. 'Well, at least you're licenced to tell women that we all secretly want a penis.'

Roman laughed. 'God bless Freud, and his sick little brain.'

'He should have known that it's not the appendage we're after, it's the equal pay.'

'Well said.'

'That and the penis.'

Roman laughed again. It was a nice sound. Deep and smooth. *West End Girls* by the Petshop Boys came on the jukebox, and his smile quickly melted into a frown.

'I hate this song,' he said.

Olivia gave him a look. 'If it's eighties music you don't like, then you won't like it here. It's only ever eighties tracks.'

'The eighties are fine,' Roman said. 'It's the Petshop Boys that I hate.'

Olivia grinned. 'Blasphemy.'

'How's about a deal, Olivia McQueen?'

Olivia sipped her Coke. 'Hm?'

'If I change the song, and it's something that you like, you have to dance with me.'

Olivia considered his offer with vague interest. 'And what if it's a song I don't like?'

'Then that should be punishment enough, surely?'

Before Olivia could answer. Tadhg leaned in between them. 'She'll do it.'

Roman Wylder smiled. It was a shark's smile. It was infectious. 'Perfect.'

Chapter Two

Olivia waited until Roman was out of earshot, before grabbing Tadhg's top and growling, 'What did you do that for?'

'Firstly,' he said, uncurling her fist from his favourite shirt. 'This is assault. You're assaulting me right now. I could press charges and then you'd be completely friendless, which would be, obviously, a travesty. Secondly, you were *vibing* with him.'

'I was not.'

'You were. You were already considering his offer.'

'I was humouring him.'

'You like him.'

You do kinda like him.

'*You* like him,' she snapped.

Nice.

Tadhg sighed. 'Liv. Honey. Baby. Listen to me. It's been a long time since Cillian.'

Olivia closed her eyes. She didn't want to think about Cillian. She nodded. 'I know.'

'You've got to move on.'

Olivia opened her eyes when she was sure she wasn't going to tear up. 'I have moved on.'

'Shutting down doesn't mean you're moving on. The only way to get over trauma is to confront it. Talk about it.'

'I know.'

Tadhg laid a hand over hers. 'It was an accident.'

No it wasn't.

'It's not your fault.'

Yes. It is.

'Nobody blames you.'

Because they don't know the truth.

Tadhg pulled away from her and nodded over her shoulder. 'Hottie McHotcakes is coming back. Be nice, Olivia McQueen, or I'll make your life hell.'

Already there.

Olivia turned and saw Roman smiling. To her surprise, she smiled back.

'What did you pick?' she asked.

'You'll see.'

West End Girls finished up with its last few robotic chords on the synthesiser. There was a hesitation before the next song queued up. There always was. The jukebox was older than The Betsy itself. Then, *As The World Falls Down* by David Bowie came on. Olivia's mouth fell open. Her parents had danced to that at their wedding.

God rest their souls.

'How did I do?' Roman asked.

'Suspiciously well,' Olivia replied.

He shrugged. 'I have a knack for these things.'

Tadhg appeared at Olivia's shoulder, like she'd grown a second head. 'Do you have a knack for anything else?'

Olivia swatted him away. Roman held out his hand and raised his eyebrows. When Olivia didn't immediately take it, Tadhg gave her a not-so-subtle shove. Olivia toppled off her stool and grabbed Roman's hand to steady her. She threw a nasty look at Tadhg as she was led away to the pathetically small dance floor.

It wasn't until Roman reached for her waist, hesitating, waiting for approval, that Olivia realised this was a slow dance.

'We could two-step?' Roman offered. 'Madison?'

Olivia didn't answer. Instead, she squared her shoulders, looped her arms around his neck, and stepped in close. His hands settled on her hips, and they danced. He was a good dancer. He had rhythm.

You know what they say about men who have rhythm.

'I know exactly what you're thinking,' Roman said.

Olivia tilted her head. 'Very much doubt it.'

'You're scoping out the exits,' he said. 'Checking to see if you have a clear path to safety in case this all suddenly goes wrong.'

Seriously, is this guy a mind reader?

Olivia didn't reply, just watched him with a guarded expression.

Roman smiled. 'Sorry. I used to be a self-defence instructor. I can spot a fellow fighter when I see one. We have a… way. What did you train in?'

'Brazilian jiu-jitsu,' she said. 'And don't take it personally. I always check my escape routes when mysterious men ask me to dance.'

'Happens often does it?'

'Actually, no.'

Roman surprised her by lifting her right arm and spinning her before pulling her back in. 'Their loss.'

Olivia smiled, but something over his shoulder caught her eye. Her feet fumbled. It was *him*. The actual guy she'd been hoping to find tonight. The man she'd been stalking for weeks. The one she'd been vetting. The man she was going to kill.

He glanced up, saw her looking at him, and quickly looked away, backing into the crowd. Olivia's arms fell loose around Roman's shoulders.

Don't lose him, Liv.

Roman looked at her, cocking an eyebrow. 'Everything okay?'

'Ladies' room,' she said, excusing herself.

He went to speak, but she didn't give him the chance. She untangled herself from Roman's arms and weaved her way through the dancefloor. Following her prey. The man peeked over his shoulder, saw Olivia following him, and picked up his pace. So did she.

Does he think we can't walk any faster? Is he dumb?

He tried to lose her by ducking out through the side exit that the band were using, but she had keen eyes. She followed and stepped through the door just in time to see him disappear around the side of the building into an alleyway.

Ah. A trap.

'He's so smart,' Olivia mumbled.

Isn't he just?

Olivia squared her shoulders and continued.

Ditch the jacket. It's too restricting.

Olivia obliged and let her jacket drape over a wheelie bin as she passed. She turned the corner, anticipating the ambush that was coming. She ducked a sloppy punch to the head, and as she came up, brought an elbow with it that rocked her assailant's world. He stumbled, putting enough distance between them for Olivia's heel to connect with his breastbone, and the man went sprawling. She followed.

The man held up his hands in surrender.

Why do they always wait until they're on the floor to surrender?

'Cormac O'Connor?' she asked.

Cormac looked up at her. 'Yes, you know I am.'

'Tidy. Just checking. I've come here to kill you.'

Cormac blinked. 'What?'

'Are you deaf as well as stupid?' she asked. 'I'm here to *kill* you, Cormac.'

'Why?'

'You know why.'

'I actually don't, though.'

Olivia stepped forward, and Cormac scrambled back through the dirt. 'Alright! Alright!'

'Why do you guys always play dumb first?' she asked, genuinely interested. 'You know what you've done. You know that *I* know what you've done. Why all the preamble?'

'Maybe we think of it like foreplay?'

'Yeah, because men are so good at that.'

'Can I at least stand up?'

Olivia considered it. Then said, 'No.'

'Why not?'

'Murderers don't get to stand up.'

'They don't?'

'Not around me, they don't.'

Cormac sighed. 'Look, do you even have any proof?'

Olivia held up her hand and showed him her palm. His name was carved into her flesh, fresh and raw but not bleeding. Cormac nodded, and she smiled and let her arm drop down again.

'Devil's debt,' he said. 'Not much arguing with that, is there?'

'Not really.'

'Can I ask you one thing, though? Before you do it?'

'Go ahead.'

'How did you know I was a demon?' he asked.

Olivia smiled. 'Intuition.'

'Come on. Have you been watching me? Spying?'

'A little.'

'Do I have a tell?'

'Kinda.'

'Was it when I ate that baby?'

She nodded. 'That was my first clue.'

'What about when I ate that other baby?'

'That was my second.'

Cormac sighed. 'Well, no point hiding it anymore.'

Olivia agreed, 'Probably not.'

Cormac changed. His skin turned as black as his coal, red veins blossoming beneath it, like lines of magma flowing through rock. From his sloping forehead, two horns sprouted, bursting through the skin and curling round on themselves. His nails fell off, making way for his talons that grew in, long and sharp, and his teeth lengthened into fangs. Last to change were his eyes. A flicker, and then they were completely red. He rose to his haunches, a good two feet taller than he was previously, and grinned.

Olivia took great joy in watching that smile disappear as she did the exact same thing. Her skin was the colour of fresh blood, dotted with black scales over her softer spots like chainmail. Her eyes blacked out, little charcoal veins spreading from their corners and blossoming across her cheeks. Her incisors had elongated into fangs that protruded over her crimson lower lip when she smiled. And she did smile. Because that *I've shit my pants* expression on grown men literally never got old. Especially when she showed them her horns, which were always bigger than theirs.

Why do they never expect that either?

'Are you alright?' Olivia asked. 'You look like you've seen a ghost.'

He blinked. 'You're... a demon too.'

'You have good eyesight.'

He licked his lips. A pause. Then, 'This is the part where you run away.'

Olivia tilted her head. 'Are you quoting *Shrek*?'

'I'm going to kill you.'

'You can *try* if it makes you feel better.'

For the second time that night, Cormac lunged at her. For the second time, she dodged. She slapped his arm away, stepped in, and landed a punch to his gut. Winded him. He doubled over and she clamped her hands together and brought them down on his neck in a double fist. He dropped to his knees and his face collided with her knee. His nose exploded, blood drenching his face.

Olivia lifted her foot and booted him, and he fell back onto his ass. She kicked him again and he skidded right back to where he originally was. His hands clutched at his face, at where his once straight nose had been, howling.

'You broke my nose!' he squealed. 'You broke my nose, you bitch!'

'Flattery will get you nowhere,' she said, reaching down to her boots and slipping the dagger free. It was an ugly thing. A sharp blade and a gnarled black handle. It did the job, though. 'Any last words?'

'You bitch!' Cormac spat. 'You bitch! You stupid, ugly, *bitch!*'

'Come on now, only one of those is true.'

'I'm going to kill you! I'm—'

Olivia opened her palm and let the dagger do the rest. It trembled in her grip for a moment, then shot out of her hand and plunged itself deep into Cormac's neck. Olivia watched his eyes bulge in surprise. He tried to speak — probably to call her a bitch again — but all that came out was a gurgle. His hands wandered from his busted nose and reached for Olivia. He swiped at her through the air, like a cat playing with string, and then they fell by his sides. Dead.

A few moments later he evaporated, leaving nothing but ash in his wake, and the dagger clattered to the ground. Olivia watched it for a few moments. Hoping it would disappear. Hoping her debt would be cleared. But nothing happened.

She sighed and fetched the obnoxious thing, stuffed it back into the hidden slot in her boot. She counted down from ten, felt herself calming, returning to her normal self. She turned to head back into The Betsy—

—and saw Roman watching her from the street, mouth agape.

Oh shit.

Chapter Three

You have to kill him.

'Shut up,' Olivia murmured.

He saw you.

'I know.'

He saw what you did.

'Yeah, I know.'

And now he thinks you're talking to yourself.

'Why is he just standing there? Why isn't he running away?'

I think he's frozen.

'Good. Frozen is good.'

Olivia put on her warmest smile. She gave Roman a little wave, and when he didn't bolt, she dared to stroll over. She stopped a few feet back, keeping that kind, well-rehearsed smile fixed into place. Roman just stood there, unblinking. An uncomfortable silence fell.

'So,' she said. 'You're probably wondering what you just saw there.'

No response.

Get rid of him, Liv.

Olivia cleared her throat and tried again. 'I can explain everything.'

Roman blinked. 'You killed a guy.'

She nodded. 'Yes. Yes, I did.'

'You stabbed him.'

'That's right.'

'And then he disappeared.'

'Poof.'

'You were like a... a...'

'Monster?' she suggested.

He nodded again. 'Yeah.'

'Well, actually, I'm a demon.'

'Oh.'

'You're taking this all remarkably well.'

'I think I might faint.'

Olivia pulled a face. 'You're pretty tall, that would be a long drop.'

'Am I in shock?'

'Quite possibly.'

'I feel like I'm going to start panicking.'

'I'd really rather you didn't.'

Roman looked down at his hands. They were shaking. 'I'm doing it. I'm panicking.'

'Please don't.'

The shakes intensified. 'Oh God, I'm freaking out.'

Olivia took a step forward, 'Roman, listen—'

Roman held out his shaking hands and stumbled back. 'Stay away from me!'

'I'm not going to hurt you!'

'Yeah, I'm sure Ted Bundy used to say that all the time.'

Olivia frowned. 'You're comparing me to Ted Bundy?'

'Who would you prefer? Jeffrey Dahmer? John Wayne Gacy? Buffalo Bill?'

'That last guy wasn't real.'

He stopped and looked at her. 'You're a murderer.'

'It's not like that.'

'You kill people. That makes you a murderer.'

'Honestly, there's more to it than that.'

Roman's hands went to his head. 'Oh my God, I'm going to be sick. I'm going to throw up. And you're probably going to kill me to keep me quiet. Then I'll just be lying here, dead, in my own sick.'

Liv, put the man out of his misery.

She shook her head. There was another way.

Oh, come on! That hardly ever works.

It was worth a try.

So was caviar, but we're never trying that again either.

It could work.

Strongly disagree.

Olivia let out a big sigh, then said. 'Roman Wylder, stop panicking.'

He wasn't listening. He was still babbling to himself.

Told you.

She tried again. 'Roman Wylder, stop panicking right now.'

Roman stopped talking.

Well, shit.

Olivia let out a long breath she hadn't realised she'd been holding. 'Roman Wylder, you will remain calm.'

Roman looked at her, wide-eyed, and nodded. 'I am very calm.'

'Good. You are very relaxed.'

He nodded again. 'Yes, I am.'

Olivia took a deep breath. 'You didn't see anything here tonight. You came outside for some fresh air. You didn't see me. You didn't talk to me. Nothing unusual happened, okay?'

Roman smiled. 'Pretty uneventful night, to be honest.'

'Yes, it was. Now you're going to go home, go to sleep, and forget all about me. Don't remember my name. Don't remember my face.'

Roman's smile melted into a frown. 'Who are you?'

'Perfect. Roman Wylder, goodnight.'

The smile was immediately back. He gave a little wave before turning and strolling away, hands in his pockets. Olivia was amazed to hear him whistling *West End Girls* without a care in the world.

That was a close one.

Olivia nodded. Far too close, indeed.

***

Olivia's flat was nothing shy of dilapidated. A student loan and a zero-hours contract at the student union could hardly set you up for anything greater than a crap-shack in inner-city Dublin. And a crap-shack it definitely was. The front door needed a kick to open, and a miracle to lock. Mould festered in the corners on the ceiling, and the brown carpet looked as though it may have once been white.

We need to move.

'We have no money,' Olivia said, heading to the kitchen.

You should start charging people for demon hunting.

'You know I can't.'

Because it's morally wrong?

'No, because I'm repaying a Devil's debt.'

Oh yeah.

Olivia chose not to think about how talking to an imaginary voice in her head that was probably, most likely, definitely not there was not exactly a paragon of a healthy and sound mind. She chose not to think about how this voice had been with her for as long as she could remember, or about how, when she mentioned it to her parents as a child, they had exchanged worried looks and then told her *not* to worry about it. About how, in her teens, therapists had told her it was most likely a sign of psychosis or something similar. And she *definitely* did not think about how it was her longest, oldest, and truest friend.

And whenever she accidentally *did* think about how talking to a made-up voice in her head was probably a bit Not Good — capital N, capital G — she gave herself an exception. She was a demon. Well, *half* demon. She had a soul, after all. It was expected for her to have a few quirks. Having a conscience that actually voiced itself in her head like having headphones in and cranked up to full volume at all times, was another one of her little peculiarities. Besides, it had always been there for her. Where most people turned away, the voice turned towards her. Guided her. Comforted her. In a way, it was like self-soothing. Home therapy. And most likely, absolutely nothing to worry about.

She hoped.

Olivia wrenched open the fridge door, nose wrinkling as the awful fridge smell hit her. The starkness of the shelves made her frown.

'When did I last go shopping?'

Two weeks ago.

'Ah.' A pause. 'Pizza?'

Pizza.

As much as she wanted to order from Dominos, the moths in her wallet were not so keen, and so Olivia ordered from the local pizzeria. *Eatily*. She didn't know what made her cringe more, the name or the one-star reviews on the *Chomp* app. Nevertheless, she ordered something called a "Mighty Meaty," took to her lumpy sofa, and put on the latest episode of *Crime Line*.

The pizza was going on fifteen minutes late when the doorbell rang. Olivia leapt from the sofa with enthusiasm that she could only ever muster for a food delivery. She raked through the dish on the table by the door and counted out €8.50 then rounded it up to €10 for a measly tip.

You can't afford to give a tip.

'But the nice man is bringing me pizza.'

She braced herself for small talk and opened the door. To her surprise, she found Roman Wylder looking at her, eyes wide.

Uh oh.

Before she could speak, he came crashing over the threshold. His arm shot out, launching a palm into her chin. She staggered back, and he swung for her again. She stepped in, arms braced over her head, and absorbed the blow before it even had time to gain momentum. She wrapped one arm around his, and her free hand sent hammer fists into Roman's face. Once. Twice.

On the third time, he caught her hand in his and twisted. Olivia yelped and her grip loosened, and Roman was able to untangle his arm from hers and crack an elbow into the side of her head. The world swam for a few moments and Roman grabbed her, wrapped her up in a clinch. Olivia squirmed, turning in his grip and used the momentum to throw him over her hip. He landed on his back with a thud and she immediately mounted him, keeping her head low, wrapping him in a headlock. She tried to pin his arms down with her knees, but he thrashed beneath her and wrenched them free.

Pain rocked through her side as he landed punch after punch in her ribs. Sweat beading on her brow, she tried to manoeuvre him into an Americana armlock. A dislocated shoulder would slow him down — or at least she hoped it would. The blows to her ribcage stopped for a blissful moment, giving her head just enough time to clear for her to realise that wasn't a good thing.

She saw the knife right before she felt it slide between her ribs. She screamed before she even felt the pain, and when it hit her, she screamed some more. Beneath her, Roman bucked his hips and easily rolled Olivia off him. This time, he mounted her. She tried to crunch up, tried to hide her head against his chest so he couldn't hit her, but her ribs screamed at her when she moved. He pinned her down.

'Who are you?' she screamed.

'Never you mind,' he replied.

Roman gave what Olivia could only describe as a perfectly polite smile before curling his hand into a fist. He reeled his arm back, ready to let her see stars.

Your necklace, Liv! Tell him that you sire him!

Without questioning, Olivia grasped the necklace at her throat and held it out to him.

'I sire you!' she shouted, having no idea what it meant. 'I sire you!'

Roman's eyes grew wide, his face falling flat. His fist uncurled and his arm dropped to his side.

'Oh shit,' he said.

About The Author

Laura Jordan is a 6ft Libran and cat enthusiast from the countryside in Kent, England. She grew up in her family cottage with her parents, brother and grandad Len. She studied ballet and performing arts for the majority of her adolescent life, thinking she would make a career of it, before realising she could neither sing, act, nor dance.

Sensing her talents may lie elsewhere, Laura set off to study creative writing at the University of Greenwich where she scraped a bachelor's degree. Laura then went on to put her degree to good use as a senior reporter and editor for a builder's merchant's magazine. However, she was fired after three months after likening her workplace to "riding a bike through hell" on Twitter.

Then Laura tried her hand at teaching. She became a Special Educational Needs teaching assistant for secondary school children, and much to everyone's surprise —not least her own— she found she was quite good at it. She kept to this line of work for three years until moving to Ireland to be with her boyfriend.

Living in Dublin with Derek, their golden retriever, and a small army of borderline feral cats, Laura spends her time co-hosting a podcast and writing books that she is still astounded that people want to read.

She is also very fond of pizza.

Acknowledgments

(Those who do not read the acknowledgments get put on Ali's bad list.)

I would like to start by saying thank you to the most important person of all: you, the reader. For your unwavering loyalty and unflinching faith in me. A strong readership, no matter how big or small, and the support they give, is the lifeblood of an indie writer. It is not an exaggeration to say that I couldn't have done it without you.

Secondly, I would like to thank my best friend, Natalie Mortimer, to whom this book is dedicated. Natalie passed away in April 2022, and it is one of my deepest regrets that she was never able to see this book come to fruition. Natalie was a force of nature, an unfettered ray of sunshine in my life, and the best friend I have ever known. She was kind, smart, utterly foul-mouthed, and I miss her unbearably every day. The character *Ali* is based off Natalie's no-nonsense approach to life, her strength, and — underneath that hard exterior — her wealth of love and compassion. She is, and always will be, the best person I have ever known.

To Derek, the great love of my life, I want to say thank you for the countless hours of listening to me talk about this book. For reading every revised chapter and for giving me honest feedback, even when it wasn't always what I wanted to hear. For loving me when, at times, it has been hard to love myself, and for showing me what true love is, so that I could write authentically about it. *You,* my darling, are *my* choice.

I want to, of course, thank my oldest and dearest friend Amy Bradshaw. I needed the character of Grace to be a paragon of light, acceptance, and understanding. I needed her to be the model of what a good sister looks like. I needed her to be radiant and effortless, and that is where Amy comes in. Whenever I need to write a character that is just unequivocally good and pure, I turn to Amy as my guiding light. Thank you for always accepting me for who I am and for keeping me sane.

I must, of course, mention Ivy Votolato, who has become a most welcome fixture in my life. Thank you for letting me steal your personality and give it to my absolute favourite character to write: Iris. And, of course, thank you for going through the finished manuscript and pointing out all the Americanisms that weren't quite right. It's taken quite some time to wrap my head around the fact that Americans call trousers "pants", but I'm getting there. Thank you for coming into my life when it was at its darkest point and for bringing all of your light with you.

To my mum and dad, who have so much confidence and faith in both me and my writing, that they never once flinched when I announced I was quitting my job, moving to Ireland, and becoming a writer. Much like Ezra's parents, they also didn't bat an eyelid when I came out as bisexual. Not everyone can be as lucky as I am to have parents that love their child unconditionally, and I am forever grateful that mine always have and always will.

I want to thank my editor, Sian, who accepts all my new manuscripts with steadfast excitement and aplomb, no matter the genre. Behind every (hopefully) great writer is an even greater editor saying, "you're probably saying the word 'fuck' too much" and "there is a *lot* of sex in this book", and for that I am so grateful. You keep me grounded and motivated.

Lastly, I want to say thank you to my favourite queer authors. To Casey McQuistin, who's books gave me the courage to be unapologetically bisexual. To Alexis Hall, whose stories make me, and so many others in the LGBTQ+ community, feel seen and heard. To Gregory Ashe whose books came into my life during a very dark time, and whose kindness, friendship, and beautifully written stories have kept me afloat. I owe you all so much, and this book is a love letter to you.

Thank you all, for everything.

Printed in Great Britain
by Amazon